SOLSTICE

SOLSTICE

P. J. HOOVER

TOR
TEEN

A TOM DOHERTY ASSOCIATES BOOK

New York

SOLSTICE

A Tor Teen Book
Published by Tom Doherty Associates, LLC
175 Fifth Avenue
New York, NY 10010

www.tor-forge.com

Tor® is a registered trademark of Tom Doherty Associates, LLC.

Library of Congress Cataloging-in-Publication Data

Hoover, P. J. (Patricia J.), 1970–
    Solstice / P.J. Hoover. — First edition.
        p. cm.
    ISBN 978-0-7653-3469-5 (hardcover)
    ISBN 978-1-4668-1518-6 (e-book)
    1. Global warming—Fiction.   2. Identity—Fiction.   3. Mothers and
daughters—Fiction.   4. Love—Fiction.   5. Persephone (Greek deity)—
Fiction.   6. Goddesses, Greek—Fiction.   7. Gods, Greek—Fiction.
8. Mythology, Greek—Fiction.]   I. Title.
PZ7.H7713Sol 2013
[Fic]—dc23

                                                            2013003721

Tor Teen books may be purchased for educational, business, or promotional use.
For information on bulk purchases, please contact Macmillan Corporate
and Premium Sales Department at 1-800-221-7945 extension 5442
or write specialmarkets@macmillan.com.

First Edition: June 2013

Printed in the United States of America

0   9   8   7   6   5   4   3   2   1

For Mom and Dad,
who raised me to believe I could do anything

CONTENTS

SOLSTICE

1

Disaster

Mom says, "Watch the heat today."

I nod and hug her and go to school like normal. Her concern's nothing out of the ordinary. And neither is the heat.

At school, after lunch, I walk through the school's old parking lot, keeping my head down so that the mist doesn't get in my eyes. The vapor sprays out from above, causing a layer of green gel to settle on my skin and hair. I run my hands through my hair to try to smooth it, but it's no use; the cooling gel only makes the curls get wilder.

Heat waves ripple over what remains of the black tar, disturbed by a random cactus here and there. A couple years ago they finally tore up the blacktop and attempted to plant some native greenery, but everything except the cactus had a hard time taking root. I take my time before my next class, soaking in the heat. Everyone else complains about it, but to me, the heat finds a way to sink into my soul and give me strength.

For the school to be spraying gel, the heat has to be extreme. Just before I walk back inside, I glance at the bright orange numbers of the thermometer plastered on the side of the school. It blinks one hundred and twenty-one degrees Fahrenheit, the uppermost boundary of the orange zone. The temperature hasn't climbed this high since we moved to Austin four years ago. It rarely even reaches into orange at all, staying below one hundred and sixteen most of the time. I pull out my FON to double-check it, and it registers the same. One degree more and . . .

The sirens start blaring in an earsplitting pattern of high and low, up and down. One degree becomes a reality. The numbers turn red. The temperature reads one hundred and twenty-two. The risk of heat-related death doubles.

I step inside, and for a second, all the kids just look around at one another, like the sound hasn't yet registered. Like they're all waiting for someone else to move.

"It's another drill," one guy to my left says.

"Didn't we just have a drill?" someone else asks.

I shake my head because I know this isn't a drill; I'd seen the thermometer. But I don't want to cause a panic. The principal comes on the intercom system and does the job for me.

"Report to your designated cooling areas immediately. This is not a drill."

Realization sinks in, and the hall erupts in chaos. Since I'm on the Disaster Student Council, I need to help out. I push my way through the crowd until I escape into the science hallway. The concrete makes the sirens even louder as the sound bounces from one wall to the next, then off the floor and ceiling and straight into my ears. I check each classroom to make sure it's empty, and then I circle back to the gym—the designated cooling area for our high school. I take up my position at the door on the far left and start directing kids inside.

We have drills every month. Drills consist of kids walking, talking, and making stupid jokes about the Global Heating Crisis. But there aren't any jokes now. Just a whole lot of pushing and screaming and everything else they tell us not to do during a real disaster. That one degree has made everyone go crazy.

My job is to make sure everyone who comes through my door is accounted for. I stand to the side of the door and try to scan each person with my FON as they walk through. But the crowd's too thick; I'll have to wait until they're inside.

Only three other student council members and I are already in position by the gym. Chloe's supposed to be next to me, but she must be trapped in the crowd. I don't want to think about her getting stuck outside in the heat. The last time she got too hot, she passed out.

I text her. where r u?

She responds in under five seconds. b there in a sec

When I look out across the crowd, I catch her waving.

My FON is almost back in my pocket when it vibrates again. I don't have to look to know who it is.

"Hey, Mom." I cover one ear with my free hand.

"Piper, why haven't you answered? I've called you five times today."

She's actually called me seven times. "I'm at school, Mom."

"You have to come home right now."

"I can't," I yell over the sound of the sirens. Two kids start pushing to get through the door faster, but one of the teachers breaks it up. I motion them inside with my free hand.

"You have to." Her pleading comes through even amid the disaster. She has to hear the sirens in the background. Does she think I'm going to just cut out in the middle of the crisis?

"I'll be home when this is over."

"Now, Piper." And she uses her commanding voice. But it only makes me want to do the exact opposite of what she's asking.

"I can't leave," I say. "They need me to help out."

"It's a heat bubble. It's covering the whole city."

I don't speak as her words sink in. A heat bubble means we could be stuck with deadly temperatures for weeks. The last time one of the pockets of hot air formed, the city was evacuated. Almost a thousand people died.

"Piper?"

"I'm here," I say, but a sick feeling forms in the pit of my stomach. Heat bubbles are the newest, worst threat of the Global Heating Crisis. Cities all around the world are testing different ways to get rid of them, but it seems like the more done to combat them, the more frequent the bubbles become. Three months ago, one formed over Central America, and a third of the population died. They suffocated from the heat. Scientists called it the most horrible natural disaster since the tsunami fourteen years ago that wiped out most of Indonesia.

"The city's going to disperse the bubble. And activate the domes," my mom says.

Disperser missiles have never been tested on a real bubble. "But—" I start.

"Take cover. And get home before they seal the domes. Please," she says, and then she ends the call.

I'm still holding my FON when Chloe shows up next to me. I give her a quick hug to reassure her—or maybe myself. "I was worried about you," I say.

"Why? You know I love the heat."

This is what I adore about Chloe. Even in disaster, she finds a way to stay upbeat. But with temperatures in the red zone, and given her last reaction to the heat, she needs to be extra careful. "There's a heat bubble coming."

Chloe hardly misses a beat. "Please tell me we're not going to be stuck at school all weekend."

I lean in and whisper right in her ear so no one else will hear. "They're going to launch a missile." And from what my mom's heard, there's no telling what a missile will do to the heat bubble. They've only been tested in the deserted regions of western Texas.

Chloe knows this. Her face pales. "They're not."

I can only nod because all of a sudden at least thirty freshmen are trying to get my attention. I give up entirely on scanning them and motion them all inside. If the city really is going to try to disperse the heat bubble, we need to get everyone behind the sealed doors.

"Let's talk later," I say, and Chloe nods.

It takes another few minutes before the hallway finally clears. Anyone stuck outside now is going to have to find some other shelter.

Once everyone's in the gym, faculty members pull the doors closed. One of the teachers swipes his FON in front of a scanner, and thick walls of plastic start lowering to the ground, forming a shield to protect us from the outside. My entire body relaxes when the shields touch the floor. We're going to be safe.

Most of the freshmen are sitting next to their friends, crying and consoling each other. I'm not going to stop them; most people do think the Global Heating Crisis will end the world. If the heat keeps getting worse, everything on Earth will die except maybe the cockroaches. Already most of the smaller vegetation is gone and people are crowding inland because of the rising sea levels.

Overhead, the giant industrial air conditioners kick in. The city has mandated they can only be turned on in times of disaster, and only then, set to cool to eighty-nine degrees. Otherwise, most of humanity has to settle for eco-friendly A/C, which cools to a toasty ninety-three degrees.

I take out my FON and scan each kid's identifier until it beeps. One by one, I make my way down the line, but I stop when I notice a girl sitting against the gym wall with her knees pulled up against herself and tears running down her face. Her arms are covered in red blisters, and standing over her is some empathy-challenged sophomore girl and her boyfriend who even in the midst of disaster tries to act like he's above it all, the heat be damned. The whole situation gets under my skin. I detest bullies.

I walk over to them. "What's going on?"

The girl and her boyfriend spin around, and their eyes widen. But she recovers her composure quickly. "Nothing," she says.

The girl on the ground scratches her blisters and stares straight ahead.

"Doesn't look like nothing," I say.

The sophomore girl puts her hands on her hips and shifts her stance. Any intimidation factor I had before is gone. She motions at the girl sitting against the wall. "She's scared. And she's freaking everyone out about it."

I shift my stance to match hers because I'm not going to have some underclassman talking down to me. "Maybe you should be scared, too." I know I am.

Her boyfriend pulls on her arm. "We should go."

"Good idea," I say. "You should go."

Only once they walk away do I squat down next to the girl on the ground. "Hey, it's going to be okay," I say.

She bites her lip, but her tears are still coming.

I point at her blisters. "You're allergic?"

She nods and then pulls her arms away and tries to move them to the inside of her legs.

She shouldn't be embarrassed. One out of every ten people is allergic to the cooling gel, but this was deemed acceptable by the city council since it helps more people than it hurts. My mom was furious about the decision, but her vote was in the minority.

"I'm Piper," I say.

The girl's eyes finally meet mine. "Everyone knows who you are."

"Only 'cause my mom's on the city council," I say.

"Yeah, maybe."

"You know my mom swears fennel tea will help reduce the allergic effects of the gel."

Hope fills the girl's eyes. "Fennel tea?"

I nod. "It's supposed to counteract the chemicals they use. We grow all sorts of it at home."

"At the Botanical Haven?" she says.

"Yeah. The Botanical Haven." Apparently everyone knows where I live, too. I guess that's the price of living in the largest private greenhouse in town. "I'll bring you some on Monday if you want to try it."

"Really?" Her face lights up like I've told her I'll be her best friend.

"Yeah, really," I say. I give her a smile and stand up and am about to start scanning more kids when, over the wail of the sirens, there's a boom so loud I feel it deep in my bones. It sounds like a bomb has dropped just outside the school walls. The ground rumbles, the bleachers rattle, and the A/C overhead gives a final clunk and turns off. All sense of order vanishes.

Someone shouts, "We're all gonna die," and people start screaming and crying. The sirens are still blaring, and the thermometer on the wall reads ninety-two. As I watch, it creeps up to ninety-three. Ninety-four.

Everyone's eyes are fixed on it, like it's some electronic symbol of their fate. I hold my breath. The sound from outside could only be the disperser missile. Maybe everyone is right. Maybe this will be the end of the world.

The temperature keeps rising. Ninety-five. Ninety-six. If the ventilation doesn't kick back in with some fresh air, we're in serious trouble. The gym won't be unsealed unless the outside temperature drops.

The thermometer clicks to ninety-seven, and I think this is it. This is going to be the end. The missile failed, and the temperature outside is still rising and it's going to keep getting hotter in here and we're all going to run out of oxygen and die.

Ninety-eight.

Ninety-nine.

The sirens go silent.

And the thick plastic walls lift.

And then there's the sound of the doors to the gym unsealing, and twelve hundred kids start cheering, myself included. Whatever the missile was supposed to do to disperse the heat bubble, it must've worked.

The principal comes back on the intercom.

"School is canceled for the rest of the day," he says.

The cheering increases, and I can barely hear his next instructions, so I check my FON for the Emergency Alert System message instead. It reads: Domes being activated. Return home immediately.

One step outside, with no cooling gel, and it's like an inferno. Even if the bubble's dispersed, it could take hours for the hot air to drift away. The domes are supposed to help force the hot air out more quickly, which is part of why they're being built, and why, once they're sealed, they'll stay that way until deactivated.

Overhead the school, the steel struts of Beta Dome extend into the sky. Twenty-four domes are being built above Austin, but only the first eight are operational so far—Alpha through Theta. Our Botanical Haven isn't inside any of them, and I don't want to be caught on the wrong side. My mom would freak, though I have to admit the thought of being away from my mom for a weekend is appealing. I could stay with Chloe. We could stay up late and watch ridiculous videos on the tube and eat popcorn and talk about which guys are hot and which ones she'd never date even if they were the last guys left on earth. But I keep walking.

I'm hardly out of Beta Dome when the glass starts to grow between the beams of steel. I can't pull my eyes away. Inch by inch, the glass forms like the shell of some iridescent sea creature. It's almost beautiful except for the fact that it's separating me from my best friend. I watch until the dome is completely sealed, take a deep breath to drink in the heat, and then head home to face my mom.

2

Opened

THE BOTANICAL HAVEN WHERE I LIVE WITH MY MOM IS ENOR-mous, with glass walls and ceilings that reach so high entire trees grow straight into the air. The lower level is filled with growing things: flowers, fruits, and herbs just to name a few. All these growing things need attention. It's what my mom and I do to make a living, and given the shortages of fresh fruits and vegetables in the world, we do exceptionally well selling to wholesalers throughout Austin and its surrounding areas. Still, it's not what I intended to do with my entire weekend.

By Sunday morning, my mom must pick up on the fact that I'm less than thrilled about not seeing Chloe all weekend. I water the early morning plants and head back upstairs to our apartment. She follows me.

"Is it really so bad?" she asks after I sink down onto the rattan sofa.

"Is what so bad?" I ask.

"Spending the whole weekend with me?"

I stop rubbing my temples. I know she doesn't want my truthful answer.

"Of course not." I give her a quick hug.

She hugs me back like she never wants to let go.

"Can I get you some coffee?" she asks.

I've already had one cup today, but I don't bring that to her attention. "Thanks, Mom," I say. "I'd love some."

"It's the least I can do for you on your birthday."

My birthday. With the domes and the heat, I'd forgotten. But suddenly the world looks brand new. I'm now eighteen. Which means I can officially do whatever I want. I take a deep breath and imagine my life of freedom. I can go off to California to college with Chloe. We can share an apartment. I can go on a real date. Maybe even have a boyfriend. I sneak a glance at my mom. She's watching me. Like she can read my mind.

My mom brings me my coffee. And then she brings out a cake. It's been a ritual for as long as I can remember. Each year the cake is different. Some years have brought strawberry short-cake with pink icing swirled four inches high. Other years she's topped the cake with plump grapes and layered fresh fruit inside. This year the cake is red velvet, and the icing is the creamiest vanilla I've ever seen in my life swirled into crests along the edges. And all over the top of it, she's decorated it with chocolate drops. Real chocolate drops from a company way up in Connecticut.

My eyes move to hers. "It's beautiful."

She smiles in reply and waits; she knows I'm going to say something else.

"But . . ." I start, because the chocolate had to cost her a fortune. The extreme temperatures and the price of refrigerated delivery trucks turned chocolate into something only the super-wealthy could afford.

My mom puts up her hand. "It's a special occasion. And any-way, we can afford it."

I don't complain because it looks amazing. I make a wish while I blow out imaginary candles, since fire is strictly regulated, and illegal fires result in huge penalties. It's only after I finish my second slice of cake that I dare to bring up the whole college thing again.

"Have you thought more about California?" I ask, regretting the words the second they're out.

My mom's face tightens like the subject pains her. "It's a bad idea, Piper. We've talked about it."

All we've really talked about are a million reasons why I shouldn't go, none of which are valid. The truth of the matter is my mom just doesn't want to be alone.

"You said you'd think about it," I say.

"I did think about it. And I decided the answer was no." My mom carries the rest of the cake to the kitchen and puts it away. As far as she's concerned the conversation is over.

I hate how she won't even consider it.

"What if I just go?" I ask. I know I'm ruining my birthday, but this is supposed to be my life-changing birthday, not just another ordinary day beginning another ordinary year in my ordinary life.

My mom walks back over to the sofa and squats down next to me. "You wouldn't do that to me, Piper," she says. "You love me too much."

She's right. I do love her. And I also know she'd probably just follow me anyway. Still, it makes me wish I were the kind of person who took more risks and didn't always listen to her mom.

Maybe my mom picks up on the fact that I need some time to myself, because after this, she heads out to collect some seeds for the Botanical Haven—without me. Which leaves me alone, sitting at the ice-cream table downstairs, reading on my tablet, and texting Chloe. Until the bell at the front of the shop rings.

I tense. On the rare occasions my mom leaves me alone, she tells me not to answer the door. Does that include today, now that I'm eighteen? I take a deep breath. Of course the rules have changed. I walk to the door and pull it open, and heat pours into the Botanical Haven.

A man dressed in a blue uniform stands on the front steps. He's got a white baseball hat on with a blue bill and blue wings painted on the sides. And even in the crazy heat, he's not breaking a sweat. His face spreads into a silly grin when he sees me.

"You're here," he says, and he flips his baseball hat around backward so the bill isn't blocking his view.

I return the smile because it's infectious. "We're closed today.

You'll have to come back tomorrow." Sunday is the one day my mom claims we need to ourselves.

The man holds out a box wrapped in white paper with a label on top. "I have a delivery."

It must not be one of our regular delivery companies since they're all closed on Sundays, too.

"I can sign for it." I move to take the box.

He pulls it out of my reach. "Not so fast. I can only give it to the recipient."

Seeing as how I never get anything delivered, I'm sure it's for my mom.

"She's not here right now," I say, even though maybe I shouldn't admit to being home alone.

He looks at the label, and his blond eyebrows pull together. "Piper Snow? Do you know when she'll be back?"

"Oh, Piper. That's me," I say.

"That's a funny last name, seeing as how it never snows." He tucks the box back under his arm. "Anyway, since you're closed today, I guess I'll come back tomorrow." And he's halfway down the steps before I can call out to him.

"Wait!"

He stops at the bottom of the steps and turns around, grinning even bigger than before. "Yes?"

I can't believe it's actually for me.

"You can leave it today," I say.

"But you're closed."

"It's okay. I promise. We're open now." And I flip the sign on the door from *Closed* to *Open*.

"Well, in that case, here you go, Piper Snow." He tosses the box to me from the bottom of the steps.

I barely react in time to catch it. I call out a quick "thank you," but he's already gone.

Sure enough, the label on top has my name, written in a flowery cursive. I try to place the writing, but I don't recognize it. Chloe always prints her notes, and my mom angles her letters the other way. I smooth my fingers over the thick white paper. It's silky, and if I tilt it just right, it shimmers. Wherever the paper came from, I'm guessing it wasn't cheap. Maybe it's even imported from Japan or somewhere equally exotic.

I shake the box, but whatever is inside doesn't make a sound. So I lock the front door and head upstairs and into my room. And then I tear off the creamy white paper.

Underneath the paper and padding is a round ceramic jar with a lid. The background is coal black, but around the perimeter, painted in red, are images of birds. Birds and flames.

There is something about the flames.

I run my hands over the jar's etched surface, wondering who would have sent this to me, but no one comes to mind. It's not like I get many presents, but if it isn't from my mom or Chloe, I have no idea who it might be from. I hold the jar up to the window and let the sun stream against it. It warms under the heat. The light bends around it, framing it in fiery beauty. It reminds me of something that belongs in a museum. Like something I've seen from my childhood.

I set the jar upright, and with my other hand, I lift the rounded lid.

My vision explodes and becomes a mass of fire, and before I know it, it's everywhere, licking my skin and burning my throat, crawling up my body. It reaches my face, my hair, my eyes. Every part of me is engulfed. I struggle to take a breath, but my lungs won't cooperate. I suck in, trying to get air, but my chest is frozen amid the searing heat.

I open my mouth to scream, and just when I'm sure my heart has beat its last, I drop the jar onto the bed, and the fire vanishes.

I look down and see I'm whole, sitting on my bed, staring at the ceramic jar. The air in the room, though humid, holds no trace of smoke or fire. Did I imagine the flames? I dare myself to touch the jar again. My fingers trace over a bird and then back to a flame; for a second, I nearly pull my hand away. But the jar is cool under my touch. Nothing happens.

I upend the jar. Something flutters out.

It's a single feather, red like the color of poppies and about as long as my hand. Somehow, it calls to me, tugs at my heart. I set the jar down and pick up the feather.

Letters swirl around in my mind. A jumble of characters blending together and forming words. They're Greek like the ones they use to designate the domes, but I have no idea what they mean. As I stroke the feather, the letters drift away, and the feather bursts into flames, burning to ash. I drop it to the floor, but by the time it hits the ground, there's nothing left of it. And then I hear the lock on the door click downstairs.

"Piper?" my mom calls out.

She's home. I need to find out who sent the jar and why, but I don't want my mom to see it. I hide it deep in the back of my closet.

3

Social Sciences

THE STEEL STRUTS RETRACT THE GLASS OF THE DOMES LATE
Sunday, reabsorbing the sand and lime for use the next time the
domes are needed, which means school is on for Monday. As
soon as I get there, I text Chloe. I hadn't wanted to text her last
night when my mom was around.

did u send me a present ystrdy?

She texts back in under a minute. no. going to give it to you
today in study hall

My fingers hover over the keypad of my FON. I'm not really
sure how to mention the jar and feather without sounding crazy.
I decide against it altogether.

I text, u r the best. c u there

Of course, all anyone talks about is the Global Heating Crisis. Everyone's trying to outdo one another with stories about
how crazy or scary or awesome their weekend was. I keep thinking about the jar, wondering how I can figure out where it came
from.

After lunch I'm late to Social Sciences because my mom calls
to remind me she has a council meeting after school. When I finally walk into class, there's a new guy sitting in my normal seat
by the windows. He looks right at me. His eyes are dark like
chocolate and filled with shadows. They make me think of mysteries and secrets and forbidden fruit. In short, he sums up every
single thing my mom tells me to avoid. So I sit down in the empty
seat next to him.

"You're late, Piper." Mr. Kaiser's already started class.

I pretend not to look at the new guy and drop my backpack onto the ground. "My mom called."

I wait for the idiotic crack from Randy Conner that I know will come. He doesn't disappoint. "Making sure you got between classes okay?"

The class snickers, and I shoot Randy my best glare. But my peripheral vision catches the new guy, and my heart tightens into something resembling a Gordian knot; he's staring right at me.

My face heats up, and I wish I could fade into invisibility. Jokes about my mom's overprotectiveness are rampant at school. I turn back around, get my tablet out, and Mr. Kaiser starts lecturing.

"Global Heating Crisis." Mr. Kaiser prints GHC in giant letters on the board in bright orange dry-erase marker, underlining it three times. "We'll finish the year with a month-long series on it." Mr. Kaiser caps the marker and turns to face us.

I chance a sideways look at the new guy and catch his mouth curving into a smile when he sees me looking.

"So your mom's overprotective?" he says.

My heart pumps into overdrive. Breathe. Must remember to breathe. Okay, so he's completely hot, but if my mom finds out I actually talked to a guy like this she'll probably yank me out of public school and homeschool me for the rest of the year. She's completely over the top when it comes to guys.

"That's putting it mildly." It's a good thing I'm already sitting because, with the blood pumping out of my legs and into my heart, I'd never be able to stand.

"Yeah, I know how it is," he says. He pushes a piece of his dark hair off his forehead, but it falls right back in place. It's funny because I know his hair will do this even before it does.

I actually let out a small laugh. There is just no way he has any idea what living with my mom is like. No one does. She wouldn't even let me go to public school until I ran away one weekend when I was fourteen. I was homeschooled until then and hardly left the house.

"You have no clue," I manage to say. I glance at Mr. Kaiser, but he's busy writing the top ten reasons global warming will kill Earth on the board.

The new guy leans in and lowers his voice, and the classroom seems to fade around us. "You feel like you have no control. Sometimes you wonder how things could have ever gotten this way. And it just doesn't seem fair."

I stare at him because I have no idea how to respond. He's looking into my soul and seeing my exact thoughts. It's like he knows me.

"Piper?"

I turn at Mr. Kaiser's voice, remembering where I am. "Yes?"

"I asked how long Earth has been in an official catastrophic state."

It's an easy question—the same amount of time I've been alive. The same amount of time everyone in this room has been alive with the exception of Mr. Kaiser, who's ancient. "Eighteen years."

"Right," Mr. Kaiser says. "Eighteen years."

I notice that the new guy isn't looking at me anymore. He's looking out the window at a gym class on the soccer field. Misters spray cooling gel into the air, forming a green haze under the UV shade coverings. The thermometer on the field outside is lit up in yellow, clocking in at one hundred and fourteen. The new guy watches the game. I vow that the next time I'm in a conversation with the hottest guy on the planet, I will actually say something more engaging. In all fairness, I haven't had much practice.

Mr. Kaiser picks on a couple of other kids, and then goes into some lengthy explanation of atmospheric stripping. I've heard it all before from my mom. My mind drifts. I wonder where the new guy moved from. Where he lives. If he has a girlfriend. I try to think of a conversation starter, but he beats me to it.

"My name's Shayne." At least this time, he's whispering.

He gives me the cutest little smile like he's got a secret he's dying to tell me. Like we're co-conspirators in a plot to take over the world. And I believe for a second we are. He flips a stylus in circles over his fingers—a skill I've tried a hundred times and never been able to master. He makes it look easy.

I glance around the room and notice that Salima and Nikki and at least half the other girls in the class are staring at him. But he either doesn't notice them or doesn't care. It's like he only has eyes for me.

"Piper," I whisper back, and this time I manage to smile at him even though my throat feels like it's about to lock up.

"Piper," he says. When it comes out of his mouth, it's like he's trying to taste it. "That's a pretty name." And then his eyes meet mine, and I see red specks inside the brown irises. They almost seem like they're moving, but it's just the fluorescent lights from overhead playing tricks.

I swallow and hold his gaze. And something creeps through me from my ears all the way to my little toes, stopping and settling around my middle for so long I know my heart's about to thump out of my chest. It only takes me a second to name it. Desire.

His hand moves like he's about to reach over and touch my hair. But he doesn't. The red specks are gone from his eyes. I blink a few times, but they're still not there. I must have imagined them.

"Don't let your mom get you down," he says. "You have a whole future ahead of you."

How can he know I dream of a future without my mom?

"Thanks for the encouragement," I say. It's the best I can come up with.

Mr. Kaiser drones on about the conspiracy theories behind global warming, which range from normal things like people not recycling plastic to the more absurd ideas like carbon dioxide being pumped into the atmosphere by an alien race trying to take over Earth. Shayne seems to be listening about as well as I am.

"What did you do this weekend?" he asks.

How am I supposed to answer that without sounding totally lame?

"It was my birthday. I had cake." I want to smack myself for how stupid it sounds.

"Happy birthday," Shayne says. "We should go out and celebrate sometime."

I can't breathe. Is he suggesting he and I go out? Like on a date? My heart pounds so hard my vision blurs. My mom would never let me date, but I don't think I've ever wanted anything more in my life than I do right now.

"Sounds like fun," I say. Actually it sounds impossible, but I leave this unspoken.

"Yeah, it does," Shayne says. And then he lets the conversation go and we sit in awkward silence until class ends.

4

Study Hall

I TEXT CHLOE THE SECOND I LEAVE CLASS. omg just met the hottest guy ever

I omit the fact that he basically ran from the room after class, no doubt a result of the wonderful conversation I carried on earlier. I'm not actually sure it qualifies as a conversation. But still, he talked to me. Suggested celebrating my birthday. I'd swoon if that weren't so pathetic.

Chloe texts back. no way. be prepared to tell me everything

I keep going over the things Shayne said. The interest he took in me. My heart regains a normal rhythm as I head to the library. I can't help but look around, hoping to catch his eye or even a glimpse of him. I stop at the water fountain, swipe my FON, and drink until the fountain turns off. I swipe my FON again, taking another turn. The water is warmer than the air around me, but my throat's dried out over the last hour, so I don't mind as long as it's wet. I wipe my mouth and glance around. Shayne is nowhere. But I do run into the girl with the gel allergy from Friday. Her blisters have dried up to the point that they've crusted over, which makes me glad I thought to bring the aloe salve for her. She thanks me like a million times and then heads to the bathroom to put it on.

Chloe's already waiting for me in the library. Her dark hair's shorter than it was on Friday, and she's got it pulled under an emerald green bandana so just the ends stick out. She's worn a bandana every day of the four years I've known her. I remember asking her why on the shuttle home from school the first day I met her. She said, "Because it looks good on me." And Chloe was right, though the bandana has nothing to do with it. She's got the body of someone who hasn't missed a day of exercise in years, and blue eyes the color of stormy water.

"You got a haircut," I say.

She touches her bandana. "It was getting out of control."

I sit down. "I don't want to hear it." As if she knows out of control. My blond hair grows curlier and longer by the day, and getting it cut only seems to make it grow faster. My mom always says it's like the plants we sell in the Botanical Haven: thick and full and gorgeous, and she combs it for me each night. I view it as a burden and stick it in a ponytail as soon as I get to school each morning.

"Okay, Piper, tell me everything," Chloe says. "And don't you dare leave out a single detail."

I take a deep breath. Just thinking about Shayne sends a chill straight down to parts I don't want to mention.

"There's this new guy in class named Shayne. Thick black hair. Amazing brown eyes. Incredible build." I leave out the part about how familiar he'd felt. Like I can almost feel his hands wrapping around me. Or maybe I just want to feel this. "And get this," I say. "He suggested we celebrate my birthday sometime."

"Like on a date?"

I twist the ends of my hair around my finger. "Maybe. I don't know. It's not like we set up a time or anything." As I tell her about it, I wish I'd come up with just a couple more clever things to say.

"He sounds totally hot," she says.

"Totally," I agree.

"I hope he asks you out for real."

A weird, queasy feeling moves into my stomach, and I realize I have butterflies at the thought of actually going on a date. I could sneak out when my mom isn't looking. But then reality asserts itself and squashes the butterflies. It's a life I've dreamed of since I knew the difference between boys and girls. But it's also a life my mom will never let me lead. In no uncertain terms, my mom has told me I can't date. Like not even work on homework together with a guy. Ever. Though more and more I wonder how long *ever* really is. Does she seriously expect me to live my entire life with her and never do anything for myself?

I push some of the unruly hair that's come out of my ponytail behind my ear. "Why? So I can say no?"

Chloe fixes her eyes on me. "Oh, come on, Piper. You're eighteen now. You have a life of your own. Your mom does not own you."

I love Chloe for saying it. She's always trying to get me to venture out. To escape from the stifling force that is my mom.

"You know how my mom is," I say. She has a way of laying on the guilt of how she raised me alone my whole life. Of how she kept me hidden from a criminal father who wanted to steal me away. But my mom protected me. Made sure I was safe.

"You need to get over it," Chloe says.

She's right. I am eighteen now. I have a whole life ahead of me. But . . .

"I wouldn't even know what to do with myself," I say. I may want to explore new horizons, but I'm afraid of what my mom would end up doing.

Chloe reaches into her backpack and pulls out a box wrapped in red-striped paper and tied with a bright red ribbon. She pushes it across the table to me. It's so thin it's hardly a box at all.

"What is it? Can I open it?"

"Of course." Chloe gives me her smile I love. "Happy birthday!"

"You didn't have to get me anything." Not that I'm complaining.

Chloe rolls her eyes. "Whatever, Piper. How was your birthday? God, it sucked that I couldn't come over."

"My mom made me the greatest cake," I say. "You would have loved it." I describe the cake, rubbing in just a little how absolutely delicious the chocolate drops were. But I don't tell her about the ceramic jar and the feather because they're just too weird. Even now, a day later, the imaginary flames still freak me out.

"Did you save me a piece?"

"Nope." My mom and I finished it off last night, eating it instead of dinner.

Chloe pretends to pout and then changes the subject. "Hey, I saw your favorite customer yesterday."

I know instantly who she's talking about. "Melina?"

Melina moved to town a couple months ago and started buying herbs wholesale from my mom and me, mostly things like mint and ginger and cloves. She opened an herb boutique downtown, and I have no real problem with her, but Chloe rags on her every chance she gets because Melina wears the most revealing clothes.

"Of course," Chloe says. "I went for a walk, and her shop was open for business, just like there'd never been a heat bubble and domes weren't covering the city. And you would have died if you'd seen what she was wearing."

"What?" I ask, since I know Chloe wants to tell me.

Chloe leans close. "Well, it was mostly see-through and silky and it had feathers draped all over it. And the way she was poking out of it, you'd have thought it was chilly out. And no way was she wearing underwear. I mean, sure, it's hot and all, but she runs around like she's naked. My mom would kill me if I dressed like that."

"My mom would never let me out of the Botanical Haven," I say. I pick up the present and begin untying the grosgrain red bow, running my fingers over the ribbed lines. I unwrap the paper and open the lid of the wafer-thin box. Tucked inside is a piece of paper. I pick it up and unfold it. It's about an inch wide and has a bunch of letters on it. Greek letters like the ones I saw yesterday. I shiver.

I hold it out to Chloe. "What is it?"

Chloe licks her lips. "The design for our friendship tattoos. We're finally going to do it."

Getting a tattoo has been my ultimate dream. A permanent sign of rebellion against my mom. Something that will last forever, like my friendship with Chloe. We've talked ad nauseam about the tattoo—where we will get one, how much it will hurt, what it will be. But I never thought we would actually do it.

"Get real," I say. And I fold the piece of paper and put it back in the box.

Chloe grabs it. "I'm serious." She holds the paper open to me. "It's ancient Greek."

Goose bumps rise on my skin even though the eco A/C is anything but cool. "What does it say?" I feel like I should be able to read the letters, to piece them together into a word that won't quite come to the forefront of my mind.

"*Giving* or *surrender* or something like that. I looked it up."

I squint at the design. "How'd you decide on this?"

"I saw it in a dream last night," Chloe says. "And as soon as I woke up, I scribbled it down just like I remembered." She holds the piece of paper up. "It's perfect."

Chloe had a dream with Greek letters.

I saw Greek letters yesterday when I opened the mysterious jar.

It seems a bizarre coincidence.

"I'm not getting a tattoo," I say. But the thought of Shayne comes back to me, and the life I want to lead flashes before my eyes. I play a vision in my mind of actually getting the tattoo. Of defying my mom. Of living my dreams.

Chloe draws an invisible band around her bicep. "Here. We're getting them here."

"I could never hide that." With every day being over a hundred degrees, tank tops and shorts have become the school's standard uniform.

Chloe looks like she's just eaten the last piece of candy in a

Valentine sampler, and I realize she's been planning this for a long time. "I know."

I blow out the breath I've been holding since I saw the piece of paper. I can't get a tattoo. Can I?

"I wouldn't even know where to go to get a tattoo."

"But my brother does," Chloe says, and I remember her brother who graduated last year has at least twelve tattoos, some in places I've only heard about and never seen.

"Chloe . . ."

"What?" she says. "You need to do something. Something for yourself. Not for your mom. Not for me. Do it for you. Make a decision for yourself."

I let the heat of the world soak into me and think about my future. With the Global Heating Crisis and all the wars and violence breaking out across the world, some people aren't even convinced there will be much of a future. What would I do if I only had days to live? Where would I go that my mom wouldn't be able to follow?

"When?"

Chloe knows she's won. "We're skipping the rest of the day. I set up an appointment for us in a half hour."

5

The Parlor

I'VE ONLY BEEN TO THE DRAG ONCE BEFORE. MY MOM NEEDED some special seeds for a plant she wanted to grow, and the only place in Austin that claimed to have them was some hippie shop located behind the college bookstore. Now, I'm back, this time without my mom.

Chloe jumps the three steps down from the shuttle, and I follow. She grabs my hand, and we start weaving our way through the beggars and musicians and peddlers. Within two steps, I'm immersed in a sea of tattoos and body piercings, shaved heads and bare chests—at least on the guys. And based on the fabric of tattoos surrounding me, it seems the Drag is the right place to come for permanent ink. The misters spray down on us, and a slick of gel forms on my skin. I imagine the tattoo there on my bicep—forever.

The steel struts are in place overhead though the glass is long gone. Alpha Dome was the first dome to be built. I guess the city figured since the college was dumping tons of money into researching solutions for the Global Heating Crisis, they should be the first to get protection. But even at that, the domes are nothing but a temporary patch; it's one of the few things my mom and I agree on. If temperatures keep rising, not even the special heat-refracting glass they grow will keep out the heat.

The clenched-up blob in my stomach increases in size with each step I take. I let go of Chloe's hand and shove both my hands into my pockets, hoping to steady my nerves. I can't believe I'm actually going to go through with getting a tattoo. Instead, I focus on the campus and try to imagine myself walking around here like one of them.

A group of three girls sits on some rocks off to one side. They've got a canopy over their heads, and a large sign is staked into the dirt in front of them.

Only YOU can stop GLOBAL WARMING, the sign reads, and it's covered with pictures of dying animals washed up on the beach and human corpses on city streets.

One of the girls stands up and walks over to me. She's dressed in cut-off jean shorts and a tank top, and she's got tattooed snakes and scorpions curling up her legs and arms. Her black hair hangs down over her white shoulders like snakes, matching the tattoos on her legs. Her eyes hide behind sunglasses, but when she gets in front of me, she flips them up.

I gasp. Her eye sockets are empty. Filled and puffed out and rimmed with lids, but there's just nothing in them. Not even skin. Just a void. I stumble backward, but she grabs my wrist. She blinks, and I see the emptiness of her eyes all over again.

"Give her the pitch, Tanni," one of her friends calls over. I can't look to see who because my eyes won't move; they're locked on this freakish empty-eye-socketed girl.

"Make her know she's responsible," the other girl adds.

Tanni tightens her grip on my wrist. "Only you can stop global warming, Piper."

When she says my name, she lets it drawl out, nice and slow, like every single letter is coming out of her mouth one at a time.

I can't tear my eyes from her face even though shivers run up my spine. "How do you know my name?"

She closes her empty eyes. "Did you hear me, Piper?"

"I read your sign," I manage to say. I think I sound braver than I feel. Because I feel like I should turn and run away—if only my body would comply. But I hold my ground. "Who are you?" I've never seen this girl before in my life.

And where is Chloe?

Tanni opens her eyes again and lashes out, grabbing my other wrist and pulling me so close to her, her features blend together into one big blurry spot in the middle of her face. Hot sweet breath pours into my own open mouth. "Do you know your fate?"

My fate? Until I left school to get this tattoo, I thought my fate was to live under the thumb of my mom forever. To hide from a father I've never met. To change cities every time he gets too close. But now I'm not so sure.

I yank my arms out of her grip. Tanni takes a step back, and her friends start laughing. Every muscle in my body is tensed up like skin stretched over a drum. I feel another hand on my wrist and whip around.

"Chloe!"

"What happened, Piper?" Chloe says. Sweat beads all over her face and neck. "I thought you were right behind me."

I let my breath out, and my muscles try to relax. "I stopped to look." I motion at the group of girls. Tanni is back on the rocks with her friends, sunglasses over her eyes. She's not even looking my way. None of them are, in fact. It's like they never talked to me, like the last few minutes never happened.

One of the girls takes a long sip from a water bottle, and I realize my throat feels like sawdust. Maybe I imagined the whole thing. Except I can't get the image of the empty eyes out of my mind or the taste of Tanni's sweet breath out of my mouth.

"They're just a bunch of freaks," Chloe says. "The Drag's full of them."

Freak seems like the perfect word to sum up Tanni.

Chloe starts walking again, and this time, I vow to stick with her, casting one final glance back at Tanni and her friends. My fate? How can anyone know their fate?

"The tattoo parlor is right around the corner," Chloe says.

I've never seen one, but there's an image in my mind of what a tattoo parlor should look like. It's a dirty dark place run by a guy wearing nothing but leather and chains. And bonus points if he's got a gold grill over his teeth. So when we walk into a wait-ing area that smells of bleach and has stenciled dots of red and purple on the walls and a watercooler off to the side, my butter-flies settle down enough to walk over and get a cup. It's one of those tiny conical cups, so I stand there and refill it five times before I finally toss it in the nearby recycler.

I think the A/C unit's stopped working because, even though the place is shiny and bright and filled with vibrant colors and the ceiling fans are on full blast, it's roasting hot. A drop of sweat trickles down my face, and I lick it when it hits my lip. It's bitter from the misting gel.

"So my brother's dating the owner," Chloe says. "He got us ahead of the waiting list." She recycles her cup, and we both sit. On cue the butterflies start up again.

Whatever my fate was before, with every second that ticks by now, it careens farther and farther off course. The school has for sure called my mom by now. With taking a shuttle down here, we've been gone almost an hour already, which makes us offi-cially late for our tattoo appointment and definitely missing from school. But the tattoo artist hasn't come out yet, so there's noth-ing to do but wait.

"I've heard it doesn't hurt that much."

I shift my thoughts at Chloe's words. "I wasn't thinking about the pain." Of all the things going through my mind today, pain hasn't come into the equation. Until now. "But thanks for men-tioning it."

"The arm isn't supposed to be that sensitive. At least not the outer part."

If she's trying to make me feel better, it's not working.

"Where is the owner?" I stand up and look around, walking over to a board covered with designs. Our Greek letters are no-where to be found; it's mostly dragons and snakes like that girl Tanni had on her legs. "You know, maybe we should forget it. If we get back to school fast enough, I could say I've been in the bathroom sick or something." The butterflies are back, and my arms shake. I won't even have to fake the sick part. My stomach is clenched so tight, I'm sure I could throw up on cue if needed.

I hear Chloe walk up behind me. She wraps her arms around me and squeezes. "Don't worry about it. You need to do this."

"Having second thoughts?" someone says.

We both turn at the sound of the voice, and Chloe lets me go. I put my hands in my pockets and try to take deep breaths but find it's harder than I thought. When I get home with a tattoo, my mom is going to kill me. I won't have to wait for global warming to do it.

"Nope," Chloe says, pulling the piece of paper with the Greek letters out of her pocket. "We're ready."

An Asian girl walks into the room. Her head is shaved, and Polynesian tattoos cover it. Tikis of all sizes and shapes. I can see the top of it because she's probably under five feet tall. She doesn't make eye contact with either of us.

"Good. Tattoos are easy," she says. "They heal fast these days. Used to be they caused all sorts of scabbing and infection. But now we seal each puncture once the ink's inserted."

I nod. Chloe's brother once told us that tattoos had been used to mark slaves, and that they were used now to barcode criminals. I wonder if my dad got tattooed when he was in prison.

"So who's first?" the girl asks, turning and walking into the next room. The red tiki on the back of her skull watches me as she goes, daring me to follow.

Chloe says, "Piper is."

6

Botanical Haven

I am right. My mom wants to kill me. As soon as I walk in the door, I know she knows. Even among the vastness of the Botanical Haven, my mom's anger finds me. Dampness settles into the air around me, and the Easter lily next to me seems to wither as if even the plants can sense her anger. She's still in the back near the rows of sinks we use to water the plants, and I have a last-minute urge to try to cover my newly tattooed left arm before she gets to me. But I know she'll still find out.

I start for the stairs to our apartment. One step. I feel her getting closer. Another. She's about to turn the corner. The tile floor echoes with her footsteps. Deep breath. I take another step. I'm almost to the cash register.

"Piper."

Her voice sounds calm. Too calm. Like it's water that she's placed inside a copper pot, but it hasn't yet boiled.

"Hi, Mom."

She comes around the corner and smiles when she sees me. But it's not her normal smile, which makes me feel safe and secure, although a bit smothered. This smile is thin. Calculated. School only let out a half hour ago, but she definitely knows I've skipped.

"How was school today?"

I shrug, keeping my left arm away from her. I can't help myself. I sling my backpack so the strap hangs over the tattoo and lick my lips. My freshly inked skin protests against the strap, but

I hold my position. "Fine. Aren't you supposed to be at your meeting?"

She looks to one side, and another plant seems to wilt under her gaze. I swear when she's mad my mom can kill plants with a glance. Apparently, it offsets my eternal green thumb.

My mom catches my eyes with hers and holds them. I can't tear them away, and I think of Tanni from the Drag, taking me captive with her empty eyes. I force myself to withstand my mom's gaze.

"Did it hurt?"

Her voice is still calm, but the anger is inside, seething just below the surface. She walks closer to me, brushing past a fern, and brown leaves fall to the ground.

"You're going to kill all the plants."

Another leaf falls from the fern, and purple flowers on a nearby iris crumple.

"I asked you a question. Did it hurt?"

I nod and tears spring into my eyes, but I fight to keep them back. "Yeah. It hurt. It hurt a lot." But it also felt blissful. Like every stick of the needle was setting me free. Giving me hope for a new life.

"I'm glad," she says.

I look around. Dead leaves litter the floor. "It's a mess in here," I say.

My mom undoes the clip holding her long black hair. It falls around her shoulders, and she smoothes it down. My mom is gorgeous and stern, and I used to want to be just like her when I was younger.

Maybe I still do, just a little. She's so sure of herself. So independent. Yet she's raised me to be the exact opposite.

"You can clean it up," she says. "I'm already late for the council meeting."

I don't bother arguing, and I don't reply. I've gotten through the worst of it, and once I hear the front door shut, I look down at my arm and smile. The black ink smiles back at me. I actually did it. My very own tattoo.

I sweep some of the leaves out of my way and move behind the register, dropping my backpack. I think about Shayne and how he'd singled me out in class. Not some other girl. Me. Talking to him was total rebellion, too. I want that rebellious life.

I brush my tattoo with my hand. The skin's raised underneath the black ink. The tattoo artist, Morgan, told us the skin would stay that way for months. Maybe even forever. She also mentioned the pain would persist at least a week, but mine's diminishing with each minute that passes. I move my hand over it and close my eyes. It's like having Braille stamped into my skin. I decide I like the bumps, and I hope they never go away. Even in the dark, I'll be able to see my tattoo. My first sign of freedom. And a permanent reminder of my friendship with Chloe.

I turn on the news so I can listen to it while I clean. The team of global weather experts is predicting another heat bubble. They flash to an image of the city council chambers where a press conference is just starting. Councilman Rendon is being escorted in. There were rumors of an assassination attempt on him this past weekend, and now he has two bodyguards flanking him. I guess the assassination attempt was real. In the background of the chambers are the other members of the council, except for my mom who hasn't made it there yet.

Councilman Rendon calls for the first question.

"Is it true that the domes are now inoperable?" a reporter asks.

Rendon looks equal parts charm and concern. My mom told me he plans to run for the state Senate next term. "Because of the heat-refracting chemicals, the glass within our dome structures needs eighteen days to regenerate between activations," he says.

"That means the domes can't be used for the next eighteen days, correct?" someone calls out.

"Yes, that is a correct statement," Rendon says. "Next question."

In the background, my mom comes on-screen and takes her seat. Even though it's impossible, I feel like her eyes find mine across the broadcast. I grab a bottle of soy juice off the shelf and sit down to watch. As long as I can see my mom on the tube, it means she isn't home.

"We've heard rumors the disperser missiles are negatively impacting the environment. Is this true?"

This is what my mom thinks, too. She claims the chemicals used to puncture the bubbles strip layers from the atmosphere.

Councilman Rendon tries to laugh. "Who here in the audience felt relief from the heat on Friday? Raise your hand if you felt the bubble disperse."

Everyone in the audience raises his or her hand.

"If we relieve the heat, we are helping the environment," he says.

Behind him, my mom stiffens. She glances away from the eye of the camera, and Councilman Rendon takes the next question. But as he talks, green the color of seaweed seems to ooze down him, starting at his head, until it covers him in a sheet of blackish fungus.

He pauses and shifts under the lights of the council chambers. Can he feel it? Can no one else but me see it?

I tap on the cable, thinking it's a problem with the input stream, but the color remains.

"How many missiles is the city equipped with?"

Rendon is about to answer when he presses a hand to his ear to listen to a private message. Then the greenish-black color oozes off him, sinking into the ground, and he returns to normal.

Rendon smiles out at the crowd. "I've just been updated with a new count. The city of Austin has produced five fully loaded missiles. And as we speak, three more are under construction. We will use missiles as needed to keep the threat of the heat bubbles away. And I can guarantee you when other cities around the world see the success we're having, they'll be begging for our technology."

I can't help but wonder, once other cities get our technology, will they also get our escalated crime rate? It's been off the charts since the dome construction started. Everyone inside the domes has plenty of food and water. But outside the domes . . . that's a different story. People fight over things that used to be taken for granted. Water recycling plants are broken into. Food storage facilities are raided. And each time temperatures reach into the orange zone, the crime gets worse.

Once the press conference is over, the tube cuts back to the global experts who rebut the use of the missiles, claiming the chemicals create instability and will cause a global disaster. It seems to me we're already in a global disaster in every way possible. Shortages of crops are causing starvation on colossal scales, and most coastal cities are now underwater because of rising sea levels. Austin used to be nearly two hundred miles from the shore, but now it's only eighty. Half of the population of Africa lives in subterranean cities, growing food in massive underground hydroponics bays. But the experts claim the missiles will bring the end faster and destroy all life on Earth, not just in Austin.

The bell on the door rings, and I snap my eyes away from the tube. I didn't lock the door behind my mom, and she didn't lock it either, which reminds me of how distracted she must have been. Still, I'm not expecting any customers. We do most of our business through mail order and wholesale accounts. A blast of heat pushes through the door when it opens, and the fans cut on to spread the heat evenly across the plants.

My heart gives a few extra beats when I see the guy there. His blond hair is rolled into tight curls that fall around his sculpture-worthy face, and he's built like he squashes army tanks for fun. From the way he's staring at me, I'm guessing he's not here to ask about any plants.

"Can I help you?" I ask. I hope I sound calm.

He walks to the counter and leans against it, swiping some dead leaves out of the way. "Okay, this is going to sound totally crazy, but you're Piper, right?"

I've never seen him before—I would definitely remember—so I'm not sure how he knows my name. "Have we met?"

His laugh is so genuine that it makes me want to join along with him. "Not yet. But my dad met your mom, and she mentioned she had a daughter about my age, and, well . . ."

My mom had been talking about me? She's so private about our lives. "Really?"

"Sure," he says. "We just moved to town. My dad is working on the domes, and your mom is on . . ."

"Yeah, I know. The city council." It's like my only claim to fame.

He nods. "By the way, I'm Reese."

"It's nice to meet you, Reese," I say.

"It's nice to meet you, too, Piper."

If his dad's working with my mom, maybe he's just here to see her. "My mom's not home," I say. It sends a flutter of excitement through me. I am actually home alone, and a guy is here also. A hot guy.

"There's a council meeting, right?"

"Right." I hold my hands at my side and attempt to remain composed. I look him right in the eye to see if I can gauge what he's thinking—why he's here. But when I do, I find I can't read anything about him. His irises are like ice. I inhale, and even above the fragrance of the entire Botanical Haven surrounding us, I can smell him. It reminds me of the thick, red wine I drink with my mom, dry with just a hint of sweetness, and it's so strong I can just about taste it.

"My mom should be back any time," I say, because I feel the need to say something.

He seems to let his guard down. With his fresh smile, his scent fades until the plants in the Botanical Haven take over again. "My dad mentioned she seemed a little . . ."

"What?"

"Overbearing?" He says it like he's not sure what my reaction will be.

"That pretty much sums it up." I laugh because I can't help it, but my laugh sounds nervous. I realize then that I'm kind of shaking because I am nervous, so I sit down on the stool behind the counter and try to get ahold of myself. Try to act like I am calm and normal.

"Back before my parents split, my mom used to be like that," Reese says. He pulls a stool up to the counter and sits on it, facing me.

Everyone always tells me this, but no one really understands. "I doubt it."

Reese crosses his arms over his chest. "Seriously. There was this one time I was out with some friends, and when I got home, she grounded me for like ten years."

His voice is helping settle my nerves, even if he is exaggerating. Still, I can't get over the fact that I'm talking to some guy while my mom's not home.

"Ten years?" I give him the obligatory eye roll, which makes him laugh.

"Fine. Not quite ten years. But she flew off the deep end. Told me never to see those friends again. She threatened to have them impaled if they ever showed back up."

"She sounds like a tyrant," I say, and for a second, I think he might actually be able to relate. "So what'd you do?"

Reese uncrosses his arms and sets his hands down on the counter, and he leans closer and smiles, which makes my nerves start up again. "I ignored her. Snuck out behind her back."

"I've never been quite that brave," I admit, though the word *quite* doesn't seem adequate.

"You should try it sometime."

I shake my head. "You don't understand—"

"You could sneak out and meet me. Like an adventure."

My breath catches at his words. *Meet him.* He's suggesting sneaking out with him. And I'm an awful daughter because a horrible part of me deep inside wants to do exactly what he's saying. The rest of the Botanical Haven seems to vanish around us until there's only me and him and an intense silence, which increases with each passing moment.

"I'm not sure," I say. There are a million automatic excuses running through my mind. My mom. Chloe. Shayne . . .

"We'd be partners in crime," he says, still trying to convince me. "It would be fun. And anyway, what do you have to lose?"

"My mom—" I start.

Reese reaches across the counter and places his hand on top of mine and squeezes it, like we've known each other forever. "Sneak out. Come on." And when he says it, his eyes fill with an excitement that makes me think it might actually be possible. Like I could have a shred of adventure. With Reese.

I open my mouth, but I'm not sure what to say. Reese's hand is still on mine. My eyes shift to it, and the next thing I know, he drops his hand back to his side. I can almost see the gears turning in his mind.

"Please? I don't know anyone in town yet," he says, and there's almost a pleading in his voice.

I let out a breath now that the distance between us has grown. I try to bring Shayne to my mind, but it's futile. All that my mind seems to be willing to focus on is Reese and the thought of disobeying my mom. It's a kind of freedom that tempts me every time I hear about other kids going to parties and hooking up and staying out all night. "I would get in huge trouble if my mom ever found out."

His face breaks into a grin. He knows I'm going to say yes. "She won't. What time does she go to bed?"

"Nine o'clock," I say before I can change my mind.

"Perfect. Friday night. Sneak out once she's asleep. I'll wait for you." Then he gives me a smile that threatens to melt my heart, and leaves.

It takes me a good five minutes to be able to think about anything else. Reese is gone, and all that's left are dead leaves scattered around my feet. I grab a broom and a dustpan and start cleaning up the mess as I play the conversation over again in my mind, thinking I've missed some vital part of it. But it's all there. Reese has basically asked me out. And without even really meaning to, I think I've said yes.

7

Hallway

WHEN MY MOM FINALLY COMES HOME, I START FOR THE
stairs. I want her thoughts on the news conference from this afternoon. But I stop when I see her sniff the air and look around.
Can she smell Reese? Just thinking about him draws his intoxicating scent back into my nostrils.

She starts toward the counter, taking one slow step after another, eyes alert. Past where she walks, fresh dead leaves drop to
the ground. Maybe it's the news conference that's got her upset.
Or maybe it's still just the tattoo. Or maybe she somehow knows
a guy's come over to visit.

After what seems like an eternity, she moves away from the
counter and starts back to her work. I watch for a few minutes as
she begins her routine, spraying leaves and packing in dirt. But
she doesn't say anything and doesn't even call out to me. Maybe
it's not such a good time to ask her about the council meeting, so
I tiptoe away.

When she finally comes upstairs, she heads right for her room,
shutting the door behind her. She doesn't offer to comb my hair
or even say good night. She's never been this mad at me before.
I'm sure she'll tell me we're moving in the morning. That I'll be
homeschooled until I graduate. That I'll never see Chloe again. I
fight the tears that threaten to form.

I think about calling Chloe, to tell her about Reese, but decide against it. It will be so much better to tell her tomorrow in
person. I get up and move to the window, looking out at the

blackness of the sky. Even in the dark, the clouds are thick, and the promise of rain hangs in the air. Rain, which is something we desperately need but causes flooding every time it comes because of the hard-packed ground.

Out back are greenhouses I spend hours reading and taking naps in. And our nearest neighbors are Randy Conner's family a quarter of a mile away. But when it's dark like this, the greenhouses and the neighbors fade into black, and it's like we're the only people in the world.

I lift the screen so it's just me and the darkness, and I let the heat pour through me and revitalize me. I wonder if another heat bubble will really come and suffocate the city.

And then I feel someone watching me.

I peer down into the darkness, but with the trees growing beyond control in our eternal summer, I can't see anything. But I know I'm not wrong. Someone is out there.

My mind shifts to Shayne. He'd been pushed to the back of my mind when Reese was here earlier. But now, with the memory of Reese fading, Shayne begins to resurface. I spoke so little to him, but I have this burning desire to get to know him better. Like the red specks in his eyes hold secrets he wants to share with me. I want the eyes out in the darkness to be his. I want him to beckon me outside. I imagine he touches me, and I don't stop him. His touches feel natural. I want to find someone I can be with forever, and I wonder if Shayne is the one.

Or is it Reese? A shiver runs down me as I think about them both, and I don't try to force it away.

As quickly as it came, the presence vanishes, leaving me once again alone with the darkness of the night. I shake my head. Whoever was out there is gone. And I'm left with only my daydreams.

A slip of paper on the nightstand catches my eye. I pick it up and open it.

Fate has smiled in our direction, and it seems we may have the
chance to meet sooner than you might think. Does that frighten
you? (Does anything frighten you?) I find eighteen years have
gone by and I don't even know what to call you. Soon all that
will change, and we'll have all the time we need.

—Your father

My father.

I read the letter three times through until the paper is shaking so hard I can't see the words anymore. My mom said he left when she was pregnant. That he got involved in some terrorist group and got thrown in prison after they blew up some giant water still that was being built in Nevada. Hundreds of people died in the explosion, and he was the person named responsible. He went to prison without even trying to deny his actions, and then he escaped less than a year later.

Now he's found us.

He knows where we are.

He's come into our home. Come into my room. He could come back at any time, even when I'm here. Dread punches me in the stomach as I think about it.

I fold the paper. I have to tell my mom. But I stop when my hand touches the doorknob. My mom isn't talking to me. She's upset about my tattoo. And if that upsets her, this letter from my father will push her over the edge. My pseudo-normal life will end. Right here and now.

It frightens me way more than the letter from my terrorist father.

I tear the letter into tiny little pieces and wash it down my sink, wishing that would make it go away. I'll tell Chloe about it tomorrow and see what she thinks I should do. If my father already knows where I am, there's no use hiding, is there? Maybe it's time to confront him rather than run away. After all, I'm eighteen now.

I head to bed and hope for sleep to take over, but my brain

seems to have a different idea. I wish for dreams of mysterious guys, but my night is sleepless. Girls with empty eye sockets fill my mind. Heat bubbles smother the city. And when I try to imagine my father, he has no face.

THE NEXT DAY I WALK INTO SOCIAL SCIENCES, BUT MY HEART sinks when I see Shayne's not there. I head to my normal seat and sit down, forcing myself not to look at the vacant seat next to me. At least today, I'm on time; my mom hasn't called me all day, which gives me a weird feeling of guilt mixed with independence.

I catch movement near the door. It's him. I stare straight ahead and pretend I haven't noticed, which is about as easy as pretending I'm blind. My heart pounds.

Please let him sit next to me. I'm not sure who I'm even praying to, but whoever it is listens. Shayne takes his seat, gives me a quick glance, and then looks away. My face burns, but I try to keep all emotion off it. The last thing I want is him thinking I am looking for him.

Mr. Kaiser starts the lecture by coming up with reasons why Earth is in a crisis state, but the sad fact is no one really knows. Sure, there are plenty of theories, but they're only that. Theories. None are proven, and there are new ones every day. The fact is winter has stopped coming. Leaves never fall from trees. The earth is in a dying cycle of drought and flooding with sea levels rising around the world. I've heard summer used to be a good thing. But all I've ever seen it as is a death sentence for Earth.

It's why my mom starts a greenhouse wherever we move. She says it's her contribution to keeping the earth healthy. To keep the smaller species of plants from going extinct. To replenish them after the trees grew big and blocked their water and sun. To help preserve the big trees for when they eventually die out, too. My mom really does care about the earth. Sometimes, she talks like eternal summer is something the world should embrace, but at the same time, she does whatever she can to help things return to normal. A normal that I've never known, since it's been summer my whole life.

I manage to zone out during lecture, and blessedly, Mr. Kaiser doesn't call on me. When class ends, I look one last time at Shayne, hoping he'll talk to me, but he's already gone. He must have been the first one out of the classroom.

"Nice tattoo."

I look up and see it's Randy Conner. He's standing there with his girlfriend, Hannah Reed, who's got one hand wrapped around his arm and the other crossed over her stomach.

"Don't tell me your mom really let you get one," Hannah says.

"Not quite." Randy and Hannah don't normally talk to me; I never knew getting a tattoo would get me attention from the in crowd.

"No way," Randy says. "You actually went behind her back?"

Randy lives next door to the Botanical Haven. He of all people knows what my mom is like. Four years ago, when we first moved in, he tried to come over and talk to me. My mom ended that before it started, threatening to peel the skin from his back if he so much as set foot near the brick fence. Needless to say, Randy never came by again. And he told the entire school my mom was a psychopathic lunatic, which, whether it was true or not, wasn't cool at all. It certainly didn't make starting at a public school very easy.

I nod, loving how Randy's words reaffirm my rebellion. I did go behind her back.

"And you got away with it?" Hannah turns to Randy. "I want to get one."

"Your mom would kill you," he says.

"There wasn't much she could do once I got it," I say, and I realize the power of a tattoo. Unless I get cosmetic removal, it's there to stay.

"Awesome," Randy says. "But you know you can't get one," he adds to Hannah, and they move on out of the room.

I pick up my backpack and head for the door.

"Yeah, nice tattoo."

Shayne is there outside the classroom. Waiting for me. I almost drop my backpack I'm so shocked by the sound of his voice. The way he says *nice* sounds like it holds a thousand different meanings, all of which I like. But the best part is he's saying it to me.

"Thanks." I attempt to think of something else to say, but nothing comes to mind.

"I waited for you," he says.

He waited for me. I record the words in my mind so I can play them over and over later. "I figured you didn't want to talk to me after you ignored me in class," I say, but I keep my voice light so he knows I'm joking.

"I didn't ignore you," he says. "I was busy . . . thinking."

"You must have deep thoughts."

"You have no idea." His smile makes me want to just stand there staring at him, but then he says, "Can I walk you to your next class?"

"I have study hall," I say before I can think about how irrelevant that is.

Shayne reaches out and takes my backpack off my shoulder. "Okay, can I walk you there?"

"Sure." I work to keep my voice calm, like I'm not over the moon that I'm being walked to class by the most gorgeous guy in the world. We turn the corner, and at least seven other girls, including Nikki and Salima from class, stare our way. Nikki shoots me a look of death and then whispers something to Salima. I pretend I don't notice. But still, I can't believe Shayne's actually picked me to walk with. I keep wanting to glance over at him to make sure he doesn't disappear, but manage to control myself.

I wrack my brain and finally think of a conversation starter. "What'd you think of the lecture today?"

God, that's so lame.

Shayne shifts the backpack so it's on his other arm. This leaves his hand dangerously close to mine.

"Tedious," he says.

"Tell me about it," I say. "If I have to hear Mr. Kaiser discuss conspiracy theory for this entire month, I'm going to pull my hair out."

Shayne stops walking, so of course I do, too. And he reaches up and takes a piece of my hair between his fingers. "That would be a complete shame. You've got beautiful hair."

I act as calm as possible given the fact that he's just given me the biggest compliment of my life. "I'm kidding," I say.

"I know." He lets go of my hair and touches my tattoo, and the shock from his touch travels up my arm and through my body, and I have a flash of a moment when he's done this before. Except he never has.

"It's Greek," Shayne says.

"Chloe says it means *surrender*. We both got one." My heart is pounding so hard, I'm sure he can hear it.

"Sacrifice," he says.

I look down at his hand. "What?"

He traces a letter with his index finger. I never want his hand to leave my skin. I try not to move.

"It says *sacrifice*."

"You know Greek?" Is that the best thing I can think of to say?

Shayne nods, and his black hair settles on his shoulders. "Sure. Doesn't everyone?"

"It's not really the most normal language to learn."

"Well, it should be." He rubs his thumb across the tattoo, and I know he's feeling the raised skin underneath.

"Chinese is a lot more normal," I say, forcing the words out, trying to be funny even though my knees are about to collapse.

"So normal is good?" he asks.

"Only if we're talking about blood pressure."

Shayne laughs. It's the best sound I've ever heard.

"There's nothing ordinary about you," he says.

There's nothing ordinary about him, either.

He rubs my tattoo a final time and then takes his hand away. "Hey, I was wondering . . . are you busy this Friday?"

Not Friday. Ugh. What are the odds? It's like the Fates have misaligned horribly. "Maybe. I don't know."

"Oh . . ." he says, and his smile falls.

"I think I have plans. Nothing big." I try to act casual, because I'm not sure what other response I can possibly give. The electricity from his touch still pumps inside me, and I hope it will never go away.

His brown eyes darken, and anger passes across his face. But then he blinks, and it fades.

"What?" I say. Anticipation and nerves blend together and flutter in my stomach.

He shakes his head. "Nothing. It's just too bad."

"I'm sorry," I say.

"Maybe we can get together some other time?" His eyes don't leave mine as he speaks.

My heart's going crazy inside my chest. I'm about to pass out. "That sounds nice." I focus on each word, making sure they come out clearly.

"Maybe coffee?"

I nod and decide against using my mom as an excuse. I skipped school to get a tattoo. I can certainly find a way to sneak in a cup of coffee. "Coffee would be great."

I hope he'll suggest this afternoon. I hope he'll suggest this second. But he doesn't. He only turns and starts walking again. And we walk the rest of the way to study hall in silence.

Shayne hands me my backpack at the door, and I sling it over my shoulder. I wonder how he'll say goodbye. I wonder if he'll name a time for our coffee date.

He doesn't do either.

"Okay, I'll see you around," he says. And in his simplicity I can't help but feel I ruined my chances with him. Maybe it was up to me to suggest a time.

"Yeah, see ya," I say, and I watch as he turns and walks away. I don't move until he disappears from my sight.

8

Bathroom

BEFORE I HEAD INTO THE LIBRARY, I DUCK INTO THE BATH-
room. There's no way I can handle study hall yet. My legs are
about to collapse under me, and I'm sweating so much a trickle
moves down my cleavage. I drop my backpack and lean against
the sink, scanning my FON to turn on the water. There are two
temperatures. Warm and hot. I go with the warm and splash it
on my face, closing my eyes, letting it wash over me. When it
times out, I turn it on again, doing this until my heart slows down.
I don't care that water has gotten in my hair. It's pulled back
anyway and tied with the red ribbon Chloe gave me.

"Do you know your fate?"

I freeze at the sound of a voice that sounds a lot like Tanni's,
from the Drag, and my chest tightens. I look up, but there's no
one in the mirror. Only me, water dripping off my face, staring
back. I don't stop looking, and my heart has started beating so
hard I feel the pulsing in my neck. I feel Tanni's soulless eyes on
me even if I don't see her.

"Do you know your fate?"

I whip around to see Tanni, empty eye sockets and all, staring
back at me. She's been there the whole time. Watching me with
those vacant eyes.

"Why are you asking me that?"

Tanni shrugs, and bracelets on her arms jingle, the sound filling the emptiness of the bathroom. "It's my job. It's what I do."

"Does this have something to do with your global warming

protest?" I ask even though I know it doesn't. Why would my fate have anything to do with the Global Heating Crisis?

She smiles and shows her teeth. They're white—almost glowing. I can nearly see through them, but I try not to stare. But not being able to look at her eyes or her mouth, I'm running out of places to focus.

"Not today," she says, licking her lips. And she takes a step closer to me.

I back against the sink. There's nowhere left for me to go.

"Who are you?" I manage to say. My throat's dry, and the water I splashed on my face is gone, replaced by a thin layer of sweat.

She takes another step toward me, and I think she's going to grab me again. I pull my arms behind me and use them to prop myself up on the sink. I could jump up and kick her and run out. But my feet are rooted to the hard tile floor.

"I'm your friend," Tanni says, and she rests her hand on my shoulder. "I want you to always believe that."

She's close enough now I can stare into where her eyes should be, and I see mist swirling behind the half-closed eyelids. She opens her lips, and mist churns inside her mouth. She leans toward me and tilts her head, and for a second, I think she's going to kiss me. But then she exhales, and the mist pours out, filling the space between us. Filling the bathroom.

I can't help but breathe it in. It's sweet, like cotton candy, and it enters my lungs, and I feel myself grow weak. I almost fall, but Tanni catches me. My knees wobble, and I can't take my eyes off her face.

"Chloe will die."

She says it as she breathes out the mist. It echoes around the room, though it's only a whisper.

Chloe will die.

Chloe will die.

The words bounce off the walls, taunting me.

"No," I say.

Chloe is my best friend. Young. Healthy. Chloe is not going to die.

"Chloe will die."

The echoes continue, like a chorus of dead souls.

This must be some kind of joke.

"Chloe will not die," I shout, even though it's only me and Tanni in the bathroom. Me and Tanni and the chorus of voices around us.

"Chloe will die."

Why won't she stop saying it? "No!" I scream, and instantly, the voices stop.

The fog disappears. Tanni lets go of my shoulders, and I collapse to the floor, hitting my head on the sink as I fall.

9

Opportunity

I'M NOT SURE HOW MUCH TIME PASSES BEFORE SOME FRESH-man finds me in the bathroom and takes me to the nurse's office. The nurse bandages my head, calls my mom, and then he sends me home on a school shuttle. I spend the whole time convincing myself that Tanni doesn't exist. She's just some far-fetched part of my mind playing out my worst fears. I tell myself Chloe won't die.

When I get home, my mom rushes over and hugs me.

"Oh, Piper, I was so worried about you," she says.

I can't hold back my tears. I let them come, flowing out of my eyes with sobs so loud the gash on my head pounds with each one. My mom holds me, lets me cry, doesn't ask questions. She locks the front door and leads me upstairs, takes my ponytail out, and helps me get into the chem-shower and change into my pajamas.

It's only when I finish getting dressed, and she pours me a deep glass of red wine and we sit in the family room, that either of us speaks. My mom watches me, never taking her eyes off me. I take a sip, waiting for the familiar relaxation in my veins. My mom has been proclaiming the life-giving powers of wine for as long as I can remember. She claims it's a gift from the Earth herself and grows grapes downstairs just to be able to make it.

"I'm so sorry." I don't even try to explain or make excuses. "I'm so sorry for everything." I feel the tears threaten to start again. I'm not even sure what I'm sorry for. I just know that I am.

"Shhhh . . ." She sits next to me on the rattan sofa. I lean into her and let her put her arm around me.

"I'm sorry." I say it again, this time managing to control the tears. It just feels so good to be here with her, knowing she still loves me.

She doesn't say anything, and I realize she's rubbing my arm, moving her fingers over my tattoo. I tense up, but none of the plants in the room seem to be dying, which I take as a good sign.

"Why did you get it?" she finally says.

I wipe my face and turn toward her, feeling relief course through me. "Chloe and I got matching ones."

"It says *sacrifice*," my mom says. "Interesting choice."

I nod, wondering if I'm the only person on the planet who doesn't know Greek.

"Chloe picked it," I say. But at the thought of Chloe, a sob catches in my throat. *Chloe will die.* Tanni said it over and over.

"What?"

My mom's eyes are fixed on me, but I don't want to tell her about Tanni. She'll think I'm too weak to handle the world without her. How could the whole incident in the bathroom have happened anyway? It's not natural. It's not possible. And I'm not losing my mind.

"Do you believe in fate?" I ask.

My mom's face freezes. "What kind of fate?"

I'm not really sure even though I asked the question. "Do you think people can know the future?" It's the best I can come up with.

"Your future?"

I shake my head. "No. Anyone's future. Do you think there are people who know what will happen?"

My mom hesitates before answering. "No. The future's uncertain. People are too complex and can act in too many different ways."

I let out the breath I've held since I asked the question. I don't want to believe in fate either.

"I saw you on the tube yesterday," I say.

"The council meeting." My mom stiffens. "He's going to destroy the Earth."

"It's the missiles, isn't it?"

My mom walks over to crack open a window. The heat filters through, but now there's a cross breeze in the room. "It's everything. Councilman Rendon is lying. He's deceiving the city for his own personal gain. It's like he wants the United States to erupt into civil war, and he wants Austin to be at the head of it."

"He avoided the questions," I say. I don't mention the green fungus I saw covering him.

"He's suppressing the results of the missile testing," my mom says. "His only concern is the election, and to hell with the fate of the Earth."

"Why don't you say something?" I can't stand by and watch everything I love be ruined by lies.

My mom leans back against the counter and runs her hands through her dark hair. In that moment, she looks so vulnerable. "Don't you think I have, Piper? It's all I can do to keep the entire council from bowing to his every whim. I've brought my concerns to the mayor, but he won't listen either. He can't see beyond the boundaries of Austin. As long his city gets shoved under those stupid domes, he couldn't care less what else happens."

I pat the sofa beside me, and my mom sits back down.

"I'm sorry," she says. "I shouldn't get so upset."

"Yeah, Mom, you should. If there's anything worth getting upset about it's the fact that they're killing the Earth." Not about tattoos, I think to myself, but I leave that unsaid. "So what are you going to do about it?"

My mom studies me. Her eyes scan over me from the gash in my hair to deep into my soul. And then she finally answers. "I don't know, Piper. Maybe we just need to resign ourselves to our fate."

It's a peculiar answer considering she just told me she didn't believe in fate. And something about the way she looks away makes me think she's keeping something from me. Like maybe she has some sort of idea how to fix things that she's not ready to share.

I suddenly let out a yawn I don't even know I've been keeping in and realize I can hardly keep my eyes open.

"You're tired, Piper Rose."

I nod and curl into her embrace. My eyelids are reminding me I didn't sleep last night.

We sit in silence, and the wine does its job relaxing me. Here, with my mom's arms around me, I believe things are once again as they should be. She's always made me feel so secure. And with her sort of accepting my tattoo, I believe she will actually let me make more choices in my life.

"You'd never leave me, would you, Piper?"

Her words reach my ears clearly, but it takes a second for my brain to process them.

"What?"

She rubs my arm and holds me closer. "You're all I have, Piper. You're everything to me." Her hands stop rubbing and press into my shoulder. "I'd die without you."

All at once, every muscle which the wine previously relaxed tenses up. And I realize my mom will never let me make my own choices. "Why would you ask that, Mom?"

As if she's caught herself, her hand starts rubbing again. "I just want you to know how much I love you, Piper."

I try to settle back into her arms, but my muscles still feel tight. "I know you love me, Mom."

"I do, Piper."

I don't respond. There's nothing to say.

"And you'll never leave me, will you, Piper?"

Her question makes me want to run away and leave her right then. To open the door and never come back. "Of course not, Mom."

"I'm glad, Piper. Now go to bed. You have school tomorrow."

I DREAM ABOUT SOMEONE COMING INTO MY ROOM AT NIGHT. I dream they watch me while I sleep. But when I open my eyes, no one is there. I fall back asleep, or maybe I never really woke up in the first place. The next morning, I think everything is back to normal until my mom stops me as I'm heading out the door.

"Wait a second, Piper. I want to ask you about something."

I rest my backpack on the kitchen table. "What?"

My mom walks over to one of the cabinets, and when I notice her hands shaking, I tense up. She sets something on the table in front of me. It's the jar. My mysterious birthday present. My face freezes. It was she. She's the one who came into my room last night.

"Where did you get this?" she says slowly, not taking her eyes off me.

I hold her gaze. Sure, I hid the jar, but I haven't done anything wrong. "It was a present." I reach for it, but she pulls it away.

"A present from whom?"

My first reaction is to lie. To tell her Chloe gave it to me. But I'm a terrible liar. "I don't know. It got delivered. But it had my name on it."

She presses her lips together and looks down at the jar, drawing her hands back as if it might bite.

But I, on the other hand, really want to touch its black surface. To run my hands over the engraved red symbols on the top and sides. The hammer and the birds and the flames, which seem to sparkle under the fluorescent lights.

"What's the big deal anyway?"

My mom reaches down, but instead of keeping her hand away from the jar, she rubs it, almost caresses it. "Did you open it?"

"Yeah, I did."

"And . . . ?"

"And what?" I reach for the jar, and this time she lets me take it. It warms under my touch, and the etched birds seem to shimmer and come to life.

"Was there anything in it?" She's looking at me like she knows the answer. But I don't want to tell her about the feather.

I lie. "It was empty."

I lift the lid, and she flinches, but I hold the jar open and show her the inside. It is void of anything except its ebony interior.

For a moment, my mom looks like she's stopped breathing. "Are you sure?"

I nod. "Yeah, sure."

"Nothing?"

"Nothing."

Silence lingers in the air. Seconds tick by on the clock. I don't move. I don't let my face betray me.

"Okay, then," my mom finally says.

She's apparently going to let this jar thing go.

I relax and scoot it away, not wanting to put the jar aside, but at the same time, not wanting my mom to see my yearning to touch it.

"I need to go away this weekend," she says out of nowhere.

I release the breath I didn't even realize I was holding. Going away is nothing new; we've gone on trips before, sometimes for the council, sometimes to buy plants. "Where are we going?"

But my mom shakes her head. "I need to go alone."

"What about me?" My mom's never left me alone before.

She gives me a weak smile. "You'll stay here."

My heart stops in my chest. She can't be serious. Me. Stay alone? Without my mom? Is it some kind of test? Is she trying to see what I will do given the chance?

"I'll make sure there's enough food so you don't even have to leave."

"When?" I manage to say, hoping that, of all the mixed feelings going through me, she doesn't hear the anticipation in my voice. I force my face to remain calm, though I'm not sure if I succeed.

"Tomorrow morning," she says. "I should be back by Sunday. Maybe Monday at the latest. I'll text you and let you know."

Tomorrow. Which means she won't be here Friday, the night I'm supposed to sneak out with Reese. Now I won't even have to sneak out. I can do whatever I want. Thinking about it makes my palms sweaty. My mom would kill me if she knew what I had planned.

"You'll be fine," she says like she's trying to convince herself. "If you get scared, you can go over to Chloe's. I'll call her mom to let her know."

"Where are you going?" I can't think of a situation extreme enough for my mom to leave me alone.

My mom looks away. "I have business to take care of."

"What kind of business?"

"You better get to school," she says.

"What kind of business, Mom?"

"Why does it matter?"

"Because I want to know."

My mom looks back at me. "I have things to talk about with your father."

My chest tightens. "My father?"

She nods.

"Where?" I'm trying to keep my voice calm.

"It doesn't matter. What matters is that he doesn't find out where you are. And I need to make absolutely certain he doesn't."

A chill runs though me. He already does know where I am. And my mom's planning to run off and meet with him alone?

"I should go with you," I say, though the thought makes me queasy. His note had been nothing short of a threat. Still, I can't bring myself to mention it.

"No. You shouldn't."

"But he could hurt you," I say.

My mom gives me a small smile. "I'm the one who's supposed

to protect you. Not the other way around. Anyway, you'll be much safer here."

I open my mouth to argue again, but my mom stops me.

"Everything will be fine. I promise. Now go to school."

10

Plans

I CAN HARDLY BELIEVE MY MOM'S GOING TO LEAVE ME ALONE.
This has never happened. Chloe is never going to believe me.

"What happened yesterday?" she asks as soon as I walk into
study hall. "I must've tried texting you a hundred times."

I push the image of Tanni out of my mind. But her horrible
words won't budge. *Chloe will die.* "Nothing."

"Nothing! I heard you got sent home. That you bumped your
head."

"I slipped in the bathroom. It was nothing." I pull aside my hair
so she can see the scab.

Chloe looks at it. "They sent you home for that?"

"Yeah. I think I passed out. Some freshman found me."

Chloe gives me a quick hug and then sits back down. "I'm so
glad it wasn't something serious."

Tanni's haunting eyes come back to me, burned into my mind,
and I think it was serious. "Yeah, me too. How'd you find out?"

"Everyone's talking about it. Well, actually, they're talking
about you and that new guy, Shayne. Nikki wouldn't shut up about
it. The head incident was just a sidenote."

My face must be turning bright red. "Really?"

She nods. "Totally. Half the girls at school are in love with
him."

I fight the instant pangs of jealousy. He hadn't been in class
today. "He is pretty hot," I say. "But guess what?"

"What?"

"My mom is leaving town for the weekend." I say it casually, but as soon as the words are out, my stomach starts flipping.

Chloe drops the stylus she's picked up. "No. Way."

I bite my lower lip. "Yeah. She leaves tomorrow morning."

"Oh. My. God." Chloe's excitement is infectious.

But I don't want the whole school to know. "Shhhh!" The kids sitting two tables over have stopped writing and stare at us.

"Piper, do you realize how huge this is? What are we going to do?"

The flipping in my stomach continues. "She told me I could come to your house if I got scared."

Chloe rolls her eyes. "I didn't ask what she told you to do. I asked what we're going to do." She knows I don't plan to sit around watering the plants all weekend.

Once I tell Chloe about Reese, there will be no getting out of it. "You're never going to believe this, but . . ."

"But what? Tell me!"

"I think I got asked out for Friday night." I whisper it because I really can't believe it's going to happen. I've never been anywhere with a guy alone.

"Like on a date?"

"Shhhh! It's not really a date."

"Shayne?" At least she lowers her voice.

I shake my head, though now that she voices it, I'm torn between wanting it to be Reese and wanting it to be Shayne. I can't believe Shayne wasn't in class today.

"Then who?"

"This other guy, Reese, who just moved to town. He came by the Botanical Haven the other day when my mom wasn't home. I guess his dad works with my mom, and . . ."

"And?" Chloe's eyes are huge. "Tell me everything."

I try to describe Reese, giving all the basic details, but my words feel insignificant. Reese made me want to do everything I know I shouldn't.

"He asked me to sneak out." Just saying it makes my stomach

tighten from nerves. Or excitement. At this point, I'm not very clear.

Chloe blows out a breath. "Oh my god, Piper. Do you realize how huge this is? You're going on a date."

I nod, realizing also how much trouble I'll be in if my mom ever finds out. "It's not a date."

She ignores my comment. "I'll come over beforehand. I can help you get ready."

Chloe looks more excited than I am. And Tanni's horrible words come back to me hard.

Chloe will die.

It can't be right. Not now. Chloe's only eighteen like me. She's got her whole life ahead of her. The whole thing was a dream. Or a nightmare. And just not real.

"Maybe I won't go—"

Chloe puts up her hand. "There's no way I'm letting you get out of your first date. You're going. We can get together Saturday, and you can tell me all about it. We'll do something fun."

"Like what?" I ask.

Chloe shrugs. "Leave that to me. So where's she going?"

I lower my voice. "She's going to see my father."

Chloe's eyes widen. "Your father?"

I nod.

"You know where he is?" she asks.

"No. But apparently my mom does. And she's not bringing me along."

"So will you get to meet him?"

I shrug, because even though everything I know about him tells me I should stay far away, I do want to meet him. He's my father, yet I don't even know what he looks like.

"I'm not sure." And then I tell her about the note. Though I've destroyed the piece of paper, the words are etched in my mind.

"He asked what frightened you? God, that's creepy."

"Yeah," I say.

"Piper, the whole note sounds creepy." She brings her hand to her tattoo and feels the skin underneath. The same way I've been doing. "He'll be seeing you soon? You should stay away from him."

She's confirmed my exact thoughts, and heaviness pushes into my mind. "Why can't I just have a normal family like yours? Why is it that, after eighteen years of running from some phantom father, he really does have to turn out to be as bad as my mom's told me?"

Chloe grabs my hand. "You don't need him. You've been fine without him this long. Let your mom take care of him. We'll go off and have our fun, and then things can just be normal."

I laugh. Like things have ever been normal. Still, Chloe can be pretty convincing when she wants to be.

"So she'll be back . . . ?"

"Sunday? Monday?" I say.

Chloe clasps her hands together in front of her. "We are going to have so much fun."

I know she's right. My mom will take care of my father. He'll stay out of our lives. And Chloe will not die. Tanni was a figment of my imagination. People don't walk around with fog in their eye sockets, spouting gloom and doom fortunes. It's just not the way life is.

11

Date

I peek outside at ten o'clock on Friday night and see Reese staring up at my window. The fact that he knows exactly which window is mine is both unsettling and flattering. I try to focus on the flattering part.

I open the front door and call to him. "Hey."

His eyes shift in my direction and light up. "Hey."

"My mom's gone for the weekend," I say. Maybe it's not the smartest thing to tell him, but the rush of freedom is intoxicating.

A grin forms on his face like he's found a way to fix the lottery. "That is perfect."

He walks up the steps to the door, carrying a bundle of pink calla lilies. At first, I think he's brought me a potted plant, but then I see they're clipped at the stems. I can't help the shock that must show on my face. There are huge penalties for being caught with cut flowers. Not to mention if my mom sees these, she'll freak.

But my mom's not here.

"I brought you flowers." He looks past me into the Botanical Haven like he's making sure I'm really alone.

Chloe left an hour ago; I don't know if I should invite him in.

"They're illegal," I say, which I know sounds totally goody-goody, but he's breaking the law. Once they're cut, they don't help the atmosphere.

"No one will see them." He looks down at the flowers. "And they reminded me of you."

"Dead?" I say before I can stop myself. Because that's what cut flowers are. Dead flowers.

Reese cups one of the blooms with his hand. "Fresh. Vibrant. Exciting."

"Okay, I guess that will work," I say.

It more than works.

"Thank you." And in that moment, they become more than just cut flowers. They become a symbol of something forbidden. I move aside, and he takes this as his cue to enter.

Reese passes the flowers to me, and I catch their scent. And something else . . . Same as before, but stronger. Red wine. Thick and dry. Powerful yet velvety smooth. Like a merlot or a cabernet. I close my eyes and take a deep inhale, pretending I'm smelling the flowers. But really it's Reese I want more of. His overriding fragrance is making me forget everything but his presence. I take another breath and open my eyes. When I do, he's watching me like my reaction amuses him.

I find a vase for the calla lilies and set them on the counter. When I turn, he's right behind me, so close I can hardly move.

"God, you look gorgeous."

Chloe told me the same thing. Well, not in those exact words. She helped me pick out the dress—thin spaghetti straps holding up black cotton fabric, which reaches to just above my knees. Red designs swirl on the black from the waist down.

Reese takes a step back and looks at me—up and down. He takes in each part of me, and I feel like I'm being savored. One piece at a time. It makes me feel like I actually am gorgeous and exciting. By the time he reaches my feet, even in the humid air, I'm shaking, and I never want him to take his eyes off me.

"You're nervous."

Nervous minimizes how I'm feeling. "Not at all," I say.

"You're cute when you're nervous."

He thinks I'm cute.

This only makes me more nervous.

Before I can respond, he reaches forward and brushes his

hand across my cheek. It causes all sorts of crazy shivers to run through me.

This is life without my mom around.

Exhilarating.

He lowers his hand and increases the distance between us.

"So where are we going?" I try to calm the emotions running through me.

He shrugs. "Anywhere."

"That's a start," I say.

"We could climb the steel struts of the domes," he suggests.

I don't know if he's kidding, but he did say his dad works on the domes, so maybe he's serious. Still, I don't want to fall to my death at the age of eighteen, or at any age for that matter. "I'm not sure I'm up for that."

"Okay, then. How about we break into the city planetarium and have a picnic under the stars?"

I laugh because this time I know he must be kidding. "Tempting. But maybe something less . . ."

"Illegal?" he suggests.

"Yeah. Less illegal."

It's like Reese actually has to consider this. "Legal can be so boring."

"How about dinner?" I say. "Will that be too boring?" I've eaten little to nothing today, and I've never been out to dinner with anyone besides my mom or Chloe.

"Dinner," Reese says. "I can work with that."

REESE HAS A CAR. HIS DAD MUST BE WAY MORE IMPORTANT than he lets on because permits for cars are rare. They're mostly reserved for CEOs and senators, and even some of the council members, though most of them opt out. I've been in cars a handful of times in my life but haven't set foot in one for at least five years.

Reese opens the door for me and helps me get in. His car's low to the ground, black, and kind of reminds me of a cockroach. But the leather seat inside engulfs my body, and I try to relax.

"It won't start unless the belts are done." He reaches across me, and his arm brushes my chest as he clips the belt secure.

I try not to flinch, but tremors run up my neck. He moves his arm away and shuts the door. I feel eyes on me as he walks around to the other side. Not Reese's. Someone is watching me. My mind flashes to Tanni and her soulless eyes. Her words come to me. I try to push them away, but they're too fast. *Chloe will die.*

"What?" Reese is already in the car, fastening his own belt.

I try to erase thoughts of Tanni from my mind. "What what?" I say.

"You look like you saw a ghost."

I shake my head. I'm half tempted to tell Reese about Tanni, but I know anything I say will sound crazy. "I guess I am a little nervous."

Reese puts his hand on mine, and his warmth erases Tanni's words. "And gorgeous."

Driving on the streets of downtown Austin at night is a far different experience from taking the public shuttle during the day. For starters, Reese's car is self-powered and doesn't have to stay on any kind of track like the shuttles. He turns down streets I've never even seen, taking us through the park and behind the theater, which is lit up like a torch despite energy restrictions. He swerves around pedestrians until he finally pulls onto the bridge that takes us across the river. The yellow numbers on the city thermometer read ninety-nine, and I can understand why there are so many people outside. With the days as hot as they are, any relief from the sun is a gift.

Reese stops on Sixth Street in front of a valet station, which clues me in to the fact that we're not headed to your average restaurant. We get out, and he tips the valet to take the car. Given it's such a primo opportunity, two guys argue over who gets to drive it until Reese finally points at one of them. "You."

The argument stops. The guy Reese pointed at jumps in the driver's seat, and the car disappears around the corner. We walk into an old hotel and take an elevator to the top floor. The air's probably fifteen degrees cooler in here, meaning they must have real A/C. Illegal A/C. I try not to look around and stare at everything. But I notice every detail's been precisely chosen. The black and white tiles. The golden walls. The bronze statues of Greek gods on pedestals in the middle of the walkway.

Before I know it, we've reached a hostess stand. The hostess tries to tell us the restaurant is full, but Reese pulls out a bill and hands it to her. She smiles at him like he's an angel and tells us a spot just came open. The snooty smile she gives me tells me I'm not good enough to be here with Reese. Like she should be his date. But she's not. I am.

The hostess takes us to a table in the back near a window overlooking the city where I can see the Capitol and four of the dome structures extending into the sky. I wonder how different it looked last weekend when the domes were sealed.

"Nice view," I say. "Good thing they were able to fit us in."

Reese sets his elbows on the table, interlacing his fingers. "Bribery works every time. Watch. They won't even card us."

Sure enough, a sommelier comes over with a wine menu and begins to make some suggestions, but Reese puts up his hand and orders a bottle of aged Chianti. I know the wine must cost a fortune; grapes are so rare these days. But, like everything else, this doesn't seem to be an issue with Reese. His dad must have made gobs of money working on the domes. The sommelier nods and moves away, taking the wine menu with him.

I've certainly had wine before with my mom. But when the sommelier comes back with the bottle, shows it to Reese, and then uncorks it, I still can't believe we didn't get carded. Reese samples the bottle, nods, and tips the guy. I'm starting to notice a pattern. Large tips get you treated like a god.

"Do you always get your way?" I ask.

Reese pours a glass and pushes it my way. "Most of the time. You just have to act confident. That's all it comes down to."

"You make it sound so easy." I pick up the tall glass by the stem and dare to sniff it. It mixes with the aroma coming from

Reese, and I want to relax—to quench the flurry of excitement running through me—so I take a sip and sit back.

"Most of the time it is, Piper. Lots of people in the world aren't really sure what they want. They dribble away little bits of their life, waiting to see what happens to them. And it makes them completely open to suggestion."

"Like getting this table," I say. "The restaurant was full."

Reese laughs. "People do love money."

The wine does its job. It inches its way through my body, mixing with the butterflies in my stomach until the butterflies mellow and the wine settles in. The waiter comes, takes our order. I get the thickest steak I can since they're so hard to come by. Just like everything else in the world, livestock is on the decline. Lots of places serve faux-meat, but I'm pretty sure this restaurant is not one of them.

"I've never been here before," I say, making conversation.

"Me, neither," Reese says. "But Councilman Rendon told my dad about it. Said we should try it. I'm sure he's mentioned it to your mom."

"Probably," I say. "But it's not her kind of place." My mom already can't stand eco A/C. If she found out about the real A/C, she'd be reporting the place.

"What is her kind of place?" he asks.

I laugh despite my nerves. They're still flaring up even with my attempts to calm them. "Home. With me. We don't go out much."

"She sounds like my mom," he says.

I shake my head. "No way. My mom is the most overprotective parent in the world. She's like a guardian angel who never leaves my side."

"But she left your side this weekend," he says.

"Yeah. It's weird. And trust me, this has never happened before. I'm pretty sure I'm going to blink and wake up. So if I disappear on the spot, you'll know why."

"But I know where you live. I'd just come find you."

For a tiny second, panic sets in. "Don't ever come by when she's home. She'd probably kill you."

He raises an eyebrow. "That bad?"

I nod. "That bad. She never lets me do anything."

"You're exaggerating just a little?" he asks.

I take a bite of my steak, licking the juice off my lips. "I'm not."

"So I'm your first date."

"You're laughing at me," I say.

He feigns shock. "Never." He raises his hand, calling the sommelier over, and orders another bottle of Chianti.

I ignore the stray thought that runs through my mind. That right now I wish I were on a date with Shayne instead. But he hadn't asked me first. Reese had. And Reese is great. And here I am.

"I'm not allowed to date," I say.

"What is your mom afraid you'll do?"

"Maybe have fun?"

Reese laughs. "Because having fun is bad, right?"

I shrug. "She just doesn't want me to be away from her. She's kind of possessive that way."

Reese nods. It's a truthful if not complete answer. But I see no need to mention my father or go deeper into my dysfunctional family situation.

"There was this time when I was little," he says. "My sister and I got into this fight."

"You have a sister?"

"Yeah. Unfortunately. She's been a pain in the ass since the minute she sprang into existence."

I'd be happy to have a sister, pain in the ass or not. "What did you guys fight about?"

Reese shifts back in his seat. "It was when she was first allowed to do things without our parents. She was always tagging along. Wanted to do every single thing I wanted to do."

"That doesn't sound so bad." Chloe had told me how she'd been the same way when she was little.

He lifts his glass and takes another sip, so I do the same. "Yeah, at first it was kind of cute. But then she stole all my friends. Turned them against me."

"I hardly believe that."

But he's not smiling, and I realize he's not kidding.

The memory seems to shift back to one of humor. "So we started this whole practical-joke thing."

Which again to me sounds like fun. "My mom's not big on jokes. She probably hasn't laughed in ten years."

"Be thankful," he says. "First my sister took every single one of my toys and melted them. She was brutal. She burned down my tree house and blamed it on lightning."

With global warming, fire is so strictly regulated, the smallest penalty is five years. I arch my eyebrows to encourage him to continue.

"So I shaved her head one night when she was asleep."

The image is a bit on the severe side. "Okay, so that does go beyond normal sibling rivalry." Chloe's brother had never shaved her head. But then again, she'd never burned anything of his.

Reese sets his glass down, and his eyes almost tear over. If I wasn't seeing it, I would never believe it. "I haven't talked to her in years. She left to live with my mom. Some days it feels like forever."

"I'm sorry," I say because I'm not sure what else I can offer except that he seems to be from a split family, too. "It's hard being alienated from family members."

Reese refills my glass, and if there were any tears, they freeze in his eyes. "Trust me, in this case, it was totally necessary. Our house was a war zone. And my mom freaked."

The idea of his mom freaking out makes me think I never want my mom to come back. And I never want the night to end. This date is way better than I ever thought possible. Reese is so easy to talk to, and I never would have thought it, but we have a ton in common.

"You're smiling." Reese reaches across the table and takes my hand. I've set my wineglass down, freshly filled and only a sip taken.

He's right. I am smiling. "Is that okay?"

Reese flashes his teeth. I try to bring Shayne into my thoughts, but he won't come. He's slipped out of my mind; there's not room for both of them, and right now, I'm totally occupied with the overpowering presence of Reese.

"You are totally sexy when you smile."

I know my face must be bright red, but his comment only makes me smile more. "You're not so bad yourself." And it's true. Reese has been perfect. Funny. Gorgeous. Reckless.

"This is going to sound way crazy, Piper, but I really, really like you."

"Reese . . ." I start.

"I don't mean to freak you out. But I have to say it. You're so full of life. So vibrant. You light up everything around you. You're perfect."

I'm sure he's joking. But his eyes aren't laughing. The blue's darkened, and the emotion behind them makes me catch my breath.

"We just met," I say.

His eyes continue to hold mine, not letting me go. "I know. But just let yourself feel it, Piper. Think how good we would feel together."

He's chipping away at the wall inside me. We would feel great together. It's like we've been together before. Freedom is such an amazing thing. "You've just had a lot to drink," I say.

"It's not that. You know it. I feel like I've known you forever."

I'm not sure why, but I feel the same way. Like part of me has known Reese since before I was even born. I can hardly form a response. "You probably say this to all the girls you date."

Reese's eyes never leave me. "Only girls named Piper who take my breath away."

Whoa. Reese is completely intense. He makes me feel alive.

And even though I'd love to sit here for the rest of my night and lose myself to him and the wine, my head is spinning and this is all moving really fast.

I stand and pull my hand away. "Can you take me home?" What I need is some fresh air. Reese has permeated my soul.

His smile returns and quells the edgy atmosphere. "Do you want to finish your wine first?"

"I think I've had enough." Actually, I think we've both had enough.

Reese stands up, leaving a few bills on the table. Large bills. "Anything you want."

We don't speak as we take the elevator down. His fingers reach out and find mine, weaving their way in between until we're officially holding hands. He pulls me close as if he wants the world to know we're together. When we reach the bottom floor and the doors open, Reese walks out first and I follow.

My heart pounds, drumming in my ears so hard I'm surprised I hear anything else. But I listen to the doors shut behind us and the elevator gears start up again. Reese keeps hold of my hand, and sweat forms between our fingers. I move to let go, but he grabs my other hand, and with a single motion, he pulls me close to him. The wine's thick and sweet on his breath, mixing with his already exotic fragrance. I can't help but breathe it in and let it fill my lungs. But once again, I think of Shayne, and the image of his face finally comes to me. His black hair covering his forehead. His dark eyes that are full of mysteries.

I shake my head.

"I hope I can see you again," Reese says.

He leans forward like he's about to kiss me. I freeze, and my mind spins. I'm searching for the right answer. Trying to decide if I should kiss him. Before I can decide, he leans in and presses his lips to mine. Even with the image of Shayne in my head, Reese's presence takes over, and I kiss him in return, letting my mouth open. I put my arms around him, pulling him into me with intensity equaling his own. He tastes even better than he smells, and my mind plays out infinite scenarios of what the future will hold. What our future will hold. What our past could have been like had we always been together.

It's my first kiss, and I never want it to stop, but I force myself to pull back.

Reese is breathless as he stares at me. "Thanks, Piper."

"For what?" I ask.

"For giving us a chance."

The valet runs as soon as he sees us, and within minutes, Reese's sleek, black car crawls around the corner. He helps me in and again buckles me up. His arm feels warm when it touches my skin, and part of me wants it to stay there. But the seat belt clicks, and he moves it away.

The car barely makes a sound when it comes to a stop outside the Botanical Haven. I've only left a single light on in the place—upstairs. Even the plants need nighttime to grow. Especially with unending summer.

I unclip my seat belt, and Reese does the same.

"Thanks for a nice evening," I say. And I'm suddenly wondering what will happen now.

Reese smiles with just a touch of humor that tells me he's not ready for the night to end. "You're not going to invite me in?"

The part of me that feels like an imposter is screaming to invite him in. To explore life a little. But I think if I invite Reese in right now, he'll never leave.

I think I don't mind.

"Maybe for a couple minutes," I say against my better judgment.

"Right. Just a couple minutes."

Reese opens his door and stands up, but five seconds later he sinks back into the seat, and his entire mood changes. He grips the steering wheel and looks straight ahead. "On second thought, I better go."

"Really?"

He takes a deep breath, holds it for a couple seconds, and then blows it out slowly. "Yeah, really."

"Why?" I couldn't possibly have done something in the last two seconds to upset him.

"I just need to go, that's all." His words are clipped, and there's no question in them.

I put my hand on the door handle and pop it open and try to pretend I don't care. "It's okay. I'm tired anyway." Which is a lie. My mind spins as it tries to figure out what happened.

Reese reaches over and pats my hand. "I'll see you around, Piper."

Just like that. Like we hadn't kissed back at the restaurant. Like he hadn't told me how much he liked me.

I push the car door all the way open. "Yeah, I'll see you around." And then I get out and shut the door behind me.

12

Desire

I'M NOT TWO STEPS AWAY FROM REESE'S CAR WHEN HE DRIVES off. I can't help the tears that spring to my eyes. It's like I've been dumped.

"Hi, Piper."

"Shayne?" I stop in my tracks and stand there and try to wrap my mind around the fact that Shayne is on my front doorstep. It's after midnight. Had Reese seen him? Is it the reason he left so fast?

He leans against the railing and gives me a hesitant smile. "I was just in the neighborhood."

I resist the urge to roll my eyes, but it's hard because his smile is so endearing. "Really?"

"Kind of," he says. "But you weren't home yet. So I thought I'd wait."

My face heats up. I don't want to talk about my date—not with him. "What are you doing here?"

He runs a hand through his hair and looks out past me at the road where Reese had just been. "Making sure you got home okay?"

My heart's pounding, and my head is spinning from the wine. What I really need to do is sit down. "I'm fine."

His face relaxes the smallest amount. "I'm glad," he says. And then he waits, like he's not sure what to say next.

"I'm sorry," I say, because I know I sounded kind of bitchy. "The last week has just been a little crazy." It's a mild way to put things. I fumble in my purse for the keys and pull them out, but I drop them on the porch.

He picks them up. "No, I'm sorry. I shouldn't be checking up on you." He hands me the keys, and I put them in the lock, and the door swings open.

"Do you want to come in?" I ask quickly, before I can over-think it.

He looks into the greenhouse. It's dim, but he takes his time looking around. "Maybe not. I should probably get going."

I step to the side and try to calm my heart when I respond. "I could make coffee." The night has been nothing but hazy, and coffee should help. Coffee is safe. Plus he'd suggested getting coffee sometime.

Shayne hesitates, but I motion for him to come in, so he finally does. The door swings shut behind him, leaving the two of us alone in the dark.

"I'd love some."

"What?" I say.

"Coffee. I'd love some."

In the space of seconds, I've forgotten all about it. "Oh, yeah. I'll run upstairs and make it."

I turn before I say something stupid and ruin the entire moment. But my hand catches on the counter, and the pink calla lilies Reese brought me fall to the ground. The glass vase shatters on the tile below, and water splashes my feet. Reese's cut flowers lay crossed over each other, staring up at me.

Not only had I gone on a date with Reese, I enjoyed it. And I kissed him like there was no tomorrow. When I think back, it's like I'm watching actors onstage. Like it was someone else and not me. For the last few hours, all semblance of common sense has vanished from my mind. It must have been the wine.

I close my eyes and blow out a breath. "Ugh."

"You broke your vase."

I can't help but laugh at Shayne's matter-of-fact tone, which

totally simplifies the whole night. "Yeah, I'll clean it up later."
And I head upstairs to the kitchen.

I make the coffee as fast as I can. Shayne is downstairs—
waiting for me. I hardly believe it's real. But I don't want to jinx
it, so I hurry and go back down.

He's near the counter, bent over with a broom. The bulb from
upstairs casts enough light to see his outline. I set the coffee on
our small ice cream table and walk over to him.

"You don't have to clean that up." I grab the dustpan off the
ground, but his hand reaches out and covers mine. I feel something move through me, starting at the hand he's holding. The
sensation is moving up my arm and into my torso, and when it
settles in the center of my soul, I have to work to make sure he
doesn't hear my breathing. His touch is so tender. So familiar.

"I don't mind," he says, taking the dustpan.

"What a mess," I say. Kind of like this whole situation between
me and Reese and Shayne is becoming. A tangle in my mind.

"No way," Shayne says. "We'll have it cleaned up in no time."
He finishes cleaning the glass off the floor and reaches for the
flowers, but I take them first.

"I'm not a big fan of cut flowers," I say.

"I figured." And his words echo truth, like he really did know
that about me. Like he can see behind my eyes. Which makes
me a bit insecure. My thoughts have always been my own.

I move around beside him and set the flowers in the sink, and
when I turn, he's looking right at me. I don't say anything. And I
don't move. His eyes settle on my face, and unlike Reese, Shayne
has no confident outer shell. It's almost as if I can see right
through him, into his soul.

The silence grows with each second until he reaches up and
touches my hair.

"You have it down." He twirls a piece of my curly blond hair
around his finger and then lets it go, watching it bounce back.

I feel my face flush but know with the darkness he can't see it.
"Yeah, I—"

I see his outline nod. "I know. Your date. Did you have fun?"

"I wished it were you instead."

The second the words are out, I can't believe I've said them. He's going to think I'm pathetic. He probably has girls flocking around him at every turn. I saw the way the girls were all staring at him at school.

Shayne brushes his fingers against the skin of my tattoo. "I wish it were me instead, too."

My face betrays me, because a grin starts to form there no matter how cool I attempt to act. But luckily Shayne smiles, too.

"The coffee's ready." I walk back toward the ice cream table. I'm not looking behind me, but his footsteps echo on the tile floor. He's following me. Which still seems unreal. I sit in the purple seat and leave the yellow one open for him. Both face the forest of plants I grow. I slide one of the cups closer to him. "Do you like it black?"

"It's the only way to drink it," he says. When he sets his mug down, I notice his eyes travel back to Reese's flowers, but he doesn't say anything.

He's so close—just across the table from me. I distract myself with conversation. "Are you guys friends?" I ask.

Shayne takes another sip of his coffee. "Reese and I?"

I nod and set my hands on the table to keep them from shaking.

Shayne's hand moves toward mine, as if he wants to take it. But he doesn't.

"It's a complicated situation," he says.

I open my mouth to ask more, but his hand lifts off the table and his fingers move to my lips. "And not the conversation I want to have with you."

I don't move a muscle because I don't want his hand to leave my mouth, but it does, so I take a sip of the hot coffee to again clear my mind. "What conversation do you want to have then?" I ask.

Shayne leans back into the heart shape of the chair. "Tell me the funniest thing that ever happened to you."

My mind starts churning as I attempt to piece out something funny that's happened in my life. "How about a different topic."

"There must be something."

"I'm horrible at telling funny stories." Which isn't quite the truth. Between being homeschooled and moving, not many funny things spring to mind. But I don't want him to think I'm a total bore.

"We'll have to practice," he says.

"It'll take lots of practice. I'm about the opposite of funny."

He purses his lips. "You have a whole lifetime ahead of you to change that."

My heart skips at the thought of my future. And I'm reminded I am eighteen now. I need to get away from my mom.

"How about you?" I say. "Tell me something funny about your life."

Shayne seems to consider this for a moment. "You'll think I'm horrible."

"No way," I say.

"Promise?"

I nod.

"Okay," he says. "There was this time when I was little. I was hanging out with my best friend. And, well, my father had this one clock that he just loved. It was huge."

"Like a grandfather clock?"

His arms circle way up toward the ceiling. "Way bigger. It was as tall as this room. My father's got this fascination with time. Can't get enough of it. He has about a million clocks and spends every waking hour making sure they're perfectly synchronized."

"Sounds like a fun hobby."

"More like a crazy obsession," Shayne says. "Anyway, this one day, my dad was gone, and my best friend was over, and we climbed to the top of the clock and changed it so it would be a few seconds off."

I can almost picture Shayne at the top of a huge grandfather clock. "That doesn't sound so bad."

"You wouldn't think so, but the first time it chimed after all the others, my dad couldn't believe it. He checked and rechecked all those clocks for days. And then he finally got them synchronized up again."

I know where this story is going. "So you changed it again."

Shayne nods. "The first time he thought it was a malfunction. But after the second time, he set up security everywhere. And then he waited."

"So what'd you do?" Every word draws me in and connects me to him. I wish I'd been a part of the experience.

Shayne shrugs. "We changed it again."

"But what about the security?"

He sips his coffee and sets the mug down on the yellow table surface. "Sure, it got harder, but that only made it more of a challenge."

"Did he ever find out it was you?"

"Nope. In fact, it kind of drove him crazy until one day I went into the room and the clock was in a million pieces." He seems to consider this for a moment. "He's probably still working on fixing it."

"There's no way I can top that." It's a way better story than Reese shaving his sister's head. I trace my finger around on top of the coffee mug and say a silent prayer Shayne won't leave.

But he pushes his chair out and stands up. "It's really nice here. Kind of like your own private oasis from global warming."

The Botanical Haven is a nice place to live with the vivid colors of all the living things around me, but I know I'm not meant to live with my mom for the rest of my life. I stand, too, and though we're still across the table from each other, it's like we're only inches apart.

"I want to move out."

His muscles visibly tense. "Where do you want to go?"

"California maybe. To college with Chloe. I want to study

law. But my mom wants me to stay here with her." Without even realizing I'm doing it, I take a step closer to him. And he does the same. And then we really are only inches apart.

"It's beautiful here," he says, and touches my arm.

My breath catches in my throat. "Maybe when my mom's not around."

His eyes meet mine, and each second that passes stretches into eternity. I hold his gaze, and even though my heart is pounding out of my chest, I don't look away. I think he's going to kiss me. I'm sure of it. His eyes hold mine, tracing over me like a whisper. His gaze is empathic. It's the most intense moment of my life, and my soul is bared.

I wait, keeping myself from leaning forward. Around us, the world holds still. The air is quiet. He shifts his body. It's so close. He leans forward. And then from outside, a branch scrapes against the glass ceiling . . .

. . . and the moment is gone.

Shayne takes a step back, but his eyes don't leave me.

"Your mom should go away more often," he says.

I laugh in an attempt to relax, which isn't going to happen. "Trust me, I wish for that all the time."

When I say it, his face falls into a cynical grin. "If only wishes came true so easily."

"Do you want another cup of coffee?" I want him to sit back down and stay here forever.

He shakes his head. "I need to go."

I open my mouth and am about to ask him to stay, but then I remind myself that I don't want to sound desperate. "Are you sure?" It's not like my mom goes away every weekend.

He looks at me and his eyes tell me he's not sure. That he wants to stay here as much as I want him to. That he wants to kiss me. But his words disagree. "Yeah, I'm sure." He grabs my hand and gives it a squeeze, and I know I can't stop him.

He lets go of my hand and walks to the door. I watch him from where I stand, and then he's gone. And I'm left in the dark alone.

I walk to the cash register, move behind the counter, and sink to the floor. It's only after I sit there for ten minutes that I'm able to clear my head. Sweat pours off me, but I can't stand up and put the fans on. My legs won't hold me, and my dress sticks to me around my thighs.

I don't move until his presence evaporates, and only then do I head back to the sink where the pink calla lilies rest. I still feel life within the exposed stems. Weakening, but they can last longer—if I want them to. An odd urge to smash them hits me. To throw them in the compost pile and pretend my date with Reese never happened, but I can't do that. Moving around the Botanical Haven, I look for the perfect container to hold them. And I move into my routine, there in the dark, watering and taking care of the plants.

13

Creek

After Shayne leaves, I hardly sleep; Reese and Shayne and my father keep invading my dreams. I twist around on my cotton sheets, hoping to quiet my thoughts of them, but then Tanni takes their place with her empty eye sockets and words of doom.

I know her words aren't true. But they repeat over and over in my head—a haunting mantra. I will see Chloe tomorrow. We have plans. She'll call in the morning.

I wake before the alarm, clicking it off and checking for messages. My mom hasn't called or texted since yesterday morning, which is so far from her normal overbearing nature, I wonder if she lost her FON. I send her a quick text to check in, but she doesn't answer. She's probably just busy. I'll try her again in a little bit.

I relax and think about the night before. Thinking of Reese leaves me disoriented. I know it's wrong to cut flowers and drink under age, but breaking the rules had been intoxicating, and I'm left with the desire to do more. He offered up a reckless freedom, one that my mom would kill me if she knew about. Not that she'd be any happier about Shayne being here late at night while I was home alone. I toss Shayne and Reese back and forth in my mind the whole time I'm showering and getting dressed, hoping the memories never fade.

It's not until I push the button on the coffee machine that Chloe calls. I mute the tube and answer.

"We still on for today?" she asks.

The sound of her voice sings into my ear. I know she won't die. She's my best friend. I touch my tattoo with my free hand and run my fingers over the imprint. But as much as I want to get out, all the reporters have been talking about this morning is the new heat bubble they're sure is going to form around the city.

"Have you seen the news?" I say. "Maybe we should stay inside."

I can almost hear Chloe shake her head. "No way, Piper. We are not staying inside the one time you get some freedom."

I glance at the tube and see Councilman Rendon talking with an image of a disperser missile inset behind him. I don't have to hear him to know he's convincing the world the missiles are safe.

"You could just come over," I say to Chloe, even though I don't want to stay in either.

"Turn it off," Chloe says.

"What?"

"The tube. Turn it off now. You need to stop watching the news," she says.

"But they're predicting the bubble will form before noon." And my thoughts go to my mom. Will she be safe from the heat wherever she is?

"So it gets hot," Chloe says. "It's hot every day. Just turn off the news and get ready."

"Fine." I click off the tube, and my mind quiets instantly. Maybe I should watch less bad news.

Chloe says she'll be by in a half hour; shuttle routes don't make it much easier than that. I have so much to tell her. About Reese. About Shayne. I can hardly wait. But when Chloe hangs up, Tanni's voice returns.

I push it away and grab a nectarine, cutting it with a knife and pulling out the pit. One benefit of owning the Botanical Haven—we grow lots of fruit, so even with the Global Heating Crisis, shortages are never a concern for us. It's sweet and juicy,

95

and when I take a bite, the juice runs down my chin, making me think of Reese's kiss. Had it really happened? And had I enjoyed it so much?

When I see Chloe walking up, I check the temperature. One hundred and thirteen. Still in the yellow zone. I can only hope the reports are wrong. Still, the second I step outside, the heat punches me like a fist.

"It feels hotter than a hundred and thirteen," I say.

Chloe shoots me a look. "We're not staying in."

"Right," I say. "We're not staying in." I clip my water bottle on my shorts and hand Chloe one of my mom's herbal heat suppressors. They're brown disks that look like cow patties, but my mom swears they help the body process heat better.

Chloe wrinkles up her nose. "Those things are disgusting."

"They aren't that bad," I say, and force it into her hand. I already had two this morning. Chloe's right; they taste even worse than they look.

Chloe takes it but puts it in her pocket instead of eating it. I opt against pressing the issue. She's pretty good about taking her sunscreen pills, so I don't have to worry about that.

I lock the door behind us, but the shuttle has already pulled away. So we sit on the bench to wait. It's not three minutes later when Randy Conner and his little sister head over to the shuttle stop to join us. As little as my mom lets me out of her sight, I'm like a phantom, but I do know Randy has a sister.

"Hi," I say, and I smile and wave.

The little girl's only about seven. But instead of the normal brightness I'd expect to see on a seven-year-old face, her eyes are hollow and don't meet my own. Randy pulls her close, and they stand off to the side, not joining Chloe and me on the bench.

"She's kind of shy," he says. And whether this is all the explanation necessary or not, it's all he gives. "So where are you guys off to today?"

Chloe used to have a crush on Randy even though he's kind

of a jerk. But that was like two years ago before he'd started dating Hannah.

"We're going exploring," Chloe says.

Randy lets out a low whistle. "Your mom is letting you out of the penitentiary today, Piper?"

I nod and stop staring at his little sister. "She's out of town." I say it like it happens all the time, like my mom leaves me to make my own choices and hang with my friends all I want. But Randy's not an idiot.

"The prison warden is really gone?"

"Yep." And even I can't keep the smile off my face.

Randy laughs. "So when does the party start?"

I laugh, too, and shake my head. "No party." I haven't even considered a party. Who would I invite? Shayne and Reese? As little experience as I have in these types of matters, the thought of Reese and Shayne in the same room equals a completely awkward situation.

Randy turns more toward us but keeps his arm around his sister. "Oh, come on, Piper. This is a once-in-a-lifetime opportunity. How about just me and Hannah and a couple of the guys from school? We'll bring our own beer and everything."

Would my mom be more upset if I drank beer with a bunch of kids at our place or if I ventured out into the city with Chloe when a heat warning had been issued? "Tempting, Randy, but Chloe and I are just going to hang out."

"God, that's boring."

I'm saved from further banter by the shuttle. Its brakes whistle, too loud to hear anything else Randy may say. He moves in front of us when the door opens and helps his sister up the steps, watching to make sure her FON gets scanned. And then he steps back down and lets us by.

"You're letting her go on the shuttle by herself?" Chloe asks.

Randy shrugs. "She'll be fine."

"That's stupid, Randy," Chloe says. "She won't be fine. She could be abducted or something."

Randy waves at his sister who's found a seat already. I have yet to scan my FON. "I told you she'll be fine," he says. "She's pretty independent."

Chloe points at Randy's sister. "Independent? What is she? Six?"

"Seven," Randy says.

I've been watching, listening, but decide to open my mouth. "Randy, seven is not independent. There are bad people out in the world."

Bad people, like maybe my father, who prey on kids and steal them away. Who ask what frightens them and then turn around and use it to do just that.

Randy fixes his eyes on me. "Piper, there are bad people every-where. She's going to be fine." And he ends every bit of question and conversation by turning around and walking back in the direction of his house.

Once he's gone, I continue up the steps to the shuttle. Chloe joins me, though not until I've scanned my FON. Randy's sister stares out the window, looking at Randy's departing form.

"Randy is crazy," Chloe says, stepping up behind me.

I catch the driver's eye and point to Randy's sister. "She's rid-ing alone," I say.

The shuttle driver nods. "She always does. She'll be fine. I'll keep an eye on her." And he smiles to reassure me until I move back and take a seat.

"Where are we going?" I ask once Chloe swipes her FON and sits down next to me. Aside from her cryptic exploring talk, I'm not sure what Chloe has in mind.

"The Greenbelt."

I don't even try to keep the smile off my face. My mom's never let me go to the Greenbelt before. She tells me it's a breeding ground for vagrants and criminals, but all the kids at school go there on the weekends since it's fresh water and hasn't yet run dry.

"How was your date?" Chloe asks.

"Which one?" I say, deciding to stall a bit. It's fun to be the one with juicy info for once.

Chloe rolls her eyes. "Puh-lease, Piper. You only had the date of the century." She puts her hand on my arm. "Tell me about Reese. I want to hear everything."

And I want to tell her everything—even though thinking about it makes my stomach flip. "I'll tell you when we get there."

"You better," Chloe says.

THE RIDE TAKES FOREVER BECAUSE FOR SOME REASON EVERY-one in Austin is riding the shuttle today. Or at least it seems that way. Randy's sister gets off at her elementary school, and I relax when I see hundreds of kids there, too, waiting to go inside. They let all the younger kids go to school on weekends during heat advisories to take advantage of the air-conditioning. The thermometer on the side of the school reads one hundred and seventeen in bright orange numbers. Four degrees more than when we left and now officially in the orange zone. I push away thoughts of the heat bubble and try to focus on our day.

When we get off the shuttle at our stop, the change is imme-diate. The shuttle has eco-friendly A/C, which may not be the greatest, but outside we're now at the mercy of the atmosphere.

"Maybe we should—" I start.

Chloe puts her hand up. "Don't even say it." And like she's trying to make a point, she takes the herbal heat suppressor out of her pocket and smashes it under her foot.

Sweat trickles through my thick hair and runs down my neck. "Aren't you hot?" I say.

She kicks at the dirt with her toes. "I feel great. Like today's the start of a whole new future."

And despite the heat, her enthusiasm infects me.

We make our way down a rocky path until I can't see the road anymore. Ahead of us is the Greenbelt, complete with trees and rocks and a trickle of water—fresh and clear—and we take off our shoes and dip our feet in. It's still early, and though I'm looking around for either vagrants or criminals, I don't see either. No one is around besides the two of us.

I look at Chloe, and Tanni's words pound into my head, causing the bump there to throb. *Chloe will die.* I push the words out of my mind, but they're persistent.

"What?" Chloe's looking at me. She still has a smile, but only half-sized.

I'm not about to tell her about Tanni's prediction. "Nothing."

"No really. You've been looking at me funny all week."

Have I been that transparent?

"You're imagining things." I reach up to her arm and feel her tattoo. "I'm just excited we got these." But I pull my hands back when I touch her. With the temperature as high as it is, Chloe's skin should be burning, but it feels cool.

"Yeah. I can't believe you really did it," she says.

My mouth falls open. "You thought I'd chicken out?"

"Let's face it. It's the only rebellious thing you've done since I've known you."

"Yeah, I guess so." I think about Reese and Shayne and the mixed-up night before.

"So what gives? Why are you looking at me so funny?"

I'm not going to tell her about Tanni. But still . . .

"Do you believe in fate, Chloe?" As I say it, the heat seems to press down on me.

She kicks the water with her foot. "Like whether we were fated to be friends?"

"Kind of." I splash some water across onto the rocks, watching it dry almost as soon as it hits. I see a tiny pool of fish, swimming circles and trying to reach the next part of the creek. So many fish have died off; only the tiniest ones still live here.

Chloe rubs my tattoo, and again, I'm struck by how cold she is. Like her body isn't processing the heat at all. She's not even sweating. "Yeah. I think we were destined to be friends," she says. "I felt that way from the first day we met."

I felt that way, too. On my first day of public school after being homeschooled my entire life, I was sure I'd talk to no one the entire day. In fact, I vowed I wouldn't. Since my best friend Charlotte had died in sixth grade, I kept my distance from people.

I decided I wouldn't make friends, and my mom would be happy. And if my mom was happy, then I could keep this small semblance of freedom. But no sooner had I found a seat on the shuttle than Chloe had plunked herself next to me.

"You aren't going to hog the whole seat, are you?" Chloe asked.

I shook my head, and down she sat.

I did my best to keep my mouth shut, but Chloe had been persistent.

"Are you new?" she asked.

I nodded, still trying to keep my vow of silence.

"So where did you move from?" she asked.

"Chicago," I finally said, thinking I could end the conversation even though this girl seemed kind of cool. "Homeschooled."

"Wow. Your whole life?"

"Yeah. Even before when I lived in Virginia," I said.

Chloe offered me a Life Saver then, giving me my choice of colors. I reached for the one on the top, trying to be polite.

She scrunched up her nose. "You really like the green ones?"

I hated the green ones. They reminded me of fish scales. "No, but that's okay."

She grabbed the green Life Saver out of my fingers and pitched it out the shuttle window, which shocked me since littering is way illegal. "Pick your favorite color," she said.

I took a red one. And we've been friends ever since.

Movement off in the tall trees catches my eye. I look through the barren trunks but see nothing. Not even leaves rustling. I slowly realize the whole world is still. And hot.

"How about death?" I say. My chest tightens even as the words come out. But I can't stop myself now. "Do you believe fate determines ahead of time when someone will die?"

Chloe turns my way, and our eyes meet. She stares at me, not saying a word. I notice her orange bandana holding back her hair, matching the burning sun overhead. She's stopped smiling, and I know she's thinking about my question.

She stands up and moves farther down the creek. It narrows to a trickle here, hardly moving over the rocks. They say the creek's been drying out for years, and once it stops flowing, the clean water source to Austin will be cut off. Chloe squats down and puts her hands in the water, bringing it up to her face, but instead of drinking it, she lets it slip through her fingers.

Chloe will die.

The light shifts, and I imagine her there, lying dead in the creek, facing downward, looking toward Hell.

Chloe will die.

I close my eyes and suck in a breath. I smell the earth around me—the rocks and the soil and the tree bark. And I smell something else. Pungent and odorous. The thick smell of rotting flesh.

"I don't know," Chloe says.

I'd forgotten she hasn't answered. I try to push the smell away. "You don't know if you believe in fate?"

"I don't know if death is known ahead of time." She reaches down again, scooping more water with her hands and letting it slip away.

Far off, in the distance, the sirens wail. I pull out my FON and confirm the deadly temperature of one hundred and twenty-two. The red zone. And the heat bubble has come.

I jump to my feet. "We need to go, Chloe. We need to get out of here."

The rotting smell is even stronger. I look at the trees, and this time I see a man, short and strong, and when he moves to the side, I see wings attached to his back. White as clouds, and so long the tips nearly touch the ground behind him.

He ignores me. He's looking right at Chloe.

Chloe will die.

The man takes a step toward Chloe. She's looking right at him but doesn't seem to notice he's there. From overhead comes the thump of the disperser missile being fired. I brace myself. All I know is I need to get Chloe away from here.

"Chloe! We need to go now!" I move to take a step toward her, but the heat presses on me. The air's so thick, I'm having a hard time finding oxygen.

Chloe opens her mouth to answer me, but her words won't come. And for the first time, panic crosses her face.

"Run, Chloe!" I know the man approaching her is Death. He's coming for Chloe.

She doesn't move; it's like her mind has stopped processing the world around her. The winged man takes another few steps, gliding so smoothly across the earth, it's like he's flying. His rotten smell permeates the air. The heat descends, and Chloe crumples to the ground.

Chloe will die. The voice in my mind chants over and over.

"Shut up!" I can't take it. I need to reach Chloe before Death does. I suck in the hot air and begin to run. But the winged man is already there, by her side, and he's grabbed her wrist.

Her face tightens, and the color drains out. I've almost reached her when I stop in the wet bed of the creek and see Shayne. I have no clue why he's here; right now, I don't care.

"Help me!"

He hears me. I know he does. The winged man shimmers and begins to fade. Chloe's fading, too. I cross the distance and break their arms apart. The man glances behind himself. He lets go. And then he stands there watching.

I manage to get my hands under Chloe's armpits and drag her from the water. She's pale and cold, but she's still breathing. My face is covered in tears, but I don't take the time to wipe them away as I sink down next to her.

"I can't," Shayne says, standing next to the winged man.

I look up, meeting his eyes.

"Can't what?" I say.

"I can't help you. She's supposed to die."

"No! She's not. She's alive." Chloe has to be alive. I know it. Why did she have to ignore the heat advisory anyway?

He shakes his head and places a hand on her limp chest. "She shouldn't be." Under his palm, I see her chest rise and fall, erratic. She's not breathing enough. And she's pale. Way too pale.

I stand and punch at him with my fists, but he catches them. "She can't die."

Shayne doesn't argue with anything I'm saying. He doesn't try to explain.

The breath moves in and out of her body. It's shallow but still there. And the man with wings has vanished.

"She's alive," I say.

Shayne reaches out and wipes my face. His fingers come back covered with dirt that's mixed with my tears. "She has to die, Piper. It's the way things are."

I shake my head and try to stay my tears, try to look fierce. "I won't let her die."

Shayne doesn't speak. He looks to Chloe, pale on the ground, but breathing. I bite my lip to keep from saying anything, trying to piece out why Shayne is even here. Why would he be here anyway?

It's only after we stand there in our silent deadlock for over a minute that Shayne finally responds. "If you had a choice, would you want her to live?"

It has to be one of the stupidest questions I've ever heard. "Of course."

Shayne looks to the trees and seems to consider something.

"I would always want her to live," I say again, just in case he didn't hear me the first time.

He turns back my way and nods. "Will you come with me somewhere? Please?"

On the ground, Chloe's stopped breathing, and I'm about to say something when I notice everything else has stopped, too. The fish I saw swimming earlier are motionless. Not even the water is moving. Every single drop is frozen in time. It's like the entire world hibernates. I squat down to Chloe.

"She'll be fine." He knows what I'm thinking.

"I should get her to a hospital. She could have heatstroke."

Shayne shakes his head. "I swear, she'll be fine."

"How can you possibly know that?"

"She'll stay just like this until we get back. No one will bother her. I promise."

"What if she wakes—?"

"Seriously, Piper. Trust me. Please." His voice is layered with frustration, and his eyes plead with me.

I want to trust him. And I want Chloe to live. And if one is tied to the other, I'm willing to take the chance. Somehow Tanni and the winged man of death and Shayne being here now are all linked.

I move forward, and Shayne wraps his arms around me and fills me with a hint of courage that wasn't there seconds ago.

"It'll be okay," he says. "Right?"

Maybe there is still some fear in my eyes. "Right." Even I hear my voice shake.

"Good."

I think I'm calm. I think maybe everything will be okay. And then we start sinking into the ground. I clench my fingers into Shayne's sides because the movement is so sudden.

"It's okay," he says. "Remember?"

I can't answer because, in the next second, I'm swallowed by the earth. But instead of dirt and grit, I'm in a silvery void of flowing liquid mercury which seeps into my mouth and ears and nose.

I'm going to drown.

I hold my breath, sure the liquid will kill me, and in seconds, my lungs feel like they will collapse. I try to hold out a little longer. Maybe the silver fluid will be over soon. But the seconds pass, and I can't stand it anymore.

I take a breath.

Instead of gagging me, the liquid fills my lungs, and they

expand and contract as if with normal air. And in that moment, I finally think that maybe it will be okay.

I shut my eyes and hold on tight to Shayne, and we seem to float in nothingness. Nowhere on Earth. Like a world all its own. Again I breathe in, searching for a taste in the silvery liquid, but it's like formless ether, liquid and gas and nothing all at the same time. Though we are floating, a current pulls on us, downward and upward, right and left. Pulling us toward our destination. When I feel cool air on my face, I dare to open my eyes.

We're in a cavern made of rust-colored rocks. Silver fluid trickles down the walls and pools on the hard-packed dirt floor. Light seems to come from the pools of silver and casts all kinds of weird shadows on the walls and ceiling above. Next to us is an underground river, and it's so dark, the water looks black. But it's bubbling, and voices come from it.

The hum of voices is freaking me out, but Shayne hardly glances at the water. He pulls a large gold coin from his pocket and spins it around on his fingers. It flashes in the dim silver light of the cavern, and I see a boat coming across the river toward us.

I haven't moved, and I realize I'm gripping Shayne's arms so hard my fingers hurt. So I loosen my grip and grab his hand instead. "Where are we?" Unlike our hot Earth above, there's a breeze blowing through the cavern that smells of burning sweetness and cools the temperature down way below ninety.

He turns to me as the boat pulls up to the dock. "Haven't you figured it out by now?"

I have, but I don't want to say it. And he doesn't press me. I can't believe it, because it can't possibly be true. Because if it is true, does that mean I am dead in place of Chloe?

The boat's tied up now, and a man jumps out onto the long dock extending into the river and walks toward us. The black water behind him extends forever.

"You have company," the man says.

Shayne nods, and with his lips pressed together, he suddenly looks as nervous as I am. "She said she wanted to come."

The man lifts a thick hairy eyebrow. "Let's hope so."

Shayne looks toward me, and I nod. My hand hurts from grabbing his so hard, but I'm not letting go. The water's still bubbling, and the voices sound more like cries. I swear I see things swimming around out there in the black water. Things with horrible faces and sharp teeth.

Shayne flips the gold coin off his thumb with his finger, and the man catches it.

"Really. You know it's not necessary." But the man pockets it anyway.

"I don't ever want anyone to say I don't pay my fare," Shayne says.

The man's face cracks into a broad smile. "No one would ever say anything of the sort." His skin looks as thick as leather, and his smile lines are so pronounced, they look sculpted. And his hair's mostly missing with the exception of a few tufts above his ears and his giant, bushy eyebrows. The smile makes me think if I weren't around, the man would be tempted to muss up the top of Shayne's hair or cuff his shoulder or something equally endearing.

"You know they would," Shayne says. He begins walking toward the dock, and since I'm holding his hand, I follow, trying to take in my situation without totally freaking myself out.

The man talks about the boat as we walk, like it's a favorite family member, and he's so friendly, I can't help but feel I've known him my whole life.

"My name's Piper," I say. The dark walls of the cavern shift and flicker around me, and the water's still moving. But the darkness wraps around me and cools my skin from the world above.

The man stops walking. "Piper." He presses his lips together. "It's a good name."

"What's yours?"

The man looks to Shayne, who gives a small nod.

"Charon. I'm Charon."

My breath catches. I've studied enough mythology in my life to know who Charon is. He's the ferryman. I turn to Shayne. "Then that means . . ."

His eyes meet mine, and I see the red specks in his brown irises again, but now they're flickering. "You're in Hell."

I ask the question that has to follow. "And you are . . ."

"Hades. Lord of the Underworld."

14

Acheron

I'M NOT SURE WHAT TO SAY. IT'S LIKE I'M A PART OF AN ELABOrate hoax, but there's no way Shayne and Charon could create this illusion. I want to turn and run away, but I can't imagine where I would go; I sank through the ground to get here.

"You're a Greek god?"

Shayne shrugs like it's the most normal question in the world. "Greek. Roman. Egyptian. Whatever. My job is the same."

"But, I mean, you're a god?"

"What?" Shayne says. "I don't strike you as the godly type?"

Okay, if I had to draw an image in my mind of what a Greek god would look like, Shayne is about as close as I'd ever get. But still . . .

"It's not that. It's just there's always been reality and mythology. And the two aren't the same."

"And you're sure about that?" Shayne says.

I'm definitely not sure about it now. Not anymore. "It's just a little mind-blowing."

Shayne smiles. "I knew if I tried hard enough, I could blow your mind."

I laugh and then immediately feel guilty. The image of Chloe's pale body haunts me.

"I should get back," I say. "Chloe needs me."

Shayne puts a hand under my chin and looks me directly in the eyes. It's like he wants to draw my discomfort away and into himself. Like he would relieve my burden at the cost of his own. "Okay, here's the thing. I stopped time."

"You can do that?" My anxiety begins to dissipate at the edges.

He rubs my chin with his thumb, and chills spill down my neck. "My father's the god of time," he says. "It's an inherited thing."

"So you stopped it now?" I ask. I ignore the father-being-the-god-of-time thing because it's just too much to process right now.

"Yeah, I stopped it now. I need to show you what Chloe could have."

I look out at the frothing river. "You mean if she dies."

Shayne nods. "You can see her place here in the Underworld, and then you can decide."

"Decide if she lives or dies?" I shake my head. "I don't need to see the Underworld. I want Chloe alive."

"It's not all monsters, Piper. Just give it a chance. That's all I ask."

I've already made my decision. If I really do have a choice here—if this isn't some bizarre dream—I won't let Chloe die. And I did see time stop. Chloe is fine, and Chloe will live. But . . .

Shayne is a god. And mythology is real. And the Underworld beckons me and draws me toward it. It wraps its tendrils around my body and calls to me with a voice I don't want to ignore. I want to see it. "Okay. I'll give it a chance."

And his smile brightens the darkness around me.

We walk to the boat, and I get in. It's large enough to carry at least ten people, and I move to a seat at the front—next to Shayne. Charon follows us in and heads to the back, picking up a long pole which leans against the smooth black wood. I watch Charon, and he catches my eye and smiles. The lines crinkle around his face again, and it infects me, forcing me to smile back. Letting me accept the mythical world around me and live in it for the moment. Helping ease my mind of worries about Chloe.

Charon unties the boat, and it begins to drift. Though the light brightens as we move, I can't see the opposite shore. The water bubbles and laps against the sides, and something jumps out of the water, catching a bubble in its mouth and swallowing it.

Hell. I'm in Hell. And Shayne is the Lord of the Underworld. "Are you the devil?"

Shayne puts his hand on the inside of my bare leg, below the line of my shorts. Goose bumps explode on my legs. "Do you want me to be?"

Charon chuckles from the back of the boat, and Shayne laughs, too.

It seems like a reasonable question to me, and I know what answer I want. "No."

Shayne rubs my thigh, smoothing the goose bumps. But it's futile. His rubbing only causes more goose bumps.

"Good. I am not the devil."

"You get asked that a lot?"

"Almost every soul who comes here. It's that whole Hell and devil association thing."

I put my hand on his, and he stops rubbing my leg. "So is there a devil?" I ask.

Shayne sighs. "Piper, let me tell you something. The devil is everywhere. Aboveground. Down here. He's evil. And he's always looking for a way in."

Just when my goose bumps were about to disappear. "A way in where?"

Shayne lifts his hand, waving it across the river. "A way in anywhere. Hell. Earth. Souls. Any tiny crack or crevice. Evil is trying to seep inside and take over."

I've been fortunate so far that evil has stayed away from my life, but I think about the escalating crime rate and the rash of fighting and war because of the Global Heating Crisis. I turn back to the water to where he's pointing—to the voices I hear there.

Send me back to my baby.

Please don't let me fall.

I'm so young.

I can almost picture faces behind the words. The water bubbles with the sound of each one, and soon they blend together. I lean over and try to get a closer look, to see the things swimming below the surface.

I didn't do it.

My daughter. Don't let my daughter die.

Each voice is different but the same. It takes me a few minutes to realize why, but then it hits me. Sorrow. Anguish for a life which will never come back.

Help us.

I want to reach in. To release the grief in the voices. I lean over and put my hands on the side of the boat. Water splashes up and sprinkles my face. I stand and try to reach farther, but my hand slips, and I fall.

A hand grabs me on the arm and catches me, guiding me back to my seat.

"Careful . . .

". . . my love."

I face Shayne. Or Hades. But he looks back out at the water.

My love. The words had been as soft as a whisper, and I wonder if I made them up.

"What are they?" I ask.

"Voices of the dead. The last thoughts and wishes of people leaving the land of the living. They stay here in the River Acheron."

They continue to call out to me, as the monsters devour them with their long snouts, some with a single gulp, some slipping through the teeth of one only to be grabbed by another. The monsters jump out of the water every so often, exposing spikes on their backs and fins that look sharp as razors. "How can you stand to listen?" I ask.

Shayne shrugs. "Better for the dead to leave their sorrows here than live with them for all eternity. It helps keep evil away."

"You mean they aren't sad after this?"

Shayne smiles and reaches up, brushing his fingers against my tattoo. It's hard to see in the dim light around us, but I feel his fingers stopping on the scar of it. "The sorrows remain here, and the souls are free to go to their place of eternal rest. Why be burdened with dying thoughts when no one can ever go back?"

"Ever?"

"No. Never."

And Chloe had almost died.

Shayne puts his arm around me, and I lean against him because his presence makes me never want to be anywhere else. I push the sorrows of the dead from my mind.

But then I hear Charon clear his throat.

Shayne turns back and looks. "Do you have something to say, Charon?"

I swivel around also so I can see him there in the back of the boat, poling us across.

"It just seems you may want to explain." And then Charon looks at Shayne, and a lazy grin covers his big, weathered face.

"Explain what?" I ask.

Charon raises an eyebrow. "The exceptions. I just think they should be mentioned."

"Charon. My rule follower."

I look at Shayne, waiting.

He puts up his hands. "Every rule has exceptions. It's the way of the world. One or two exceptions do not mean people can come back from the dead." Shayne's eyes blacken, and I see the red flashes.

"People can't leave the Underworld. That is the rule. But of course, as Charon has been so kind as to point out, there have been a couple exceptions over time." He looks back at Charon. "A long time. And we never make a habit of it. And there are always consequences."

I begin to ask the question I've been thinking, but the words won't come out. I think it's because I'm not sure I want to hear the answer.

"What?" Shayne asks.

"Nothing. It's nothing."

But he persists. "Tell me."

I take a deep breath and force the words out, realizing even as I say them that I will be in the Underworld forever. Even if I haven't died, I will remain here. No one leaves. And the thought hardly fazes me except I'll have to leave Chloe. "Am I dead instead of Chloe? Will I be able to leave?"

Shayne surprises me. I figure he'd break it to me gently. But he starts laughing. "Do you want to leave?"

I glance back again at Charon who's also smiling. "Maybe," I say.

Shayne stops laughing. "Maybe." He licks his lips and squeezes my hand. "Well then maybe you can leave. Unless we decide to keep you here forever."

I'm not sure I'd mind. Right now, being here with Shayne is perfect. But I think of Chloe. How close she came to dying. And Shayne saved her.

"But why Chloe?"

"It was her time."

"No!" I push his arm off my shoulder. "It was not her time."

He meets my gaze. Again, I see the red flashes in the brown of his eyes; they've started back up. Fire behind the darkness of Hell. "Yes. It was. Fate told you so herself."

"Tanni? So she is real?"

Shayne nods.

"But you saved Chloe."

He glances back at Charon who turns away. He's avoiding the conversation.

Shayne's voice is quiet. "I know."

He did save her.

"So what happens now? What if I choose to have Chloe live?" Which I know I will. It's not even a choice.

"It will be an exception," Shayne says.

What would Chloe's sorrow have been had she died? What would she have left for the monsters to devour?

Shayne pulls me back toward him, erasing the distance I've put between us. "Just give the Underworld a chance, Piper. Letting Chloe die may be the better choice."

"I doubt it."

Shayne cocks his head. "Maybe so. But try to be open-minded."

There's a magnetic ball in the pit of my stomach drawing me to the Underworld. I want to see it and right now I want to be with Shayne. But as I sit there, I remember something. Something I'm not sure I want to ask. Everything I know about the Underworld has made one thing clear. Hades is married to Persephone. And they rule the Underworld together.

I open my mouth, but I'm not sure how to bring it up.

"What?" Shayne says.

"It's nothing," I say.

"No really," he says. "You were going to say something."

I let out a long breath and finally let the question come. "I've studied mythology in school. I always thought . . ."

"She's gone," he says. "She's gone and she's not coming back."

I'm not sure how to respond. "What happened?" I finally ask.

"I don't want to talk about it. Please just don't ask, okay?" His tone leaves little room for debate.

"I'm sorry," I say.

"I was, too," he says. "But I've moved on."

With the interest he's showing in me, I have to believe he's telling the truth. I drop it so I won't risk him changing his mind. Maybe he's left his sorrows here in the river, too. I settle against him and watch the feasting of the monsters, and push Shayne's past romances out of my mind.

We travel from the dark cavern and then through a swamp so hazy and gray I can't see the front of the boat. The haze dissipates, and we're out into the middle of an ocean with a sky overhead that sparkles like a crystal. Two suns pound down from above, but unlike on Earth, the heat they generate finds that perfect in-between space of warmth and cool. It's like what my mom told me spring used to be like, back before the Global Heating Crisis started. She said autumn was a season of dying, and winter brought horrible temperatures so cold people froze to death, but that each spring, life returned to the earth.

I don't realize we're approaching the far shore until clouds form in the crystal sky and the monsters in the water diminish. The voices weaken, as if no sorrow is permitted to reach the banks. And then I see the trees and feel the humidity. Limbs twist over the water, dripping below, and as we pass under the weeping willows, droplets rain down on me, falling in my thick hair. Far above, grackles call out, talking amongst themselves, jumping from branch to branch. And when I see the cerulean-blue sky complete with clouds, I know we're no longer in a cavern but in some other world entirely.

Shayne jumps out first when the boat pushes its way through the reeds and cattails and hits up against the dock. He grabs the rope and loops it around a post, and I can't help but notice his muscles moving beneath his shirt. He catches me staring. Above him, the canopy of trees holds back the light from the suns of Hell, and shadows play on the hard wooden surface. Then Shayne extends his hand toward me, and I grab it, letting him help me out.

Charon flips the gold coin, which Shayne catches high in its arc. "I can't take your money," Charon says.

Shayne laughs and puts the coin back in his pocket. "I know." And their exchange makes me wonder if Charon is like a father to Shayne.

"You're going back already?" I ask Charon.

"My work is never done. And when I say never, I do mean

never." Charon laughs, and I imagine him crossing the river thousands of times each day. The same routine over and over again.

The image of the gold coin flashes in my mind. "You must make a lot of money."

"Not as much as you might think," Charon says.

"Nobody buries people with money anymore," Shayne says. "We've had to start a donation fund within the assembly of gods."

"There's an assembly of gods?" I ask. And I wonder if it's filled with the same corruption the city council has back home. Does someone like Councilman Rendon lead it and make every decision based on his own gain?

"Everyone needs rules and government," Shayne says. "Especially immortals."

"And you're on it?" I ask.

"Yeah," Shayne says. "I'm on it." He unties the rope and tosses it back in the boat. Charon uses the pole and turns the boat around, already pushing it through the reeds, toward the other shore, away from the overhanging branches and back into the river of sorrow.

15

Crossroads

I'M TOTALLY UNPREPARED FOR WHAT HAPPENS NEXT. SOMETHING bounds out of a tunnel ahead of us and leaps for Shayne, knocking him flat to the ground and landing on his chest. It's a black dog the size of a bear with three heads, all of which are licking Shayne's face, shoving each other out of the way. One begins to growl at another, and pretty soon, Shayne's pushing the dog off him.

"Cerberus! Be careful!" He looks to me and laughs. "One of these days, he's going to get carried away and bite my ear off." He stands up and reaches out with both hands, scratching two of the dog's heads. The other head nuzzles against his arm until he scratches it behind the ears.

"You have a dog?" I know I'm stating the obvious, but it's just such a bizarre scene, I'm not sure what else to say. And the word *three-headed* does not seem to be a necessary descriptor.

"Cerberus guards the entrance to the Underworld."

Cerberus looks my way, and his tail goes into overdrive. He turns, and I know he's going to run for me and knock me over. I imagine the three heads licking me, and my lips lift into a smile I can't hold back.

But Shayne moves first, grabbing the neck in the middle. "Not yet, Cerberus. Let her get acquainted first."

Cerberus wriggles and tries to break free. He whines and pulls and tugs, but Shayne holds firm, and I see the muscles in his arms flexing, veins showing, sweat covering them.

"He likes you."

My smile grows, and I walk toward Cerberus. "I like him." I scratch him behind the ears of his left head like I'd seen Shayne do. His tail flaps back and forth, moving so hard his backside slams into Shayne. And then Cerberus jumps up, placing a paw on either of my shoulders, which sends me flying to the soft, muddy soil. All three heads begin a licking frenzy.

"Cerberus!"

He keeps licking. I'm laughing so hard, I can't do anything but move my head from side to side, trying to evade the three sloppy tongues. Completely unsuccessfully.

"Cerberus! Stop right now!"

He stops licking, but his paws stay on my shoulders. One of his heads swivels in Shayne's direction. I manage to stop laughing long enough to speak. "It's okay. He's a good dog."

He wags his tail and moves his heads back to start licking again.

"Cerberus!"

Shayne grabs hold of Cerberus around the middle and lifts him off me. I can breathe again. Shayne walks to a rocky wall, still holding Cerberus, and takes something out of one of the wooden supply chests stacked there. He tosses it across the way and releases Cerberus, who bounds off after it, disappearing into a pitch-black tunnel. Shayne comes back over to me. I've managed to stand up and brush some of the dirt and slobber off myself. It's gotten everywhere, even inside my ears.

"Nice dog." I laugh, trying to shake my ears clean.

Shayne combs his hand through my hair. A clump of dirt falls to the ground. I must be covered in it. How can he look so clean? He's been slammed in the mud also.

"He's a bit on the excitable side. But there's no better dog," Shayne says. "Plus he eats people who try to sneak in."

"Remind me never to sneak in," I say.

Shayne smiles, and I'm struck by how completely hot he really is. Like maybe I can believe in Greek gods, because the guy standing in front of me totally qualifies. But it's not just his looks.

It's every single thing about him. The way he moves with such confidence. The way he looks at me like he understands me. Even as I stand here next to him, talking about his dog, I feel like we're connected on a way deeper level. Like there is so much more we could be talking about. It takes my breath away.

"You wouldn't be sneaking. You have an open invitation," he says.

I look back into the dark cave to distract myself from my thoughts, and then I take a few steps back so I can see more of the rocky wall. There are ten tunnels cut into the rock that look identical.

"Where do they go?" I ask.

"Different parts of the Underworld."

I point to the one where Cerberus just disappeared. "So this one leads to . . ."

"My home." He reaches for my hand and moves it so it's pointing to the tunnel on the far left now. I try not to think about the amazing sensation his touch sends through me. "Except now it's down this way."

"So it changes?"

He nods.

"Why?"

"Security. Only I know where they lead at any given time."

"You and Cerberus," I venture.

Shayne laughs. "Yeah, me and Cerberus." He points one tunnel over from where we stand. "And now it's down there."

I step up to the tunnel he's pointing at and look inside. My eyes adjust, and I see there's nothing but blackness ahead, and I know that's the way we're going. Excitement runs though me.

We start down the tunnel. There's a breeze blowing through it, and each time it touches my arm, it caresses me. Even though I can hardly see him, I feel Shayne walking next to me, almost like he has some sort of energy field. I sidle closer to him because I want to touch him again. The darkness gives me courage, and maybe it does the same for him because he stops walking, and then I'm up against the cave wall.

"Piper." His voice catches when he says my name.

He's pressing against me, his warmth at my front, and the cold, hard stone wall behind me. His breath covers my face, and I'm tempted to move forward and kiss him.

But he puts a hand on my cheek. "I need to ask you something."

"What?" I dare myself to put my arms around him. I trace my fingers up his back, over his shirt, feeling his hard muscles, which shiver at my touch. It's like Shayne puts me in a place of comfort I've never known existed.

"Do you want to be here?"

I nod in the darkness.

"Do you want to see my world?"

I do. For reasons beyond my explanation, I am drawn to Shayne. To Hell. Even the stones in this tunnel seem to draw me in, making me feel like I belong.

"You have to answer me. Even if you weren't here for Chloe, would you want to be here?"

"Yes." And I lean my head forward again, and this time, our lips finally meet, and we kiss, and his mouth tastes like burning sweetness. There is no way I've only known Shayne a week. Our kiss—the way it tastes and makes me feel—is so familiar. I trace my fingers up his spine, and he lets out a small groan. I wouldn't have thought it possible, but he pushes himself closer until every bit of our bodies touches. Against my chest, his heart beats, joining the pounding of my own. His hands are at my shoulders, then my neck, then down at my waist.

They start to travel downward to my hips, but then he stops, pulling his head away. He steps backward, taking deep breaths matching my own. I can't move, because I can't get enough air to make my mind think, and we stand there in silence in the dark of the tunnel.

"That's nice," he says when his breathing has slowed.

I still can't move—though if I could, it might just be back to him. "Yeah, really nice."

"Thank you," he says.

"For what?"

"For trusting me. And being with me."

"I might never leave," I say.

He lets out a laugh. "And I might never let you."

He takes my hand, and we again walk down the tunnel. The warmth grows with every step we take, but the breeze continues, making it almost balmy. Soon the tunnel begins to grow lighter, and I see flickering, like flames of a fire, ahead in the distance.

"We're almost there." He gives my hand a quick squeeze, and then we turn a final corner, and the world erupts in light ahead of us.

"You live here?" When I thought of Hell in the past, I always figured it to be black and fiery.

He leads me down a couple steps into the room before me. The smooth, white walls look like they get polished hourly. The pristine floor is decorated with a giant mosaic in tiny black and red tiles stretching the entire distance of the room. It's a design of red flowers growing off black vines—a design that reminds me of drawings I made as a child. In the center of the room sits a coffee table with cut gems inlaid in the circular top and red and black chairs surrounding it. The colored gems of the table are arranged in bouquets of flowers—lotuses and orchids, with stems twisting around each other, forming a continuous design.

"Did you expect something else?" Shayne asks.

I turn to him, dragging my eyes away from the table and the amazing mosaic floor. "Well, yeah. Look at this place."

He looks around. "You don't like it?"

"Of course I like it. How could I not like it? I mean, it's fantastic."

Shayne smiles and sits on a black chair. "Someone with impeccable taste designed it."

An enormous pang of jealousy rockets through me when I realize he must be talking about Persephone. And I think that even if she is gone like he's said, I may never be able to compete with any memories of her. I stem the envy running through me.

He gestures at a red chair, and I sit down, sinking into the plush leather, letting it swallow me like I want this whole world to do with each second that passes. Shayne waves his hand over the table, and a bottle of wine and two glasses appear on the bed of colored flowers.

"Isn't there some myth about eating or drinking in the Underworld?"

Shayne picks up the bottle. He uncorks it and fills the two red crystal wine goblets halfway. At this point, I don't mind drinking it if it means I could stay here with Shayne forever.

"Yes, a myth." He hands me my glass.

I take it but don't put it to my lips. "Is it true?"

"Do you want it to be?"

I put the glass to my mouth, taking a long drink. "Yes. I want it to be." I think about my mom for some reason, right as I drink it, and try to imagine her reaction to what I'm doing. Sitting with Hades in the Underworld drinking wine. And she expected me to stay in while she was gone.

"Something funny?"

"It's not really funny. I was just thinking about my mom."

Shayne takes a sip of his own wine. "I'm guessing your mom has serious issues."

It's funny he should realize this after knowing me for such a short period of time. But it's not like I can deny it. "She's not that bad." Which is a flat-out lie. She is that bad.

"Maybe we shouldn't think about your mom."

Shayne's right. Thinking about my mom and what she would do if she saw me now is laughable but also a mood dampener. So I push her out of my mind.

I look around the room. The far wall holds a bookcase stacked with volumes of leather-bound books. I stand and move toward it, bringing my glass of wine with me. It's so different than the wine I had with Reese last night. Sweeter and warmer.

When Reese pops into my mind, my heart races. I turn to Shayne, who's looking at me but doesn't say a word, and I pray mind reading is not a skill the Lord of the Underworld possesses. I look back to the books.

"You have a nice collection."

Shayne gets up and joins me. His hand brushes across the nape of my neck, sending a shiver down to my toes. "I like to read."

It's an amazing response from an amazing guy.

Inset in the bookcases is a framed map. "What's that?"

"The Underworld." Shayne traces his finger over the network of rivers on the map. "There are five rivers in the Underworld. Boundaries between the lands." He points across one of the rivers. "And here are the Elysian Fields . . ."

"The what?"

"Elysian Fields. They're kind of like the nice place," he says. "The place you get to go when you've been really good."

"Like Heaven?"

"Some people call it that."

A lump forms in my throat before I can stop it. "Is that where Chloe would go?"

Shayne's hand settles on mine, and he nods. "Of course."

"I don't want her to die."

"I know," he says. "But you promised you'd at least consider."

The lump stays in my throat. Chloe is my best friend. But I did promise. "I want to see it."

"Anytime you're ready."

I reach for my glass and take a final sip of wine. It seeps through me, tickling as it goes. "I'm ready."

Shayne sets my glass on a shelf along with his own—two red glasses on a shelf of black. He reaches out his hand, and I place mine in his, remembering how I held Reese's hand only last night. But I push Reese far from my mind, because he has no place here right now. Shayne brushes my cheek with his other hand. "Then let's go see paradise."

16

Paradise

WE COME OUT OF A TUNNEL AND WALK TO THE SHORE OF A river. Tree limbs hang low, covered in ice crystals that sparkle everywhere, bouncing off the snowy ground under our feet. Dampness is thick in the air. This river is frozen, and even though we've entered a winter wonderland, I look at Shayne, now bundled in a sweatshirt and jeans and looking amazing, and frown.

He waves his hand in front of me, and my clothes change. I'm now dressed in jeans, boots, and a shearling wool coat covering me to my knees. I barely remember the last time I was so covered up.

They say there used to be stores that carried nothing but winter clothes, but now the only places that have them are indoor resort areas. Back when I was eight, my mom took me and my friend Charlotte to a resort in Virginia. Once I got past the awe of seeing fake snow fall from the ceiling, we spent the day skiing and skating and making snowballs. My mom even skated, though she spent most of her time falling on her butt. It was only years later that I realized the day must have cost her a small fortune, but she never said a word about it.

Shayne takes a step from the snowy ground out onto the ice. "It's solid. You can jump on it if you want."

I look down at myself and then stare at him. "You can change my clothes?"

He laughs. "I'm a god, Piper. I can do anything."

I narrow my eyes. "Anything?"

Humor plays on his face. "Well, there are rules, but it's fun to find ways to break them."

I reach a foot out, barely touching it to the slick ice. But my foot slips out from under me, and I fall on my butt.

Shayne laughs.

"What? It's not like I've had much time to practice ice-skating in Texas." Austin used to have a public rink, but it went private when energy rates got too high, and then it closed entirely. Even with solar power, the cost of the A/C was exponential. I put my hands on the ground and try to get up, but I fall again, and Shayne only laughs harder. So I kick my leg out and swipe it against his feet, sending him falling to the ground next to me.

"That's not fair," he says. But his eyes sparkle as he reaches out and tries to grab me.

I slide backward and push myself up on my hands. "It seems fair to me."

Overhead, a breeze comes our way, rustling the frost-laden branches and sending handfuls of frozen crystals raining down onto the ice. It sounds like a symphony of bells and continues for over a minute. I look upward at the trees, letting the chill in the air and the warmth of the sky hit my face, and I suck in the fresh air. I know Shayne's watching me. But I don't look, instead closing my eyes and enjoying the song.

When it's over, I try to move again, and within a few steps, I remember how to walk on the stuff. Standing there, stable, I actually have time to look out across the ice. "Why is it frozen?"

Shayne slides over to me. "It's Cocytus. The river of lamentation. But there's nothing to be sorry about when you're going to the Elysian Fields, so it's frozen over to make crossing easier."

"Easier than what?" Because nothing about this icy surface so far is easy.

The ice is thick, and far below I see the monsters, trapped but still moving. If there were no ice, what would these monsters feed on with the sorrows all gone?

I shift my eyes away from the monsters and back to the shimmering world in front of me. "I never thought there would be ice in Hell." And certainly not an icy wonderland, especially since my mom's always talking about how horrible winter used to be. But even in my coat, I shiver when a blast of cold air hits me. Shayne moves closer and wraps a warm arm around me under my coat.

"So you thought it would be all fire and torture?"

I nod, and he laughs.

"So there's no fire and torture?" I ask.

"We have our share of that, too. But we're not going to Tartarus today."

"What's Tartarus?"

Shayne leans close and whispers in my ear. "It's where the bad people go." And then he turns my face toward him. "It's what gives Hell such a bad reputation."

"Sounds intriguing." I laugh when I say it, but part of me does want to see the fire. To see if it really is as scary as all the images of Hell I've been fed my entire life. I want to see everything in Shayne's world.

"Intriguing is a good word for it," Shayne says. His exposed skin's picked up an icy layer which makes him look like he has smoke curling off him.

"I'd like to see it."

His face falls a bit, though he tries to hide it behind a quick smile. "Let's just keep you out of Tartarus. It's a nasty, dirty place." He says it casually, but his voice tells me it's not a suggestion.

Which makes me want to see it more. Does he really think I'm so weak I can't handle it? "It's part of your world. You said you'd show me."

"Not Tartarus. Not this time."

He drops it, so I pretend to drop it. And soon, we're on the other side.

Shayne slides up to a dock, implanted in the thick ice, and gestures with his arm to the shore—to the people there. "Piper, this is paradise."

Every single person in the Elysian Fields looks like they're having the best day of their lives. I guess really it would be the best day of their deaths, since everyone here is dead. But if a single person is sad about being dead, they aren't showing it. I spot three beach volleyball games, at least fifteen couples making out, and enough sandcastles being built, it's like an entire kingdom made of sand. And all I can think about is how much Chloe would love it here. We could play on the beach and not have to worry about the scorching sun overhead.

But I wouldn't be here with her, and I don't want her to leave me.

"So what does it take to get here?" I know billions of people have died over the course of history, but paradise isn't that crowded. There must be some sort of entry requirements.

"Well, getting on my good side can't hurt."

I tilt my head, trying to look sweet. "Am I on your good side?"

Shayne brushes my cheek with the back of his hand. "Definitely."

I motion with my hand at the beach. "And all these people got on your good side?"

"Sort of." Shayne links my arm, and we start walking on the long dock. It's slick with the frozen ice of the river, but my booted feet grip the grainy wood underneath. "It's the people who've done something to help others that mostly get here. The ones who don't only think of themselves. People like Chloe."

I nod but don't trust myself to answer. Even if this is paradise, it's not time for Chloe to die. She can live the rest of her life, and then, when she's old and gray, we can come to the Elysian Fields together.

I step down from the dock, and my feet warm at once, making my boots unnecessary. It seems the boundary between the icy cold of Cocytus and the warmth of the Elysian Fields is immediate. I look at Shayne. "So . . ."

He looks back. "Yes?"

I motion down at my clothes: the jeans, boots, and coat. "Are you going to change my clothes again?"

He gives me a look that makes me want to both kiss him and punch him in the stomach at the same time. "Are you coming on to me?" he says.

I start to pull off the coat. "In your dreams." I wonder what I have on underneath the clothes, but I never get the chance to find out. Shayne waves his arm again, and I'm back in my tank top and shorts.

I close my eyes and let the heat of the two suns warm my skin. Shayne touches my arm, brushing my tattoo, and a chill runs down my body.

The tattoo looks lighter, like it's vanishing, but the skin is still raised underneath.

"It's fading." I'm not sure what it means. "Is Chloe—?"

"—fine." Shayne rubs the tattoo again, and the color returns, each Greek letter darkening at his touch. "She's just like we left her. I gave you my word."

I stare at the tattoo. "Have we been gone long?" Is the fading a bad sign for her? Is she dying—again?

But Shayne shakes his head. "No time has passed. I promise." He holds my chin with his thumb and forefinger, and his eyes meet my own. In his eyes, red flashes within the chocolate brown.

"Thank you," I say. His words settle the lump that's been surfacing in my throat every time I think of Chloe. The image of her and the horrible, beautiful winged man.

"Piper!"

I turn at the sound of the voice, and I see a child running toward me on the beach. She's wearing shorts and a T-shirt, and her long brown hair trails after her as she runs.

"Charlotte?"

She laughs, and when she reaches me, I let go of Shayne and grab her into a giant hug because I can't really believe she's here. She was my best friend from childhood, but when the first flu pandemic slammed into our overcrowded city, it took her away from me in sixth grade. But now that she's here, I never want to let her go.

"Piper! You're so pretty. So grown-up."

"Charlotte . . ." I'm not sure what to say. I feel like I'm back, six years ago, running around, watering plants in our shop. We were inseparable—my mom even approved, and then Charlotte left me. Like Chloe almost left me today. "I'm so sorry."

Charlotte pulls back from me. "You're crying." Her face is soft, and her hand moves up and touches her mouth as if she's trying to make sense of my words.

I realize I haven't been clear. "You were so young. You had your whole life ahead of you. And then it was over. Just like that."

Charlotte's face lights up, and her smile returns. "Don't cry, Piper. I'm so happy. Even Mr. Kibbles is here with me." And on cue, the Yorkie she used to have is next to her, pawing at her leg for attention.

I scratch him behind the ears. "Remember how sad we were when he died?"

Charlotte shakes her head. "He never died, Piper. He's here. See?"

It takes me a few seconds to process her words, and I realize she only remembers good things about life.

I bend down, and Charlotte wipes my cheeks, and I gather her again into a hug. "Everyone missed you so much. You had the loveliest funeral. It was perfect." I think of her funeral, the only one I've ever been to. I told my mom I'd seen Charlotte there, up by the altar. Like a ghost and an angel blended into one. So small, but shining and looking right at me.

My mom told me I'd imagined it, and she made me promise never to talk about it again.

"Your parents missed you, Charlotte. Everyone did. Even my mom." I'm rambling now, but I want her to know how much I cared. What an impact she had on my life. If not for Charlotte, I may never have had a true friend before Chloe. And seeing Charlotte, I know I can't let Chloe go, even though I know Chloe would be happy here. I may be the most selfish person on the planet, but she's the only real friend I have.

But Charlotte shakes her head. "It doesn't matter."

I feel a hand on my shoulder and turn to Shayne. "Humans can't escape death. The best they can hope for is to leave their sorrows behind at the River Acheron and come to live here," he says.

I look around at the world I've come into and wonder what Charlotte's sorrow was. Does someone that young have a true sorrow? "But everyone doesn't make it here," I say.

Shayne shakes his head. "And everyone doesn't deserve to either."

Charlotte's dancing back and forth on her feet like she can't contain herself. "Are you coming, Piper?"

I look to Shayne who gives an "I don't know" shrug.

"Coming where?" I ask.

"The sculpture contest," Charlotte says. And then she and Mr. Kibbles run off before I can say another word. I'm struck by how different our reactions are. She's acting like we were just hanging out yesterday, yet I watched her die and be buried and have lived six years since.

I turn to Shayne. "Can we go?"

"Of course," he says.

We catch up to Charlotte, who grabs both our hands and pulls us along. "Come on. They're just about to judge."

We run after her as she moves through the people. I worry about bumping into someone, but it's like a path has been cleared just for us. We head up a dune and down the other side to the contest.

There are about fifteen sand sculptures scattered around the beach. The first I see is a giant head resting on its side with a crown of leaves around it. Its eyes are closed like it's sleeping, and hanging above it is a giant hand pressing it downward. My face heats up when I see the next sculpture. A man and a woman are in a moment of complete ecstasy. The woman sits on top of the man with her mouth wide open, and birds flying out. I glance sideways at Shayne, who looks over and grins. I roll my eyes in response. Charlotte leads us through all the sculptures, and we stop at each one until we finally reach the smallest. My heart almost stops when I see it. It's a perfect replica of the ceramic jar that had been delivered to the Botanical Haven. The lid is wide open, and there's a bird flying out. The sun sits just above the head of the bird such that the rays of light and the feathers of the bird become one.

"Do you like it, Piper?" Charlotte asks.

I nod. I can't pull my eyes from it.

"I made it just for you," she says.

"For me?" How could she have known I would be here?

Shayne smiles at Charlotte. "It's definitely the best."

And as if everyone in the contest can hear him, they all start cheering. I take this to mean Charlotte's won the contest, and I'm not about to disagree. All the sculptures are amazing, but hers rises to the top.

Shayne takes my hand. "Are you ready to go?"

"Where?" Charlotte's already back with a group of friends, running and playing and living her perfect life in paradise.

"I want you to meet someone," Shayne says. "It shouldn't take long."

As if I'd say no.

"I'm ready," I say, and we walk away from the beach.

17

Rhadamanthus

WE WALK OVER THE DUNE TOWARD A HOUSE I HAVEN'T NO-
ticed until now. In fact, the more I think about it, the more sure
I am that it wasn't here two minutes ago. Maybe in paradise,
things can appear out of nowhere.

"Who lives here?" I ask. As we get closer, the beach clears
until it's just Shayne and me walking side by side. He reaches for
my hand and holds it. I pretend my heart isn't beating like crazy.

"Rhadamanthus," he says, like it's a name everyone should
know.

I guess he sees my blank look.

"Overlord of the Elysian Fields." Shayne gives my hand a
squeeze. "And my best friend."

My stomach fills with jitters when I think of meeting Shayne's
best friend.

"You'll love Rhadam," he says. "Of the company in the Underworld, he's the best. Though I'll be honest, the competition isn't
too tough."

The thought that Shayne wants me to meet his best friend
warms me. Like he wants to show me off, when, in fact, it's me
who would want to show him off. Though, aside from Chloe, I
have only my mom to show him to. And I can imagine her reaction.

"What's so funny?" Shayne asks.

"I'm not sure *funny* is the right word," I say.

"What?"

I laugh again at the absurdity. "I was just thinking of how my mom would react if I brought you home to meet her."

Shayne's face goes deadpan. "She'd probably try to skewer me." But then he gives me a playful smile. "So can I take that as an invitation?"

I figure the question doesn't even need an answer. Ahead of me in the sand, I spot something dark, and when we reach it, I bend down to pick up a black oyster shell.

"So much of the sea life is dying . . ." My voice trails off, and I look upward. I'm not sure how to phrase it.

"Aboveground?" Shayne finishes for me.

I nod. "It's hard to find any shells at the beach."

I remember the beach back in Virginia. It scarred me. Dead fish littered it, and the birds that fed on them coated the sand like filth. It was one of those images that never goes away. I can still remember when the alarms sounded, signaling that the sea level was rising. Everyone was supposed to evacuate the beaches because there was the threat of a tsunami. And most people did. The bodies of those who didn't washed up for weeks afterward.

But the sea life never had a chance. Contaminants rushed in with the rising water and killed armies of species. Later, my mom and I walked the coastline for hours, and all we saw was death.

Shayne must be able to read some of the horror on my face. "You've been to the beach?"

I reach down, picking up another shell that curves in on itself until I can't see anything but a single dot in the center. I try to focus on it instead of the memory of dead fish.

"We used to live by a beach. Back in Virginia, when I knew Charlotte. There was a lot more beach back then. Now it's underwater." And so is all of Florida and most of Louisiana.

"I never knew that."

"Why would you? Are you omniscient?" The thought of Shayne knowing everything sends a rush of adrenaline into my chest.

"If only." He shakes his head, and for a moment, he looks so vulnerable. So normal. "Omniscience is not within the power of the gods."

I laugh. "That's a good thing, I think. Anyway, my mom never wanted anyone to know who we were or where we lived."

"So why'd you move?" He's casual, reaching down, grabbing a handful of sand, letting it fall through his fingers. Each grain sparkles in the sun, and it's so white, when it hits the ground, it reminds me of powdered sugar. But he wants the answer. I hear it in his voice.

"It was right after Charlotte died." My heart starts pounding when I begin to tell him, catching me totally off guard.

"What happened?" He's looking at me now, coaxing the words out with his eyes.

"Nothing." I throw up my arms. "I don't know. I mean, one minute we're there going to her funeral. And the next thing I know, my mom's telling me to pack my bags. That my father had shown up at the funeral. That he was coming to take me away. And we're leaving that night."

Shayne takes the hand not holding the black oyster shell. "Did you see him?"

I shake my head, and though my heart is still pounding, it feels good to get it out. "My father? No. I was only eleven. I don't even know what he looks like. But I've heard it my entire life. That if my dad found me, he'd take me away and never let me see my mom again. That he was a dangerous terrorist and was wanted by the government. She told me we needed to be more careful. It was always the same old story." I want to forget about the letter so I don't mention it to Shayne.

"So you never met your dad?"

"No. My parents got divorced when I was a baby. Or maybe they weren't even married. Sometimes I wonder if I can believe my mom." I flip the oyster shell over with my other hand, studying the pearly gray of the inside. It's reflecting a thousand different colors, and I wish I could keep it. Keep part of the Underworld forever.

Shayne smiles and reaches up to my cheek. "Maybe you shouldn't believe her."

I know he's right. But still, it's not like I want to hear him say it. She's my mom. My problem. And I love her.

He starts walking, holding my hand. "What do you think of the house?" he asks.

I look up to where he's pointing and try to make sense of what I see there. "I'm not sure it's really a house."

I guess in the most technical sense of the word, it is a structure. There are four walls, a roof, and probably a hundred windows, but none of them touches. Each piece floats in the air of its own accord.

"Rhadam is a bit unusual."

This turns out to be a huge understatement. Rhadamanthus looks like a knight getting ready for a jousting competition. It's not just the leather pants and undershirt he's wearing. It's the fact that, when we walk into the atrium of his home, he has a sword in each hand and is fighting off two invisible opponents.

"I'll take your spleen this time." Thrust. He whips around, his long brown hair flying. "You think you can sneak up behind me." Stab. Back around. "The spleen wasn't enough? You've come back for more." Thrust.

It's like he's totally unaware of our presence. Shayne clears his throat, but it doesn't help.

"Your head comes off this time." Swipe.

I can almost see a head rolling away into the corner of the atrium. Turn. Kick. Thrust. Twist.

"Is he fighting anyone?" I whisper to Shayne, wondering if there are actually ghosts he's battling or something else invisible to me.

Shayne shakes his head. "Rhadam just has a really good imagination." He clears his throat again.

Still no response from Rhadam. "You can join your companion." Swipe. I envision the head flying through the air, landing with a thud next to the other one.

Maybe I just have a really good imagination also.

Only when both invisible opponents are defeated does Rhadam turn around.

"I hope you came to fight," he says. "It's impossible to find good competition these days." Rhadam's face cracks into a grin that makes it obvious he does a lot more smiling than frowning. And he looks like he lives life exactly how he wants to, kind of like Chloe. She'd go nuts over him. I can almost picture them together.

Shayne—or Hades, I have to keep reminding myself—lets go of my hand and walks over to Rhadam, where they do some handshake thing that makes me think they're trying to kill each other.

"No fighting today," Shayne says.

"Scared?" Rhadam asks.

"Please. If I kill you, who am I going to get to watch over Elysium for me?" Shayne punches Rhadam in the shoulder, but he's so solid he hardly moves.

Rhadam punches Shayne back. "And if I killed you, I'd have to take your place ruling the Underworld." His eyes flash over my way. "But maybe that's not a bad thing. The Underworld seems to have nice spoils."

Blood rushes to my face, and I know I'm turning seventeen different shades of red. I smile back, hoping I don't look like too much of an idiot in front of Shayne's best friend.

Shayne purses his lips. "Spoils. I like that." He walks back to me and takes my hand, leading me over to Rhadam. "This is Piper."

Rhadam lifts my other hand to his mouth and kisses the back of it, which, even though I'm sure I'm already at the stage of infinite red, still makes me blush deeper. "You're even prettier than Hades said."

I look at Shayne. He rolls his eyes and looks away, so I turn back to Rhadam.

"He's mentioned me?"

Rhadam laughs. "Gods, he hasn't talked about anything else all week. It's been 'Piper this' and 'Piper that.' I feel like I've already met you twenty times over."

My eyes flicker back over to Shayne. It's his turn to be embarrassed. I can't resist. "I had no idea the Lord of the Underworld could blush." But the mere fact that he's been talking about me this week to his best friend is making my stomach flip around in all sorts of ways I never thought possible.

Shayne clears his throat and gives Rhadam the evil eye. "Rhadam may be exaggerating just a bit."

Rhadam takes my hand away from Shayne's. "Trust me, I'm not exaggerating." And he starts walking with me following at his side.

I look at Shayne who, though still bright red, winks and follows on after us.

Rhadam leads us out of the atrium and into the house. With the structure of the house, we slip between where walls should join, move through doors that don't come close to shutting, and walk up onto the roof on individual stairs that don't connect.

"I moved the house because of the view." He motions out to the water, which now looks like it has waves big enough to capsize the *Titanic*. But behind the ocean, like a giant monolith, a glacier fills the horizon. It's blue and green and white, and the suns above reflect off it, making it look almost neon. It's so much ice all in one place and like nothing I've ever seen on Earth.

"I don't blame you." Shayne stands next to me, so close our legs touch. He takes my other hand, leaving me standing between him and Rhadam. Shayne gives the hand Rhadam still holds a suspicious look, and Rhadam lets go of it.

"There's so much ice," I say.

Shayne traces his thumb along the back of my hand. "Sometime we should visit what's left of the polar caps."

I love that this implies there will be more of *us* in the future. "I'll hold you to that," I say.

"Good," Shayne says.

Rhadam clears his throat. "Of course. I'd love to come. Thanks for asking."

"You can leave?" I ask.

He sighs. "No, not really. It's one of the funny things about paradise. I can't ever leave, but whatever I want, I get." He glances away from the glacier and turns back toward the beach, but instead of being up high, we're again on ground level. We leave the house and start walking back in the direction of the beach party.

"So how did you die?" Rhadam asks.

It takes a second for his words to make sense. I look down at myself to make sure I'm all still there. "I'm not dead."

Rhadam laughs, and I realize he's joking. "Don't worry. You don't look dead. You don't even smell dead."

It makes me wonder how dead people in the Underworld smell. I haven't noticed anything, but then again, I'm not sure I'd know what to smell for.

Rhadam purses his lips and then looks to Shayne. "It's too bad, you know. You should do something about it."

It's like Shayne is actually considering it. But then he replies. "I'm not sure that's the best way to win a girl's heart."

"Definitely not," I say. Though he's already got the heart part pretty well under control.

As we walk, people fill in again until the beach party is back in full swing. Shayne is like a rock star. People rush up to him constantly, telling him how happy they are here in paradise and how their only wish is that he would visit more often. He glances at me out of the corner of his eye as if to apologize, but he doesn't push them away. In fact, he lets go of my hand so he can have more space.

I'm fighting stabs of jealousy because so many of the girls are gorgeous when Rhadam leans over and whispers in my ear. "They love him here."

I pretend I'm totally fine with all the attention Shayne is giving them in return. "I can tell." I can't help but wonder if that's how Chloe would act if she were here, all fawning over him and stuff, but I push the thought aside since Chloe will not be here.

As we walk, I decide to ask Rhadam everything I want to know about paradise. Like where people live and if they get married and do they have to work. He tells me about how people fall in love all over again and how weddings are held barefoot on the beach and how everyone has some purpose for his or her existence, whether it's constructing sand sculptures or trying to get their golf swing just right. He talks about friendships that bond over eternity and children who are reunited with their parents once they pass on. And even though he answers my questions endlessly, what I really can't understand is the judging criteria. What makes one person better than the next?

"What if someone is kind of good? What then?" I ask.

Maybe I ask too loudly because Shayne pulls away from his most recent group of adorers and comes back to my side. "They get judged," he says. "Just like everyone else."

I press him. "Who judges?" I glance to Rhadam, but he has his lips pressed together like he doesn't want to be part of this conversation.

Shayne stops walking. "I judge."

"Everyone?"

He nods. "Every single soul that comes across the River Acheron gets judged."

"Isn't that kind of a big job?" I ask. I've never heard the exact numbers, but I know tens of thousands of people die each day. And that number's only increasing as the Global Heating Crisis continues. I can only imagine how world disasters and war affect the death toll.

Shayne's eyes get a faraway look, and they aren't meeting mine anymore. "I've had help. But it's still a big job."

"And an even bigger responsibility," I say. After all, trying to decide who gets paradise and who gets stuck with eternal torment could probably keep someone up at night.

"True. But don't you ever get a feeling about people?" he asks.

"Like what?"

"You know. Like you can look into their soul and see what they've done wrong."

I grab his wrist. "All the time. I swear. My mom tells me I'm imagining things, but I just have this way of knowing who's to blame." It's the reason I want to go to law school once I get out of college. Whether it's bullies at school or criminals on the tube, I get so sick of seeing people get off with no punishment. And I think of the black fungus on Councilman Rendon, like a visual confirmation of my feelings.

"That's how it is for me, too," Shayne says, and motions out across the world. "But it's just on a bigger scale here. And judgments last forever."

We cross another dune, but instead of the beach, the world shifts once again, and we wind up on top of a hill filled with a rainbow of unadulterated color. Trees and bushes grow on rolling hills, and flowers of every size and color fill the spaces in between. Meadows of them—purples and yellows and even my favorite reds. Set underneath the treetops are tree houses and hobbit holes and stone cottages. It's a world of nature and beauty, and it reminds me of what I imagine our own Earth looked like before it got paved over.

"Chloe would be happy here," Shayne says, glancing over at Rhadam, who's visiting some of the nearby houses.

"What if I say no?" There's not really a *what if* about it.

"Then Chloe will live."

It's the answer I want. "And then when she dies much later on, she'll come here?" I think of Chloe and me here together enjoying paradise. Forever.

Shayne's words shake me from my thoughts. "She'll have to be judged again, Piper. She'll live her life tempting fate, and when her time comes again, I'll have to make that decision."

"But of course she'd come here." I can't see that it's really a question.

"Near death can change people," Shayne says. "I don't know what will happen if you let Chloe live."

I close my eyes and put death aside and fall into a half sleep there on the grass, thinking about Chloe, but I'm woken by the sound of voices. I pretend to still be asleep, but I crack open one eye so I can see. Rhadam's come back, and he and Shayne are sitting across from each other talking.

"I'm not trying to tell you your business," Rhadam says. "But you have a serious problem."

"Like what?" Shayne asks, and suddenly I'm wide awake, though I try not to move.

Rhadam's eyes flicker over to me then back to Shayne. Out of my peripheral vision, I see Shayne nod. He doesn't know I'm listening.

"I talked to Minos yesterday," Rhadam says. "I borrowed help from him to move the house. And he mentioned he had a visitor." His words are staid, and I know it's because I'm just a couple feet away that he doesn't want to speak freely.

Shayne's whole body stiffens. "What kind of visitor?"

Rhadam leans in close. "Okay, he started drinking, and you know how Minos is when he drinks."

"Everyone in the Underworld knows how Minos is when he drinks," Shayne says.

"Right. So, he started bragging. Saying he knew how to return memories and get souls back across the river."

"He's lying," Shayne says.

Rhadam puts up his hand to silence Shayne.

"Maybe. But then he told me he'd been talking to Ares. That Ares found a way to get through the boundaries of the Underworld."

Shayne's fingers dig into the ground. "That's impossible."

"Impossible, but it happened," Rhadam says. "And you need to watch out."

Ares is the god of war; I know this from mythology. His name causes my skin to prickle while at the same time making butterflies form in the pit of my stomach.

Shayne stands up. "Tell me how the god of war has managed to enter my domain." His eyes bore into Rhadam. "Tell me that."

Rhadam is silent for a moment while I watch. People getting into the Underworld without Shayne's knowledge can't be a good thing. Didn't he just tell me Cerberus would eat them?

Finally, Rhadam sighs. "He must have help. Some back door in."

I decide it's time to enter the conversation. "There are back doors into the Underworld?"

Shayne keeps his eyes on Rhadam and doesn't even blink at the fact that I'm awake. I wonder if he's known all along. "There are no back doors into the Underworld," he says. "Everyone has to go by Charon."

Rhadam shakes his head. "Except Ares."

"How?" I ask.

"Ares is working with someone on the inside; he has to be," Rhadam says.

Shayne runs a hand through his hair. "I still say it's not possible. The boundaries should be secure."

"So this is a real problem?" I ask.

Shayne looks at me then and tries to give me a reassuring smile, but I see how white his face has gotten. "It's nothing. Just normal stuff going on here in the Underworld."

He's lying. The Underworld has issues just like the world above. And he really wants me to send Chloe here? "But other gods are getting in."

"Yes," Rhadam says at the same time Shayne shakes his head.

"So why now?" I ask.

Shayne's eyes meet mine. "Good question. Why now?"

I glance at Rhadam whose eyes are fixed on me, waiting. Why would others be coming to the Underworld? I figure the Underworld can't be much different from any world. "They want control?" I say.

Rhadam nods. "My thoughts exactly. Ares is already doing everything he can to cause the next world war aboveground. And now he wants to claim the Underworld for his own, too."

"The day Ares takes over the Underworld, I'll tear his entrails out inch by inch and knit them into a chew toy for Cerberus," Shayne says.

Rhadam opens his mouth, but hesitates.

"What?" Shayne says.

"You should go to the assembly," Rhadam says. "Get a warrant out for Ares."

"I'm not taking my problems to the assembly of gods," Shayne says. "We've been over this."

"Why not?" I ask.

Shayne turns to me. "Because it's the ultimate show of weakness. There's no better way to lose control than to admit you need help."

I'm not sure if I agree with this logic, but I doubt Shayne wants to argue about it with me. Besides, he's the one in charge here, not me.

He turns back to Rhadam. "Thanks for watching my back."

Rhadam nods.

And then Shayne reaches out for my fingers and intertwines his with them, rubbing his thumb softly on the back of my hand. "Are you ready?"

"Are we leaving?" Not that I mind. As charming as Rhadam is, the conversation has put a certain chill into the air, even here in paradise. A chill of gods and battles over mythical domains.

Shayne nods.

"I'll see what else I can find out," Rhadam says. He looks at me, and his smile from earlier returns. "Piper, can I just say how great it is to finally meet you?"

When he takes my hand and kisses it, I feel like I'm on a stage with a million eyes watching me.

"It was great meeting you, too. Maybe I'll be back sometime," I say.

"It's a pretty nice place to come visit," Rhadam says.

Shayne actually laughs, and a giant weight lifts off my chest. He grins at Rhadam. "Especially if you're overseeing Elysium."

Rhadam lets go of my hand. "It's a hard job, but I sacrifice for the greater good." And then Rhadam vanishes.

"So what did I miss?" I ask Shayne.

"Nothing," he says.

It has to be a lie. He must not want me to know. And, of course, this only makes me more curious.

18

Disease

PARADISE IS PERFECT, BUT CHLOE IS WAITING FOR ME. "ARE
we going?" I ask.

"Almost," Shayne says, and he leads me down from the hill. I
guess he's still trying to convince me to let Chloe come here. He
must know by now it's pointless. Or maybe he's just trying to stall
for time. If it's the latter, I don't mind.

We walk until we reach a path of manicured greenery. Trees
have grown along the sides, forming a tall arbor with a grass walkway below. It slopes downward, and water bubbles in a stream at
the bottom. The green is so vibrant, so different from the world
I know back aboveground. That world hangs on the edge of
extinction. And this world thrives. It's ironic how the world of
the living is dying, and the land of the dead is alive.

Out of nowhere bounds Cerberus, who knocks into Shayne
and sends us both flying. After I wipe my face from Cerberus's
exuberant licking, we get up and stroll down the path, Cerberus leading the way. He stops every so often to snap at a passing bird with one or all of his heads, but either has really bad aim
or isn't trying all that hard to catch one.

Once we're out of the arbor, we reach a stream that flows over
rocks in a white froth until it clears them and settles into an
even flow. To the left is the source of the water—a waterfall cas-
cading down from a small cliff cut into a hill. The sun catches
the water, reflecting a blaze of light around the entire valley.
Vines climb up the rocks on the side of the falls, creating curtains

that bloom with vibrant flowers. Mist hangs in the air above the crash of the water, forming a cloud of rainbows which holds steady even as the mist within it shifts and settles.

With each step I take, I want to move to the Underworld and stay here. To have Chloe actually come to paradise. To make it my new Botanical Haven away from the stifling presence of my mom. To live with Shayne forever. I follow him off into the trees, and pretty soon we come to a clearing planted with all sorts of orange and purple and electric-blue flowers. Saffron yellow. Cherry red. Vibrant colors. Colors I love.

I look at Shayne. "This is your garden?"

"It's a new hobby. I've only been at it for a few years."

I walk into the center of the garden and look at the abundance of life sprouting out of the earth around me. "And I thought I could grow things."

He walks over and joins me. "But there is this one that won't grow."

Around me is nothing but life. I smell each plant. I almost hear nectar pumping through stems, feeding them. But then I catch it—the scent of death, here in this beautiful garden. So misplaced that, as soon as I smell it, all other aromas go away. I close my eyes and begin walking, following my instincts, and soon I find myself in front of a tree which, although still alive, is not in bloom like the rest of the garden. It seems to be coated in a thick layer of yellowish-green mucus. When I reach my hands out to touch it, the mucus disappears.

"A pomegranate tree?"

Shayne nods and reaches up to touch a branch with green leaves. "It won't produce fruit."

I run my hands over the bark. At home, in the Botanical Haven, I can nurse almost anything back to life. I can make fruit grow from even the ficklest of breeds. My mom says it's been that way since I was born.

The pomegranate tree is breathing. I feel it under my palms.

But it's missing . . . something. Something fertile in the soil hasn't made its way to the roots. Or has been removed entirely.

"I built the garden around it," Shayne says.

I hear him but don't turn. "What happened?"

In his voice, I hear the resignation. "It just started dying."

Slowly, I turn. "The soil around it is empty."

"I do fertilize." Shayne seems to be reading my thoughts.

"Then why isn't it working?"

He shrugs. "I figured you could ask the tree."

Again I place my palms on the hard bark and try to reach my spirit into it. It seems to tell me it's missing a vital ingredient, but I soon realize maybe this isn't quite the truth. I recognize something, and suddenly, I feel like falling to the ground and crying.

My mind slips out of reality, and I'm walking in a field. And aside from the grass that reaches well past my knees, the pomegranate tree stands alone. Awake. Aware. And bursting with life. The branches hang low to the ground, plump with fruit. Light radiates from it as I draw near. I take a few steps closer until I can brush the bark with my hand. So healthy. So unlike the reality of what I've felt.

I lift my hand and reach for a fruit. It pulls against my touch, but then it gives and comes loose in my hand. It's the color of red wine, and I peel it until I can see the seeds inside.

And then, all at once, I'm being pulled from the tree. I reach out toward it, but it's moving away, and so am I. Leaves fall and fruit begins to drop. I'm so far away the tree is only a brown shape in the distance. Oppression hits the tree like a fist. My reality returns. And I'm back in the garden of flowers with Shayne.

I take my hands off the tree and turn to him.

"I thought you said there was no sadness here in the Elysian Fields."

"There's not. At least, there isn't supposed to be."

"This tree is full of sorrow." I think of the River Acheron.

And deep inside me, the origins of the sorrow twist and form, growing like roots. "Why is this tree sad?"

I see tears in the corners of his brown eyes; they shine when the red flashes. "A lot of the Underworld is sad. We've been that way for years." He looks away and reaches out to touch a nearby red flower.

A breeze blows through the valley.

"Should we go now?" Shayne asks.

I nod because the initial happy thoughts of paradise have vanished. I'm trying to hold on to them, but the tree's dug its sorrowful roots inside my soul. We walk out of the garden and head back the way we came. It's only when I see Cerberus's three heads looking our way that my sorrow begins to diminish. I push it away, but part of it sticks, as if echoes of the sadness will never leave me. Like it's a part of me I'll never understand.

19

Departure

I CAN TELL SHAYNE'S PENSIVE. HE'S GOT HIS LIPS PRESSED together, and he doesn't even skate when we cross the river. Instead, we walk hand in hand in silence. Shayne must realize he's been quiet, so he starts to make chitchat, but my mind drifts to Chloe, back aboveground, at the side of the creekbed.

"I need to leave," I say once we reach the winter wonderland on the other shore.

Shayne turns to me, and his eyes soften. "Please don't go." He brushes my arm. "Not yet."

I think if he asks me right now, I'll stay with him forever.

"Please?"

I nod, and he pulls me in and holds me. My body presses up against his on the edge of the River Cocytus, under the icicle trees. His muscles are hard, and they mesh into mine. I feel the beating of his heart in his neck, my forehead is so close to it. His skin is warm enough to melt every bit of ice around us; I let the heat soak into my body.

He kisses the top of my head, and a chill spreads down me, having nothing to do with the frozen river we've just crossed. He lets go of me and backs up so I can see his face. His soft, gorgeous, dark face. A face of mysteries. A face of secrets. I want to know his secrets. Want to share them with him.

"I really like the Underworld," I say.

"I really like you," he says.

I want to sink back into his warm arms. But he's one step

ahead of me. He pulls me to the snowy ground, letting my coat fan out below me, and moves to me. His lips find mine. My arms snake around him and pull him close to me.

His kisses are hard and fierce, and his hot breath explores my mouth. I gasp for air when I can between kisses, but don't twist away because if it's a dream, I don't want to wake up. His hands move to my hair, breaking the ponytail holder with a snap, and he runs his hands through the tangles that have accumulated. Against me, I feel him, and I want him to be a part of me more than anything else.

His hands travel down my sides; I don't want to stop anything with Shayne. I lift his shirt and let my hands move over his skin. Each touch is electric, and his kisses taste of singed sweetness. Being with him here in our winter paradise is more perfect than the Elysian Fields, but Shayne stops way too soon and rolls off me. He jumps to his feet, grabs one of the supply chests near the dock, and throws it. It smashes into the rock wall, and the pieces scatter everywhere. And then thunder rumbles around us.

I stand up and try to force away the yearning that pulses hard through my body. His back is to me, and I'm not sure if I should go over next to him or keep the distance between us. "Is it something I did?"

Shayne whips around, and his eyes are flashing. The red beats and throbs inside, and the brown is so dark it looks like ink. His teeth are clenched, and for a second, it seems he wants to kill someone.

"Gods no!"

I'm relieved and baffled all at the same time. "Then why did you stop?"

Shayne closes his eyes and tries to get his anger under control. His hands are balled in fists, but when he reopens his eyes, he relaxes his hands, and the red flashes settle down. "Because . . . it's too fast. It's just not right."

I bite my lip to keep from offering my thoughts on whether it's right or not. It seems right to me. Everything about Shayne seems right, from the level of comfort I reach around him to the feelings his touches evoke. And even though he denies it, I'm sure I've done something to upset him.

Shayne whistles, and soon Cerberus comes bounding out of the dark tunnel ahead. He runs to Shayne who reaches down to scratch Cerberus's left head. His ears go back, and his eyes close as Cerberus leans forward. "It's just hard, Piper. I need to be more patient," Shayne says. Our eyes hold each other until finally he breaks the contact. "I do think you're right about one thing."

Finally. "What?"

"It's time for you to go. At least for today."

I nod, though at this point, I don't really want to leave—ever. But Chloe's waiting for me back at the creek. "Can I come back sometime?"

"Piper, you can come back any time you want." And he kisses me again, deep and sweet, and once more, I'm struck by the connection I feel to him.

Shayne takes my hand. We start walking back down a tunnel, turning a few times, until we come out, and I see the banks of the River Acheron ahead of us. A boat approaches—Charon, coming to get us.

"How? Do you have a FON?" I have a hard time imagining that the city issued Shayne his own Functional Operating Node.

He laughs. "No, no FON. But just call me. I'll be around."

I find the thought that Shayne will be around both comforting and mildly unsettling. He can't possibly be around every second of every day.

"Always?"

"No, not always," he says. "That's impossible. But enough."

Our trip back with Charon is quiet. I sit in the front wrapped in Shayne's strong arms while Charon guides us across the bubbling river of sorrow. I hear the voices as we move through the water, see the monsters feasting on sadness, but I ignore them, instead thinking only of Chloe waiting for me and Shayne's burning warmth next to me and his odd but intense burst of anger back on the shore.

Charon smiles when I get off the boat, and for a moment, I want to reach out and hug him. He holds his feet firmly in one place, though, and since I don't see an opening, I brush the weird urge away. I chalk it up to the fact that I've just been in Hell for the day and I think I'm in love with Shayne, who is actually Hades, Lord of the Underworld. Not the most normal day, though certainly it's been the most memorable.

Shayne walks me away from the shore, and I recognize the place where we first arrived.

"So . . . ?" he asks.

Paradise will be waiting for Chloe later. Her time isn't now. There has to be a reason Tanni warned me about it. "I want Chloe to live." And with those words, I am officially the most selfish person in the world.

Shayne nods. "And I stand by my word. She'll live."

The words sound almost like a death sentence.

"Are you ready?" he asks.

I look up, but all I see is packed dirt and rock hovering above us. "How do we get through?"

"Just you this time."

I look away from the hard ceiling, back to his face. "You aren't coming with me?" And all of a sudden, I don't want to leave.

"Chloe needs you. Not me," he says.

"You'll be at school?"

Shayne smiles, and it lights the dark cavern. At least for me. "School. The only good part of it is seeing you when neither your mom nor Reese is around."

Reese. I'd almost forgotten about him. My face burns when I think about kissing him. Was it just last night? It feels like a lifetime ago.

"Just promise me you'll be careful," he says. "So many things aren't what you think."

"Like what?"

"Like Reese for starters. His only reason for existing is to cause conflict, and he's already doing a pretty good job."

It takes me a second, but then it comes together in my mind. Because if Shayne is a god, then maybe Reese is, too. And maybe he's the one Shayne and Rhadam were talking about. "He's Ares, isn't he?"

Shayne nods. "The god of war. And apparently a bigger threat than I estimated." His eyes darken again, and the red sparks flash. "Please just stay away from him."

I nod. Now that I've been here with Shayne, I can't imagine being with anyone else.

Shayne puts his fingers to my lips. "And promise me you'll always trust me."

It's a strange request. And my mind flashes to our conversation with Rhadam. The secrets I know Shayne's keeping. "Of course."

Shayne smiles. "Thank you." He moves away from me and leaves me standing there alone.

I look back up at the packed earth above us. I know I need to go, yet I want to turn back and run to the Underworld. To Shayne.

But Chloe needs me. And my mom needs me. So I clear my mind, thinking only of my return, and soon I'm amid the swirling liquid silver, floating in it and breathing it in.

I feel myself drifting back—back to the world above. I'm overwhelmed with the urge to fight against the drift, to kick my way back to Shayne and the Underworld. But I know life is waiting for me on Earth. And so I continue on, losing myself in the cool fluid until I'm once again on hard-packed ground.

20

Shock

THE WORLD COMES ALIVE LIKE A NIGHTMARE. I'M BACK IN THE Greenbelt; there's a stillness, and the sky is dead gray. And then there's some kind of sonic boom, and the air around me starts to hum and vibrate. Just before I left, the disperser missile launched. And now it's like there's some rebound effect going on. Some kind of switch has been flipped. A blast of cold wind slams into me, and goose bumps explode on my bare arms.

Chloe's where I left her. Lying on the rock-covered ground. Still unconscious. I blink my eyes a few times, and the smell of the earth around me registers. What just happened?

Hell? I've been to Hell?

I look around, but there's no sign of the winged man who'd come for Chloe. His putrid odor is gone. He's gone.

And so is Shayne.

Shayne is the Lord of the Underworld.

Chloe breathes normally, but she's pale. I head to the creek and grab a handful of water, holding it in my cupped hands. When I get back to her, I drop it on her face, rubbing it into her cold, white cheeks. She stirs, but doesn't wake, so I get some more and do it again. It's not until the third time that her eyes finally flutter open. Overhead, rain begins to fall. But it's hard, like tiny pellets being flung from the sky.

"Piper?"

She looks right at me, though her eyes don't see me. But she's alive.

I take her hand. "Hi, Chloe." I wipe the rain from her forehead and help her sit up.

She turns her head and looks toward the creek. "What happened? What am I doing here?"

"I think you collapsed from the heat."

She shudders as another gust of cold wind hits. "It's so cold."

I nod, though I want to forget about the weather. I want to forget about this whole global warming disaster we live in. All I really want to do is hug Chloe. To never let her go again. But she's still so dazed, and I don't want to startle her. "They launched another missile."

I don't think she's even close to feeling the panic that's starting to creep through me. Something is seriously messed up with the weather. The temperature has never dropped this quickly since I've been alive. But it's like Chloe doesn't even hear me. She shivers and wraps her arms around herself, and I notice her tattoo. Fading—like mine had done in Hell. I touch it, and the ebony ink revives under my fingers until it's as dark as the day she got it. Just like mine did when Shayne touched it. I take this as a good sign.

Chloe pulls her arms closer, and her teeth begin to chatter. I realize she's in shock.

"We need to get you home." And like the Fates are against us, the sky picks that moment to open up and begin dumping on us. Something hard hits my head and then bounces to the ground in front of me. I pick up a thick ball of ice. Hail—that's what we learned it was called. But it hasn't hailed since the Global Heating Crisis started.

I grab Chloe, and we make a run for the shuttle stop. She's like a rag doll but lets me lead her. We dash under the UV covering at the shuttle stop, but it's not UV I'm worried about right now. The hail is coming down like stones. The thermometer at the shuttle stop has dipped to fifty-four. I think there has to be a mistake. It drops as I watch to fifty-three then fifty-one. But fifty never comes because a giant piece of hail smacks into the yellow

LEDs so hard, both Chloe and I jump. I think she's shivering, but then I realize I am, too. The world is crashing in on us.

It takes forever for a shuttle to come. When it does, the driver has his hands gripped on the steering wheel because the road is solid ice. We're the only ones on the shuttle, and he instructs us to sit down and not say a word. Chloe's not talking because I think she must still be in shock. I'm about to ask him if we can stop at the hospital because she's so pale, but the driver looks like he's seen death himself, so I keep quiet. Chloe will be fine. She's alive.

The shuttle makes three more stops before we get to Chloe's house. At the first stop, Randy Conner gets on. He gives us a nod and then sits behind us.

"What the hell's up with this weather?" he says.

Chloe doesn't even look at him. She's pressed against me, but I turn my head to talk to him.

"The missile," I say. "It did something to the weather."

"You think so?" Even in a disaster, Randy's still a sarcastic jerk.

I ignore him and turn back around. The shuttle is sliding everywhere; we can't get around a single turn without almost running into either a tree or a brick wall. Finally, when we get to Chloe's stop, it plows right into the UV covering at her shuttle stop, sending pieces everywhere.

I stand up to help her off, and for a second, she looks normal.

"Thanks, Piper," she says.

"For what?" She can't know I saved her from death.

Chloe reaches her palm up to my cheek. "For looking out for me." And her words seem to convey something deeper, like maybe she does know what's going on. On Monday, I'll ask her about it. I'll tell her about Shayne and the Underworld even though she'll think I'm nuts. Because I feel like I have to tell someone or I'll burst.

"You're welcome," I say. I'm about to ask the driver to wait while I walk her to her house, but Chloe waves me away.

"I'm fine," she says.

"You sure?"

She nods. "Call me later." And she walks down the steps of the shuttle and runs to her house.

The driver backs up out of the debris of the shuttle stop and starts down the road. I go back to my seat in front of Randy and sit down.

"You think school will be canceled on Monday?" he asks.

Overhead, the hail pounds down on the roof of the shuttle like a storm of bullets. I look out the window to where the ground has already picked up a layer of whiteness. I grip the back of the seat as we slide from one side of the street to the other.

"If this keeps up," I say.

"Let's just pray we make it home alive," Randy says.

It seems we will. The shuttle pulls up to the curb by the Botanical Haven without running into anything and stops. I stand up but notice Randy's still sitting.

"You're not getting off?" I ask.

He shakes his head. "I'm gonna go pick up my sister." And for a second, it's like there's a side of Randy he's never let me see before. He's such an arrogant jerk on the outside, but he's going to the elementary school to make sure his sister gets home okay. I blink, and his image shifts so he's layered in blue moss. It covers his face and hair, his hands and arms. I hold my eyes open, staring at him to make sure it's really there, but when I finally have to blink, it vanishes. Just like the mucus on the pomegranate tree.

"Keep her safe," I say, because I can imagine what a little kid would think of a storm like this.

"I always do," Randy says.

I wave goodbye to him and then get off the shuttle.

The first thing I do when I get inside is text my mom. Even if she is off with my father somewhere, she's got to be freaking out about this weather. I'm shivering, so I grab the comforter off my bed and wrap it around myself. It helps, but all the glass of the Botanical Haven makes the cold seep right into my bones.

what's going on? I text.

I make some coffee and wait for a reply, but none comes.

I text her again. weather's gone crazy.

Still she doesn't respond. It's been over a day since she's been in touch, and I can't help but let it put me on edge. Something has to have gone wrong. She would never stay out of touch this long. I sit at the ice cream table with my coffee and listen to the storm rage on the glass above. It's shatterproof, so I'm not worried about it breaking. I try not to focus on my mom. In the next hour, I text her five more times.

The storm pounds down for the better part of the day until, in a single moment, it stops.

Just. Like. That.

Dark clouds turn to white, and a blue sky creeps back out from behind them. And then the sun comes, and everything starts to melt. Water cascades down our glass roof and pools on the ground outside.

My FON chirps. My mom texts. Finally. i'm fine, piper. stay safe. stay inside.

Relief and guilt hit me in equal doses. I've completely betrayed her instructions. I text back, so glad ur ok. was worried abt u. safe here.

She texts again. i may be a couple more days. miss u

A couple more days. That's all she's going to say? Nothing about my dad? Nothing about where she is?

I text, miss u too, and wait for her response.

She doesn't text back.

I flip on the tube to see what kind of trouble the storm has caused. Around the city, roofs and walls have caved in everywhere. Downtown, about fifty people are trapped beneath the debris of a building, and most of the coverage centers on this, though reports of wrecks and flooding are sprinkled in. I watch the news as each new horror is revealed. Rescue crews pull dead bodies from the building and flash to family members who find out their loved ones are dead the same time I do. I wonder where in the Underworld each person will go. I wonder how Shayne can handle all the sorrow.

When I can't watch any more of the misery, I turn off the tube. And then I go downstairs and start tending the plants and flowers even though they don't really need it. They've been protected from the devastation outside. Like an oasis.

Reese's pink flowers are still alive, though they've sucked up most of the water in the container. I move to water them, but then I stop. Should I really keep them alive? This is the god of war we're talking about. I should pick them up and toss them into the compost heap, erasing all memories of him and our date. But he'd been completely nice to me. And not a threat at all. And I have to wonder if Shayne could be wrong about him. I go ahead and add water to the stems because that's what I do. I take care of plants.

THE NEXT DAY, ASIDE FROM FLOODING, THE COLD SPELL IS A memory. Temperatures are back at one hundred by seven a.m., and the weather stations predict humidity will get to dangerously high levels because of the melting. Precipitation is good in that it helps plants grow, but in such mass amounts, the ground and city can't handle it. I text my mom, but she doesn't text me back. It's totally out of her character to not get back to me right away, especially with the weather issues. She'll probably text me later this evening. Let me know when exactly she's going to be home.

I call Chloe next, but her mom tells me she's sick. Her mom doesn't sound worried about Chloe but keeps me on the FON for five minutes to talk about the storm. I assure her I'm fine here alone at the Botanical Haven and that if I have any problems, I'll come over. But I try to get her off the FON. I don't want to spend my day talking to Chloe's mom, so I ask her to have Chloe call me later. Once Chloe gets better, I'll tell her everything. I think she'll have a hard time believing I traveled to the Underworld and came back to talk about it. I have a hard time believing it. But as the hours tick by and she doesn't call, I start to think this conversation will have to happen tomorrow at school.

I'm about to lock the door and take a nap when the bell rings. I glance out the glass to see who's here because, at this point, anyone is better than no one. It's Melina, the consistently half-naked girl who owns the herb boutique downtown. She's come to the Botanical Haven every other week in the two months she's been here, but always when my mom was home. When I open the door, humidity pours in like thick gel.

"Hey, Piper." Melina's lips lift into a cherry-ice-cream smile, pink and round and perfect. She peeks her head in and looks around, letting her blond cornrows fall forward over her blouse, which dips so low in the middle I see her ribs. Each cornrow is capped with a shell that jingles against the others, creating a song as she moves. Melina looks like she belongs on the cover of *Cosmo*, except she's so pretty no one would believe the photos are real. "Is your mom home?"

"She's out of town."

Melina's eyebrows shoot up her beautiful forehead, making the green of her eyes stand out like emeralds. "Seriously?"

It's like the entire world is aware of how overprotective my mom is. "Just for a couple days," I say. I don't want to seem like a naïve child in front of Melina.

"Odd timing," Melina says.

"What do you mean?" I ask. There's something about the way Melina's asking me questions, like she doesn't want me to realize how interested she really is.

"You know, with the storm and all," Melina says. "I hope you were okay."

"I was fine."

"You weren't out in it, were you? It was horrible out there. Councilman Rendon said tons of people died."

I'd love to be able to argue with her and tell her she's wrong, but all anyone has to do is watch the news. "I didn't have any problems," I say.

Melina shrugs like talking about thousands of people dying is no big deal. "So what have you been doing?" she asks.

My mind flies to my date with Reese and my journey to the Underworld with Shayne. "I went out with some friends. Nothing big."

Melina laughs. "That's good. I know your mom would be furious if you got in any trouble."

Unfortunately, I know this, too. "Maybe," I say.

A perfect smile forms on Melina's perfect face. Her body reminds me of a minx, sleek and supple, and with her low-cut blouse, I see every curve.

"Hey, I have an idea," she says. "Let's go for a walk together. I know we've talked a few times, but I feel like I don't even know you at all."

The air from outside reminds me I haven't been out in over a day. And I guess there are worse things I could do besides taking a walk with a customer. At least my mom might approve of this, and when she asks what I did, I'll have something valid to tell her. "Sounds like fun," I say, and I try to make it sound upbeat.

"Perfect." Melina reaches out a golden arm and opens the door wider, and the sunlight catches the fine, blond hairs, making her arms shimmer.

Once I'm outside, Melina lets the door swing shut. And then she links arms with me. There's no one around to see us, so even though my reflex is to pull back from her, I let it be. I don't want her to think she intimidates me.

We pass the smaller greenhouses out back which are steamed up from all the humidity; I can't even see inside. I head for the path in the woods, walking under the trees. There are puddles everywhere from the storm, and no matter how hard I try to avoid them, my feet are soaked in seconds.

Outside, I see how sheer Melina's clothes really are. In the sunlight, I can see right through the blouse. Her thin skirt falls into the space between her legs, outlining her thighs, and it's clear she's not wearing any underwear. I glance at her sideways, unable to take my eyes off her. Imagining the effect she must have on guys.

"Crazy weather," she says. If she's aware her clothes leave little to the imagination, she doesn't show it or doesn't care. She stops near a large crop of limestone and sits on one of the bigger rocks, spreading her legs to let her skirt hang in between. And then she pats the place next to her.

I sit down next to her, pulling my eyes from her chest. "My mom thinks the atmosphere is being stripped away."

Melina draws her pouty lips together. "I guess that's one theory."

"What's another?" I ask.

She seems to consider this. "Maybe the Global Heating Crisis is just coming to an end. Maybe the whole thing has just been the natural progression of weather on Earth."

"Maybe," I say, though I don't for a second believe it. Global warming has been talked about for the last seventy years. It's not just going to disappear by magic.

"Or maybe it's something else entirely," Melina says. "Maybe it's those air diverters they've been trying out in Japan."

"My mom thinks those are just as bad," I say.

"But what do you think?" Melina asks.

"I think she's right." Everything I've read about the air diverters suggests that all they're doing is redistributing the heat. Nothing really gets rid of it. They just move it around. I pick up a pebble and throw it, trying to hit a puddle. Instead, it lands on a slope, and I watch it tumble down a few feet and stop in the mud.

Melina puts her hand on my forearm, causing goose bumps to form. "Councilman Rendon disagrees," she says. "He thinks all the changes going on are good."

I bite my tongue to keep from giving any theories my mom has about Councilman Rendon. "Everyone's entitled to an opinion," I say, shaking my arm to get her hand off. "And since the people in charge get to make the decisions, fate is in their hands."

Melina sets her hands behind her and tosses her head back, letting her cornrows fall until they touch the rocks. "My husband thinks fate is for the weak."

Husband! I can't believe Melina is married. She looks like she's only a couple years older than me, and I can't imagine a perfect enough guy to be her match; it seems every creature on Earth would feel inferior to her.

"I didn't know you were married," I say.

Melina nods. "For a while now." She stretches her arms, and for the first time, I notice the thick band on her ring finger. Patterns twist it into knots.

"Was it love at first sight?"

Melina laughs and settles her hands in her lap. "Not hardly. Let's just say it was a marriage of convenience."

I'm not sure what could be convenient about marrying someone you don't love—especially if you're the most gorgeous creature on the planet. "So do you believe in love at first sight?" I ask. I think of Shayne. Of the first time I saw him in class. And the desire that moved through me.

Melina's eyes widen, and this time, they look violet. I shake my head, knowing the sun must be playing tricks on me; eyes don't change color on demand. But the lilac glimmers in the sunlight and picks up the iridescence of the shells hanging from her hair. "Do you?" she asks.

I nod.

Melina lifts an eyebrow, moving so her breast brushes my arm. I flinch but don't pull away. "So do I. I believe there is some love so strong nothing can stand in its way. Love is the only certainty in the whole universe."

I sigh and, unable to take it anymore, scoot enough so we aren't touching. "That's exactly how I feel," I say.

She nods and breaks eye contact, closing her beautiful eyes and looking back up to the sun. "I felt that way about someone once."

"Not the guy you married?"

Melina shakes her head. "I loved this one guy, and he loved me. The world stopped when we were together."

"So what happened?" I barely breathe the question.

Melina angles her head. "He fell in love with someone else."

"I'm sorry," I say because I can't think of anything else appropriate.

Melina turns to me then and holds my eyes. "Are you really, Piper?"

"Of course," I say. Though I've only known Shayne for days, my world would shatter if I found out he loved someone else.

Melina points to her gorgeous body. To her perfect face. "Look at me, Piper."

I'm not sure how I could look at anything else, so I nod.

"It happened to me. It could happen to anyone."

I let out the breath I've been holding. "I'm sorry," I say again.

Melina lets it drop. We chat for a few more minutes but then say goodbye. I leave her there and head back to the Botanical Haven by myself and lock the door behind me.

I stop at the sink in back for a quick drink of water. Outside, it's getting warmer by the second; the thermometer's well over one hundred and five. It's like the ice storm was a fantasy. I want to flip on the tube to make sure it really happened, but I can't bring myself to watch any more bad news. I finish my water, set my cup on the shelf above the sink, and head to the stairs. But I'm no sooner up four steps when the bell on the door rings yet again. I walk back down and open it, sure it will be Melina. But it's not Melina at all. Instead, it's the same delivery guy from last Sunday. The one who'd brought me the wrapped jar. He's in his blue uniform and has the same white baseball hat on with the blue bill and wings painted on the sides.

My senses go on high alert, but I hope nothing shows on my face.

"Another delivery?" I ask, and flip the sign from *Closed* to *Open*.

He holds out a package. This one, unlike the other, is wrapped in bright pink paper and has pink twine tied across it and in a bow on top.

"Piper Snow. Just for you," he says, meaning he remembers

who I am and that whatever he's holding is for me and not for my mom.

"What is it?" I ask. The package looks like an art decoration itself.

The man flashes a grin that is part cheesy, part flirty, and part eternal amusement. "It's not my job to open them. Just to make the deliveries." And he passes the package to me.

"Do I have to sign?" I ask, but he's already down the steps and halfway across our yard. So I close and lock the door behind him and carry the gorgeous package to the counter. Sure enough, tied to the twine is a tag with my name printed in large block letters, completely different from the curvy script of my last delivery. I untie the twine and pull off the paper and underneath is a golden box with a name stamped on top that, based on the two little dots on top of the *u*, looks German. The box is flat and square, and the lid lifts off easily.

I gasp when I see what's inside. Nine dark chocolate truffles sit nestled in paper, each with a large *P* stamped on them. Like they've been personalized for me. I glance back over my shoulder just to make sure no one is watching. Sure, chocolate is rare, but it's not just that. Importing it from other countries is illegal, so smuggling is the only way to get chocolate from Germany here to America. And I know in that moment who it has to be from.

I pull out the card tucked into the top and flip it over. It's written in the same block letters as the tag on the box.

DON'T BELIEVE EVERYTHING YOU HEAR ABOUT ME. AND PLEASE
GIVE ME A CHANCE. WE WOULD BE PERFECT TOGETHER.
P.S. EAT THEM FAST BEFORE THEY MELT.

I stare at the chocolates, trying to decide if I should be flattered or upset. Reese had illegal chocolate smuggled into the country for me and had it delivered to my house. Reese said we'd be perfect together. And Reese asked me not to believe everything I heard about him. But it's not like Shayne would lie to me, would he?

The scent of the chocolate wafts up to me. My finger traces over one of the engraved initials. I lift a truffle out of the box, and before I give it any more thought, I take a bite. I let it melt and then chew it slowly. When I finish that bite, I have another until the entire truffle is gone. Only then do I reread the note from Reese. It does nothing to help resolve the conflicts in my mind. I fold it slowly and hide it in my room.

21

Death

SUNDAY NIGHT, THE CITY COUNCIL HOLDS A PRESS CONFER-
ence. The council room looks empty without my mom sitting
there. The Botanical Haven feels even emptier. I haven't heard
from her all day, and no matter how much I try to convince myself she's okay, with each passing hour my worry doubles.

Councilman Rendon gets up to the podium and talks about
the rescue efforts downtown and how nearly everyone was pulled
from the debris of the collapsed building. He lists only fifteen
casualties of the fifty people trapped. His math reminds me of
the cooling gel the city uses in the misters. Ten percent allergic
to the gel is acceptable. I think he figures as long as he gets the
majority of the vote, he'll win any election.

After he's talked on and on about how well everyone responded
to the emergency, the questions start.

"How many deaths were reported?" the first reporter asks. It's
always right to the worst of the worst.

Council Rendon clears his throat and uses his most serious
expression. "Reports as of late afternoon are that two hundred and
eighty-seven lives here in Austin were lost in the ice storm."

Two hundred and eighty-seven deaths in Austin alone. It's a
horrible number. I can't help but wonder, of those two hundred
and eighty-seven deaths, how many will make it to paradise.

The reporters jump on this response and begin grilling him
on the details: how many died from roofs collapsing, how many

died from accidents on the road. But the next question is the one everyone, including myself, has been waiting for.

"Is the disperser missile to blame for the ice storm?" the reporter asks. She stands there and stares at Rendon until he gives his reassuring smile and motions for her to sit down.

She stays standing. "We need to know, Councilman. Is it to blame?"

"Of course not," he says. "The university has been doing tests on the missiles for months now. I've stated before and I'll state again. The missiles are not the cause of the atmospheric disturbances. The missiles are helping."

I almost laugh at his simplification of the disaster our world is in. Atmospheric disturbances. Two hundred and eighty-seven dead, and it's a disturbance. I know he's lying, and as I watch, I see the thick green fungus spread over his skin. Every single word coming out of his mouth is false; not even he believes them. And I think this is the kind of man who would never make it to the Elysian Fields. I watch his lies for another few minutes and then try texting my mom again. There's no reply.

WHEN I GET TO SCHOOL ON MONDAY, I IMMEDIATELY KNOW something's wrong. Tension hangs in the air like black crepe at a funeral.

"Randy Conner's dead."

Someone whispers it in the hallway.

"What happened?" Another whisper.

"It was the ice storm."

"The shuttle wrecked."

"He died instantly."

Oh my god. I had been with Randy on the shuttle. I talked to him just before I got off.

"Is his sister okay?" I ask. He said he was going to pick her up. No one seems to know.

My stomach flips over, and I almost throw up. I can't believe

Randy's really gone. Dead. And unlike Chloe, Randy will not have anyone to bring him back.

When I get to Social Sciences, I see the empty chair where Randy normally sits, and I can't help but notice Shayne's chair is empty also.

Mr. Kaiser walks in and tells us what he knows. Randy Conner is dead. He'd been one of the unfortunate two hundred and eighty-seven people to die in the city this weekend. I'll never have to worry about any more wisecracking comments about my mom's overprotectiveness from him. I ask about Randy's sister, and Mr. Kaiser tells the class she's fine. She was with him when he died, and then her parents came and took her away. The funeral's going to be held Wednesday, and anyone who wants to attend gets out of school early for the day.

And I wonder: Will Randy Conner go to the Elysian Fields? Because at this moment, if I had to judge, I would say yes. He'd been taking care of his sister when he died, and if that isn't something that deserves paradise, then I don't know what is. I feel like that's what the blue moss was trying to tell me. And the more I think about it, the more certain I am about it.

I look again to Shayne's chair, trying to command him to appear, but I don't want to call his name. I want him to be there on his own.

Mr. Kaiser lectures on everything needed to construct an underground city, but my heart's not in the lecture. I don't think anyone's is.

After class, I head to study hall. I need to talk to Chloe about everything that's happened. She'll help me understand what's going on. But now that I'm thinking more rationally about it, maybe I should leave out the mention of Hell and Hades and anything three-headed or dead; I'm not really sure. But when I get to the library, she's not there.

I figure she's late, but five minutes later, she's still not there. So I get out my FON and call her. Nobody answers the first time so

I leave her a message, but then I dial again, and she finally picks up on the third ring.

"Piper?"

"Hey, Chloe. Where are you?"

"I'm at home."

"It's a school day. Are you still sick?"

Chloe seems to hesitate. "Maybe. I feel really light-headed, Piper. My brain's in this total funk."

I think of Shayne's comments on near-death experiences. About how they can change people. "I'm sure it'll pass," I say.

Chloe lets out a laugh that sounds like she's about to cry. "I hope so. I keep doing really screwed up things."

My breath catches, and I'm almost afraid to ask. "Screwed up like what?"

A pause. "Like I unplugged everything in the house yesterday."

"That doesn't seem so weird," I say to minimize it, and I try to laugh.

But Chloe only sounds more frantic. "Every single thing. And then when my mom plugged everything back in, I broke the lightbulbs."

"All of them?"

"All of them," Chloe says. "There were a hundred and thirty-four if you count the ones in the microwave and refrigerator."

"Why?" I ask.

There's panic in Chloe's voice. "I don't know. It's like I keep getting these weird urges, and I can't control them."

"Maybe you're just in shock, Chloe," I say. I'm trying to convince myself, too. "Is your mom there?"

"She just went out to fill a prescription for me," Chloe says. "And all I want to do is get the hammer and drive nails into the mirrors."

"Don't, Chloe." I glance at my watch. There's no way I can get to her house and back before study hall is over, but I don't care. "I'm coming over."

I can almost see her shake her head. "No, Piper. I'm fine."

I scowl even though she can't see me. "You're not fine. Just wait there for me."

In the FON, I hear someone talking.

"It's okay, Piper. My mom just got home."

"Can I talk to her?" I ask.

Chloe actually laughs. "No. I'm fine. Really. I'll take some medicine and take a nap, and I'm sure I'll feel much better."

Still, I don't want to let it drop. "Can I come by later?"

"How about I call you, Piper?"

"I could just stop by after school," I say.

Chloe blows out a breath. "I'll be asleep. Seriously."

"Are you sure?"

"Totally. Anyway, I gotta go."

Her mom is there, which is some consolation. She should be able to keep Chloe from doing anything destructive. "I'll see you tomorrow?" I say.

"Yeah," Chloe says. "Tomorrow." And she disconnects.

At least Chloe is alive.

MY MOM DOESN'T COME BACK THAT DAY. NOR DOES SHE CALL me or text me or anything. I must call her and text her twenty times, but I don't get any response. And other than that I have no idea how to reach her. She didn't even tell me where she was going. And I wonder if somehow, by wishing she'd go away forever, I've made her do just that.

My heart sinks Tuesday when I walk into Social Sciences. Shayne's still not there. I stare at his chair for probably the entire hour, wondering when he'll decide to show up. But wondering doesn't help. Mr. Kaiser spends the lecture talking about alternatives to the missiles and underground groups that are fighting against the city, but the class feels dead; I don't even want to listen, but I force myself to.

He starts with a list of alternatives. I manage to come up with the Japanese air diverter option, and someone else mentions the reverse tornadoes they've been dreaming up in South America.

But I swear for each item listed, Mr. Kaiser has at least three reasons why it does more harm than good. Finally, I can't take it anymore.

"So what's your solution then?" I ask. All he does day after day is give us a million reasons why nothing will work.

Mr. Kaiser sets the orange dry-erase marker down and leans back on his desk. "For starters, we stop everything we're doing."

"Everything?" Nikki says.

"Everything." He points at the list. "Let's imagine that none of these tactics had ever been tried. Where would Earth be then?"

"Dead?" Nikki suggests, and I have to admit it's a valid point. When temperatures reach into the red zone, the risk of death increases by sixty-five percent.

"Not so." Mr. Kaiser slams his fist down on the desk. "That's exactly the kind of propaganda the city council has been feeding you. But who's to say the heat bubbles would even exist as a threat?"

"Councilman Rendon," I say. He'd say the bubbles would still be around. But he's a liar.

"Right," Mr. Kaiser says. "Councilman Rendon and others like him will continue doing anything and everything they can without enough long-term experimentation. And when they keep it up, the only viable solution will be for everyone to move underground."

Underground. I actually have to suppress a smile at this. We'll be underground one way or the other. Either everyone will be dead and in the Underworld, or everyone will be alive and living in an underground city. Like somehow the worlds will be merged no matter what happens.

AT LEAST TODAY CHLOE'S IN STUDY HALL. SHE'S AT OUR TABLE when I get there, and I pull out my chair, dropping my backpack on the ground.

"How are you?"

She's wearing a red bandana, crisp and ironed, like she's taken extra care in making sure it's folded perfectly. She looks up, and I notice how pale her face still is.

"My mom told me I was sick."

I try to get her to relax. "Yeah. It was the heat."

Chloe shakes her head. "That's what my mom told me. But I don't remember it. It's like the last three days have been a blur."

I decide not to bring up our FON conversation from yesterday. Maybe if she doesn't remember breaking lightbulbs, it's for the best. I take her hands, but they feel like dead, clammy fish in mine. "But you're better now. That's what matters."

But even as I say it, Tanni's haunting words telling me *Chloe will die* slam into me so hard the air is punched out of my stomach.

But Chloe didn't die. She's here in front of me. She's cheated death, and Tanni's horrible words will never come to pass.

I realize my face has frozen into a frown, and I'm sure Chloe's going to call me out on it, but she doesn't seem to notice.

"Is your mom back yet?" Chloe's words snap me back to the present.

I shake my head. "It's weird. She's texted me a couple times, but she's still not home." And even though my mom and I have our differences, another day has passed, and her absence has started to grow a lead anchor of guilt in the pit of my stomach.

Chloe purses her lips together. "So no word from your father?"

"Not since the note."

"Maybe your mom won't come back," Chloe says.

I think Chloe's joking, but she's not even smiling. "She'll come back," I say.

"What would you do, Piper?"

My mom has always been around. But if she weren't—if she really didn't come back—I know what I'd want to do. I'd go back to the Underworld. But now, a few days later, it seems unreal. Almost like it didn't happen.

I decide now's as good a time as any to start telling Chloe about everything, but I'm not sure how to start. "Well, I'd wear really bright colors every day," I say. "Like red."

Chloe smiles and tugs at the ends of her bandana. "Red is the color of blood."

My face freezes. "Yeah. It is." It seems like a whacked-out comment. "And cherries," I add.

"Blood reminds me of death."

Chloe will die.

Chloe tents her fingers in front of her face. "Remember when you asked me about fate, Piper?"

I nod. "Sure." I push Tanni's words away.

"I don't think someone can escape fate," she says.

Chloe did. Shayne had given me a choice, and I'd saved her. And she'd cheated fate. Stayed alive. "They can, Chloe." But even as I say it, it strikes me as false. Like I'm lying to her and myself all at the same time.

"There's a funeral tomorrow," Chloe says.

I nod. "Randy Conner. Are you going?"

"I want to see it," she says. Which is a weird reason for wanting to go to a funeral.

"Why?"

"I want to see the people." And then she grabs my hands with such force, my pinkie finger feels crushed against the rest of my hand. "Have you ever wondered what someone would say at your funeral?" She looks at me, and it's the first time today her eyes meet mine and really see me.

I shake my head and try to break my hands free. But she won't let go. "No. I haven't."

"Do you think he'll be there?"

"Who?"

"Randy." She says it like it's the most natural question in the world. "Do you think he'll be there watching?"

"Chloe, he's dead."

She doesn't hear me. "Would you watch your own funeral? Would you want to know who came?"

The blood's being cut off from my fingers, so I make another move and tear both my hands free. Chloe's obviously still in shock. Maybe I should tell the nurse so he can send her home.

I shake my head. "No, I don't think I would."

But I see Chloe's answer in her eyes. She'd want to watch. She would be there. Watching over the crowd. And in my mind, I see Chloe's funeral instead of Randy's. Her mom and dad. Her brother with his multiple tattoos. Maybe the tattoo artist, Morgan, would even come.

I look at Chloe's tattoo, and like black worms crawling on her skin, the letters shift under my gaze. They swirl and twist, and I can't make them out. They seem to slither off her arm, holding on by only a tendril. I'm tempted to reach out and catch them, or try to steady them at the very least. But then they settle into a string of symbols, none of which I can read. Still, somehow, my mind knows what they say. It can sense the word.

Death.

I look again, but the letters stay the same. Morphed from *sacrifice* into *death.* I glance down at my own tattoo, but it's stable and solid. And it no longer matches Chloe's. When I look up, Chloe watches me. Her eyes flick down to my tattoo, and she smiles.

"You know what I love about you the most, Piper?"

I hardly dare to breathe, but I answer her. "What?"

She unties her bandana. Her brown hair falls over her shoulders, and she twists the bandana around in her hands. "You always believe me."

I nod, which she takes as encouragement.

"I know no matter what I do, you'll believe me and trust me." She reaches across and takes my hand. "And that means everything to me."

I squeeze her hand in return and chance one more glance at her tattoo, holding my breath. But I'm sure it still says *death.* A death which Chloe escaped.

I need to change the subject. "I never told you about Friday night," I say. That seems like a good place to start.

Chloe just smiles. "I want to hear all about it, Piper. But can we talk about it tomorrow? I have so much homework to catch up on."

"Yeah, sure."

"Good." And she spends the rest of study hall pretending to do homework, though all she does is trace her finger in circles over the screen of her tablet.

22

Funeral

WEDNESDAY AFTER SECOND PERIOD, I HEAD TO THE FUNERAL.
I wait for one of the shuttles in front of the school, and I keep
scanning the crowd, looking for either Chloe or Shayne, but it's
like I'm in a sea of unfamiliar faces. I know almost everyone
around me, but I can't focus on any of them. I say hi to a couple
of the kids in my classes, but otherwise stick to myself.

My back's already drenched in sweat, and heat presses down.
But there haven't been any reports of impending heat bubbles,
and for now, I think the city will be spared any more disasters.
This still doesn't keep other kids from talking about it, and someone even starts taking bets on when the next bubble will hit.
One sophomore guy claims it will be tomorrow; he swears he's
developed some equipment in his home lab that can predict to
within the minute when the bubble will form. Given the random
nature of the bubbles I've seen so far, I highly doubt he's right,
but on the off chance he is, he could make a killing. If nothing
else, the kid's got everyone hanging on his every word, juniors
and seniors included. I hop a shuttle while he's still talking and
head to the funeral.

When I walk into the church, I can't find Chloe anywhere.
But it seems the rest of the city has turned up. Every seat is taken,
and the standing and greeting areas are packed. I look down the
long front aisle and see Randy Conner's family at the front. From
the back of the church, I spot his seven-year-old sister with her
face turned enough that I can see her eyes are dry and her lips

are pressed together like she's holding back a river of tears that she never plans to let loose. I see the backs of his parents, his mom leaning away from his dad, toward his sister, and shaking with silent sobs. And as if he knows I'm watching, Randy's dad turns, and our eyes meet. Anger flashes there, rooted so deep it's wrapped and coiled around every bone and sinew in his body. It tears at him and eats him alive day after day. It's a black mold around him, smothering him and everyone he touches. And for some reason, I remember Acheron—the river of sorrows.

I shift my eyes, not wanting to empathically share his anger, and spot Randy's girlfriend, Hannah Reed, there in the front. She sits on the side opposite from Randy's family and won't even look their way. Her wide dry eyes scan the crowd, not seeing anyone; if she notices me, she makes no acknowledgment.

What was Randy Conner's final sorrow? What did he leave behind on his way to the Elysian Fields?

An usher sees me and tries to find me a spot. I end up standing against a redbrick wall tucked into the place where they light candles. I move to the far back corner and wait. I'll find Chloe later, after the Mass.

Mass begins with a song. "Amazing Grace." It's the same one they played at Charlotte's funeral so long ago. Charlotte had been my best friend, but I never really knew Randy at all. He was a face in the hallways and a voice at the back of the classroom. A shadow next door after my mom threatened to skin him. But when the casket begins its trek down the long aisle, the sobs coming from the crowd around me bring an unexpected lump to my throat. I feel like I should have taken the time to know him better.

The priest motions everyone to sit when the song ends, so I lean back against the bricks but turn when I feel someone next to me.

"Shayne?"

He's dressed in black, appropriate for the occasion, and his hair's combed neatly behind his ears. He squeezes my arm but doesn't smile.

"Where have you been?" I whisper, almost under my breath, forcing the lump out of my throat.

"Busy."

"Will you be back tomorrow?" I hate the thought of sitting through another Social Sciences class wondering where he is.

He gives the smallest hint of a smile. "We'll see tomorrow." He reaches for a pack of matches set near the candles. According to my mom, the Catholic Church got a special dispensation for matches and candles.

"You promised you'd be around."

Shayne nods and strikes a match. The immediate sulfur smell hits the air. The flame flickers as he moves the match to an unlit votive candle. It takes a couple seconds, but the wick catches in a burst of light. Then he moves the still-burning match close to his mouth and blows it out. "Do you have any special intentions?" He holds the pack of matches toward me.

I take them, pulling one out of the box. "What was your intention?" I ask.

His hand reaches up, brushing my arm. "I can't tell you."

"Like wishing on a star?"

Shayne nods. "Right. If you tell what you intend, then it won't happen."

"Then I won't tell you what I want either." But I hope he wonders.

I move the match to the box, ready to strike it, when a flame flashes out of nowhere and the match ignites. I'm so startled that I drop it into a candleholder. I stare at it, watching it burn and melt the surrounding wax until it sputters and extinguishes on its own. And then I turn to Shayne.

He's staring at the match, now covered in cooling wax. His eyes shift to mine, and he smiles. He's playing tricks on me. Using some god power from the Underworld to light the fire. So

I take out another match, push the box closed, and prepare to strike it. Yet this time, it doesn't ignite until I pull it across the scratchy paper. I dip it down, lighting the candle and letting the sulfur again enter my nose. And then I blow it out.

"So where have you been?" I ask.

He shakes his head and puts the pack of matches back in the recess. "I've been around."

"But I haven't seen you." And if I haven't seen him, he may as well not be around.

"You haven't called me."

He's right. I haven't, and I'm not entirely sure why. "You're busy," I say. It's the best reason in my mind. I opt not to mention the chocolates Reese had delivered. I'll sort out Reese on my own.

Shayne nods. "Never too busy for you."

I smile whether he means it or not.

"I almost came by yesterday," he says.

My heart flutters. "Really?"

"I got to your front door," he says. "I almost knocked."

Had I felt his presence? I'd been so worried about Chloe, I hadn't thought of much else. "Why didn't you?"

His lips tighten. "I thought your mom might be home. I didn't want her to see me."

"You're not scared of my mom are you?" Though in actuality, he probably should be. I'm scared of my mom.

"I'm not sure *scared* is the most appropriate word," Shayne says.

"So why not just come to class?"

Shayne leans close and whispers into my ear. "It's hard, Piper. I'm trying so hard to be patient and stay inside the boundaries, but more than anything in the world, I want to tear them down. And I can't. No matter what that ends up meaning."

"What boundaries?"

Shayne only responds by kissing my ear. It comes out of nowhere, and I'm pretty sure I've died and gone to the Elysian Fields. But when I look around, I see we're still here in the church, though a small hidden corner of it. Taking part in Randy's final blessing.

My corner of happiness vanishes when I feel eyes on me; they fill me with dread. Slowly, I turn around toward the back of the alcove. Tanni—Fate—stands next to a statue of the Virgin Mary, her eyes matching the empty eyes of the statue. Her friends stand on either side of her, sunglasses on but watching me.

The statue's hands are extended out in front of her, reaching to implore those who would listen. Tanni's arms lift to match.

The church around me enters a bubble of muffled words and fades into the background. Outside of the bubble exists only me, Shayne, Tanni, and her two friends.

My body tenses as rage builds inside me. "You were wrong," I say. "Chloe didn't die."

Next to me, Shayne stiffens. "Don't talk to her, Piper."

It's too late for that. Tanni's soulless eyes look at me, but it's like she didn't hear me. "It's your fault," she says.

Shayne pulls on my hand. "Let's go."

I pull my hand away from his. I don't need him telling me what to do right now. "Chloe did not die," I say. I want Tanni to hear me. I want everyone to hear me. I know I'm yelling, but I don't care. Chloe is alive.

Tanni's eyes shift to Shayne. "You have no reason to be here," she says. And just like that, he vanishes.

I stare at the spot where he was. "What did you do to him?" I demand.

Tanni shakes her head, and her hair moves from side to side in a cascade. "It's all your fault, Piper."

"What's my fault? And where is Shayne?"

Tanni steps forward and grabs my wrist, and her cold steel grip is like a vise. I'm not sure why I bother struggling, but I do, trying to break my wrist free until it hurts.

"Randy Conner is dead," she says.

I nod, and with her grip and her words and the fog circling behind her empty eyes, she's got me. I'm rooted in place.

"And it's your fault."

"What is?" But something's starting to come together inside me. A nasty itching sensation in the back of my mind. I don't want to face it.

"You killed him."

I open my mouth, but nothing comes out.

"You killed Randy Conner. It's your fault."

"How?" It's the only thing I can manage to say.

"Someone had to die. It wasn't his time. It's your fault."

I stare at her now, and I can't pull my eyes from her face. The truth slams into me like a freight train. I saved Chloe. But at what cost? Randy was one of two hundred and eighty-seven people to die. Would he really be alive right now if not for me?

"It's your fault." Tanni says it a final time and then lets go of my wrist. She walks back and joins her friends at the Virgin Mary, and they fade until they're gone.

The bubble around the world slips away, and the church is reanimated. Mass has ended, and six of Randy's friends carry out his casket. No one has heard anything. And Shayne is gone.

My fault. I hear it in my head. Is Randy Conner's death my fault?

23

Reunion

MY MOM IS HOME. THE SECOND I WALK THROUGH THE DOOR, a giant heaviness lifts from my shoulders. She's not dead. I can voice this concern in my mind now that I know she's okay. The cold feeling in my gut I've been carrying around since she stopped texting me dissipates. I didn't even realize it was there, weighing on me.

She moves around in the Botanical Haven, cutting dead leaves off plants all over the place. And she's taken the calla lilies Reese gave me and set them on a table at the front of the store. The glass container shimmers from the sunlight coming through the windows. I'll have to explain why I have illegal flowers. Maybe I can lie and say I cut them myself.

"Hi, Mom."

She gives me a sideways glance and then looks away. Snip. Snip. More leaves fall. Some aren't even dead.

I walk in and decide to go ahead upstairs. Let my mom have her time and then come talk to me when she's done. After all, if either of us should be angry about something, it's me. My mom should have been home days ago. She didn't call. Didn't give an explanation. Didn't do anything except not show up. Yet, even with all that, my stomach is clenched in fists of guilt.

"Did you miss me?" she says.

I turn, halfway up the steps. She's at the bottom looking up at me, scissors in hand.

"You stopped checking in. I was worried."

My mom sighs and pulls off her gardening gloves, tossing them onto the counter by the cash register. "Things got complicated."

My heart skips a beat. "With my father?"

She nods, and I notice she glances at my tattoo. I look down at it and focus on the bumps faded from redness into just the black of the ink.

"Who is he?" I haven't asked in years. A lifetime. Not since I got over the dream of living a normal life with a normal family.

My mom turns away and walks to the door, locking it from the inside. It's early. No one who went to Randy Conner's funeral went back to school afterward, but if my mom knows about the funeral, she doesn't say anything.

"Who is he?" I repeat my question, wondering if I'll ever know.

"It doesn't matter, Piper."

I throw my backpack to the ground, watching it tumble down the five steps I've already gone up. "Yes. It does. You spin me some story about how he's some escaped terrorist and then you spend almost a week with him. And then you come back here and tell me it doesn't even matter who he is. It doesn't add up, Mom. If he's so bad, why have you been gone so long? What's complicated anyway? What complications could there possibly be?"

My mom's eyes meet my own, and it's like she's begging me to drop the subject. To stop asking my questions. I don't want to stop. I'm sick of living a life filled with her mysteries. Or lies. They seem to blend together.

I start up the steps again, leaving my backpack lying at the bottom.

"It's about custody, Piper."

Her words freeze my feet in place. "Custody?"

"I can't lose you, Piper. Not now. Not ever."

"He wants custody?" How could a father I've never known want custody of me? I'm eighteen now. Custody shouldn't even be a concern. Not to mention an escaped criminal could never even take the case to court.

"He wants to take you away from me." My mom's voice is coarse as sandpaper. "And I'll never let that happen. I won't share you."

Share me? It seems such an odd thing for her to say. Sharing her adult child with an estranged father. The father who left me a note in my room. The father who said we'd have all the time we need to get to know each other.

"Why did he do it?" I ask. "Why did he leave?"

My mom laughs. "He never wanted to be a part of your life from the very start. We were nothing to him. So he left and got himself in trouble and escaped from the burdens of a family."

My father never wanted me?

"So why now?" I whisper the question, but she still hears it.

"Why now indeed?" My mom walks toward the counter, shuffling through the dead leaves on the ground. More drop off around her as she walks. "Because we haven't been careful enough." She laughs. "I haven't been careful enough."

"Careful? How much more careful could we have been?" I suppose if we completely removed ourselves from the grid that would have been more careful. But even my mom hasn't been that extreme. At least not yet.

"We'll have to move again." She pulls out some junk from a drawer and begins shuffling through it.

"No."

She ignores me. "Yes, that's the only answer."

"No, Mom."

My mom swivels her head and stares through me. "No what?"

I look to her eyes, but she won't meet mine. "No, I won't move again."

She turns back to the stuff from the drawer and flips through it like she's looking for something. "Yes, you will."

I won't. I tell myself this over and over in my head. I have a life here. I have Chloe. And now there's Shayne. I don't have to live with my mom forever.

The bell rings. Someone's trying to come in. The knob shifts, but it won't open since my mom's locked the door. I look through the glass to see who's visiting.

Reese. I have Reese.

I look at my mom, and she's staring right at him.

"I wondered where the flowers came from." My mom's voice is so calm it sounds crazy. Each word drawn with perfect precision.

"Open the door," he says. And I know this is so very bad that my worlds are about to collide.

My mom faces me again, and I am compelled to walk down the steps until I'm at the bottom, near the counter.

"This is not what I was expecting." She uses her crazy-calm voice again. And more leaves drop from plants.

I only want her to get rid of Reese, not kill him. "Mom, it's no big deal."

She thrusts her finger out and points at the door. "He is a big deal. How dare you try to tell me he's not?"

Reese knocks again and twists the knob. I hear the metal crunching inside it.

I throw up my hands. "He's nothing. I swear it." I tell this to my mom and myself at the same time. Reese is nothing. It's Shayne my mom should worry about.

Or am I lying to myself? Should my mom be concerned with Reese also?

"He gave you these." And in a single move, she grabs the pink flowers from their holder and throws them down on the tile.

When she turns back to the door, her mouth twists into a frown. Reese stands there in the doorframe, dwarfing it. He looks every bit the god of war.

I can't believe he's the god of war.

"You don't belong here." My mom narrows her eyes at Reese, and I realize she knows him. Maybe he came by when I wasn't here or something. But she can't possibly know who he really is.

He walks a few steps toward us, so sure of himself. I'm thinking there might still be a way for me to get out of this situation gracefully when he says, "Did Piper tell you about the great time we had Friday night?"

My eyes almost fall out of my head. I can't believe he's gone and said this.

My mom turns to me, and I know she'd like to lock me away. Forever. Somewhere no one will ever come. "Piper has told me nothing of the sort."

"Do you want me to tell you about it?" Reese takes another step, and his foot smashes the pink petals of the calla lilies.

My mom picks up her shears, and if they were only bigger, I know she'd cut his head off. "I'd like you to leave," she says.

"How do you know each other?" I say, but neither of them looks at me. It's like I haven't even spoken.

"You can't stop it," Reese says. "You know Piper and I are going to end up together." And he looks at me, and all at once, our eyes lock, and his intoxicating scent pours into my nostrils. God, I could die in that smell and be happy. I totally remember his kiss.

He can tell I remember it; it must be all over my face. He smiles.

I want to make the thought go away. To force Reese out of my mind. But his scent flows through me like the wine we also shared on Friday. It reaches into the parts deep inside me that tell me how much fun life can be and settles. I try to force myself to look away from him but find I don't want to. So I take a step back to increase our distance.

"I think you must have misunderstood." My mom's voice sounds certain. She has no idea what's going on inside my head. I don't either, because even though I don't want to be with Reese, there is something almost supernatural pulling me toward him.

Reese won't take his eyes off mine. Won't free me. "I didn't misunderstand anything," he says.

My mom moves closer to me and settles her hand on my

shoulder before answering him. "Piper is going to stay with me," she says.

I decide they've both gone nuts. I squeeze my eyes shut, breaking the contact. "Would you both just leave me alone?"

And I run for the door before either Reese or my mom can react.

24

Threat

I run out of the Botanical Haven, past the green-houses, and into the trees, pushing deeper and deeper until I can't see anything but a forest of bark around me and branches high overhead. Even then, I keep running, trying to put as much distance as I can between myself and the craziness of my life. Chloe is totally freaking me out. My mom and Reese know each other. And Tanni claims I'm responsible for Randy Conner's death.

I stop when I see a Spanish oak in front of me; one of its long branches twists so low to the ground I can rest against it. It's only then that I catch my breath, letting the hot, clear air around me replace memories of Reese. He's like a drug. I'm feeling drawn toward him in a crazy way even though I know that's the completely wrong thing to do. I let the heat of the world soak into me to erase him from my thoughts, because I don't want him there.

"Shayne," I whisper, praying that wherever Tanni sent him, he can hear.

In seconds, he's there next to me.

"I was afraid . . ." I say. "Tanni . . ."

"It's okay," he says. "I was worried about you."

We stare at each other. Neither of us moves. I feel like I've betrayed him. I feel like I've been with Reese. But I haven't. I ran away from the Botanical Haven before I got too close.

I take a small step, and this is all it takes. Shayne pulls me to him, and I bury my head in his neck. I can feel him breathing in my hair.

"God, I missed you," I say. How could I miss him so much already? But it felt like a part of me was lost.

"I missed you more," he says. "Way more."

I don't think it's possible.

"Reese came to visit," I say.

Shayne stiffens. "When?"

I shudder amid the warmth of the world around me. Reese and my mom. Have they started after me yet? Will they even follow? "Just now. It's like they know each other," I say. "How can that be?"

Shayne rubs my back but doesn't answer, and then he tenses up, and I know why. I smell Reese. He's followed me from the Botanical Haven.

"Oh, you can't be serious." Reese actually sounds surprised.

Shayne lets go though I really want to keep holding on to him. "Go away," he says.

Reese puts his hand to his chest in mock surprise. "You're kidding, right?"

"Go away now," Shayne says. "I don't want you anywhere near Piper."

Reese looks at me and catches my eyes, locking them in place. "Piper doesn't seem to mind."

As soon as he says it, his smell amplifies, creating a wave of memories in my mind. Memories of smiling with Reese and laughing with Reese. I fight, with every muscle I have, to stay rooted in place. I lean back on the Spanish oak and pray it will grow limbs and hold me so I don't go to him. But his scent brings to the forefront of my mind our night out. Our kiss. It draws me forward.

Shayne turns to me, and I want to die when I see the confusion in his eyes. He's watching the struggle inside me. I don't want to be anywhere near Reese; I want to be with Shayne.

I want to be with them both.

Shayne opens his mouth, his beautiful lips pulled back in a snarl around his teeth. "Just make this easy and leave."

Reese laughs.

"What's so funny?" Shayne says.

"Everything's funny, Shayne."

I hear the bite when Reese says the name.

"What?" Shayne takes a step away from me. A step closer to Reese. And his hands are tightened so hard into fists they're white.

Reese sneers. "I was just thinking how funny it'll be when you're trapped in your own tortures. A suitable end for the ex-Lord of Hell."

Shayne takes another step toward Reese. The last thing I want is for the two of them to start fighting. My memories are telling me I want to run to Reese, but my heart wants to grab hold of Shayne and leave this place now. The sooner the better.

But Shayne's such a freaking guy. He wants the fight. "Stay away from Piper. Go away now, or I won't wait for permission from the assembly. I'll set Prometheus free and give you his place. Let the birds eat your liver for a few millennia. We'll see how you feel then."

Another wave of Reese's aroma hits me. More memories stir. I can't even tell which ones are real anymore. I see myself walking on a beach with Reese. Having a picnic with Reese. Kissing Reese. I remember how sweet he'd been. The nice things he said. The presents he'd given me. How special he made me feel. But I know I've never done these things with Reese. We've only just met. I turn my face away, trying to block the scent, but it's not like I can stop breathing.

"Your threat is worthless." Reese's teeth gleam under the smile that forms on his mouth.

"Watch and see," Shayne says.

"The assembly backs me." Reese flexes his fingers and then relaxes them. "But of course you'd know that if you ever came to any assembly meetings."

"I have more important things to do," Shayne says. "Like run the Underworld."

Reese laughs at this. "Maybe you're not doing such a great job. I'm sure you've heard I've been to visit."

Shayne glares at him in reply.

"It's true," Reese says. "But I can tell you want to deny it. I'll tell you what."

"What?"

Reese puts a hand to his chest. "I left you just a little sprinkle of proof. Look for it when you get home."

Shayne takes a step forward, and I'm pretty sure this is it. They're going to kill each other. "You visit and you die," Shayne says.

Reese just gives a wave with his hand and then turns to me. "Piper, I'm sorry about Randy Conner. You did hear he died, right?"

Randy is dead because of me. I might as well have wrecked the shuttle.

"I heard," I manage to say. The memories keep twisting around: Reese consoles me. Reese laughs with me.

"Now let's see, Shayne, where would you put someone like Randy Conner?" Reese puts his finger to his mouth as if he's considering the question. "The Elysian Fields?" He shakes his head. "No, that's not what my sources tell me."

But it has to be. I know in my heart Randy belongs in paradise. The thought helps clear my head. The memories try to sort themselves out.

"Shut up, Reese," Shayne says.

"So Randy didn't make it to paradise." Reese snaps his fingers. "Asphodel then."

I glance at Shayne and can tell from his pursed lips that Reese is right. That somehow Shayne didn't see the good in Randy that I saw. There's been some oversight. I haven't been to Asphodel, but I know it's not paradise.

"Shayne." I find my voice and manage to get out his name, trying my best to ignore Reese.

He turns to me, fists still balled. "What?"

"I need to get out of here. Now." Even if he has no clue about the struggle in my mind, he's got to hear the strain in my voice. If I don't get away from the two of them, I'll go crazy.

Reese laughs. "I'll see you soon, Piper, okay?"

"Not okay," Shayne says. He scowls at Reese and then wraps his arms around me, and we start sinking, through the dirt and damp and rock and then into the river of liquid mercury that carries us until we're there on the bank of the River Acheron. Charon's just pulling the boat up to the dock when Shayne and I arrive. Charon's face cracks into a leathery smile which pulls his white eyes almost shut.

But before we walk over to join him, I turn to Shayne. "About Reese—"

Shayne leans over and kisses me, stopping my words.

"You don't have to make any excuses for him," he says once he pulls back.

I'm not sure how to explain it. "My mind started playing tricks. Like I couldn't remember what was real and what wasn't."

His eyes darken. "He doesn't play fair, which is exactly why I told you to be careful around him. He can't be trusted. Ever."

I know he's right but wish he weren't. The memories felt so real. It was like I really lived those moments . . . with Reese.

"Why won't you talk to the assembly of gods about him?" I ask.

The light from the silver pools shifts, causing shadows to flicker on Shayne's face, giving him a serious look. "Let's just say some members of the assembly and I are not on the best of terms right now."

"Why not?" I ask.

"Because we're not. End of story."

I gather not to press him any more.

I remember what Reese said about Randy. If he'd been trying

to get under my skin, it had worked. "Randy should be in the Elysian Fields," I say.

Shayne shakes his head. "I judged him. He's in Asphodel."

I glance at Charon who's watching our conversation but not interrupting. "You judged wrong." I've never felt so sure about anything.

Shayne takes my hand, which I've balled up into a fist. "How do you know?"

I shrug and try to relax my muscles. "I just know. I talked to him before . . ." I can't believe I was probably the last person to talk to Randy Conner.

"Before he died?" Shayne asks.

"Yeah." I tell Shayne about the ice storm and about how Randy was watching out for his sister, making sure she got home okay. "He just didn't seem like such a jerk," I say. "It was like I could see the good in him." I don't mention the blue moss I'd seen on him, but I know it's a sign. I don't need anyone's confirmation on that.

Shayne purses his lips, but he doesn't say he's going to change it. Instead, he reaches into his pocket and pulls out a gold coin, which he flips off his thumb. Charon catches it and pockets it without even looking.

"You know you don't need to pay," Charon says.

Shayne grins. "Don't want anyone to say I don't pay my fare."

I watch the conversation and attempt to relax. Try to shake away life's worries. But I worry I've killed Randy Conner, and Shayne's doomed him to Hell for eternity.

Charon flips the coin around in his pocket. "Nobody would dare say anything of the sort."

It's the same banter from before, and I realize this must go on every time Shayne makes the water journey. Eternal friendship.

"Can you move Randy?" I ask.

I hear Charon let out a whistle under his breath.

"No, Piper. I can't. He's been judged. He has to stay there."

"But don't you ever worry that you're wrong?" I ask.

Shayne looks out across the water when he answers. "If I worried about that, it would consume me. I judge and move on."

I process this thought as we get into the boat. There has to be some way I can get Shayne to move Randy. Charon boards last and picks up the pole to move us.

"How long have you and Charon known each other?" I ask. We sit on the bow of the boat, side by side, still in the darkest part of the cavern. I look out to the black water, seeing the sorrows there bubbling to the surface. Seeing the creatures shimmering below the froth, eating what sorrows they catch. Far ahead, the sky brightens where I know the two suns shine down from above.

"Forever."

"That's a long time."

Shayne pulls me closer. "An eternity."

"So who do you live here with? Just Charon?"

Shayne glances back at Charon whose face is frozen as if he's trying to not blink. But Shayne quickly turns back to me and smiles. "Don't forget Rhadam."

I smile at the memory of the energetic overlord of the Elysian Fields.

"And Cerberus. Not to mention the billions of dead souls keeping me company."

I think of the sorrows of all those souls, left behind here in the river to be devoured by creatures of the Underworld. "What was Randy Conner's last sorrow?" The question forces its way into my mind. I can't pick Randy out of the chorus. All the voices blend together, shifting in rhythm when one gets swallowed by the creatures. Moving to fill the empty space.

Shayne is rigid against me all of a sudden. "You don't want to know."

"Yes, I do." I think of the shuttle accident. Randy's girlfriend and tons of friends and classmates at his funeral. His miserable family. And I remember Tanni and her friends by the Virgin Mary. I press my eyes closed and try to find his sorrow on my own, but it won't come. "I just want to know."

"Maybe you should let Randy be."

But I know I can't let Randy be. "I want to know."

Shayne sighs and looks to the river, and I see a bubble rise to the surface. It grows larger and begins to float, and the things under the water stay away from it.

I lean toward the edge of the boat, hoping to hear, but I feel Shayne's hands grab my arms.

"I want to hear." I need to hear.

"You'll be able to."

So I lean back into him and close my eyes again.

If I die, who will protect them?

I gasp when I hear it, and images fill my mind. My eyes fly open, remembering his family at the funeral. His little sister with dry eyes. His mom shaking with sorrow, leaning away from his dad, not touching him. And his dad, with a black aura of anger pulsing through his veins. I see his dad's anger in Randy's sorrow. Anger his dad can't control. Anger that makes Randy's dad hit his wife and children.

Tanni's words pound into my head.

"It's my fault."

I don't even realize I say them aloud.

"No, Piper."

The bubble pushes again below the water and disappears. My fault. Randy Conner's death is my fault.

"I made you save Chloe."

But Shayne grabs my shoulders and turns me to him. "No, it's not your fault. You can't think that way."

"Then why?"

Shayne looks away. "The Fates determine who will die next. Not you. Not me. Chloe lived, and they chose Randy Conner."

It's all tumbling around in my mind. "But if Chloe had . . ." I can't even bring myself to say it. I don't want her dead. More than anything, I don't want her dead.

"Randy may still have died." His eyes shift back to me. "It's all a game to them, watching lives fall apart." His eyes have narrowed to slits, but the brown irises inside start to stir with flecks of red.

"And you do whatever they say?" I know it comes out harsh, but he's just taken Randy and delivered him for eternity to the wrong place.

His defenses go up. "What do you mean?"

"When they die. You take the soul away from whoever the Fates say."

An icy look runs across Shayne's face, and his arms tense. "I don't take anyone's soul away."

I motion around with my arm. "But this is your world."

Shayne is holding anger just under his skin. "Yeah. My world. And my responsibility. But not my doing."

"But I thought—"

"—wrong." Shayne's eyes won't meet mine. "My job is to judge and maintain control. And trust me, that's a big enough job."

I feel like I've slapped Shayne. My cheeks burn, and I wish I could take it back. "I'm sorry."

Shayne's face softens, and he gives my shoulder a gentle caress. A shiver runs down my spine. "I'm the easy person to blame."

"Doesn't that bother you?"

His lips curl up in a wry smile. "It does get a bit old having every single death in history blamed on me. But it goes with the job."

"So why is Randy in Asphodel?"

"It's not so bad there, Piper," Shayne says.

Bad or not, if I've fated Randy to die and doomed his family to suffer under an abusive father, then at least I need to see the product of my actions. My choice to save Chloe. "I want to see."

Shayne rubs my shoulder and pulls me close. "I know."

I hardly remember Charon is on the boat. His presence seems to evaporate when Shayne and I argue. When the boat bumps against the dock and Charon jumps out, I remember him, and my heart sinks; I've hardly spoken a word to him.

But he's the one who helps me out this time, and when his

hand grabs mine, he gives it a quick squeeze. Something stirs inside me, and I reach out and hug him. He lets go of my hand and grabs me in a bear hug so fierce, my lungs feel like collapsing. His weathered face cracks into its smile, which, even after two visits, I love.

"Have a wonderful time."

I smile back, and Shayne gets out of the boat behind me. "I will." The Underworld feels more welcoming than my real home back at the Botanical Haven, even with all its scary river monsters and haunting sorrows.

Once our feet hit the swampy shore, Cerberus runs over, weaving through the trees, tail thumping so hard it's like his lower half is another head with a mind of its own. He jumps both front paws up onto Shayne, and they wrestle around until Shayne finally falls to the ground.

"Does he wait for you every time you leave?"

Shayne reaches over to rub Cerberus's belly, which causes him to flop down, roll over, and expose every bit of his giant stomach. Even with three heads, he's just a dog.

"Pretty much. Man's best friend, right?"

I laugh. "You mean god's best friend."

"I may be a god, Piper, but I'm still just your regular, average guy."

All it takes is one look at Shayne to know there's nothing average about him.

We turn and wave a final goodbye to Charon. He's already far away from the dock, out in the reeds and cattails, but the warmth of his smile even at that distance broadens my own.

"Charon likes you," Shayne says.

"I like Charon."

Shayne laughs. "That's one thing not many people will say. Most people aren't happy about dying. Everyone knows they don't live forever, but when it's actually their time, they almost never want to go."

I think of Randy Conner. "Randy didn't want to go, did he?"

Shayne shakes his head. "No. I crossed with him. It was pretty rough going at first. But once he got to the other side . . . well, it always changes."

We reach the end of the tunnel, and ahead, I can see the flickering from the fireplace inside Shayne's home. Cerberus is already curled in front of the fire, and instead of sitting next to Shayne on the sofa, I plop myself on the ground next to Cerberus and start scratching between a couple of his ears. I feel Shayne's eyes on me.

"So you missed me?" He tilts his head and waits for my answer.

I move my hand, scratching a different head. "I missed your dog."

Shayne laughs and comes down to sit on the ground next to me. He touches my earlobe, which causes a tingle somewhere that is definitely not my earlobe. And he pulls my ponytail holder out, letting my hair escape from its bonds.

"I'm glad you came back."

My chest is tight, and I don't dare look at him. I could melt into Shayne and this world and stay here forever. "I am, too." I lean my back against him, and we sit there, me still scratching Cerberus, and Shayne running his hand through my hair. The fire never dies. It crackles and spits sparks into the air, and despite the burnt aroma, I feel more like I'm in Heaven than Hell. And I never want to leave.

"Are you sure you want to see Asphodel? We could go back to the Elysian Fields. Rhadam's been asking about you."

Shayne's words snap me out of the paradise I'm living. It's not that I want to see Asphodel. I need to see it. I look at Shayne; his lips have pressed into a smile. "I'd take paradise forever," I say. Here with him.

"Most people would, when given the choice."

"But they don't get a choice, do they?"

He shakes his head, and orange embers from the fire reflect off the blackness of his hair. "If they did, no one would choose Tartarus, would they?"

I consider this. "Maybe the really bad ones would."

His eyes shift to the side for only a second, but I notice. "No one would choose that life, Piper. Trust me. To end up in Tartarus is like picking the short stick in life. Or death, as the case might be. And the worst part is it lasts forever. There's no getting out."

I sit up. "Never?"

"Never. There are two basic rules down here. Once a person has been judged, they stay where they are placed forever."

Like Randy Conner. Stuck forever in Asphodel. But I'm not ready to accept this yet. "And the second?" I ask.

"No one can ever leave the Underworld."

I raise an eyebrow. "Except the exceptions, of course," I say. "And me."

Shayne rolls his eyes. "I'm not talking about you. You haven't died. Not to mention you came here by your own choice, and you are my guest."

His guest. I like that. "Too bad." I'm joking, but only kind of. "If I couldn't leave, I'd have to stay here forever. And my mom couldn't do anything about it."

Shayne's face tightens, and it looks like I've made him mad.

"What? I'm only kidding."

He shakes his head. "It doesn't matter."

But my mind tells me I should know why he's upset. "What did I say wrong?"

"Wrong?" Shayne stands up. "You didn't say anything wrong." He walks away from the fireplace—away from me. I watch his feet step across the red and black mosaic floor—the floor I love as if I created it myself.

I stand up and follow him. He reaches a table set against the far wall. It's black wood, buffed to such a high polish I can see his reflection in it. A picture hangs overhead, oil painted on canvas, with souls and angels and demons and the Underworld partitioned into regions with rivers flowing throughout. "Then why are you upset?" I ask.

Shayne turns and leans against the table, which rocks under his weight. All at once, his eyes shift. Flickering, but so fast they're like sparks in a fire. Like the air around him could ignite if he wanted it to. He's holding a helmet of some sort. I hadn't noticed it before, but it's made to cover only the crown of the head, and it shines of pure gold.

He holds it out to me, and the air crackles around him and it. "Piper, do you know what this is?"

My breath catches in my throat. I do. I know exactly what it is. And even though I've seen this object many times before, I don't remember any of them. "It's the Helm of Darkness."

Shayne's face relaxes as if the weight of the helmet has been removed from his head. "Yes. It's the Helm of Darkness."

My mind forms the words for me. "It makes its wearer invisible."

Shayne nods and turns, setting it back on the table. "Do you know who I am?" He turns back when he says it, and it looks like he's going to take a step closer to me, but he doesn't.

My feet feel planted in the ground; I can't move. "Shayne. You're Shayne."

"And . . . ?"

I take a deep breath. I'm not sure why I have a hard time saying it—even to myself. "You're Hades. Lord of the Underworld."

Shayne's eyes bore into me, and I take a step back without even thinking about it. "And who are you?" he says.

I don't know who I am. I want to be someone else, but I'm not sure who. Someone who lives a life of tattoos and danger. Someone who doesn't obey every small command her mother makes. I want to be that person, but I'm not.

"I'm Piper," I say, but I feel like there's more.

Shayne's eyes stay locked on mine, but something disappears from them. Something hopeful and mysterious. "Yes. You're Piper." He walks toward me, and his eyes return to normal. He leans forward and kisses me on the lips gently. And I know whether he claims to be a god or an average guy, I love him.

"Are you ready to see Asphodel?"

With Shayne, I'm ready for anything. "Tell me about Asphodel."

"It's the place in between," he says. "For the souls who aren't so good and aren't so bad."

"Like Purgatory?"

He seems to consider this. "Purgatory. That's one way to look at it."

Shayne smiles, and I never want him to stop. His smile has a way of filling me with a comfort I haven't felt my entire life. I link my arm around his, and we start walking. "Except no one minds being there. They don't even think about it."

"So Randy is happy?" Maybe I can just find him in Asphodel and say goodbye. Tell him I'm sorry.

Shayne's smile turns wry. "I'm not sure I'd go quite that far. But I'll let you decide for yourself." And then he walks back to the table, picks up the Helm of Darkness, and clips it onto his belt, and we move out of his sanctuary into the blackness of another tunnel.

25

Asphodel

FROM THE MINUTE WE REACH THE BARREN, RED SHORE, I KNOW this: Asphodel is a hell. Not like the eternal torture Shayne tells me is Tartarus. But a hell all the same.

The thick scent of musty clay hits me from the first step. I screw up my nose and look out from the mouth of the cave. "Which river is this?" I motion out beyond the dried-up red river-banks to the churning rusty water in the middle, and I see monsters again, but they aren't staying under the surface. They're jumping above, baring their fangs, snapping at each other. Their razored fins slice at each other, and when they bleed, their blood blends with the red water.

Shayne presses his lips together. "The River Lethe. Passage-way to the Asphodel Meadows."

Clay cakes under my feet, pulling at my sandals until I toss them aside altogether, letting my toes sink into the oozing red-ness. Along the shore lie skeletons of boats marooned in the thick clay, falling to pieces. It's a dead world and a dead river with nothing alive except the monsters waiting for us. It makes me think of how my world will look should the Global Heating Crisis and the ensuing wars continue. And there's no reason to think they won't. I imagine the Botanical Haven as a singular oasis amid a world of barren desert because I know my mom would never move to a city belowground. And I know she'd want me by her side.

Will the world really come to that? Will my life really come to that?

Shayne and I walk to the dock; its piers aren't even submerged until halfway out, and when we reach the water, thankfully the monsters stay away from Shayne. It's like he's got an invisible force field surrounding him, and I happen to be lucky enough to be ensconced in it.

I motion to the monsters. "They never bother you?"

Shayne unclips the Helm of Darkness and holds it out. The monsters retreat. "The Helm makes the wearer invisible, Piper, but it also helps maintain control of the evils here in the Underworld. It's one of the final gifts from the Cyclops. One of the only few that still exist." As he moves it, the monsters shift, keeping the distance constant.

Cyclops. Just when I think I have this mythology stuff under control.

"They're more active than the others," I say, and I let out a small laugh that even to me sounds like my throat is shaking.

"They're fed well." Shayne steps down into the mud-caked boat, and I follow, not waiting for his hand. I don't want to spend even a second too far from him with these things flying around.

"More sorrows?" I ask. Like the monsters in the River Acheron, I figure these monsters must eat sorrows.

But Shayne shakes his head and shoves the boat off from the dock. He hoists the rope in, and it drops on the floor of the boat with a thud.

I scoot away, not wanting a drop of the tarnished water to touch me.

"Memories," he says. "When souls head to Asphodel, they leave everything behind. And the monsters eat it all."

"Everything?"

"Everything. Names. Happiness. Fears. Goals. Every piece of thought that makes a soul what it is stays behind in the River Lethe." Shayne clips the Helm of Darkness back onto his belt. The monsters edge in closer but still stay outside our boundary.

"And that's what happened to Randy?"

Shayne motions back to the red river. "He left everything here. Randy doesn't even remember who he was."

I bite my lip, trying to piece this out. "Then I can't talk to him?"

"Why would you want to?" Shayne asks.

I push the lump in my throat back down. "To tell him I'm sorry."

Shayne shakes his head. "It's not your fault."

But I know it is. Even if Shayne wants to deny it, I cursed Randy to this place as surely as if I've killed him myself. And somehow I'll make it up to him. "Does the Helm only work here?" I ask.

"It works anywhere. The sea. The Earth. The Underworld." He links his fingers with mine. "And trust me—there are monsters everywhere."

We ride in silence. The only sound is the snapping of the monsters' jaws. They bump against the boat, some hidden below the thick red of the river and some jumping until I fear they may join us in the boat. But none do. Overhead, the sky is as lifeless as the world around me. There's no sun to speak of. No light, but also no darkness. Only that in-between gray of a lifeless world.

I lean against Shayne, feeling the muscles of his arm holding me. I try not to focus on the death around me, but my mind can't help the comparisons that keep forming.

"Do you think Earth is going to die?" I ask.

He brushes his cheek against my hair. "From the Global Heating Crisis? Yeah, lots of it will die." There's not a bit of doubt in his voice.

"What about the other gods? What do they think?"

Shayne looks out across the red water. "They're divided. They have been for years. Some of the members of the assembly fight to do everything in their power to restore the world to how it was. And others . . . they think the crisis is a good thing. They think change on any kind of massive scale is needed to keep humanity moving forward. They relish the struggles for power, and they enjoy choosing sides."

"Like Ares," I say.

"Yeah, like Ares. He wants the Global Heating Crisis because with it comes war. And war is what he feeds on."

I turn so I can see him better, but he's not looking at me. "So which side are you on?"

Shayne lets out a low chuckle. "Neither, which is the root of my problems with the assembly."

"Why neither?" Because if I had to guess, I'd be sure that Shayne wants to restore Earth to how it had been before the Global Heating Crisis ever started.

"Because I have enough problems of my own, Piper. The Underworld keeps me plenty busy. I don't need two worlds to take care of."

I'm not sure this is valid reasoning, but I don't argue. Who am I to tell Shayne he should do more? But maybe he can read my mind.

"You think I'm horrible," he says.

"No. Not horrible. Just . . ." I struggle to come up with the right word.

"Obsessed?" he suggests.

"Dedicated," I say. "You're dedicated to the Underworld."

"Someone has to be."

I look across the water, and soon I see the opposite shore and Asphodel there beyond it. We're almost to the dock, and the souls wait for us. As we pull up to the dock, empty stares surround us. One grabs the rope Shayne throws, tying it to a wooden pier. Another clears the path in front of us.

Shayne walks like he is Lord of the Underworld. He holds his head high; he doesn't look anyone in the face. I make the mistake of doing so and am met with eyes that seem to penetrate right through me without seeing me. But then one face in the crowd catches my eye, and I gasp when her eyes meet mine.

"Chloe!"

Shayne turns to face me. "What?"

I point into the mass of faces, but she's gone. "Chloe. She was right over there."

Shayne looks, craning his neck over the crowds, searching. "Chloe isn't here, Piper."

I realize I haven't taken a breath since I saw her, so I inhale. "I saw her. She looked right at me."

He shakes his head. "You couldn't have, Piper. Chloe is back above. Alive. You know that."

I do know that. But it had looked so much like her. And there had been recognition in those eyes. It had been Chloe. "She knew who I was."

Shayne takes my hand. "She couldn't have. Even if it were Chloe, people here don't have memories, remember?"

"But she looked right at me."

Shayne narrows his eyes and searches the crowd again. I see the same thing he does. An ocean of empty faces. Thousands of them, pressed in on each other. None of them familiar. And none of them meeting my eyes. I must have been wrong. Chloe is still alive. Back on Earth and waiting for me. And then I catch the scent.

"He's here," I say.

Shayne's face turns away from mine and back to the crowd. He's smelled it, too. Reese's aroma hangs in the air like thick mist. I hold my ground, promising myself I will not show my emotions. I will keep Reese out of my mind. And then I spot Randy Conner's face looking back at me.

"There." I point to Randy Conner, but when Shayne turns to look, Randy disappears. And the scent shifts to the right. My head snaps over, and again I see Chloe. But instead of casual recognition, her face is painted with malice. Cold. Hatred. She despises me with those eyes. She blames me for her death. A death that never came. A death I helped prevent. But her face is steel. And her look is poison. It's a look I never want to see on Chloe's face.

Shayne must see it, too. "Stay here."

And before I can protest, he's off, putting the Helm of Darkness onto his head; he vanishes in front of my eyes. As I watch him disappear, Chloe's mouth turns into a sneer, and she laughs. And then she's gone also. But the scent remains. Reese's scent.

I'm alone then, in the middle of a growing crowd of empty ghosts pressing in from all sides. I steady my nerves, which threaten to send me running for the clay river. But thoughts of the monsters halt me. I can do this. I can wait for Shayne who should be back any moment. I can keep my thoughts from Chloe who is safe aboveground and from Reese who is looking for a tunnel into my mind.

Reese's smell surrounds me and pushes its way into my nose, but it's only teasing me. I shift my feet as if firm footing will steel my resolve. The scent plays with me, bringing fresh memories into my mind. Memories of sneaking out to meet him. Of feeling his caress on my skin. Of laughing and touching. My minds spins because the memories feel so genuine. I don't know what's real anymore, and the scent comes at me from all angles. I squeeze my eyes shut and hold my breath to keep it out.

"Piper."

The voice is a whisper.

"You remember us, don't you?"

Reese sounds like a melody, but I stay in place, not breathing. Not opening my eyes to see if he is really there.

"Don't try to forget."

I want to grow my feet into the ground. I want to close my nostrils and live without air. But instead I inhale, trying to get as much of it as I can.

"We can be great together. I can give you everything."

Could Reese give me everything? I don't want to fight him. I want to stop fighting. I want to live in the memories that stir around in my mind. I take another breath, tasting his scent, looking for more. But then it's gone. His voice fades along with his aroma.

All at once, Shayne is at my side. He pulls off the Helm of Darkness and appears next to me.

"Reese was here." I can hardly get out the words. My mind tries to settle, but it's still so foggy. Reese's smell is a drug, and every time I get around it, it only leaves me more confused.

"I don't understand how." His face twists in frustration. "The Underworld may be weakening, but nobody should be able to penetrate it. Not even Ares." He attaches the Helm of Darkness back to his belt and takes my hand.

"But he was here."

"It had to be some kind of shade," Shayne says. "He couldn't have been here physically."

I glance around. "So he won't be back?"

Shayne's eyes settle on the mass of dead faces. "No. He won't be back." And even though Shayne is trying to sound confident, he can't know for sure. Not if what Rhadam said is right.

I push the thought of Chloe out of my mind, wanting to erase any connection between her and this godforsaken place as fast as possible. It wasn't her. Only Reese . . . Ares . . . playing tricks with my mind. Chloe is alive, though living on a stolen life thanks to me.

We're on a paved walkway, and ahead are buildings with walls made of gears as big as houses. One connects to another and then to another, and they turn like a perfectly synchronized clock. It's like a giant metal creature. The scent of oil hangs thick in the air, and the gears crunch over and over with clicks and whirls. "What goes on here?" I whisper, but even my whispers draw stares from the dead faces around us.

Shayne tightens his arm around me. "Everything happens here. Asphodel keeps most of the Underworld running."

"Running? Like doing what?"

We walk to the largest building in the front. Shayne has to wait until the gears click past, and only then is there an opening we can fit through. No sooner are we inside than the gear moves behind us again and seals out the light. Inside, we're greeted by dead faces that are attached to people who are buffing and polishing metal everywhere. Control panels cover the walls, but they have so many buttons and lights, I can't even distinguish one from the next. Red blurs into blue and green. People sit in front of the controls, and their hands move in the same motions over and over.

"The Underworld is a world," Shayne says. "There's plenty to do. Just because almost everyone here is dead doesn't mean there's no effort involved in running it."

"But look at these people." I motion around at the scene in front of me. The residents of Asphodel stare back at me with their stygian faces filled with only emptiness. It's like they aren't even aware of the tasks they're doing, and yet they have to do them forever. "This is depressing."

Shayne shrugs. "They don't know they're unhappy. They don't know anything. Not even who they used to be."

I can't believe his lack of emotion. "How can you stand this? How can you stand to even come here?" Is Randy just another one of these people, oiling some giant machine?

Shayne considers this. "I have to come here. Whether I like it or not. It's my job, and there's no one else to do it."

"But why this? Surely there's some better solution."

Shayne lets out a laugh which doesn't reach his eyes. "Let's face it, Piper. Not everyone deserves to be in the Elysian Fields. Being sort of nice won't get you there."

The dead faces surround me. These faces used to be people. People with lives and families and dreams. People like Randy Conner. "Well, that stinks," I say.

"Maybe. But being sort of bad won't get you sent to Tartarus, either, so it's kind of like a compromise."

It makes sense, though I don't want to agree with him out loud. "How many souls come here?" The dead are packed in like cockroaches; they can hardly move.

"Lots of people have died over the years, Piper. But the Underworld grows to fit them all." Shayne stands a little straighter when he says this, and I realize he must be proud of his world.

"Isn't that convenient? And when you say lots, you mean like . . . ?"

". . . billions. And most are here in Asphodel."

We leave one factory and then another. I'm pretty sure I've seen all Asphodel has to offer. The entire place seems to be a city paved over with machines. Shayne tries to tell me how each machine has a purpose, but it's all just so industrial. There's no nature and no weather. Asphodel is a giant void layered with metal. Shayne leads us farther into the city, away from the sanctuary of the boat—a sanctuary surrounded by a clay river infested with voracious monsters.

"What are we doing now?" I ask. I don't mention Randy because I know he's not the reason Shayne brought us here. As we walk through the city of factories, they seem to fly by around us. Like they're all in fast forward and we're not. They're a blur in my peripheral vision.

We step to the side as some kind of robotic car comes driving by. It's carrying five dead people who don't even seem to notice us.

"Checking in with the management." Shayne stops and turns his head so he's looking at me. "Do you mind coming along?" The way he angles his head lets me know he's curious what my response will be. Like he's testing me.

Something about his question makes me laugh.

"What?" When he asks, the red flecks in his pupils flash.

"I'd say that I'd follow you to the ends of the Earth, but that doesn't seem like enough."

Shayne's smile lights up the gray world of Asphodel around us. "No, it doesn't, but it still sounds nice to me."

"Well, as tempting as it may be, I'm not going to let you leave me here alone."

Shayne raises an eyebrow. "Scared?"

I glance back at the lifeless city. "I'm not quite sure that's the right word." The truth is I want to see what else is out there. I want to see more of the Underworld. And I want to find Randy—the real Randy—even if Shayne tells me there's no point.

"Good," he says.

And I know I've passed his test.

We start walking again in our fast forward way, and before long, we pass through a flat, metal plane populated with the dead, empty-eyed souls. As soon as I see them, every bit of laughter and happiness is sucked right out of me.

"You get used to it."

I guess it shows on my face. But I shake my head. "I don't want to get used to it."

I don't expect him to respond, but he does. "It's reality, though, Piper. Just like above. Look at Austin. Some parts are nice, and you'd feel safe going out at night alone to walk your dog. But try to do that in the wrong area, and it could be the last thing you ever do."

"Not if Cerberus were my dog."

Shayne smiles and pulls me closer with his arms. "I could loan him to you."

The image of me walking Cerberus around on the Drag fills my mind. Of course, there, he'd probably fit right in. "My mom doesn't give me much opportunity to hit the seedier areas of town."

Shayne leans over and kisses my cheek, making me want to press into him. "So maybe next time Reese comes around, you could employ Cerberus."

Would tearing the god of war apart kill him? How do gods die? I almost ask Shayne, but then decide it's not a conversation topic I want to bring up given our bleak surroundings.

"Rhadam mentioned there's been trouble in Asphodel," Shayne says.

"What kind of trouble?" I think of the pomegranate tree dying in the Elysian Fields. That had been trouble for Shayne also. Things shouldn't die in paradise. And I think about what else

Rhadam said. About bad things brewing in other parts of the Underworld: secrets being kept and plans being made.

"Things not working right. Souls misplaced. Machines breaking. Even attempts to cross the river." Shayne points to a house far off ahead of us. It's up on a hill away from the city, and unlike the rest of the bleak Asphodel, the air seems fresh around it, and rays of light actually touch it. "And we're going there to find out why."

As to why Shayne decided to take me on this task, I have no idea. He can't possibly think this is some kind of romantic date, and the closer we get to the house on the hill, the less I want to go. Even though it's clear and crisp outside, the house itself seethes evil. But there's no chance I'll venture back through Asphodel without him. And anyway, if he is testing me, I don't want to back down now. I want to prove to Shayne I'm tough like he is.

"Who lives here?" We're at the top of the hill now. Almost at the front door. It reminds me of a retro Hollywood home. Lots of glass windows and steel beams, but the front door is ten feet tall and made of thick black wood—like the door of a fortress.

"Minos. An old Cretan king. He's the overlord here in Asphodel."

"A king from Crete runs Asphodel?" I ask.

"An ancient king runs each of the territories. Minos here. Rhadamanthus in the Elysian Fields. And Aeacus in Tartarus."

"Rhadam is a king?" I never thought to ask this when I met him.

Shayne shakes his head. "Was a king. Here in the Underworld he's an overlord. They all are. I'm the only king." He scowls. "Which more and more seems to be a point of confusion among the lords."

I remember Rhadam's deference to Shayne, so solid a part of their relationship it could never be in question. "Not Rhadam?"

"No, not Rhadam." Shayne brushes his sleeves, and dirt vanishes off them. "He and Charon are about the only people I can trust."

We're at the imposing door now, but Shayne doesn't open it. Can he sense the evil that touches each and every one of my nerves? He lets go of my hand, and I look at him, ready to open my mouth and ask another question. But I stop. In a single moment, he's ceased to be Shayne, the guy I'm sure I'm in love with, and has become Hades, supreme King of the Underworld. A force to be reckoned with.

He lifts his hand and knocks on the thick door—a knock so hard I hear the echoes through the windows inside the house. Nobody answers, but Shayne doesn't knock again. Instead, he waits, and we stand there in silence until, after what feels like eternity, a lock clicks, and the door creeps open. Dead eyes greet us from inside.

"I'm here to see Minos." Shayne's tone makes it utterly clear it's not a request.

The man who's opened the door stares at Shayne. He's got sandy-blond hair, and from his engorged biceps, it's obvious this guy spent way too much time in the gym back when he was alive. But now, here in Hell, does it really matter how much time someone spent in the gym? I wonder if he spent more time with his loved ones and less time working out if he'd have ended up in the Elysian Fields instead of Asphodel: Land of the Walking Dead.

"King Minos is busy."

It's the first time someone in Asphodel has spoken. Until this point, I wasn't even sure they could speak.

Shayne's face hardens, and I almost hear electricity sizzle off him next to me. "Tell Minos that King Hades demands to speak with him." He omits the word *king* in front of Minos.

The man doesn't nod or agree or shake his head. It's only when he walks backward, away from us and toward a long hallway, that I realize he's simply obeying Shayne's command. The command of the King of the Underworld must supersede commands from one of Shayne's minions.

Shayne and I stand there, still on the doorstep, watching him leave.

I lean close to him and put my lips to his ear. "Why don't you go in and find him?"

He whispers back, not turning his head away from the room ahead. "Because even in Hell, we have courtesies."

"It doesn't seem like Minos is being very courteous to you."

Shayne gives his head an almost imperceptible shake. "No, it doesn't."

Another ten minutes later, and the blond shell of a man returns. "Follow me."

26

Minos

WE FOLLOW THE STEROID-RIDDEN GHOST MAN IN SILENCE. HE has his back to us as he leads us first down a hallway, then through a breezeway to another wing of the house. Every step I take, a sense of dread weighs heavier inside my stomach. I look down and realize I'm clenching Shayne's hand so hard my knuckles are white.

But Shayne doesn't turn to me or comfort me aside from a brief squeeze of my hand. His face is frozen in a hard stare straight ahead. At the end of the breezeway, we stop in front of a glass room overlooking a flat, gray ocean with nothing else in sight.

"King Minos will see you in here." The man moves aside and gives us a clear view of the room ahead. Every wall is glass, and in the center is a stone chimney so large a Spanish oak could burn inside without being cut.

Shayne doesn't acknowledge our guide as he opens the glass door. He walks in, and I follow. I can't see anyone in the room, but Shayne doesn't hesitate. He skirts around the giant fireplace and stops at a chair on the other side. Amber liquid sits in a crystal tumbler on a table next to the chair.

"Minos." Shayne's voice sounds like razors slicing glass.

"Hades." Minos doesn't turn to face us; instead, he's facing out the windows overlooking the dull ocean. "So you finally decided to grace us with your presence here in Asphodel?" Every word Minos speaks scratches in his throat as it comes out, making it sound like it pains him to talk. A hand reaches from the chair and picks up the glass. He swirls it, making the ice inside clink up against the crystal.

"Unlike you, I have other duties here in the Underworld." Shayne lets go of my hand and shoves the side of the chair around, causing Minos to spin and face us. The drink flies from his hand and crashes to the ground, and the air is filled with the sweet smell of alcohol.

Minos looks at Shayne but manages to keep his face impassive. But when Minos's eyes find me, they grow as big as the gold coins Charon collects. He half stands up, but Shayne throws an arm in front of me. "Sit down!"

Minos continues to stare at me but obeys the command.

"To what do I owe this honor?" Minos forces his eyes away from me, but they dart back every so often as if he can't control them. He gestures toward an empty chair, but Shayne stays standing, and I follow his lead.

"We can start with the escape attempts." Shayne's fingers are unclenched, but he shifts them around like they are prepared for battle.

I'm starting to wonder just what Shayne's gotten into here. What he's gotten me into.

Minos waves a hand. "A couple restless souls crossing the river. So what of it?"

Shayne grits his teeth. "Why are they crossing the river, Minos? They shouldn't have anything to cross back for."

Minos looks at Shayne and narrows his eyes. "You tell me, O wise ruler of the Underworld. Why would anyone want to leave Asphodel?"

"They wouldn't." I can hear Shayne's breath now, and his presence has shifted to something feral. "Unless someone's been telling them to."

Minos spreads his arms wide, palms up. "Why would anyone in Asphodel tell the dead souls about their past? And besides, as we've seen from the recent attempts, crossing the River Lethe only results in being devoured by the monsters." His eyes shift to me again. I meet them, and he stares at me with such cruelty, I'm forced to look away.

Shayne moves in closer to Minos. "I think somebody's trying to exchange souls. Trying to get people out of Tartarus."

The silence that descends on the room is so real, it pushes at me from all sides. My heart is beating so fast, I'm pretty sure everyone both below- and aboveground can hear it.

Neither Minos nor Shayne looks away from the other. The heavy quiet is so oppressive, I feel like something needs to be said, and neither of them is going to say it.

"Nobody can leave Tartarus, right?" I'm not sure how the words manage to escape my mouth, but when they do, Minos turns his head and looks at me. Shayne leans away from Minos, and the silence is replaced with something even worse. Lies and secrets fill the air around us, so thick they're like real creatures.

I'm trying not to look at Minos, but I see him still staring at me, and then he licks his lips. "So the beautiful criminal speaks."

Criminal? He's talking about me? I glance at Shayne and notice his fingers are now balled into fists. And I'm pretty sure by speaking, I've messed everything up.

"It's not her fault." The words come out of Shayne's mouth slowly and clearly, as if he wants to make sure Minos doesn't misunderstand a single one. I have no idea what he's talking about, but I'm smart enough to know now's not the time to ask.

Before I know what's happening, Minos jumps up from the chair and grabs me, pressing something hot and sharp to the softest part of my neck. It's not cutting me, but it's so tight, I don't think I can breathe. Minos holds me like a vise with his other hand. And he spins me to face Shayne.

"You know the penalty for killing a phoenix." Minos's scratchy voice snarls in my ear, mixing with the sound of my pounding heart.

My eyes flash to Shayne, but he doesn't meet them. He's staring at Minos and looks like he's ready to pounce on a kill.

"Let her go." It's a direct command, and the part of me that's not worrying about staying as still as possible wonders if Minos will obey it.

Minos's hot breath seeps into my ear. "You know the penalty." And though I don't think it's possible, Minos presses the knife even closer until I feel it cut into my skin.

"Let her go. Now."

I can't believe how calm Shayne's being, especially when I feel a trickle of blood moving down my neck. The knife is so close, I can hardly get air out, and my heart pounds in my ears so loudly the room seems to spin.

"Consider this a direct order." And Shayne is every bit the king when he says it.

I feel Minos's muscles tighten, and I know he's about to either slit my throat or let me go. In a single move, he shoves me away, lowering the knife, but not before drawing a thin line under my ear with the blade. Warm blood pours from the cut down my neck.

Shayne catches me, but still, he doesn't look at me or talk to me. His grip is like steel, but it also fills me with comfort.

"She belongs in Tartarus." Minos moves away, widening the distance between Shayne and himself. I think he knows he's gone too far.

"*You* belong in Tartarus, Minos. No more warnings. Consider this your last." Shayne turns his back on Minos. I'm not sure if this is a good idea, but Shayne is the king here. I try to convince myself he knows what he's doing. And all I really want is to stop my heart from exploding and get out of here now.

I try not to run, but Minos doesn't follow us as we show ourselves out. The blond ghost man waits outside the door, but a single look from Shayne, and he doesn't follow us, instead heading back into the glass room where Minos is. And it's not until we leave the house completely and get down the hill that my heart slows down enough that I'm able to speak.

"What the hell was that all about?" I'm holding a hand over

the cut in my neck, already healing, but I still feel the warmth of my blood. I want to stop and rest, but I don't dare suggest it. If Minos really does want to send me to Tartarus for some unknown reason, I don't plan to help him.

Shayne takes a deep breath. "Minos is getting power hungry."

I squeeze my eyes shut and shake my head. "No! I mean the part about him trying to kill me and dump me in Tartarus. He said I'm a criminal. And yeah, I may not be the best person in the world, but I certainly haven't done anything worthy of eternal torture."

Shayne actually smiles. "No, you haven't."

"So what did he mean? Criminal?"

Shayne looks back at the house, which is still and haunting, and then back at me. "It means there are things I can't tell you."

"Can't tell me? To hell with that! I'm sick of hearing that!" I pull away from him and slam my fists down on his chest.

"If I tell you, it could kill you." He grabs my hands and holds me. For all the anger in my voice, his is a whisper. And I want so badly to know what he's talking about. What secrets and mysteries are being kept from me? Before I can stop it, the tears come. His arms are around me, and he's stroking my hair. Holding me tight. Why does it seem like there's so much I don't know and no one will tell me anything?

We stay like that in Asphodel, and the ghosts avoid us. I'm not sure when I stop crying, but by the time all my tears are cried out, all I want to do is lie down and sleep. I don't even want to find Randy anymore. I just want to find out why my life has gone crazy. But we still need to get out of this hellish purgatory and back across the River Lethe. Back to the safety of Shayne's sanctuary. I don't try to press him or question him on our trip back. I'll figure out a way to get the information I need from him, because whatever it is, he knows it, and I plan to find out.

27

Phoenix

SHAYNE PRETENDS HE'S GOT HIS ANGER UNDER CONTROL, BUT the red flashes in his eyes so fast it looks like sparks.

It's only when Cerberus pounds through the clay, meeting us on the bank of the river, that Shayne's eyes finally stop their flickering madness and his muscles relax. I, on the other hand, can't stop thinking about Minos.

Criminal.

Tartarus.

His haunting words keep coming back to me.

Killing a phoenix.

We walk down the long tunnel, Cerberus only steps ahead of us as if sensing Shayne's unease. We're almost to his sanctuary ahead. Already, I smell the fire. Once we're inside, he pours us each a glass of wine. I finish mine in one long sip, and he refills the glass, but already the wine's moving through my veins, flushing the fear out of my body.

Shayne lets out a long sigh. "Your visits haven't gone so well, have they?"

I glance at him but don't respond.

"I'm sorry," he says.

"What does a dead bird have to do with anything?"

"Nothing. Everything." Shayne gets up and walks to the bookcase. He pulls a red leather book from the shelf, bringing it back over to me. Flipping it open, he stops on a page with a hand-drawn purple and red bird amid a mass of flames. I suck in my breath when I see its tail: five long red feathers—feathers that look identical to the one I found in the mysterious jar that had been delivered to me on my birthday.

"What?" Shayne has turned away from the page and is studying me.

I shake my head. "Nothing." But images of the jar and the feather stay in my mind.

He doesn't press me but turns back to the picture. "The phoenix lives for a thousand years, but when it's time for the phoenix to die, it bursts into flames, burning until it's nothing but ashes. Once the ashes have cooled, the phoenix is reborn again, all on its own."

It bursts into flames, like the feather had done in my hand.

I look down at the picture, studying it. "Does that mean it can't be killed?"

And why did someone give me a ceramic jar with a phoenix's tail feather in it?

Shayne flips the book shut and turns to the fire, which crackles when he looks at it. "It's almost impossible to kill a phoenix."

"But it can be done?"

Shayne nods. "Yeah. It can be done."

"And for someone who kills a phoenix . . ." I know how the sentence will end, and I don't want to finish it.

Shayne takes a long breath. "The penalty is eternity in Tartarus."

I've never seen a phoenix, and part of me doesn't even believe they exist. But here I am in Hell drinking wine with Shayne— Lord of the Underworld—and I know it's possible. There was a feather to prove it. Or maybe it was a feather to prove my guilt.

"Did I kill a phoenix?"

Shayne moves so close, the warmth of his body smolders next to me. He takes my hands, and the smell of the wine on his breath sends a wave of exhilaration through me, blending in with his sweet burnt taste.

"No. You did not kill a phoenix."

I let out the breath I've been holding and can't stop the smile that's hiding behind my lips. Finally, an answer. "So Minos was wrong."

Shayne nods. "Yes. Minos was wrong." And then he's leaning into me and kissing me, and I forget about phoenixes and Minos and Asphodel. He traces his fingers up my spine, and I respond by pulling him down onto the floor. Between the embers and Shayne, I feel like I'm on fire myself. I run my hands over his chest, his arms; I don't want to believe we ever have to be apart.

We stay there forever, and even at that, it's not long enough. I never want to go away, but as the wine leaves me, I know I have to. I need to get back to reality, to take care of Chloe, to deal with my mom. And then, of course, there's Reese. It's only once Charon takes us back across the River Acheron that Shayne mentions him again.

"Please stay away from Ares." The concern in his eyes and voice is enough to catch me off guard.

"I will. There's nothing to worry about." I'm telling myself this as much as I'm telling Shayne because, when I say his name, I remember the kiss we shared and the chocolates he sent and all the other memories that flooded my mind, and I wonder if I'm being honest with myself.

"I'm serious, Piper. Ares will trick you and deceive you and do whatever he needs to do to win you."

"To win me?" I stare at him. "Is there some kind of competition I'm not aware of? Am I a prize or something?"

"No, Piper. Nothing like that."

"Then what?" I need to know. "You can only win something when you're competing against someone else."

"Look. Ares doesn't care about you. He only cares about war and conquest. He thrives on it. You can think whatever you want, but just remember that. He's the god of war."

I roll my eyes. It's not like this is some kind of amusement park game and I'm the giant stuffed animal up for grabs. This is my life.

"I have no plans to go near Reese." And it's true. I can only hope he's gone by the time I get back home and that I never see him again.

Shayne twists up his lips. "Yes, but I'm sure he has plans to go near you."

I cross my arms. "I'll be careful. As long as he doesn't hold me at knifepoint and threaten to throw me into Tartarus, everything should be fine."

Shayne doesn't laugh. He caresses my ear, sending a wonderful chill down below my stomach. And then he gives me a wistful smile and walks away, leaving me to return to Earth above.

28

Hurricane

I RETURN FROM THE UNDERWORLD AND FIND MYSELF BY THE Spanish oak. Reese is nowhere to be found. Overhead, the birds flutter through the trees. Birds. Phoenix. I look up and imagine I see a purple and red bird overhead bathed in flames. But there's no fire. There's no sun. A giant gray cloud fills the sky, and the wind picks up and starts blowing leaves off the tree.

I know I need to go back home and see if my mom will tell me what's going on. She's keeping secrets from me about who I am. Who she is. It's like I don't know her. And I don't even know myself.

I try to piece it out in my mind, but there's just nothing that makes sense. I've lived with my mom my entire life. That's all I am. Still, there has to be something more. Otherwise, why would two Greek gods suddenly be fighting for my attention?

A gust of wind slams into the tree, and a cracking sound cuts into the air. I hardly have time to jump out of the way before a branch from the Spanish oak falls to the ground. Would it have killed me? Would I be judged just like Randy Conner? I try to think of the good things I've done in my life. Are they worthy of paradise?

As I walk out of the woods, the wind starts to really pick up, so I run until I'm in front of the shuttle stop. My tattoo aches, and it's turning red again. The ink has faded a few shades, but the raised scar underneath remains. And I think of the face I saw in Asphodel. Like a shadow of Chloe. It reminds me too much of the fading tattoo. I brush it with my hand, and it deepens again.

When the shuttle stops, I hop on and head for her house. The wind's blowing so hard it pushes on the shuttle, but the driver has his hands tight on the wheel. It's getting dark outside, almost like night, and I think most people will be heading inside. But around the steel struts that reach upward to form Beta Dome, there are work crews everywhere. I get off the shuttle at Chloe's stop, but before I walk the remaining distance to her house, I move closer to one of the steel legs and try to see what's going on.

There's a panel open, and one of the workers is guiding a sand truck that's dumping into it. My mom told me they use sand to help grow the glass in the dome, but I thought the domes needed time to recharge. I walk up to the nearest worker and tap him on the shoulder. He turns around to face me.

"What's going on?" I ask. From above, tiny drops of rain begin to fall down. They're heavy and sparse, and I can see each drop when it lands on the concrete surrounding the steel supports.

"You need to get inside." He looks back at the panel.

"Why? What are you doing with the dome?"

He flips the control panel he's been working on closed and finally looks me in the eye. "Running tests," he says, and I see his lie thick on him.

I wipe the rain off my face. They shouldn't be doing anything with the domes. I pull out my FON and text my mom. I'm still freaked that she knows Reese, but I'm not going to ask her about that now. It's not like I can text the message why do u know the god of war? and get any kind of real response.

what's going on with the domes? I text her instead.

She responds in seconds. get home. talk when u get here

I start to type out the next message, to tell her about the sand, but then stop. I'm not ready to head home yet. I pocket my FON and sprint to Chloe's house. The wind has started blowing hard enough I have to fight against it as I run. My hair's blowing every single way and getting in my eyes, and anything not tied down is starting to move.

Chloe's sitting outside when I get there, arms wrapped around herself, legs drawn up into her. It's like she doesn't even realize the wind is blowing. Overhead, a tile blows off her roof and crashes to the walkway where it shatters. The streets are littered, and where any trees still stand, branches snap off and fall.

"It's freezing here," she says. "Have you noticed how cold it is?" She doesn't even look up at me, but she has to know I've arrived because there's no one else around she could be talking to.

I stand over her. "Chloe, we need to get you inside." More tiles pull from the roof. We're under the patio cover, but the way the wind is blowing, one good gust and it could be gone.

"The world feels like ice."

Ice. I think of the River Cocytus between Hell and the Elysian Fields. Frozen over, but still the wraithlike monsters swim underneath, hoping for an opening but never finding one.

Chloe lets me help her up, and then we walk inside. Her mom shuts the door behind me and starts telling me how she's been trying to get Chloe inside for the last half hour. Chloe's mom is normally a calm person, but she's freaked. Her eyes look bloodshot from worry, and she keeps hovering over Chloe.

The rain comes down in sheets then, pounding on the roof of the patio. I'll have to stay at Chloe's house until the storm relents. My mom may want me home, but she won't want me walking or taking a shuttle in this mess. I text her a quick, waiting til storm stops, and leave it at that.

Chloe's mom finally goes into the kitchen to make us some coffee, leaving Chloe and me alone. We sit on the sofa, and I try to figure out how to start this conversation with her. There's been so much going on, I don't know where to begin. So much has happened even just today. This hurricane is only the most recent part.

"I missed you at the funeral," I say, and put my hand on Chloe's.

But I yank it back at the touch. She is freezing. Like she's kept her hand in an ice bin to numb it. I force myself to reach back out and put my hand on hers, rubbing it to warm her. I try to ignore the sound of the wind beating against her house and the memories of Minos accusing me at knifepoint.

"I was there. In the back."

"I didn't see you," I say.

"I saw Randy." She turns to me at this, and her eyes dig into mine, but they look odd. Like her pupils are tiny dots in the center of giant, oversized irises. Irises so big they should touch the boundaries of her eyes. But there's white all around—encompassing them. I remember something I heard once about white showing all around the eye. Something about violent death.

My heart skips a beat, and I'm afraid to look away. Like Chloe might vanish on me or something. Sink down right now into the ground and be swallowed up. "Randy's dead," I say. "It was his funeral."

And Chloe cannot be seeing ghosts.

But Chloe shakes her head so furiously, I'm actually happy. It's the first bit of emotion she's shown since her near-death experience. "No! I saw him there. He was watching. Listening." And she grips my hand with such force my knuckles feel like they might pop.

Her mom walks back in the room right then and sets two cups of steamy coffee down on the table. She gives me a small smile, but then a boom of thunder hits. We all jump, and Chloe's mom bumps her hand into one of the cups, splashing coffee over the side. I pull my hand away from Chloe's and reach for a towel to wipe it up.

Chloe's mom mouths me a silent "thank you."

I nod in response, and then she leaves the room.

Chloe takes a long sip of coffee and then rubs her hands together, warming them. "So what's going on, Piper?"

This is it. I can tell her about everything. Reese. Shayne. The Underworld. But as I go over the phrasing, it just feels so off. I'm walking around in a world of mythology; who is going to believe that?

Outside, there's a groaning, like a giant metal monster has just woken up. Chloe and I both jump at the noise because it sounds like something is going to crash in on us. I look to the window, but she has the shades pulled. And then the sound stops.

I wait for my breath to return. "I'm not sure where to start," I say.

Chloe gives me a smile. "Start anywhere. I feel like I've lost the last week."

It's like it's the old Chloe. She's back. And Death has left her behind.

I scoot closer to her and relink my fingers with hers. Her hands have warmed up again, and her tattoo is normal. I look to mine and see they match. Black and solid etching the word I know means *sacrifice*.

For some reason, Minos's words come back to me. *You know the penalty for killing a phoenix.* I ignore them.

I start with something easy. "My mom got back today," I say, grasping for straws. "She said my father wants custody."

"Custody?" Chloe's voice echoes my own amazement.

"Yeah. Weird, huh?"

The metal outside groans again though not as loud. I think the wind must be hitting against the metal beams.

"Totally weird. You're eighteen. Parents don't get custody at eighteen."

"That's what I thought, too." And then I lean closer though no one is around to hear. "I have to admit I'm a little curious, Chloe."

She moves her fingers until our thumbs press together. "About your father?"

I nod. "I might get to meet him. And he wants me in his life."

Chloe purses her lips. "I don't know, Piper. He got convicted as a terrorist."

"That's what my mom says. But maybe she's lying. Maybe she's just been keeping me away from him."

Chloe doesn't answer. She knows if it were up to my mom, I'd live with her until I was a hundred years old.

"Seriously, Chloe. I want to meet him."

Chloe doesn't seem to hear me. Or she chooses to ignore me. "He was so sad, Piper."

"My father?"

Chloe shakes her head. "Randy. His father beats his mom. And his little sister. Did you know that? She's only seven."

The blood freezes in my veins at her words, and the chill that runs through me knocks the wind out of me. How could Chloe possibly know Randy Conner's final sorrow? How could she know about his abusive father? I lived next to him for four years, yet I had no idea.

"He asked me to help. Wanted me to do something." Chloe looks away, and I can finally blink when her enlarged eyes leave mine.

I believe her. She's talked with Randy Conner's spirit as surely as I've gone to Hell. "What can you do?" When I say it, I'm not really asking her. I'm asking Shayne, but I know he won't answer. His realm is the Underworld, not abusive dealings of the world above. He's made that clear.

Chloe sighs, but she doesn't answer. She wraps her arms back around herself and turns away. "I did it again, Piper."

"Did what?" I ask. At this point, I have no idea where Chloe's disjointed conversation will take me. And I realize she's not ready for me to tell her anything about my life just yet.

"It was this weird urge," she says.

"Weird like how?"

Chloe actually lets out a laugh; there's not an ounce of humor in it. "I cut my sheets into thin strips."

I try to hold my face steady and act like maybe this is a normal thing. "Oh. Why?"

Chloe shakes her head, making her brown bandana fall askew.

But she doesn't straighten it. "They felt so dirty. I washed them but it didn't help, so I cut them up. But I still can't sleep on the bed, Piper, so I moved to the floor."

My breathing has stopped, but I manage to get words out. "Why did they feel dirty?" Out of nowhere, I imagine Chloe sleeping with someone on her bed and then needing to wash the sheets afterward. I know Chloe's slept with two guys before, but there's no one I'm aware of at the present.

Chloe doesn't turn to me and doesn't reply.

"What's wrong, Chloe?"

In profile, I see a tear creep into the corner of her eye, but her lips stay together. I'm tempted to press her—to ask her again. But the wind slams into the house again, and this time, it hits the window and sends glass scattering into the room. I jump up but Chloe doesn't even move. I hear her mom from the kitchen calling in to ask what happened.

"Are you going to be okay?" I ask.

"You need to leave, Piper."

Hurt runs through me. I start to ask why, but she stops me.

"Now, Piper. Just please leave now."

29

Retribution

I NOD AND STAND UP AND WIPE THE TEARS THAT SPRING INTO my eyes. Chloe acts like she's two different people. But she is right. I need to get out of here. I need to get out of the city. The metal groans again, and all of a sudden, I know what it is. They are opening the growth slats on the domes; they're going to try to grow the glass. Even though the domes haven't had time to regenerate, they're still going to try.

I take a step for the door, but Chloe doesn't even look at me. Maybe the sheet-ripping thing was just like the lightbulbs—just some near-death recovery thing. It's only been a few days. Chloe just needs time to recuperate. I'm almost at the door when it blows open. From the kitchen, I hear Chloe's mom call out again, but I don't want to talk to her, so I run out the open door.

The sky is furious. Clouds as black as the River Acheron spin in the sky, and rain comes down so hard, it hurts when it strikes my face. The blast of sirens is almost muted from the storm. I glance up at the steel struts of Beta Dome. Glass is growing fast. In the seconds I watch, it grows downward by a foot. I need to run to get out of the city. I take off and don't look at anything around me. I don't look back at Chloe's house; she'll be fine once the dome is sealed. She'll be fine when she gets some rest. Debris fills the streets, but no one is around. There's no sign of the work crews that had been there earlier. And I'm willing to bet a shuttle won't come.

Litter flies past me and tumbles down the street. Something

hard strikes me on the back and knocks the wind out of me, but I can't turn to look. I have to get out of here. I'm vaguely aware of my FON vibrating in my pocket, but I ignore it. My mom's calling, I'm sure, and given this storm, I don't blame her. It's like nothing I've ever imagined before.

I'm almost beyond the last steel support of Beta Dome when the metal groans a final time. And then shards of glass start to fall to the ground. I dig into my reserves and run like I'll die if I don't. Once I'm free and clear and fifty feet away, I spin around and watch the destruction of the dome the city had prided itself so much on. Glass showers down, mixing with the rain until I can't tell one from the other. My FON is going crazy in my pocket, so I stop under the overhang of a house's roof and pull it out.

b home in a few, I text my mom. She's got to be absolutely nuts with worry.

please tell me ur ok, she sends back.

fine, I text.

i love u so much piper. i never want 2 lose u, she writes, and I surprise myself when a lump forms in my throat and pushes tears upward to my eyes. Her words are simple, but she cares so much.

I wipe my tears and wait until the storm begins to subside. I stand there under the patio roof of the house and watch as the clouds first blow away east of Austin and then nearly evaporate from the sky. The rain stops next, and when it clears, I see that most of the glass from Beta Dome is gone, too. All that's left is the shattered skeleton near the sides of the steel beams. The sky transitions first from a dark gray to a creamy butter and then to a denim blue. Then it's back to the color of topaz, and the sun shines down from above, reflecting off every bit of glass littering the ground and the sky. The transformation is so sudden, so complete. There's been a hurricane in Austin, and now, only its destruction remains.

The city is a wreck, but I don't head back to Chloe's house or anywhere near the dome. I need to get home to my mom. Because even with everything that's happened, I want to be near her. I want her to tell me there's been some mistake. That she was just angry and that she has no idea who Reese really is. But as I walk home, my stomach starts to turn queasy. My mom knows I went on a date with Reese. They know each other. And she wants us to move. Again. She's been to see my father, and whatever path we lived on in the past has changed. I just don't know to what extent yet.

The first thing I see when I get home is Reese's pink calla lilies, still smashed on the floor, and nearly every pink petal missing. I pick a single stem up, and before I think about what I'm doing, I infuse life back into it.

The blossom moves under my energy, and even the green stem is given rebirth. Power flows out of my hands into the flower, and it bursts into color and vibrancy. I touch the bottom of the stem, and roots grow and twist around my hand and fingers. In turn, I pick up each of the remaining flowers and do the same, and when they've all reformed, only then do I stop and realize what I've done.

The cut flowers, once dead, are alive. I feel their life with my hands. I've had a green thumb my entire life, but this is paranormal. But then again, so is everything else that has been going on in my life recently. If gods walk the earth, then why can't flowers regrow in seconds? I stick them back in the water-filled container on the counter.

"Maybe you should just let them die."

I turn and see my mom standing there watching me.

"I can't."

"Throw them out, and tell him to never come back." She shifts, like she wants to say so much more than she is. Like she wants to run to me and hug me.

I set the vase on a shelf next to the sink. "Didn't you already do that?" I walk past my mom, brushing her shoulder on my way.

"Of course, Piper. But he won't give up." Her voice shakes as she talks. "He'll keep coming back because he thinks he has some right to be with you."

"But why?" I ask.

My mom throws her hands up in the air. "I don't know. I just don't. He showed up here and said he was supposed to take you away. And I can't let that happen."

"Who am I, Mom?" I have to ask the question even though it sounds absurd to my ears.

My mom doesn't even hesitate. "You're my daughter, that's who you are."

I shake my head because her answer's just so frustrating. "No, really. Who am I?"

My mom comes over and pats my shoulder. "Piper, you're beautiful and you're smart, and to me, you're the most perfect thing this world has ever created. But that's it. That's all you are."

"No," I say. "There has to be something else. Something special."

She looks at me like she feels sorry for me. "There's nothing else, Piper. There's nothing special about you at all."

Her words sting. I feel them like worms digging into my heart. If she notices she's hurt me, she doesn't show it.

"We need to move. To go away," she says.

"No." I don't raise my voice or argue or even try to make it sound like a compromise. I'm not moving. Not again. If I move anywhere, it's going to be away from my mom—alone.

"Yes," she says. "Your father will find you otherwise."

"Beta Dome shattered," I say because I don't want to talk about moving or my father.

My mom stares at me a second, and I finally let my eyes meet hers. And then she pulls me into a hug. I don't break away, but I don't hug her back.

"I was so worried about you, Piper." She puts a hand on my cheek, and the tears in her eyes tell me how much she loves me.

"I was fine," I say.

"You were out there in the storm. Councilman Rendon called

a virtual meeting to tell us about his plans. He went ahead and activated the domes. He said there was a hurricane approaching Austin." She shudders like even the memory is too hard to live with.

"I went to Chloe's," I say. "The glass shattered. It's everywhere."

Anger flashes into my mom's eyes. "It didn't have time to regenerate. How does he think the glass will sustain a hurricane when the growth proteins haven't had time to bond?"

I don't answer because there's nothing I can really say.

"He's killing the city," my mom says. "He's killing the world. He's pulling it apart with everything he does."

I know it's true, but it seems a little unfair. "It's not like he started the Global Heating Crisis."

My mom's nostrils flare. "No, he didn't. It doesn't matter at this point how it started, just how we deal with it."

I'm not sure I agree, but my mom doesn't leave it open for debate. We head upstairs and flip on the tube. Reports of damage from the hurricane are still coming in. I try to ignore it because most of the images they're showing are horrific. People are dead everywhere. The shattered glass from Beta Dome caused so much destruction, they estimate it will take weeks to clean up. Councilman Rendon is scheduled to give a speech in a half hour to talk about the tragedy. I text Chloe to make sure she's okay, but she doesn't answer, so I call her mom who tells me they're all fine, that aside from some missing roof tiles and the broken window, they got off lucky. I assure her I got home safely and am with my mom.

I attempt to go about my normal routine until the news conference starts. Changing my clothes. Brushing my teeth. It's only when I pick up a comb and begin to yank it through the blond snarls that my mom comes over. She takes the comb from me and sits me down, pulling each and every tangle out one by one until they're all gone.

"Maybe I should get a tattoo also."

Her words catch me halfway into a trance state. I'm sure I've heard wrong. "What?"

"A tattoo." She touches it. "We could both have one."

I laugh at the absurdity of my mother getting a tattoo. I wonder how *overprotective* would be spelled in ancient Greek anyway. But maybe the time away from my mom was a good thing. Maybe she's starting to relax. To be less protective.

"We could get matching ones. Mother and daughter. Together forever."

All hopes of my mom relaxing disappear. "That sounds more like something saved for couples," I say. "Not mother and daughter."

She holds the comb steady, feeling each tine with her fingers. "We're an exception, Piper. You'll always be my little girl."

"I'm eighteen now, Mom."

She moves the comb to her own head and runs it through her dark hair. Even when it catches on a tangle, she keeps her eyes on me. "Eighteen is only the beginning, Piper. We have our whole lives to be together."

I decide not to respond. There's nothing I can say to agree with her. I want my own life, but the impasse is she wants it, too. My silence prompts her to kiss me on the forehead and turn back to the tube. The news conference will start in minutes. But there's something I need to ask my mom.

"Mom, do you know what a phoenix is?"

She freezes, and I see she's stopped breathing. She knows. As surely as I know Randy Conner's death is my fault, she knows what a phoenix is.

"It's a bird." She makes it sound casual like everyone in the world should know.

"What kind of bird?"

"A bird that only exists in legends, Piper."

I don't get a chance to say anything else, because at that moment, the news conference starts. My teeth grit when Councilman Rendon comes on, standing at a makeshift podium there in

Chloe's dome. He's supposed to give some speech about how the domes were activated by accident, which I know is a lie. The area is lit up like midday, and the ground is swept free of glass. He gives his signature smile and motions with his hand for the crowd to be quiet. He announces he's going to be speaking and won't be taking any questions. Of course, questions come anyway.

"Councilman, how could the domes be accidentally activated?"

"Is it true growth materials were refilled today?"

I think of the sand I saw being poured into the metal struts.

"What's being done to remove the glass from the domes that didn't shatter?"

The news reports showed these domes. Chloe's was the only one to crack and fall, but the other operational domes only grew about one-third of the way closed. If I lived under that glass, I'd be freaked out, too. One gust of wind, and the glass could all come crashing down.

Next to me, my mom's staring intently at the tube. Her lips are pressed thin, and I think she hates this man.

He starts a prepared speech, but when the questions don't stop, he gives up and starts with the answers.

"The accidental activation occurred due to a programming error," he says. "I can assure you it won't happen again."

My mom stiffens next to me. "Lies," she says. "Flat-out lies."

He goes on to deny growth materials being refilled today even though I myself saw the work crews dumping the sand. But his last lie is the worst.

"I can assure the city of Austin with all faith that there is no risk of glass shards continuing to rain down on the city. Sealant has been sprayed from above." He gives a small laugh like he's trying to win over the crowd. "The real question will be: How do we get the glass down now that it's up?"

"He makes me sick," my mom says.

The questions from the crowd start fresh, but they're halted at the sound of metal groaning on metal. I recognize the sound the second I hear it, and I know what will happen even before it does. The groan waxes, and then there's a cracking sound. And we watch as a single shard of glass comes careening down from above straight for Councilman Rendon's head.

He moves fast.

Wicked fast.

The glass smashes into the ground.

And it's like the whole thing doesn't even faze him. He stands up, brushes off his clothes, and fixes his false smile right back on his face.

"Oh my god," my mom says.

I turn and see her face is the color of ash. Every bit of blood has drained out of it, like she's seen a ghost.

"That was scary," I say, because she must just be freaked out by his near death.

She doesn't answer.

The tube fades into the background.

"What's wrong, Mom?"

Finally her eyes move away from the tube and fix on me. "What did you just see, Piper?"

"The glass," I say. "It started falling, just like we were talking about. He was saying it wouldn't."

"When it fell," she says. "What did you see then?"

I think of how fast Councilman Rendon had moved. How no ordinary human could have gotten out of the way. How, like Shayne said, there are gods who are trying to bring about the end of the world. Trying to make it happen faster. My mind spins. These gods could be all around us. They could be people we know.

"He moved out of the way," I say with as calm of a voice as I can manage. "What did you see?" I ask to test my mom.

Her face is still the color of ash, but she tries to act like my answer has appeased her. "I saw the same thing you did."

But I know she saw more, just like I did. There is no way Councilman Rendon is a normal human.

30

Dinner

THE DAY AFTER THE HURRICANE, SCHOOL IS CANCELED. CREWS have been cleaning up the city nonstop, but there's not supposed to be any travel to or from Chloe's dome. We text back and forth a couple times, and it's weird because she doesn't even remember the hurricane. She just claims she's tired, that she'll see me tomorrow at school. She acts like she didn't tell me to leave.

When I look outside the Botanical Haven, the Global Heating Crisis is back in full force. Temperatures are over one hundred and eight, and my mom's been called in for an emergency city council meeting. She pretends nothing happened on the tube yesterday and that we never had any kind of conversation about it.

"Rendon will be there?" I ask because I'm trying to gauge her reaction. To see what her suspicions really are.

"Of course," my mom says. "But there are lots of rumors about the domes. He's going to have some tough questions to answer."

"Tough questions you're going to be asking?" I smile, and my mom returns it.

"You'll stay in? Keep the door locked?" she asks.

What she's really asking about is Reese. And we both know a locked door won't keep him out.

"I'll stay safe," I say.

My mom gives me a kiss on the forehead and makes me promise to text her in an hour. She leaves, and I lock the door. I text

Chloe again, seeing what she's up to, but her answer only confuses me.

have a meeting to go to. tell u about it l8r. ttyl

A meeting? What kind of meeting? All school activities have been canceled for the day. My fingers hover over the keypad. Chloe is keeping secrets from me. I don't respond. Instead, I grab my tablet and pretend to read for the rest of the day even though my mind doesn't focus on a single word.

My mom finally gets home close to five.

"They're taking down the domes," she says.

"Taking them down?"

"Deconstruction will start this weekend." She walks upstairs and I follow her.

"Why?" I ask.

My mother almost smiles when she answers. "Some underground terrorist group delivered a threat. Said if the council didn't stop destroying the atmosphere, they'd blow up the dome structures."

I put this together in my mind. "So instead of waiting for the domes to be blown up, the city's taking them apart first."

My mom nods.

"What about the missiles?" I ask. If a terrorist group is against the domes, then they're certainly against the missiles.

My mom grabs her hairbrush and starts pulling it through her dark hair. She brushes it first behind both ears, then only behind one.

"The missiles will still be on standby," she says.

My mom fiddles with her hair some more and then moves to her jewelry box and pulls out a necklace I've never seen her wear.

"Are you going somewhere, Mom?"

She clasps the necklace and turns to face me. "How does it look?"

It's a leaf with glittering green gems sparkling against her skin. "Gorgeous," I say.

She gives herself one more look in the mirror and then turns to me. "Get ready."

"Where are we going?"

"We're going out for barbeque, Piper."

My mom hates barbeque. She doesn't eat meat. And we almost never go out. I tilt my head, trying to read her expression.

"Mom?"

Her eyes look past me. "What?"

"You hate barbeque."

Her face is a mask, but there's a certain light in it I never see. "So tonight I've changed my mind."

I bite my lip while looking for more in her face. But there's nothing there. Nothing she is willing to let me see. "Okay. Barbeque. Who with?"

My mom arranges the jewelry on her counter and then finally looks at me. "Your father, Piper. He can't wait to meet you."

Everything my mom's ever told me about my dad starts spiraling around in my head. Because if he's such a bad person, why is she bringing me to meet him now?

WHEN WE WALK INTO POK-E-JO'S BARBEQUE, THE OVERwhelming aroma of smoked meat hits me; I focus on it to keep my mind off how nervous I am. I'm going to finally meet my father—something I've dreamed of since I was a little girl. And now it's really going to happen. I close my eyes and suck in the smell, picking out the sausage, the brisket, and even the macaroni and cheese from the air. This is going to cost a fortune.

I look over at my mom and see her nose is wrinkled up.

"Don't you even like the smell, Mom?" I ask because I need to say something. My stomach is a ball of lead inside me.

"I had a bad experience with meat once," she says. She keeps checking her hair. Touching her lips. I wonder if she's as nervous as I am.

It's dark already, and every single booth is taken. My heart skips a few beats as I scan the room, wondering if I can pick out my dad. My eyes settle on a man with a receding hairline and a pair of bright blue eyes staring at me. His hair is spiked and blond and looks like he should wear a hat to keep his scalp from burning. Even with his retreating hairline, he hardly looks thirty.

I turn to my mom and see she's gazing at him also. The ball in my stomach turns into an iron fist which begins to tighten. My father. The man sitting in the booth is my father. The lines of his face are familiar because they match my own. I open my mouth to say something, but my throat constricts.

My mom puts up her hand. "Let's just get our food and sit down. The sooner we get this over with the better."

I nod, not that I want to get the meal over with. After eighteen years of not even knowing who my dad is, I don't want to rush the meal. I have a father, and he's sitting in a booth waiting for me. He doesn't look like a terrorist or a criminal. And he doesn't look like a kidnapper either.

I manage to walk through the line, ordering my food without even thinking. My mom orders only a salad, holding my arm at the elbow the whole time. Like she's afraid my dad's going to snatch me away or something. It makes me feel like I'm five years old all over again.

I scoot into the booth, across from my father, and my mom slides in next to me. The red vinyl crunches under my legs as I cross them, and already I can feel it sticking to me and sweat forming. If the restaurant has eco A/C, they aren't using it. Or maybe I'm just nervous. Or both.

My father looks over and cracks a grin that reaches far up his forehead. "You like the heat, Piper?"

It seems a funny question to be the first words spoken between my dad and me—simple chitchat about the weather.

I nod. "Yeah. I do. The hotter the better." I reach across the table for the barbeque sauce. The sausage here is too dry without it. My hands shake, but I don't want him to see I'm nervous. I want him to think I'm brave and independent and someone he should be proud of.

My father smiles. "Now that sounds like a daughter of mine." He grabs a different bottle and passes it over to me. "Here, try this instead. It's my own special blend."

Before I can reach for it, my mom's hand grabs the bottle. "No."

My mouth drops open. It's barbeque sauce. What's the big deal?

I watch my parents—my father raises an eyebrow and looks at my mom. She stares back, and it's like she's trying to shoot arrows out of her eyes. They stay there, locked in silent combat until finally my mother speaks.

"Piper doesn't need anything from you," my mom says.

My father inclines his head. "And what does Piper need from you? Let's answer that question first."

My mom's eyes flash. "I have given Piper everything she's needed. For eighteen years, I've been more than she could ever hope for."

His eyes shift to me. "And maybe more than she wants. Too much if I could venture a guess."

It's like he can pick the memories of my oppressed life right from my mind. But I'm not opening my mouth to agree or disagree.

"Piper loves me."

A smile breaks onto his face. "And Piper will love me, too." He places one of his hands on my mom's. "Piper can try the sauce, darling Lucia. It's okay."

It's rare I hear my mom's real name. I never call her anything other than Mom, and we're so seldom around people when we're together. Lucia. It seems way old-fashioned and almost foreign. And I wonder where my parents met.

My mom's eyes soften, and in that moment I'm struck by how truly beautiful she really is. How guys must have always thought so, even my dad.

She lifts her hand off the bottle. "I'll choose my battles."

"You always have," my dad says.

I take the bottle of sauce and dump it over the sausage and brisket, letting it spill so some dribbles into the casserole. My stomach is clenched hard again, but the sauce smells like ambrosia laced with pepper. I know I'll love it because when it comes to sauce, hotter is better.

"Thanks." I cut a piece of meat and put it to my lips, inhaling the fat and smoke blended together.

"You can't buy sauce like this anywhere," my father says. "I make it myself."

I nod. "It's really good." There are at least three kinds of peppers in it. Habañero. Chipotle. And something else I can't identify.

He leans forward onto his elbows and stares at me. "So this is the daughter who's been hidden from me her whole life."

Inadvertently, I lean back.

"What kind of father would you have been anyway?" my mom says. Unlike me, her posture matches his. She leans forward and fixes her eyes on him. They are equals in this discussion about me.

I look at my father. White-blond hair gelled upward. Led Zeppelin T-shirt with a splotch of barbeque sauce on it. Three-meat platter in front of him. On first glance, it seems to me he'd be a lot more fun as a parent than my mom.

My father holds my mom with his gaze. "Well, for starters, I would let Piper have her own place in the world."

Next to me, my mom shudders. "Piper's place is with me."

My dad stays forward, holding his pose and my mom's attention. They wrestle back and forth with their eyes, and silence is their battleground. I chew slowly, thinking I shouldn't draw attention to myself even though I am the center of attention. After an eternity, my father sits back and looks to me. "So, Piper, tell me about yourself."

I force myself to laugh, though my muscles are rigid. I'm clenching my fork, so I set it down and think about the difference two weeks can make. If my father had asked me this question two weeks ago, I'd have given some pretty boring answers. Still, I'm not about to spill on my date with Reese and my journeys with Shayne to the Underworld.

"Oh, you know," I say.

His smile encourages me. "No. I don't. But I'd like to."

I grab my spoon and scoop up some green bean casserole. "Well, I'm eighteen. I'm a senior. I have a best friend."

"Eighteen, huh?"

I nod, eating the casserole.

He looks to my mom. "And I see you have a tattoo."

"I got it a week ago." I hold out my arm so he can see my left bicep.

He raises his eyebrows when he reads it. "Sacrifice."

Again, I realize everyone knows Ancient Greek except me.

He reaches across the table to touch it. "It's fading."

I nod. "I think the artist may have messed up. I may have to get it reinked." But my stomach clenches when I say it. I know the fading has nothing to do with the ink and everything to do with Chloe almost dying.

My father pulls up the sleeve on his T-shirt. "I have a tattoo also."

That's putting it mildly. I lean over to get a better look. It looks like every natural disaster possible has been inked on his shoulder. There are cosmic reds and greens and bright yellows, blended together into a pattern that almost seems to shift and change in front of my eyes.

"Wow. It's the most amazing thing I've ever seen."

He nods and rolls his sleeve back down. "Thank you, Piper." And he winks at me.

"Did you get it in prison?" I ask, because Chloe's brother told us about all the people who get tattoos in prison.

He raises an eyebrow and looks sideways at my mom. "Prison?"

My mom remains silent.

"I thought you were in prison," I say. "That you caused the water still explosion out west and you got caught."

My father actually laughs. I think most people would be furious at an accusation like this, but he laughs. "And let me guess. Your mother told you that."

My mom twists up her face. "Well, what was I supposed to tell her? That you didn't have time to raise a daughter?"

"You can tell her what you like, Lucia. I'm sure Piper will find the truth on her own."

I know in that instant everything my mom's told me about my dad is a lie.

Next to me, my mom slams her fork on the plate. It clatters like a bell such that, four tables over, people turn and look. "Are we done here yet?"

"Done?" My father laughs. "I'm only getting started. So tell me, Piper, do you have a boyfriend?"

I almost drop my spoon at the question, catching it before it lands on my lap. But I do manage to get a giant drop of sauce on my leg. I wipe it off, licking my finger.

"Piper does not have a boyfriend." My mom answers for me.

I open my mouth to protest but then stop. I have Shayne, and then there's Reese. But neither of them are appropriate conversations to have given the present company. So instead, I nod. "Right. No boyfriend." I glance over sideways at my mom who smiles like a fox that's gotten away.

"Oh, come on now. A pretty girl like you? Certainly you have young men declaring their undying love for you every day." And his blue-steel eyes meet mine and hold them.

My heart begins to pound; I feel it in my temples. But I hold my face steady and force a smile to my lips. "Only in my daydreams."

He grins, and I feel like we've shared some secret. A secret even I don't know. "Well, you have your whole life ahead of you." He grabs his beer bottle and lifts it to his mouth, drinking the remainder down in one large swallow. Even though I don't drink beer, it's still impressive.

"Piper has no need for boyfriends." My mom spears a cherry

tomato with her fork and puts it in her mouth whole. She chews it, and we both watch her, waiting until she's finished. "We have each other and that's all we'll ever need."

My father slaps the table, causing the plates to rattle against the silverware. "Nonsense. Piper, how would you like to come stay with me for a few months?"

My mom rockets up out of her seat. "How dare you? Piper is not going to stay with you."

My father looks at her, commanding her to sit down with his eyes. She glares at him but settles back into the booth.

"Why not, Lucia? You and I both know Piper would benefit from some time away from you."

I guess this means my father is aware of my mom's desire to control me. But I have to admit, the thought of getting away, of getting to know my father a little bit better, is like new flowers planted in a garden. Like tendrils of the life I want to lead are breaking into my world, trying to lay down roots. And I plan to give them as much room as they need.

"Well, for starters, Peter, what would your wife say about that?"

My face freezes at the question. Whether it's the fact that my father now has a name or that he is married I'm not sure. But of course, I'm eighteen years old. Why wouldn't he have a wife? And there could be other kids in the mix. Half brothers and sisters I've never met.

"My wife, if you must know, will tolerate it." He waves his hand, and a waitress sees it. He holds up his beer bottle, and she turns to get him another one. "She'll argue at first, but you know she'll come around. I can be very persuasive."

Is that how my mom was, too? Did she give in to his persuasion?

"How did you two meet?" I take a sip of my iced tea after I ask, wondering if either of them will bother answering. And then I watch their faces.

My mom tries to harden her look, and I'm sure she'll start in on some story of how she was horribly wronged by this awful man here at the table with us. But after meeting him, I know in my heart this can't be the truth.

At the question, however, my father's face softens. "Your mother is quite a charmer, Piper. Did you know that?"

I shake my head and look at her. The hardness falls from her face, and she actually blushes. "No. I had no idea," I say. *Charmer* and *mother* are two words I never would have put in the same sentence.

But my dad nods. "Yes. I fell in love with her the moment I saw her."

My mom laughs, but it's not the snide laugh which up until now has permeated the conversation. There's a longing in her voice, and I think maybe she fell in love with him the moment she saw him also. "You fall in love with everyone you see," she says.

My father angles his head. "Not untrue. I do admit it. I have an eye for beautiful creatures. But of them, your mom rose to the top. If I weren't already previously engaged, I may have married her on the spot. Instead, the day we met, I took the one moment of bliss I could and left it at that."

The truth hits me. My mom and dad were never married. And beyond that, I was nothing more than the result of a one-night stand. My mom. The woman who acts like Earth will implode if I so much as utter the name of a boy at school. She slept with my father the moment she met him and ended up pregnant.

I turn to her and wait. Wondering what she'll say. Wondering if she'll deny it. Or defend her actions. Or anything. But my old mom returns, and she deflects the conversation. "Piper will not be staying with you. You're a bad influence, and besides, she and I have been talking about moving anyway. Having her out and about will not do at all."

My father raises an eyebrow. "Lucia—"

She interrupts. "I'm serious about this. I don't think you want me to be more clear, do you?"

My father shrugs. "Would things be any worse than they are now?"

I have no clue what he's talking about. But I'm not about to interrupt.

My mom nods. "Yes. Things will be worse. Of that you can be sure."

The waitress comes over, holding another beer. My father takes it, but at the same time, my mom stands up. "Piper, we're leaving."

I look to my father. His grin has come back, and he lifts the beer in a "cheers" sign. "Darling daughter. It's been a true joy meeting you."

I don't want to stand up. To leave. But my mom's eyes are on me. "Will I see you again?" I ask my father.

"Absolutely." He stands and turns to my mom. "A kiss for old time's sake?"

She scoffs. "Please." But her face is flushed; even I can see it.

"You're still just as beautiful as you were so long ago, darling Lucia." My father reaches out and cups her chin with his fingers. Something inside me stirs as I remember Shayne doing the same thing to me. And then my father leans over and kisses my mom full on the lips. Her body freezes, but her lips relent, and she kisses him back with everything she has. It's a part of my mom I never would have believed existed. But here it is, right in the middle of Pok-e-Jo's Barbeque.

And more than ever, at this moment in time, I want to travel back to Hell. To be with Shayne forever. To live a life of love and happiness I've never known before. And I wonder if, underneath her façade, my mom doesn't crave something similar.

31

Tears

TEACHING IS POINTLESS ON FRIDAY. THE TEACHERS GIVE IT A try, but all anyone wants to talk about is the hurricane. I look for Chloe at lunch, and when she doesn't show, I text her.

will u b in stdy hall? I send.

Her response is short. Too short. can't. have plans

what plans?

crazy. ttyl

I'm not sure what she's referring to when she says *crazy:* her plans, the world, or herself. I send her a quick response and head to class.

When I walk into Social Sciences, my heart flips over in place a few times. Shayne's sitting there, waiting for me. He moves his arm off the chair next to him so I can sit down.

"Don't the teachers wonder why you're here so little?" In the last couple weeks, he's been in class all of three days. I'd wonder where he was if I didn't already know. But even still, being in Hell doesn't explain why he can't make it to class. Especially if he really does want to see me.

Shayne looks at Mr. Kaiser. He's just uncapping his dry-erase marker—purple this time—and the smell drifts through the air.

"Being a god does have its powers, Piper. The teachers hardly notice me."

I smile, and in a moment of utter insanity, I lean over and kiss him lightly on the mouth. It's something I've seen other kids do-ing in school and always wanted to experience for myself. It makes me feel so alive. Shayne tastes like a rustic campfire mixed with something so intense it pulls at every part of my insides.

"I like that," he says when I pull my head back.

"I like that you like that," I say. And this time he leans forward and kisses me.

Mr. Kaiser clears his throat and starts class. It's not like Randy and Hannah weren't always making out before class. But now, with Randy gone, that won't happen again.

"So what are your powers?" I whisper.

Shayne keeps his head close to me. "Making you fall madly in love with me."

I can't tell if he's joking. I think he is. I also think he's right. Still, I fix him with a look that tells him he's full of crap. "I hardly call that a power," I say.

A smile plays on his lips. "What would you call a power?"

"Hmmm . . ." I put my finger to my mouth, pretending I'm in deep thought. "Maybe breaking down brick walls. Or climbing up the sides of buildings."

"I'm a god, not a superhero," Shayne says.

I hear Mr. Kaiser clear his throat again. With Randy Conner dead, the class has been drained of all comedic relief, and Shayne's laugh stands out like a wart.

"Would you like to share what's so funny, Piper?" Mr. Kaiser says.

I look around and realize the whole class is staring at me. Now why hadn't he asked Shayne to explain the joke? I shrug. "We were valuing the powers of superheroes." I glance sideways at Shayne and see he's twirling his stylus on his hand.

Mr. Kaiser raises an eyebrow and then turns and writes the word SUPERHERO in large purple letters on the board behind him. He caps the marker and turns back around. "So what power would you want if you were a superhero?" He's not asking me, but the whole class in general.

"How about flying?" someone suggests.

Mr. Kaiser turns and writes *flying* on the board. "What else?"

"Invisibility—'cause then I could sneak into the girls' locker room," someone else says.

It's a stereotypical male answer, and it garnishes a stereotypical female reaction of eye rolling, name calling, and laughter. But Mr. Kaiser writes *invisibility* on the board nonetheless.

Most of the answers are funny, even expected, such as my climbing buildings or breaking down walls. There's an enormous sense of release descending on our Social Sciences class, and I look over at Shayne and grin. He reaches out across the aisle, takes my hand, and squeezes it.

The whiteboard is just about full when Mr. Kaiser says, "How about one more thing?"

"I'd like to bring people back from the dead."

It's Hannah, Randy's girlfriend. I still remember her face at the funeral—frozen into a state of repressed sorrow.

Silence falls on the class faster than a flash flood in a dry creekbed. I have no idea what to say, and I'm pretty sure no one else does either. Shayne's still holding my hand, but lets it go and turns around to face her.

"Why?"

It's a simple question but an unexpected one all the same. I can't believe he's asked it.

"Why what?" Hannah's staring at him, and I know their eyes are locked.

"Why would you want to bring someone back?"

Hannah lets out a gasp of exasperation, and for a second, I think she's going to get up and come punch Shayne. The silence in the class is so solid, I can hear the mercury in the thermometer rising.

Hannah breaks the silence. "I think that's pretty obvious."

But Shayne keeps at it. "What if Randy is at peace? Why would you want to bring him back?"

Hannah jumps to her feet. "How could he be at peace? He's

left his family here with that monster of a father. He's left me here." She glares at Shayne, and I think she's trying to evaporate him with her eyes. "Did you know I'm pregnant?"

When she says it, I realize my heart is pounding in my chest, and I've forgotten to breathe. I don't want to move. Don't want to draw any attention to myself.

"Yes." Shayne's so calm it's like a violent contradiction to the rage and sadness pouring off her.

I'm staring at Hannah, watching her face. It's red, but her eyes are dry—just like at the funeral. And she's carrying Randy Conner's baby.

"Yes what?" she demands.

"Yes, I knew." And whether Hannah, Mr. Kaiser, or anyone else in the class believes Shayne, I do. "But why would you want to bring him back?"

I can't believe he's pressing her. I almost open my mouth at this point and tell him to stop, but my mouth feels pinned shut.

Hannah doesn't speak. Her mouth's opening, but nothing's coming out. And I realize in that moment how much Hannah and I are alike. Except I was able to bring Chloe back from the dead, and Randy will stay in the Underworld forever.

"It's not like things are perfect in this world. Why would you bring him back here?"

Hannah stands there looking at Shayne. Her eyes grow lighter, and soon tears pour down her face. They flow like the River Acheron, full of sorrow, and I know this is the first time she's cried since Randy died. Her hands move to her stomach as she cries, and I think about the baby. It'll grow up without a father. Just like me. But its father will be dead, unlike mine. And its father will not abuse it like Randy's.

"Because I miss him." Hannah manages to get the words out between her tears, and within moments, Salima gets up and helps her out of the room.

I'm staring at the place where Hannah was, watching the door swing closed. And when I look at Shayne, he's staring forward, twirling the stylus on his hand. I want to say something to him, but he's not looking at me, and if he knows I'm trying to get his attention, he's ignoring me. So I turn forward and see Mr. Kaiser erasing the whiteboard. With the purple dry-erase marker, he writes *GHC: WHAT YOU CAN DO* at the top of the board, underlines it three times, and we get on with the lecture.

32

Sleep

SHAYNE WAITS FOR ME AFTER SCHOOL. I THINK HE'S LEFT, BUT
when I get to my locker at the end of the day, he's there holding
it open already.

"I don't know if you helped Hannah or made things worse."
I've been going over it in my head since class let out. On the one
hand, Hannah finally released her sorrow. On the other hand,
she did it in front of the entire class.

"I think I helped."

My mind's been telling me the same thing, but I want to hear
Shayne say it. "You're always so sure of yourself," I say.

Shayne gives a small shrug like he's trying to not act cocky.
"Not always."

"Lots of the time."

"Yeah, lots of the time," he says.

"I can't believe Hannah's pregnant," I say. "I had no clue."

"Only she and Randy knew," Shayne says. "Randy told me
when he crossed."

It's just one more piece of his memory for Randy to leave behind in the River Lethe.

Shayne shuts my locker and takes my hand. "Can I walk you
home?"

"Of course." Chloe's skipping, so I can't take the shuttle with
her. But we're hardly ten feet away from my locker when I catch
Reese's scent in the air.

A wave of darkness covers Shayne's face. "Why won't he stay away from you?"

I lift my head and see Reese, here at our school, across the corridor. When our eyes meet, he winks at me.

Shayne's hand tightens like a clamp on mine, and he takes a step in Reese's direction.

Reese's eyebrows arch like he's surprised Shayne would challenge him. I wonder if Shayne will start a fight right here in the middle of school with so many people around. If so, Reese must be up for it because, in five quick strides, he stands directly in front of us.

Reese glances at Shayne and then reaches over and brushes my cheek, sending a flurry of goose bumps down my neck. I'd be lying if I said revulsion was the sole cause of those goose bumps because with his scent in the air, my memories of him return. It's immediate this time. False memories mix with real ones, and I have no idea what is true. I scoot backward to get out of his reach.

"I really missed you, Piper," Reese says.

I open my mouth to tell him I wish he would leave me alone, but the words won't come out. Shayne's hand feels like it will snap the bones in my fingers in half. I wince, and he lets go, though he stays close.

"You need to leave, Reese," Shayne says under his breath.

I glance around; we've gathered more than a couple stares. Distance forms between our bizarre triangle and the observers who want to watch but must not want to get caught in the middle.

Reese ignores Shayne and keeps his eyes focused on me. "I wish you'd give me a chance, Piper. I swear I'm not as bad as he'll make you think." He steps forward again—or maybe I do—because his hand moves to my lips.

I remember a million other times just like this. Reese touching me. Caressing me.

"Are you busy tonight?" Reese asks.

I glance at Shayne out of my peripheral vision. His face doesn't move, but he's turned so I can see his eyes and the red in them like fireworks.

"Yes, she has plans. Permanent plans." Shayne's words catch me. I've started to drift. To succumb to the memories; they're clouding every bit of judgment in my mind. "Now leave, Reese."

Reese laughs. "Leave? Piper doesn't want me to. Maybe you should leave."

My lips part even before I can stop them. My date with Reese had been fantastic. The memories and his aroma pour through my whole body. I have to fight with my own mind; it wants me to go to Reese. I force myself to take a step closer to Shayne and grab his arm, trying to root myself to him, away from Reese. Reese is screwing with my brain. The memories aren't real. I don't want to be with him.

"Never. Touch. Piper. Again." There's no chance Shayne is going to be misunderstood.

But this doesn't seem to stop Reese. He turns to Shayne and glares. "I don't think you can stop me." His thumb brushes across my lips, sending a chill through me.

I hate that he's having this effect on me. It's making me crazy.

In a flash, Shayne swats Reese's hand away. It flies backward, making a sickening crunching sound like bone on bone. And then Shayne punches Reese right in the nose. The odor of blood is immediate, and the memories in my mind start to clear.

I hear the kids around us gasp, which further helps erase the memories of Reese, and I force clarity into my mind.

Reese grimaces and lets his hand fall to his side. There's blood running from his left nostril, but all he does is wipe it with the back of his hand. And then he reaches up to touch my lips again. I step back, out of his reach, and lean close to Shayne. For whatever bizarre reason my body is betraying me, but I will fight it. "Can we go?"

"You know Piper wants me." Reese's voice is like nails trying to pierce Shayne's armor. "Her body is aching for me. Just look at her. And it's killing you."

In one step, Shayne moves forward until he's directly up in Reese's face. "Know this, Reese. Come near her again, and I will kill you."

"You don't have the power," Reese says. And then he spits on Shayne.

Shayne doesn't flinch. "I dare you to test me."

Reese takes a step back and smiles. "Sounds like a dare I plan to take." And then he gives me a final smile and walks away, pushing his way through the crowd, leaving only his haunting scent in his wake.

I'm afraid to move, unsure what Shayne will think. He watches as Reese leaves, and pretty soon, the smell evaporates, too, leaving me somewhat in control there in the hallway next to Shayne. And after a few wayward glances, everyone starts to disperse. I don't know what to say.

"I asked you to stay away from him, Piper." Shayne's voice is filled with fury.

"I have."

"Then why does he keep coming back?"

I spin on him and unleash my own fury, keeping my voice low. "Because he's the god of war. You said it yourself. He'll never give up. So stop blaming me."

I kick the nearest locker and then storm toward the doors of the school.

Shayne catches up to me in seconds. "Wait."

I stop. "What?"

"I'm sorry," he says. "That's not fair."

I only nod in response. He's right. It's not fair.

"We never got along," Shayne says. He clenches his teeth as he speaks. "Not since the first time we met."

"That doesn't surprise me," I say. A friendship between Reese and Shayne seems as unlikely as my mom deciding to let me move out.

Shayne waits until we get outside. The heat hits me, but the misters take over quickly, spraying gel on me until I've cooled to a normal temperature as much as I can with the memory of Reese spinning in my head. I stop for a minute and let the gel and my thoughts collect.

"He's always hated me. Been jealous of everything I've had. He's trying to mislead you to get to me."

I turn to Shayne. I've had secrets and lies and half-truths enough. "It's not like you're bubbling over trying to tell me the truth either." It's not like anyone is. Not my mom. Not my dad.

Shayne tries to take my hand, but I pull it back.

"I want you to know the truth," Shayne says. His eyes pierce into me, but I fight inside, not daring to let myself sink into them, knowing I want to more than anything in the world.

"Really?" It's almost laughable.

Shayne nods. "Look at everything I've shown you."

"But all I have now are more questions." Like why my life was ordinary until two weeks ago, and now I'm being accused of kill-ing mythological birds. And why Greek gods are walking the Earth. And why my dad wants custody. I know I'm scowling, but I'm angry at Shayne for not telling me anything. I'm angry at Reese for asking me out in the first place. I'm angry at Chloe for drifting away from me. And I'm angry at myself for letting her. "Everything was fine before. Things used to be normal."

Shayne reaches out again, and I let him take my hand this time. "Do you want things to go back to how they were?"

I bite my lower lip and meet his eyes. "Maybe." But it's a lie.

Shayne's face falls, and guilt hits me hard in the chest. I don't seriously mean it, but before, at least I knew what was going on in my life. Now, my best friend has almost died, and I'm pretty sure I'm in love with the Lord of the Underworld. And though I desperately wish Chloe were back to normal, I'd never trade any-thing for knowing Shayne.

But I don't open my mouth and tell Shayne this.

"I can't tell you anything else," he says.

I've been expecting his words, but I still hate them. "Why not?"

"Because if I tell you, not only could I be doomed to Tartarus, so could you. I didn't make up the rules, but I still can't take the risk."

"Then I'll ask Reese." My heart speeds up. Reese will tell me what's going on.

"No." Shayne's word comes out like a command, and my face must react because he softens his voice. "I don't want to lose you."

"But I need to know what's going on." Even to my own ears, I sound like a desperate child. "What if I'm willing to take the risk?"

A breeze blows, and Shayne's dark hair moves across his face. The red has started flashing in his eyes. "I can't let you, Piper. It would destroy me."

"I need to know." I have to know.

"I don't want you to find out from Reese," Shayne says.

I ball my hands up in fists. "I don't care what you want," I say. "I'm sick of people telling me what to do." And with that, I turn to run back in the direction Reese went. I'll find him and make him give me answers. But before I can move, I find myself face to beautiful face with a winged man.

The man reaches out, and before I can even cry out or think about running, he touches me. The world spins, blackness clouds my vision, and I fall to the ground.

33

Charon

I WAKE UP IN MY BED, COOL COTTON SHEETS SURROUNDING me, fans on overhead. I look down and realize, even though it's dark outside, I'm still in the same shorts and tank top I wore to school on Friday. I don't remember coming upstairs or falling asleep, or even the sun setting.

I sit up in bed and blink my eyes a few times, waiting for them to acclimate to the darkness. The bright green letters of the clock by the bed tell me it's close to three o'clock in the morning. And then I see the day and realize it says Sunday instead of Saturday. I pick it up, thinking it must be wrong, but unless the geosynchronous satellites rotating around Earth are out of sync, it's really Sunday morning, and I've slept for over twenty-four hours.

"Mom?" Her room is only down the hall, so I don't call too loudly.

There's no answer.

"Mom?" A little louder this time.

Still nothing.

I stand up and find my sandals by the bed, right where I normally leave them, and after I slip them on, I open the door and walk to my mom's room to check for her. Her bed is empty. I stare at it to make sure, but she's really not home. I have no clue where she is. Actually, the more I think about it, the more I realize I have no clue what's going on at all. Like how I got to the Botanical Haven. And how I slept for an entire weekend. Something hazy sits at the back of my mind but won't reach the surface, so I head to the bathroom to wash my face.

I turn on the cold water full force, ignoring the ration rules, and splash it on my eyes, trying to clear the fog moving around in my brain. I look up into the bathroom mirror and reach for the towel. And when I do, I see the red line on the side of my neck, near my ear, and remember Minos in Asphodel. He threatened to send me to Tartarus. For killing a phoenix. Shayne promised me I hadn't killed anything. That I wasn't responsible for Randy Conner's death.

And then it all comes back to me. We were at school. Shayne wouldn't tell me anything, and he didn't want me to ask Reese. We argued, and I threatened to talk to Reese anyway. I know I was being irrational, but even now I can feel my frustration. I need to know what's going on. But before I had the chance, Shayne summoned a winged servant from the Underworld. Not Death, who'd been summoned for Chloe. This one had been summoned for . . .

"Sleep," I say to my reflection in the mirror, and anger builds inside me. I can't believe he did that. He put me to sleep. I want to let the rage push through and take over; I want to scream at him for what he's done. But the fear in his eyes moves to the surface of my mind, and my anger won't take root.

I feel wetness on my toes and realize the sink is flooding over. I turn off the water, undoing the stopper so the water will empty. I watch it as it goes down, swirling faster once it gets near the bottom.

I walk out of the bathroom, back down the hallway, and head into the darkness of the downstairs. The steps seem to last forever, taking me from the emptiness of our upstairs to the forest that is our home below. Two places so near to each other, but so different. Among the plants, I've always lost myself. Like it's another world.

As soon as my feet hit the tiles, I know what I need to do. Shayne asked me not to talk to Reese. But he didn't mention anyone else. I need to go to Hell and talk to someone there. Maybe Charon. Or Rhadam. One of them might tell me something. Minos enters my mind, but I shove him aside. His brutal eyes had caught mine and accused me, and I know I can't go back and see him again. Not alone, and hopefully not ever.

But I will go to Hell. Alone. Without Shayne. And I will get my answers.

I CALL TO THE UNDERWORLD BECAUSE I CAN SENSE THE RIVER of silver skimming under the surface of Earth. It almost seems to reach up and pull me to it, like it could seep into my veins and make me part of it. I'm not sure if it will work, if I'll be able to go without Shayne, but the earth opens up for me. It recognizes me and accepts me, swallowing me whole and holding me close on my journey to the Underworld. Silver liquid fills the void around me, and then I'm there on the banks of the River Acheron. I see Charon by the dock, waiting. He's got his eyes closed—like he's taking a catnap, but when I look in his direction, they flip open and grow wide. I guess he wasn't expecting to see me. I'm not sure I was expecting me to make it here either, yet now that I'm here, everything feels as it should be.

I walk to the dock, trying to pretend I belong here. Trying to play my part. I'm not sure if Charon will take me across the river based on his reaction, but he recovers well and waves. Relief floods through me when I see his familiar face, and I know he'll help.

"I wasn't expecting you." He pulls the boat up against the dock and moves aside so I can get in.

Only then do I remember the payment. My face falls, and I shove my hands in my pockets, trying desperately to find some kind of coin. But my pockets are empty.

"I can't pay you."

Charon takes a step back and bows low to the ground. "I could never take a single drachma from you. I wouldn't be able to live with myself."

Relief floods through me; everything is falling into place. For a second, I feel like a coconspirator. "Does that mean you're really alive?"

Charon stands back up, and his face creases into the smile I love. "It's been up for debate many times."

"And . . . ?" I step into the boat.

He unties the rope, and I sit down, in the middle this time, near enough to Charon so I can talk. After we get out on the water, I plan to ask him my questions. To see what I can learn.

Charon shrugs and picks up the pole, already shoving it in the water to move the boat forward. "Let's just say I don't think I'll die anytime soon."

I see my opening. "Will I?"

Charon looks at me, and our eyes catch. The smile sinks away, and then finally, he looks out toward the water. "The monsters are a bit restless these days."

He's trying to avoid talking. But I've got him pinned like a mouse in a labyrinth with no exit, and I'm not going to lose my opportunity, even if he is poling faster, trying to reach the shore sooner.

"Do you know who I am, Charon?" I figure I can't get much more direct than that.

Charon looks back at me and nods. "You're Piper."

Before I can say anything else, a monster bumps into the side of the boat, sending a spray of water up and drenching me. At the touch of the water, a wave of sorrow overcomes me, and I break down crying. I don't expect Charon to come near me or comfort me, and he doesn't. He's probably seen this a million times before.

"It'll pass, Piper. I promise."

"I just want the lies to go away." I'm still crying, but as the water drips off me, the sadness slips away with it.

Charon doesn't say anything, and we cross in silence. Before I know it, I'm jolted when the boat bumps into the dock. But I don't stand.

"Aren't you getting out?" he asks. He's hopped out ahead of me and has already tied the rope, holding out a hand to help me.

I sigh, but it comes out mixed with a sob. Am I destined to never know anything? "Maybe I should just go back home."

Charon purses his lips. His eyes flicker around—at the shore with the giant trees towering above, toward the empty tunnel in the rocks ahead, then back at the water. The wails of the sorrows tear at me, and each time I hear one, I see a monster jump up out of the reeds and snatch it from the air.

"Piper."

I turn back to Charon. "What?"

He's not looking at me. His eyes are still focused on the tumultuous water. Overhead, the grackles call out their song, echoing around from one tree to the next. "Things in the Underworld haven't always been this bad."

I hold my breath. Maybe he's going to tell me what I want to know. "In what ways?"

Charon points to the water. "The monsters are vicious now. The realms are getting out of control. Even the Elysian Fields. There's talk of other gods gaining entry. Not to mention the overlords are seizing more power every day."

I think of Minos. Of Ares appearing in Asphodel, if only as a shadow. Of Hell not working correctly. "How long have things been going wrong?"

Charon turns, and his milky-white eyes meet mine. "Eighteen years."

When he says it, it's like I've been punched in the stomach. It's the same amount of time my Earth above has been in the Global Heating Crisis. A hell of its own with a sun that only gets more powerful by the day. Eighteen years. There's something connecting my Earth above and this hell below. Eighteen years. It echoes in my mind.

It's the same amount of time I've been alive.

Are the secrets I crave somehow tied to the physical sufferings of the worlds both aboveground and below? And am I somehow involved?

I open my mouth to respond, but I can't think of anything to say.

"Please be safe," Charon says.

I snap out of my thoughts and see him reaching back into the boat. I stand up and give him my hand so he can help me out. And no sooner am I on the dock, walking away from the boat, than I know it's already slipping away through the reeds and the swampy water behind me. And just like everything so far, I only have more questions and still have no answers.

34

Sisyphus

I STARE AT THE TEN TUNNELS. I DON'T KNOW WHICH ONE TO choose. I don't even know where the others go. And Cerberus is nowhere to be found. I think he would lead me in the right direction.

The sixth tunnel is the one we took last time, but when I walk up toward it, I'm hit with hatred. A red fungus suddenly covers the edge of the cave's mouth. I turn from it because the thought of taking that path makes me want to vomit. I step in front of the tunnel to its left, and the nauseous feeling is replaced by happiness. Green ivy covers the opening.

I stare through the illusion of ivy down the dark path. I count my heartbeats.

I don't need happiness. I need answers.

This tunnel must lead to the Elysian Fields, but after Charon's staid words, I know Rhadam won't tell me much either. No one will. I focus on the ivy, which I think is an illusion, but I feed my anger into it until it bursts into flames. I watch it burn. And then I locate the tunnel with the hatred again and take a step inside.

Voices greet me.

Come to us.

Visit us.

I cover my ears and close my eyes but soon realize they're inside my head, like specters floating around, trying to latch on to something real.

We need you.

Each word is a chorus, beckoning me. I haven't moved since my initial step inside the tunnel, and I want them to go away. I turn, thinking I'll leave. Knowing this is a bad idea. But the opening where I came from is no longer there.

Piper.

They know my name. I shake my head and take another step forward, trying to move as far away from the haunting sounds as possible.

"Stop!" I say it aloud, but the voices ignore me.

Piper. It's only fair.

We want to see you.

When they say it, I know where they're coming from. Tartarus. Hearing the sounds helps me realize why Shayne didn't want me to go there. They're tearing at my insides, devouring my brain. I can't get them out.

Visit us.

It's been so long.

We miss you.

You belong with us.

My heart skips around in my chest, and a hollow feeling of dread settles on my stomach. I just want them to go away. Squeezing my eyes shut again, I think of Shayne. Of Chloe. Even of my mom. Anything to make them depart.

We'll tell you secrets.

My eyes snap open, and the voices stop.

They know they've got me.

I don't even think about what I'm doing as my feet move me. The voices lead me to Tartarus. The ground feels like gravel under my feet, and the farther I get into the passageway, the less I can smell the comforting banks of Acheron and the more I can smell something close to burning flesh. But I don't care; I need to get there.

I see the flickering redness of the flames and feel the heat long before I round the corner of the tunnel, and when I do come around, the river is on fire.

A name rings out in my head from deep in my memories. Phlegethon. The river of fire leading to Tartarus. I tie my hair into a knot, hoping to keep any stray flames from catching it. My mind screams at me to turn around. To run to the comfort of Shayne's home. But I need answers, and Tartarus seems willing to give them to me.

Like the other rivers, the dock extends into the water. It's surrounded, yet untouched, by flames. I want to turn and run, to get away from the flames at all cost, but the voices beckon. I step forward, forcing myself to move until I'm on the hard wood of the dock. The flames hiss up over the sides of my sandals as I walk on the wood, but somehow they don't burn me. I wrap my arms around my middle and step into the waiting boat, and before I can change my mind and turn around and leave, it begins to move, and I'm out in the middle of the river of fire.

Burning souls. I know Phlegethon is an initiation into the place of eternal torture. The flames taunt me, but why they don't touch me, I'm not sure. Even my curly hair seems safe tied up at my neck.

Come to us.

Be with us.

As I move across the burning river, the voices start up again. I open my mind and let them in, wishing I could make the boat move faster. Tartarus holds my answers. I'm as sure of it as I am that there are questions. And that secrets have been kept from me my entire life.

We've missed you.

I miss the voices, too. I've never known them, but I miss them. They are a part of me. And I wonder if I do belong in Tartarus like Minos said. If I did kill a phoenix.

The boat seems to be on fire as it moves. The wood is red hot like the embers in Shayne's hearth, and around me, sparks crackle.

But the heat doesn't harm me, and soon, it's carried me to the dock on the other side. Ahead, all I see is a wall of flames, and for a second, my stomach tightens, and I wonder what I'm doing. Nothing good happens in Tartarus.

Come, Piper.

A single voice calls out, and I know it. I can't place it, but it's drawing me, pulling me through the wall of flames. I close my eyes and walk forward, and then I'm on the other side and immediately the smell of rot and filth hits my nose. I force myself to take a deep breath, and my stomach lurches until I'm on my knees heaving up nothing but bile and emptiness since I've been asleep for over a day.

When I stand up, I wipe my mouth on my bare arm and look around. A desert stretches before me, and I start walking straight, knowing I'll end up somewhere soon. Somewhere besides the rancid-smelling barrenness surrounding me.

I walk for miles, and the desert moves by in fast-forward, the same way it did in Asphodel, except there's nothing to see around here, and soon I begin to doubt myself. The voices have left me, and there's not a soul around. Maybe I should turn and go back.

Answers. We have answers.

The voice comes out of nowhere, and I shift right, moving in the direction I know it's coming from. Its promises make the ball in my stomach tingle, and with one step after another, I'm soon approaching a mountain range with a medieval castle high on the top. It's where I need to go.

I start toward the mountain, taking another mouthful of the rot around me, and force myself to take breath after breath until my stomach no longer reels. But something grabs my foot from behind, sending me flying face-first to the hard-packed sand.

I kick with the other foot and look down, seeing a skeleton hand clenched around my Achilles tendon. Another hand pops out of the earth and grabs at my leg, and they pull me until I'm up to my knee in the gritty sand. A wave of panic rolls over me when I realize I can't even kick my leg anymore. The hands grasp harder, and sharp pieces of bone cut into my flesh. I lift my head, spit out the sand in my mouth, and try to grab my leg and pull it out myself. They're cutting and clawing, and more than anything, I wish Shayne were here with me. But he doesn't even know I'm down here in Hell. Not to mention in Tartarus. And I can't tell him, or he'll take me away, and I'll never get my answers.

"Let go!" I scream when I realize I'm thigh-deep in the sand. I'm going to suffocate, and no one will ever even know where I've been. I can imagine my body hidden beneath the sand forever in Hell.

But at my words, the skeleton hands obey me and let go. I twist around until I've yanked my leg free then get up and run for the mountain, trying to get off the deadly desert. Sand is caked on my sweaty face, and I claw it off as I run. I will not die before I get my answers. I need to know what Shayne knows. Whether he wants to tell me or not.

I'm halfway up the mountain when I see a naked man with shoulders so wide, I'm sure he could pick me up and snap me like a dehydrated stick given a chance. But I have no intention of giving him a chance. He's standing there on the mountainside supporting a boulder nearly as huge as he is with only his sheer mass holding it in place.

I move around to the side, trying to hide behind a large pile of boulders. Like my Earth above, there aren't any bushes or shrubs around. Too much heat must kill them off down here also. From my vantage point, I see the sweat pouring down his dark naked body, tracing patterns through his hairy chest, and my chest tightens when I realize I have no way to get around him unseen. I'll have to wait for him to move.

"Come out and play with me."

His voice is not what I'm expecting. Actually, I'm not expecting his voice at all but had I been, the sweet, melodic tune is so unfitting the massive man, I don't even try to pretend I haven't heard. I lift my head slowly above the rock pile and see the man looking my way. His face is covered with a smile so inviting, I find my legs carrying me around from my hiding place and over to him.

"Lovely. Simply lovely."

Heat floods my face when I realize he's talking about me. He turns sideways, propping his boulder up with the side of his body, and I can now see his exposed parts hanging there between his legs.

He chuckles, and I lift my eyes, realizing I've been staring directly at them. But my eyes keep trying to look back down as if they've got a mind of their own. I pull them away against their will.

"It's okay to look." He shifts, and I catch a glimpse out of my peripheral vision. "I don't mind at all." And he reaches down and brushes his hand against himself.

"I'm only here to get some answers." I point toward the top of the mountain, happy to have something to focus on. "I'm heading up there."

"Ah." The man laughs again, and I hear the melody pulling me in.

"Do you know who lives there?" I ask. I'm still looking at the castle, and this close, I can see the orange and purple storm clouds swirling overhead and the lightning striking so close, it must be hitting the stones.

"The master of Hell, of course." The man wipes his forehead and blessedly turns away from me. "Do you mind if we get going? I still have to get this boulder to the top." He doesn't wait for an answer. Instead, he leans over, places both hands on the black rock, and begins to push.

"Do you mean Sha"—I catch myself—"Hades?"

The man barks out a laugh followed by a huge grunt. The vein on his temple bulges out so far, I think it might burst. "Not that master." And for the first time, his tone has a hint of disgust in it.

"Then who?"

He turns to me, holding the boulder in place while his eyes gaze my way. But he's still smiling. "You know."

It's not a question. He knows I know. And I realize when he says it that I do. "Aeacus." Another of the ancient kings ruling over the domains of the Underworld.

The giant of a man nods and turns back to the boulder.

I motion at the rock even though he's not looking at me. "Why are you doing that?"

"Somebody needs to. And seeing as I've been unfairly accused and left in this place of eternal damnation, I find it's my job."

"Unfairly accused?"

He gives a giant shove, pushing the boulder a good two feet ahead. And he's fast; he moves up before it can slip even an inch. "Accused of killing innocent people. Travelers and guests to my house."

He's got the boulder moving at such a clip, I'm having a hard time keeping up. He's almost jogging behind it. "And did you?" I ask.

Out comes another laugh, though, at this point, I notice it's missing most of its humor. "Of course not!"

"So you didn't kill anyone?"

He turns to me and shakes his head, sending sweat flying in all directions, some landing on my arms and chest. I notice his private parts shake when he does this, and I avert my eyes, looking instead at the rock. But he catches me looking and smiles.

"What is this? A trial?"

I don't answer. I'm certainly not going to apologize for asking.

"Fine. Yes. I killed many, many people. But every single one of them was trying to kill me first. Or cheat me. Or rape my wife. And so I killed them all." The man turns to me and licks his lips, and his body reflects his excitement and pleasure. "And might I just say I enjoyed it immensely."

My face freezes, and I know without a shadow of a doubt this man belongs right where he is. Here in Tartarus. Spores of evil coat him. I'm ready to leave him, and a weight lifts off me when I see we're only steps away from the top.

His melodic voice sings to me. "I don't believe I caught your name."

I shake my head. "No, you didn't." I don't want to give this monster my name.

"I'm Sisyphus." And with a final push, the boulder crests over the top of a ridge, hitting a plateau. Sisyphus moves it around, making sure it's resting perfectly on flat rocks. He bends down, propping it in place with some smaller rocks to keep it from moving. And then he turns to me, and when he opens his mouth, I smell his breath—foul like he's been feasting on the bodies of his victims. He narrows his eyes, and my skin begins to crawl.

Every part of me wants to run away. But I know I need to finish this.

Sisyphus licks his teeth and smiles. "I know who you are." The melody has vanished from his voice.

He takes a step toward me, and I take a step backward.

"You do?"

Sisyphus nods. "Uh-huh. Even in your disguise. You can't fool me. And I know why you're here."

"Why?" My throat's so dry I can barely squeak it out.

"You're checking in for him. I knew you'd come. Aeacus said you wouldn't. Said he'd be lord forever. And maybe that's your biggest mistake. You never should have come."

He takes another step toward me, but my head shifts at a sound. I look past his broad shoulders and see the boulder rock on its pedestal. Sisyphus hears it, too, and turns, but too late. The boulder moves again, shifting around the rocks underneath it. Sisyphus lunges backward, throwing his arms out, but the momentum can't be stopped. His fingers scrape as the boulder pulls out from underneath his grip. And then it begins to tumble, picking up speed, until it's a blur on the side of the mountain.

"No!" Sisyphus doesn't even look my way a final time. He's off and running so fast, he blends into the mountainside, and I'm left alone on the plateau with the dark castle ahead.

35

Aeacus

When the slick naked form of Sisyphus disappears, I expect to be able to breathe again. But as I face the dark castle, my chest tightens so ferociously, I can't force air into my lungs.

"Come inside."

"Come to us."

"We've missed you."

The voices again. But they aren't in my head this time. They're seeping out of the walls of the castle, as if a chorus of dead souls has been used to form the stones.

I want to turn and run, but I need to go in. Sisyphus said he knew who I was. And I want to know. Need to know. My answers are only footsteps away. I lift my right foot, forcing the knee to bend, and plant it in front of me. Dust lifts from the ground, swirling at my feet and then growing until I'm standing amid a nebula of dead ground. I lift my left leg and plant it ahead of the right. My feet feel like stones. The dust engulfs me. And all my senses are screaming at me to flee.

"Yes. Come closer."

The voices pull at me, and I am a slave to my own curiosity and to their promises.

"We have answers."

"We've missed you."

Overhead, thunder booms, and purple lightning hits a high tower, electrifying it for a moment—outlining it against the stormy orange sky. The castle holds in the electricity as the stones sizzle, unwilling to let it go, but finally the outline of the building disappears, and the tower remains unscathed.

One step at a time, I make my way forward. I'm almost there when a skeleton hand reaches out of the ground. It doesn't grab for me but instead beckons with a long, bony finger. Drawing me forward. Another one comes up beside it, and then another off to the left and closer to the thick doors. All around me, I see the bony hands, palms up, fingers curling inward, making me move. They stay out of my way, and soon I'm at the side of a moat, and a drawbridge slams to the ground.

I jump back but only for a second. Once the dust settles, I set my feet on the wooden planks; my legs tremble under me.

"Never leave us."

"You belong with us."

The voices come from every part of the castle. The stone walls. The wooden drawbridge. The cobblestones up ahead. I close my eyes, trying not to think about Minos and the dead phoenix, and I remind myself—they'll tell me what I want to know. What I need to know. And then I'm out on the cobblestones, and the drawbridge rises behind me.

I stand in the middle of a courtyard with only the smell of death to keep me company. Fountains sit in the four corners, but they're dry and cracked like the fountains in my world aboveground. My feet crunch on the gravel underneath, but when I look, I see it's not gravel at all. It's broken pieces of bones.

I think of Sisyphus. Of his nakedness and of his melodic voice. And then there were his words. *I know who you are.*

"Who am I?"

I don't realize I've said it aloud until I hear the echoes of my whisper all around me.

Who am I? Who am I?

It taunts me as it mixes in with the other voices. It blends into their chorus. I put my hands over my ears to hold out the noise, and then another voice takes over. One that drowns out the rest.

"Come join us. We'll show you."

To the left, a carved wooden door gapes open. Yellow light pours out from inside, and I know I need to go there. I steel myself against my fears and walk across the bones toward it.

I shield my eyes when I walk in, but the door slams, and the blinding yellow light extinguishes. I'm left standing in a room with just enough light from the torches on the walls to see a long wooden table ahead of me and three men seated around it. My eyes move from one to the next, trying to figure out what I've gotten myself into. But before I can take them all in, the man at the head of the table stands up.

He's got a close-cut dark beard, and on top of his thick curly brown hair sits a golden crown covered in gems, which send reflections of color across the table and the room. When he stands, I notice he's holding a golden goblet decorated with gems equaling the ones on his crown.

"I certainly hope Sisyphus didn't scare you." His voice is in my head and in my ears, and he raises the goblet to his lips and takes a long drink, leaving a red stain on the hair of his close moustache.

"He did. He did." The man on the right cackles when he says it. "Look at her eyes. Such pretty eyes. Tasty eyes. One at a time. Savor them." His own eyes cross when he speaks, and his lips are so dry, the skin is cracking.

The man—the king—at the head of the table whirls on the man who's spoken. "Tantalus, we shall not eat our guest. It's not polite."

Tantalus, the man on the right, rubs his hands together. "But look at her neck. Like a pearl. And her breasts." He licks his lips and reaches for a plate of fruit on the table.

I want to turn around and run out the door. I glance over my shoulder but can't see the door anywhere. It's vanished—blended into the stone wall behind me.

The king slams his goblet down on the table, sloshing thick, red liquid over the sides. "Can't you see she's scared, you idiot?"

He raises a hand and points it at the man, and the plate of fruit moves until it's just out of his reach.

Tantalus screams like he's been wounded, and his fingers claw at the table, snapping against the hardness of the wood. There are scratch marks decorating the wooden planks in front of him. I force my eyes away from him and back to the king.

"Please excuse his rudeness, my lady. We don't make a habit of eating our guests," the king says.

The man on the left laughs. It's the first time I look at him, and my breath catches. He's about my age with light brown hair that reaches past his ears, and is muscular and sculpture-worthy. He's clothed in a toga, and when he looks at me, his green eyes sparkle with humor.

"Perhaps Tantalus would make a habit of it if he could eat anything," he says.

The king picks his goblet back up. The wine is back at the top, somehow magically refilled. "May I please introduce myself and welcome you to my kingdom?"

I still don't trust myself to speak, so instead I nod, biting my lip until it hurts. The pain helps stem the fear I feel is about to bubble over.

"I am Aeacus, King of Tartarus." He motions to the right. "You've had the pleasure of meeting Tantalus already."

"And don't forget about me." It's the man on the left talking. The one so good-looking I can almost forget Tartarus is a place for the eternally damned.

Aeacus laughs. "How could anyone forget about you, Pirithous?" Aeacus extends his arms wide. "My lady, may I present the honorable Pirithous to you?"

I force myself to flash a brief smile, barely showing my teeth.

"Oh, her teeth. Her teeth. And what of her tongue? Just one glance of her tongue."

I shut my mouth at Tantalus's words and cross my arms over my stomach, trying to hide as much of myself as I can.

Aeacus motions, and a chair at the end of the table nearest

me slides out, its heavy stone scratching against the hard floor underneath. "Please sit and join us."

I don't want to sit. I want to call for Shayne. I want to go back and hang out with Chloe. I want to be with my mom. To let her comb my hair. But I also want answers, and so, against every nerve in my body, I walk forward and sit in the cold, stone chair.

Once I'm seated, Aeacus sits also. Pirithous pours a goblet full of wine, sliding it down the table to me. I watch his fingers as he pours, noticing how long and powerful they look. Veins pop from his arms as he flexes his muscles. Unsure what to do, I catch the goblet when it reaches me and raise it to my lips.

"Her lips. Must have her lips. So red. Always so red." And Tantalus lunges up, nearly jumping across the table to me. His eyes roll around in his head, and his hand almost reaches my arm. I look down at his skin and notice it's shriveled like a grape left out in the sun.

"Tantalus!" Aeacus's voice booms through the chamber, and Tantalus freezes inches from my arm. His chair grows long tendrils that reach out and grab him, yanking him backward so fast it's like he's disappeared and then rematerialized.

Tantalus begins crying. "Just one taste. One small finger."

I curl my fingers under my palms and look away. The only positive part of this is Aeacus doesn't seem to want to let Tantalus eat me.

"The little flower is scared," Pirithous says, and he reaches over what seems like an impossible distance, and his fingers touch my closed fist, caressing it.

Shock runs down my body, and I look away from him, hoping he doesn't notice. But with the shaking in my body, I have about as much control of myself as a feather in a hurricane.

"My lady." Aeacus straightens his crown. "Why have you honored us with your presence?"

My mouth falls open, revealing my chattering teeth. "I thought you knew."

Aeacus forms a lazy smile on his face. "Of course I know. It is my job to know." And then his eyes harden, and he looks into my soul. "But do you know?"

My stomach flips around, trying to settle, but it won't. I lift the goblet and take another sip of wine. I wait until I swallow to answer. "I want some answers. I want you to tell me who I am."

Aeacus's eyes soften. "Good, my lady. You have come to the right place." He motions, and plates of fruits appear along the table with cheese and crackers scattered in, all out of the reach of Tantalus. Aeacus reaches out with a knife, cuts a thick slab of something that looks like Brie, and lifts it to his mouth on the knife. "Do you know what the penalty for killing a phoenix is?"

A rock forms so fast in my stomach it knocks the wind out of me.

"Ah, I see you do." Aeacus cuts another piece of Brie and holds it out to me on the end of the knife. "Would you like some cheese?"

I shake my head, wondering what I've gotten myself into, but can't find my voice to reply.

"Do you see how white her shoulders are?" It's Tantalus again.

I close my eyes to shut out the noise.

"I could feast on just one shoulder forever."

"Enough!" Aeacus's voice pounds across the room, and Tantalus covers his eyes and cries.

"Life in Tartarus."

At his words, I turn to Pirithous.

"With me. Forever," he adds.

Aeacus laughs, then pulls the knife back, eating the moldy cheese himself. "Yes, Pirithous. Life in Tartarus. With all of us."

I open my mouth, but nothing comes out.

"Our flower is so excited, she's not sure what to say," Pirithous says. His hand is still on my fist, and when I realize this, I pull it away as fast as I can.

And then I manage to find my voice. "I didn't kill a phoenix."

Pirithous's face falls, but Aeacus laughs. "Ah, but somebody did. And a price needs to be paid." He motions around the room.

"And since you've been so kind as to join us, it only makes sense that I extend the invitation to you."

But I shake my head. "I'm not here about a dead bird. I want answers." I can hear the anger building up in my voice; I will not listen to this madness anymore.

Aeacus purses his lips together. "It seems your flower has a temper, Pirithous."

"I am not his flower!"

This only causes Pirithous to laugh, and before I know it, my chair is sliding around the table. My goblet falls out of my hand, spilling in a bright red stain in front of Tantalus. He moves his face down to lick it, but the liquid recedes. And then I'm right next to Pirithous, so close our arms touch.

"Ah, yes, that's what Theseus said also. But I knew my time would come." And Pirithous grabs my hand, pinning it to the table.

I decide I've had enough, but my feet and legs feel like lead. I can't scoot the chair out and get up.

"Your flower wants to leave." Aeacus watches me closely as if wondering what I'm going to do next.

"Share her!" It's a desperate plea from Tantalus.

I'm directly across from him, and I can't take my eyes off his crazy face and cracking lips.

"No!" Pirithous shifts so his arm is around me now. His other hand snakes out to grab mine, and I'm locked in place.

I need to leave.

I have to get out of this hellhole I've managed to get myself into. I need to get back to Shayne, who doesn't even know I'm in Hell in the first place.

I pick my right hand off the table, and put it on the edge to scoot myself back. My heart is pounding so hard, I'm sure all three of these crazy men can hear it. Three crazy criminals, whose crimes were bad enough that they've been sentenced to Tartarus for eternity. But when I push with my hand, my chair won't move.

"Let me go!" I turn to Pirithous. How dare he hold me here?

Pirithous laughs. "I will never lose you again, my flower."

"Let me go now!" I shove his arm off my shoulder and push again, but even with his arm gone, I'm immobile.

And then all three men around me begin to laugh. I look down at my lap, but instead of the normal flesh and clothes I expect, all I see is stone. Cold, hard stone from my waist down. Panic sets in, and I look to Pirithous's chair. His body is the same way. Flesh from the waist up, and solid rock below.

Their laughter pounds in my ears, echoing through my mind, and it won't stop. My throat constricts, and I can't force a scream or even words out. I'm going to end up in Tartarus forever after all. Penance for a phoenix I didn't even kill.

Shayne flashes through my mind. I'm lost to him and to myself. All the protecting my mom has done my whole life, only for me to end up here. As I sink into the madness around me, my vision starts to cloud until all I see is a dark tunnel ahead of me and red on all sides.

36

Retrospection

THE ROOM EXPLODES WITH LIGHT. PIRITHOUS SCREAMS FIRST, and within seconds, my chair is scooting away from the deafening cry. And then the burning begins. Even with the horror I've just witnessed, I have to turn my head at the sight of Pirithous. He's covered in flames, and the smell of burning flesh is so strong, I need to retch. But my legs are still stone. Part of the chair.

Tantalus stands up, as if trying to escape out the now open door. But tendrils from his chair reach out again, and this time, I see they're snakes, hissing and biting him, wrapping around his arms and legs, and forcing him to sit. He's sobbing, but it doesn't help. Fire erupts around him, and through the flames, I see his crossing eyes roving around the room.

"My Lord."

I turn my head to Aeacus. He stands up, ignoring the burning bodies of his two companions. His eyes have grown as wide as golden drachma, and every bit of color has drained from his face.

"How dare you!"

Shayne's voice booms across the room like thunder. The wall to my right explodes, sending rocks flying in all directions. A piece hits me on the arm, slicing into me.

"I was only trying to answer a few—"

But Aeacus doesn't get a chance to finish his sentence. He screams, and the crown on his head begins to melt, gold dripping down his face. A ruby falls into one eye socket and an emerald into the other, and the gold melts and hardens around it, until even his screams can't be heard through the hardening metal. He's clawing at his face, but it's only a mask now. I want to pull my eyes away from him, but with the burning bodies on either side, there's nowhere else to look.

It's only when I feel hands on my shoulders that I snap my head around. And when I see Shayne, I begin to cry.

"It's okay," he whispers. "I'm here."

"I'm so sorry." I sob between every word, and when my tears hit my legs, I realize they are no longer stone but have returned to the soft human flesh from before. "I'm so sorry."

"Shhhh . . ." He pulls me into an embrace and holds me. "There's nothing to be sorry for."

"I wanted answers."

"It's okay." Shayne rubs the back of my head. "I understand."

I'm not sure how we get out of Tartarus. All I know is that one minute I'm amid the muffled screams of Aeacus and the burning flesh of Pirithous and Tantalus, and the next minute I'm on a boat, crossing the flaming River Phlegethon. And Shayne is by my side, holding me the entire time. I can't stop my tears.

When I get off the boat, my legs are shaking so fiercely, I fall to the hot sand. Shayne picks me up, carrying me down the tunnel to his home.

The fire is burning when we get there, and Shayne sets me down in front of it. I prop myself up against a chair and take the glass of wine he offers me and watch as it shakes in my hand, threatening to spill. Cerberus comes over and licks my free hand until I scratch him behind a set of his ears. Shayne sits down across from me, and Cerberus moves away, closer to the fire.

"So you decided to come visit?"

I am such an idiot. Shayne knows this, and I know it. "How—?"

But Shayne gives a weak smile before I can finish. "Charon told me. If I can't count on Charon, then I may as well pack it up and move out of here completely."

"You knew the whole time?"

Shayne takes a sip of his wine, licking his lips afterward to get the final drops off. "I was in Asphodel." His face hardens. "And almost too late."

I shudder. "Tartarus is a horrible place."

Shayne nods. "The worst of any world. Why do you think I didn't take you there?"

I look down, playing with the crimson stem of my wineglass, trying to calm my tremors. "I thought you were keeping the truth from me."

Shayne sighs, and then moves over until he's sitting next to me. "You're shaking." And he puts his arms around me.

I remember Pirithous's arm and shake even harder. "They're horrible men."

I feel Shayne nod his head. His hair is so close, it brushes on my cheek. "They were horrible men while alive, and now they pay for it with torment for eternity."

"They tricked me." I feel the overwhelming need to defend myself against my stupidity.

"Of course they did. You can never trust the souls of the damned."

I shake my head and try to stop the tears threatening to flow from behind my lids. "I wanted to believe them."

Shayne turns to me, taking the glass from my hand and setting it on the ground. He reaches out until we're face-to-face, holding hands. His presence holds back my tears for the time being. "Did you get any answers?" he finally asks.

There it is. Hard in my chest. The sad truth. "Nothing. I didn't learn anything."

But Shayne doesn't take his eyes off me. They bore into mine and flash red. I can't look away.

"Who am I?" he asks.

"Shayne. Hades. Lord of the Underworld. We've been down that path," I say.

His eyes don't falter. "Who are you?"

I sigh in frustration and move to get up, but his hands hold me in place. His mouth is so close to me, I feel the heat from his breath on my cheek.

"Who are you?"

I squeeze my eyes closed, trying to focus on his words. Everyone in Hell seems to know who I am. Shayne knows. Reese knows. Even naked Sisyphus knows. But I don't.

"Think. It's important. Who are you?"

He moves close, and a vein in his neck throbs. He waiting for an answer I don't have. For eighteen years, I haven't even known who I am.

Then, in my mind, I see my mysterious birthday present. The jar with the red feather. And Tanni's voice rings in my head, but not with the haunting words of doom she's spoken to me in the past. I see her soulless eyes filled with fog. Like she's here in the room with us, but only in my mind.

Open the jar. Free yourself.

I remember opening the jar, finding the feather inside. The swirl of Greek letters. The wave of emotions that flew through me. I relax and give myself over to the secrets once contained in the jar, and the truth takes shape in my mind.

I open my eyes, and see Shayne's gaze has shifted from determination to hope. He's trying to draw the word from my mouth.

"I'm Persephone," I say.

It comes out solid. All at once.

I am Persephone.

37

Confusion

PERSEPHONE.

It's a name I know.

I play the sounds over in my mind. Four syllables. Melodic. Exotic.

Shayne leans forward and kisses me, soft at first, but I don't want to be hesitant. Being with him fills a piece of me that's been missing for the last eighteen years. I'm never going to let it go again.

He runs his hands down my back, through my hair. "You have no idea how much I've missed you," he says.

I don't get the chance to respond because he kisses me again. I return his kisses and pull him close and melt into him until we feel like one person. For the first time in my life, I am complete.

Between kisses, Shayne keeps finding excuses to use my name.

"Do you want more wine, Persephone?"

"No, I'm okay."

He nibbles at my ear. It feels incredible. "Something to eat, Persephone?"

I shake my head.

"Are you cold, Persephone?"

That is it. His arms are wrapped around me and flames roar in the fireplace; he knows I'm not cold.

I turn to face him. "You're just trying to say it."

Shayne cocks his head. "Say what?"

I punch him lightly. "The name."

Shayne acts as if he's gotten the punch line to a joke. "Oh . . . Persephone." He smiles. "I just haven't used it in a long time."

The problem is that knowing my real name has only made me more confused. "So I'm the Queen of the Underworld."

"Next to my side." Shayne's breath is on my shoulder. He leans into me and kisses my neck, sending a ripple of chills through me once again. God, I love that.

I recover and look around the room, remembering how much I like it. "And I designed this room?"

Shayne nods. "I told you it was designed by someone with great taste."

"And so, we're . . . married?" It's weird even to say.

"Hmm . . . well . . . kind of."

I narrow my eyes. "What do you mean . . . kind of?"

"Think about it."

"I'm trying not to. It's making my head hurt." Because how can I be Persephone when I've been Piper my entire life?

"Maybe we can figure it out together." Shayne pulls me up onto the sofa; we're never more than inches apart. Cerberus pads over and puts a head on each of us, begging for a bit of attention. "See, Cerberus remembers you."

I smile at Cerberus. "And I remember him. Though I'm not sure how."

"So what do you remember?" Shayne asks.

I sink back into the red leather and force myself to think. "I remember growing up. For the last eighteen years. As Piper."

"And what else?" He's hoping for something more. "Do you remember when we met?"

I sigh. "I don't know. I remember parts of being Persephone. Parts of this world. But it's like it was another life. A piece of my past but not a piece of Piper."

AN IMAGE FROM AGES AGO PLAYS THERE BEFORE MY EYES LIKE a movie on the tube. Of a mountain and a hidden area away from my mom. Even back then, she never wanted me to leave her. She thought I should stay by her side always. Earth was warm then, too, but my mom controlled the seasons. Winters were cold, and summers bright. But there were no extremes. No global warming. Plants prospered and flourished and flowered and bloomed. And I infused life into them just by my mere presence.

My mom tried to trust me. She let me venture out into the wide-open spaces. And maybe I felt oppressed then, too, because I left her every chance I got. I had friends who met me and helped me sneak away. I had other gods vying for my attention. And though I toyed around with the idea of one day picking someone to spend my life with, no one drew my interest. Not Hermes and not Hephaestus and not Ares. Though Ares was always the most persistent.

That morning my mom told me she would be spending the day traveling the earth in Apollo's chariot. As the goddess of all living plants, my mom had responsibilities way bigger than most of the other immortals. And so she left, and I met my friends in the meadow.

"Have you heard the rumors?" Peisinoe said.

"What rumors?" Aglaope asked.

I leaned forward, wanting to catch their excitement. After all, it wasn't every day my mom left me alone for so long.

"The Underworld is leaking into our Earth," Peisinoe said.

"Leaking?" I asked.

Peisinoe moved her head forward so all four of our heads nearly touched. "They say monsters are coming out into the world."

Thelxiepeia put her hand to her mouth. "Monsters!"

Gods, she was always such a drama queen.

Peisinoe nodded. "Through the caves around Mount Othrys. They're coming out into our world. The gods are all trying to control them."

I covered my mouth. "My mom should know. She's out there."

Aglaope looked over at me. "Persephone, that's what your mom is doing today. She's checking to see if the rumors are true."

Aglaope had taken every opportunity possible to make me feel stupid. Of the three, Peisinoe was my only true friend.

I shook my head. "She's just on a random patrol." But the idea made sense. Monsters escaping might be momentous enough for my mom to leave me alone.

Aglaope tossed her hair over her shoulder. "You are so naïve, Persephone."

"I am not," I said, even though I knew it was true. But with my mom controlling my every step, how could I not be? "What caves, anyway?"

And Peisinoe told me.

I waited until they left; I made an excuse about needing to help some dogwood trees blossom. And then I started walking. Maybe I was naïve. And overprotected. And if so, then what better way to begin my escape from that shell than to see exactly where these monsters were coming from anyway? Maybe I could help stop them. I could become more than just some girl who helped plants bloom.

It had taken over an hour to get to the caves. Not only was it through scrub and rocks, but it was halfway up a hill and hidden behind a couple boulders. In fact, I almost gave up on finding it entirely, but then I felt the waves of heat. And I followed them until I found the mouth of the cave.

It took a bit of convincing myself, but I finally summoned the courage to go inside. I took one step and then another and entered the blackness.

"Haven't you heard the rumors? There are monsters around."

I turned at the sound of the voice even though it was too dark to see.

"I'm not scared of monsters," I said, though my heart went into overdrive.

He laughed. "Really? Then why is your voice shaking?"

Deep breath. Whatever I'd gotten myself into here, I was a goddess. I could handle anything thrown my way. "I'm just cold," I lied.

"Maybe you should come closer then."

"Maybe you should keep better control of the Underworld," I said. Even though I'd never met him, I knew this could only be Hades. My mom had told me all about him. About how he kidnapped small children and sacrificed stray animals and drank blood from a hollowed-out skull every night for dinner.

"I'm in perfect control of the Underworld," Hades said. "I'm always in control." He stepped out from the shadows just enough that I could barely see him. But instead of the scary images my mom had always conjured up for me about how Hades was a monster himself, complete with eyes made of flames and breath like acid, I saw the most amazing thing. Hades was completely gorgeous. And sexy. And looking right at me.

My stomach flipped. "So why are monsters getting out then?" I asked, trying desperately to keep my voice even. Why had my mom lied about what Hades looked like? Could she be wrong about the things he did, too?

He stepped closer, and even though he looked completely in control of the situation, for a second, his face shifted just enough for me to see that he was nearly as nervous as I was.

"Because I wanted to distract your mom," Hades said.

"Why?" My voice was barely a whisper.

He took another step toward me. He lowered his voice, and the edge of confidence vanished. "Because I wanted to meet you," he said.

And in the biggest moment of rebellion in my life, I closed the distance between us.

Now, BACK IN HIS HOME, I RUN A HAND THROUGH SHAYNE'S inky hair, remembering it was longer when we first met. But otherwise, he looks exactly the same. Immortal. Gorgeous. Perfect.

"You let monsters out so you could meet me."

Shayne doesn't look the least bit guilty. "Your mom never let you out of her sight. I had to try something."

I remember how flattered I felt. Like I was the most special person in the world. He made me feel that way every single day.

"My mom was furious when she found out."

Shayne laughs. "And nothing ever changes, does it."

Things had only gotten worse. "She started the rumor," I say. "She said you kidnapped and raped me."

"And she turned your friends into Sirens," Shayne says. "They never got over that."

They hated me afterward, even Peisinoe, spinning the kidnap and rape story out of control. Everyone believed it.

I shake my head, remembering my mom's ensuing wrath. The barrenness of the earth for months at a time. The droughts. The ice storms that froze the earth over. That she knew I wanted to be with Hades made her actions all the more extreme.

"My mom never changes," I say. "But I still don't get how I'm Persephone and Piper."

"And I don't either. All I know is that your identity was cursed. If I told you who you really were, we'd have both ended up in Tartarus. You had to remember on your own."

Which is why Shayne refused to tell me. "But who cursed it?" I ask. And how is it tied to the ceramic jar?

Shayne takes a sip of wine. "That's a great question."

"How do I find out?" I ask.

Shayne sets his glass down on the end table and reaches to pet Cerberus again. "I'd start with your mother or father."

My memories are coming back, filling in the gaps. "My mother is Demeter."

Shayne nods. "Who still hates me, I might add."

"Let her," I say. I'd much rather spend eternity with Shayne than with my mom. I felt that way from the minute I met Hades so long ago, and it had driven my mom crazy.

Shayne nods, and his eyes flicker red amid the brown. "I will. And how about your father?"

"My father." I can't say it. I think of the man from the barbeque dinner. The man whose face looked so much like my own. It's too much. Too hard to believe.

So Shayne says it for me. "Zeus. King of the gods."

I work my mind around this fact. My father is the king of the gods. Not the king of Earth or the sea or even of the Underworld like Shayne. He is the king of all other kings. The ruler of everyone and everything. And I am his daughter. Every god on earth should bend toward his will—with *should* being the operative word here.

As memories flow back to me, I remember plenty of times when gods defied him. I remember plenty of times when I defied him. But I also remember talking endlessly with him over a campfire or by a mountain lake or in the dense trees of a jungle. My father never told me what to do and when to do it. He gave me advice and let me make my own decisions, so unlike my mom and her domination. She controlled everything from the number of ears of corn a stalk might sprout to how long I could spend in the gardens away from her each day. If nothing has changed with my mom, I'm willing to bet nothing has changed with my father either.

"He made up the thing about the pomegranate," I say, remembering the story my father told my mom after one of my visits to the Underworld.

Shayne grins. "Definitely a victory for us."

Zeus lied. That was all there was to it. He made up the whole superstition that food couldn't be eaten in the Underworld. And that if it was, the person who'd eaten it could never leave again. He told my mom I'd eaten six pomegranate seeds and had to stay in the Underworld one month out of the year for each seed I'd eaten. That she should be thankful I could return at all. That he was doing her a favor.

My mom was livid. She threw Earth into the coldest winter it had seen since the Ice Age. And my mom couldn't set foot in the Underworld, so Zeus never had to worry about her finding out the truth. I married Hades, and we lived together for half of each year in bliss, while my mom tormented the world above.

"Did she ever find out the truth?" I ask.

Shayne finishes off the rest of his wine. "I can't imagine who would have ever told her any differently. And she did let you keep coming."

She did. Even though it pained her each and every time. She adored me all spring and summer and then mourned me when I left. And I endured her all spring and summer, losing myself in the plants and flowers on Earth, and then, even though I loved her, I rejoiced when I departed.

"They'll have answers," I say.

Shayne smiles, but there's a hint of sadness in his dark eyes. "They should. All I know is you've been gone from Hell for eighteen years now, and all of the Underworld is suffering as a result."

My suspicions are confirmed. "Because of me."

Shayne pushes some of my out-of-control hair behind my ear. "Yeah, because we missed you." And his lips find mine again.

We walk back to the River Acheron, and it's as if lenses have been lifted, making a world where I feel comfortable turn into a world where I belong. The Underworld is as much a part of me as Shayne is. Love for it is rooted in all parts of my body. I ache when I think of all the time I've spent away. Time in which monsters have grown strong and boundaries have weakened.

When we reach the banks of the river, Charon's face breaks into a smile. I run over and hug him, never wanting to let him go. He's been my friend since the first time Hades brought me down here, thousands of years ago. He talked to me when Hades was gone. He listened to me blather on about anything, only stopping me when souls demanded his attention. He treated me like a part of Hell even before I was.

"I've missed you so much," I say. Charon has been like a father to me. I love him as sure as I'm Persephone.

When we pull apart, tears run down his face, and his already milky eyes seem translucent. "And I've missed you, my Queen." He seems to have a hard time getting the words out, and before I can think, he's hugging me again like he wants to make sure I won't vanish.

My Queen. I was Queen of the Underworld.

I remember walking the fields of Elysium and the meadows of Asphodel, maintaining order and keeping control. And I even remember Tartarus. Delivering punishment to those damned. I think of Sisyphus and Tantalus and Pirithous. Punishment is deserved for evil like theirs.

Tantalus cut up his own son and served him in soup to the gods—to my own mother who actually ate it, which explains her aversion to meat.

Pirithous tried to steal me from the Underworld to make me his bride.

Sisyphus carved up travelers and guests for pleasure, keeping them alive as long as possible to prolong their suffering.

They deserved their fates in Tartarus. And I was happy to ensure their eternal torment. I delivered their sentences with pleasure.

Charon gives my hand a final squeeze and then takes us across the river. I look to the bubbling sorrows, and realize I can see faces with them now, not just hear words. I see Randy Conner's face with his sadness. I see deaths and miseries and longings, all left behind. But the sorrows don't tug on me as before. I dip my hand toward the water, confident the monsters won't harm me, letting them come to me and trying to offer calmness in return. And when my hand touches the water, the monsters disperse, and the mad, frenzied bubbling of the sorrows stops. Within seconds, the River Acheron is calm.

Shayne and Charon both stare at me.

"The water hasn't been calm in eighteen years, Piper."

I smile at my name, and Shayne starts laughing.

He puts up his hands in compromise. "I'll call you whatever you want." And then he motions back out to the water. We bump into the dock, the boat causing the only ripples on the now smooth surface. "Just remember, we need you down here. I need you down here."

When we step out, he holds me, and I never want to leave. "I want to be here. Forever."

Shayne laughs. "And this is the root of the whole problem. It always has been."

I pull back and look at him. "What do you mean?"

Shayne rolls his eyes. "Talk to your parents. But just promise me one thing."

I nod. I'd promise Shayne anything. "What?"

"Promise me you'll come back."

It's my turn to laugh. "Promise you'll take me."

Shayne smiles and gives me a kiss. And then I'm moving through the earth and the silver divide, rising up from Hell back to the Botanical Haven above.

38

Awake

I check the clock on my FON; it's Sunday afternoon.
While it felt like an eternity in the Underworld, it's only been
about twelve hours of real time. And aside from me, the Botanical Haven is empty; my mom isn't home.

My parents are gods. I am a god.

I look at the plants in the Botanical Haven around me and
realize, from the changes in weather we've been having and a
weekend of neglect, half are on the verge of dying. A raw humidity presses in from all sides; the glass is so wet with condensation,
I can't see out. At the sink in the back, I fill a glass of water for
myself, drinking the whole thing and refilling it before turning
to the plants. They need moisture, so I throw open some windows. I notice dark clouds hanging in the west over the Hill
Country, but they aren't moving. They stay still like a threat that
could descend on Austin in a second.

The heat pumps in through the windows, and I'm moved by
the powers inside me. Around me, life returns to everything.
Leaves grow, and flowers bloom. I change them with a mere
thought. Pinks become blues. Yellows become reds. Life blossoms
and flourishes, limbs grow to the ceiling, and roots dig out of
pots and reach for the floor. The Botanical Haven is a thing
alive and under my control. It flexes and bends to my will. I grow
vines around the railings and hang flowers from the rafters. Fruit
blossoms and then bursts into being on orange and cherry and
avocado trees. Vines produce tomatoes and kumquats and black

grapes. It's a power I've always had though I've never known how to harness it like this.

A knock on the door shakes me from my zone. My mind immediately flies to Reese, coming to visit again. Knowing my mom isn't home somehow. He knows I'm Persephone. He's been waiting for me to find out. He's been courting me forever, since even before I knew Shayne. And of all the gods who'd pursued me before Shayne, Ares never gave up. Once I made my decision, Hermes and Hephaestus and Apollo acquiesced and recognized me as Queen of the Underworld. But Ares remained unwavering. Biding his time. Always nearby.

I glance around a tall tree and look through the glass. But I don't see Reese. I see Chloe. I rush to the door, unlock it, and throw it open. Chloe's standing there with her arms wrapped around herself, shivering even though sweat beads down her face and arms. The humidity's so thick, the air around her seems hazy.

"Chloe!"

She doesn't move. I grab her and try to pull her in, and she finally lets me. I take her upstairs, drape a blanket across her bare arms even though it's well over a hundred, and start some coffee brewing. It's only when she's sitting there at the table that she finally seems to realize where she is.

"Piper."

I fill a cup of steaming coffee and slide it over to her. "You're shaking."

Chloe nods. "My body can't seem to keep up with the temperature changes."

My mind can't seem to keep up with anything. "It's like autumn is coming," I say.

I try to think of something to keep the conversation going. Having Chloe here with me soothes something deep inside me. Like everything else about my life is off but Chloe is still the same. She's just been freaked out recently; that's all. She's getting better.

"If autumn is coming, that'll blow a lot of scientists' global warming theories right out of the water."

"My mom says people used to play in the snow," Chloe says. "They skated and made angels."

I think of the frozen River Cocytus, of doing just that. "It sounds like fun, Chloe. Maybe if we went far enough north—"

Chloe smoothes the top of her bandana. "You think there's still snow anywhere?"

I want to tell her about kissing Shayne on the snowy banks of the river. I want to tell her about blowing icy breath. And trees with icicles. And a glacier beyond the ocean. I want to tell Chloe everything. "I'm sure there is. I think there are winter wonderlands just waiting for us."

She pats my hands. "That sounds so nice, Piper. Like paradise."

"Yeah," I say. "Just like paradise." I'm trying to find a way to start. To explain the oddities which have become my life.

But Chloe doesn't give me the chance. Instead, she looks at her arm. "My tattoo keeps changing."

I'm looking at it, too. Pure black. Ebony. And with my new memories, I clearly read it. It spells *fate*.

"It's probably just the light," I say.

Chloe's holding her coffee cup with both hands, but she hasn't taken a sip. I pick up mine and put my lips to it, hoping she'll take my lead and do the same. But she sits there unmoving, her eyes still fixed on her arm.

"Did you know Hannah Reed is pregnant?"

So Chloe's heard about the classroom incident also. I'm sure it's all over the school by now. "Yeah, I was there when she told everyone."

"Do you think she'll keep the baby?"

I try to grasp what Chloe is saying. "Yeah, I think she'll keep it. She misses Randy a lot."

Chloe nods and finally takes her eyes off her arm and looks me directly in the face. "Randy misses her, too. I asked him about the baby." She sets the coffee mug down in front of her.

I hold my breath. Chloe's been talking to Randy Conner again from the dead. But Randy is in Asphodel; he shouldn't have any memories of who he is.

"He wants me to tell Hannah to keep the baby." And then Chloe's hand flies out like lightning and grabs mine. "But what if she doesn't listen?"

I don't look down, but her grip is icy. "You can't control other people, Chloe. You can't make her keep it."

Her clutch loosens. "Do you think the baby would go to Hell? Do you think Hannah would go to Hell?"

I pry my wrist out of her hand, and she hardly seems to notice. I don't want to think about Hannah or her baby. I want to stop this conversation now and get back to Chloe. To me. To us. "Hannah will keep the baby."

Please, Hannah, keep the baby. Because I don't want Shayne to have to judge something so small and innocent, the way I used to help him judge all souls that came to the Underworld so long ago. He's had to judge alone for the last eighteen years. He's had no one to share the burden with.

This seems to be good enough for Chloe. "Randy asked me to do something for him."

I hold my breath. "Something like what?"

Chloe picks up her coffee. Finally. She takes a long sip, the steam pouring out around her lips. "He asked me to kill his father."

I'm right to hold my breath. I'm afraid to move. I wish I could snap my fingers and make this whole encounter go away. Make Chloe normal again. I think I should have let her die by the creek.

"So I did."

"No, Chloe, you didn't."

"Yeah, I did." She says it as calmly as if she's telling me about a lecture she fell asleep in. Like she couldn't care less.

"No." I breathe it out. Chloe can't be a murderer. I know what happens to murderers in Hell. Not that Randy's father wouldn't deserve death. If he did make it to the Underworld, I'd place him in the chamber with Aeacus and Tantalus and Pirithous. I'd strip the skin from his body and then set him to burn for eternity. I'd feed his eyes to Tantalus and cut his hands off so he could never hit anyone again. And I'd visit him every week to make sure things hadn't become too bearable for him.

"Yes," Chloe says.

I shake my head. "Please tell me you're lying, Chloe. Please. Just tell me you're lying." Persephone passes judgment on murderers. I know what will happen. I have designed those punishments myself.

Chloe laughs. "Don't worry. No one will ever know."

I'll know. And that's worse than anyone else.

"You didn't do it."

But Chloe nods, and whether she did or didn't, she believes she did which is almost as bad. "Randy asked me to. He told me how to do it. It's why I'm still here, Piper."

"What do you mean, why you're still here?" Her words are like crazy words spinning around in my head. How can everything have changed so much in such a short time?

Chloe shrugs. "It's why I didn't die. I needed to do this. It's why Thanatos didn't take me."

She says the name Thanatos, assuming I know who she's talking about. I do. He's the winged man who collects souls and brings them to the banks of the River Acheron. But I pretend I don't know. "Who?"

"Death. I saw him there. That day by the creek. But he left me, and I knew there was a reason. And killing Randy's father was the reason. Don't you see that, Piper? God, it makes such sense now."

She saw Death, but she acted like she didn't? Or did she only remember him afterward?

"I think you need some sleep, Chloe."

Chloe sets down her coffee cup, now halfway empty and still steaming. "Yeah. You're right." She stands up and heads for the stairs, leaving me there at the table. "But I just thought you'd want to know."

I watch her leave. I do want to know. And I don't want to know. And I know whatever else I do in life, I cannot let Chloe end up with an eternity in Tartarus because of my selfishness. No matter what.

39

Choices

THE MORE I THINK ABOUT CHLOE, THE MORE CERTAIN I AM she didn't do it. She did not kill Randy Conner's father. He may be an abusive monster and deserve to die a slow, painful death and suffer an eternity in Tartarus, but Chloe did not kill him.

It turns out I am wrong—partly. When I get to school Monday morning, the word is out. Randy's father is dead. One of the terrorist groups made good on its threat. They planted a bomb under the steel struts of Gamma Dome and then blew it up. Hundreds of people died in the explosion and in the fires that came afterward, and Randy's father had been one of them. And now they're threatening to blow up more if the city doesn't dismantle all the disperser missiles.

It was a terrorist casualty. Chloe could not have been responsible.

The humidity from the day before has doubled, and smoke from the fires mixes with it. It feels like we're living in a giant brick oven. It feels like every bit of rain that poured down during the hurricane has lifted into the air and hangs there smothering the city of Austin. Normally, I'd text my mom to see what the city council plans to do in response to the terrorist threat, but today is not a normal day, and my life is far from normal.

I head to first period, trying to do the things I'm expected to do, but how can I when everything has changed? I'm not even the person I thought I was. My life to this point has been a fabrication.

The tube is already on when I get to class. That kid from our school is being interviewed, the sophomore who claimed he could predict when the next heat bubble was coming. He's sitting by a table with a giant piece of equipment on it that looks like some kind of satellite dish connected to a coffeemaker. I have to wonder where he got the materials to make it.

The camera zooms out, and I recognize the city council chambers. My mom is pointedly absent.

The second I spot Councilman Rendon, I recognize him as Polemos, one of the minor war gods. He was always trying to claw his way into the good graces of Ares, like a leech looking for blood. I can't believe I didn't recognize him before. It's so clear to me now. And here he is now in my city still trying to cause conflict.

"So what you're saying is that you were approached by one of these terrorist organizations?" Councilman Rendon asks the kid.

The kid, whose name, Toby Garcia, flashes below him on the screen, nods. "That's right. They came to my house Friday night when everyone was sleeping. They grabbed me from my bed and started asking me all sorts of questions."

"What kind of questions?" Rendon asks.

Toby pats the equipment beside him. "Well, they wanted to know all about the HB Predictor."

The words *Heat Bubble Predictor* flash on the screen.

Rendon nods to encourage him to continue.

"So I told them about it. Told them how it can predict the bubbles."

"But it didn't work this week, did it?" Rendon asks, and the way he enunciates it, it's like he's happy the HB Predictor is flawed.

"Something else happened," Toby says. "Something happened to change the weather. Because a bubble was coming; I guarantee it."

Rendon looks down at his notes and nods. "Yes. Fine. So tell us, after that what happened?"

"They told me they wanted me to work for them. They wanted

me to predict the bubbles so they could cause malfunctions when the bubbles were coming."

This just feels off. Terrorist groups normally do the things they do because they think it will help their cause, even if it normally ends up happening in a destructive sort of way. I glance around the council chamber again and wonder where my mom is. Why isn't she watching this, too?

"What did you tell them?" Rendon says.

Toby Garcia looks directly in the cameras, and not an inch of fear shows in his eyes. "I told them to get screwed. That I'd never help their psycho organization."

When the show cuts to commercial, I get a bathroom pass and leave. I can't take it anymore. All people are going to do is talk about the terrorist attack. I need answers. My mom's not home, but I don't want to hear her lies anyway. Our relationship is built on lies. My blood boils when I think of her. What I need is to find my dad.

I walk out to the breezeway, and when the heat and smoke hit me, I embrace them, letting them soak into me. The heat of the Earth is not enough to bother me. I've dared the fires of the River Phlegethon and the torments of Tartarus. But it's still laughable. I don't know who I am. How can Piper be Persephone?

I head to the concrete bleachers around the soccer field, and even though there's plenty of shade covering them, I find a spot out in the sun. It burns my legs when I sit, but I force myself to tolerate it. Down on the field, there's a man in a baseball cap spreading chalk on the fake grass. Mr. Kaiser's talked about how fields used to be made from real grass before the Global Heating Crisis, but now they'd never waste water for such an unnecessary purpose.

The man moves in a line, heading away from me. He reaches the end, then turns around and heads back, a few yards over. When he's almost done with the line, he looks up at me as if he knows I've been watching. And then he waves.

My father. He's heard me asking for him even though I haven't uttered a word. I wave back, unsure if I should go meet him or wait here.

But he puts up his hand. "I'll be right up. Just give me a second to finish this line." His words find their way to me even though he's far away.

I've given him eighteen years; another minute or two shouldn't matter. So I nod in acknowledgment and rest my elbows on my knees to wait.

Zeus finishes the line, and then the chalk canister disappears into thin air. He looks at me and smiles and then climbs the bleachers to sit by me.

"Talk about humidity . . ."

It's the second time we've spoken, and again he starts the conversation by talking about the weather. I want to begin it by talking about me. "Who am I, Dad?"

He smiles. "You're my daughter, Persephone." He grins at me, and it's so infectious, I want to join in with him. But I resist the urge, instead holding my face as impassive as I possibly can.

"Yes, I've managed to figure out that much on my own."

"So what do you need me for?"

"To tell me the rest. To tell me what I don't know," I say.

"Like . . . ?"

"Like who is Piper?" It's an obvious question, but there's been no obvious answer I can figure out.

"You haven't talked to your mom yet?" Zeus asks.

"My mom's been gone all weekend. I thought she might be with you." A spark of worry creeps inside me.

"About that," he says. "The assembly of gods found out she's had you hidden, and they brought her in for questioning. Lots of gods are unhappy about the last eighteen years. Of course, just as many don't care. They love the impending war. They crave the coming change."

"Like Councilman Rendon," I say, referring to the god I now recognize as Polemos.

"Smart girl," my dad says. "There are immortals like Polemos all over the Earth, taking advantage of the situation, looking for ways to gain control."

"And you're letting them?" I ask.

Zeus feigns shock. "You might have forgotten, but I'm patient. And always planning."

I, apparently, have not inherited the patience gene. "When will my mom be back?" I ask, not sure what answer I want.

"Soon," Zeus says. "But right now it's just you and me."

"And by me, do you mean Persephone or Piper?"

Zeus takes off his baseball cap and holds it in his hands. His skin is tanned to a perfect shade of gold contrasting against his platinum hair. "How about both?"

I nod. "That's a good place to start."

"You are Persephone."

"Fine. But I remember the last eighteen years of my life as Piper."

"That's because eighteen years ago, your mother did the unspeakable."

I know what he's talking about as soon as he says it. "She killed a phoenix." But I'm still not sure how it relates to me.

Zeus nods. "She sacrificed a phoenix. When Hermes brought you back from the Underworld, she sacrificed a phoenix, and you were reborn as Piper. A brand-new baby from the ashes of Persephone and the bird itself. It's a horrible sin, but one containing the power of rebirth. The bird died, and Persephone died—for a time. But then she came back. As you."

The blood drains from my face. I know I'm staring at him, but I can't get my mind around what he's saying. My tattoo. Sacrifice. My mother killed a phoenix.

And my mother killed me.

My mother is the one who belongs in Tartarus.

It can't be real.

"What's going to happen to her? Will she go to Tartarus?" I now know the price for killing a phoenix.

"She should."

"Will she?" Even with what she's done and how she's been the most overprotective, overbearing mother in the whole world, I can't stand the thought of her in that horrible place.

Zeus puts up his hands in defeat. "The assembly's split on it currently. There are some who would love nothing more than to strip her rank and cast her into Tartarus."

"But not everyone?"

"Not everyone. There are others who recognize that what she did, she did for love."

"What happened after she killed the phoenix?" I ask.

"She hid you from us. Locked your identity away inside a jar crafted by Hephaestus himself."

A jar . . . like the one I received on my birthday.

Zeus continues. "It wasn't until the first equinox came and you didn't show up in the Underworld that I realized what she did. Nobody did. But by then it was way too late. You were gone."

I blow out a breath slowly, trying to calm my voice and keep it from shaking. "I never went back, did I?"

"No." Zeus looks up at the sun which is moving behind a cloud. "And autumn never came. Nor did winter."

The pieces of the truth move together and take shape. "The Global Heating Crisis is entirely because of me?" It doesn't even sound real.

But Zeus looks at me and chuckles. "Well, of course. If you never go away, then your mother has no reason to make Earth change seasons. It's year-round summer as far as she's concerned." He wipes his forehead. "And a year-round sauna for everyone else."

"So you're saying if I go back to the Underworld, fall and winter will come?" Could it really be that easy?

"Things are pretty out of whack right now," he says. "It's going to take some time. And just to make it clear, you don't have to go back to the Underworld. You just have to reside in the domain of another god where your mom can't get to you."

The domain of another god. "Like when I went to visit Shayne?"

Zeus nods. "Exactly. But you don't have to stay with Hades. In fact, the earth would probably be much better off if you didn't."

I narrow my eyes. "What do you mean? I love Shayne."

Zeus rolls his eyes. "Don't overrate love. You have choices."

"What choices?"

He tries to act like he's considering this, but I know nothing he's saying is unplanned. "Well, how about Ares for starters?"

"Reese?"

"Yeah. He's been pining for you since day one. I figured with the arguments he and Hades used to have, we'd be looking at another world war."

With Ares vying for the Underworld and the Global Heating Crisis in full swing, it seems the next world war is imminent.

"He's a little on the pushy side." And I realize so, too, is Zeus, king of the gods.

"But he thinks you're gorgeous. Not to mention, he's loved you as long as Hades."

Ares was pushy ages ago. And Ares is pushy now. Not much has changed.

"You want me to be with Ares," I say. "Why?"

"I just want you to keep your options open," Zeus says. "You have a new life and new choices. Don't feel like you have to make the same ones as before."

"I'm not interested in Reese," I say to make sure he's clear on it. Or maybe to make myself clear on it.

Zeus pretends to think some more. "I guess there's always Hermes. Or Apollo. Or . . ."

"Why don't you want me to be with Shayne?" To me, Shayne seems like the obvious answer.

Zeus leans back, and resignation covers his face. "Tell me about the world, Piper."

"It's hot," I say, annoyed that he's toying around with my mind.

"Right. It's hot. It's hot because of the Global Heating Crisis. We all know that. But what else can you tell me about it?"

It's obvious he's trying to make some kind of point, so I go with it. "Okay. Fine. The coastlines have receded. Plants have trouble living . . ."

Zeus puts his hand on my shoulder to stop me. "Go deeper."

And so I close my eyes and go deeper. I try to put global warming aside and focus on all the other problems. Crime is out of control, and disease runs rampant because of overcrowding in the cities. Terrorist groups blow up city domes and recycling plants and food storage facilities. And then there's the war. With all the fighting breaking out everywhere, the earth is on the brink of the next world war.

"Oh," I say.

Zeus nods. "Yeah. Oh. If global war comes, everyone on Earth could die. And as things are now, I'm not willing to stand by and let that happen."

"But what does that have to do with me?" I ask. I figure my part in this whole mess has to do with the climate. I can't do anything about the wars.

Zeus runs a hand through his hair. He's staring out at the freshly chalked turf. "Piper, do you remember how Hades used to be?"

"Of course," I say. "Just like he is now." I leave out the gushy descriptors because they aren't for my dad's ears.

"No," he says. "Before you two were together. You never knew him then, did you?"

I shake my head. The first time I met Hades had been in that cave so long ago.

"Hades was angry. And unjust. And the Underworld was a place to be feared. Other gods were scared to visit, and each year that passed, things only got worse."

"He was never like that," I say. My dad must be mistaken.

"He was. Until he met you."

"I don't believe you," I say.

Zeus only continues. "He changed. Everything changed. You brought to Hades the power of freshness and life. You calmed his anger and helped him understand how to judge fairly. You made paradise what it is today. Without you, the good parts of the Underworld may never have survived. Why do you think I spun the whole rumor that let you stay there? I needed to do something to keep you down there. But now it's not the Underworld that needs you. It's this world. It's Ares. He needs you. Your light. Your life. If he doesn't change, war will erupt on a massive scale, and this world will be destroyed."

I shake my head, but I'm not sure how to respond. What he's saying can't be true. I had no power over Shayne. And I wouldn't have any over Reese either.

"But I love Shayne," I say. "And I loved being the Queen of the Underworld."

Zeus looks me right in the eyes. "I'm not going to tell you what to do, and I'm not going to force you into anything. All I ask is that you think about your choices."

Choices. When have I ever had choices? Had I had them back when I first fell in love with Shayne? Or did my mom and my dad control everything about my life even then? Was that all Zeus's fabrication, too?

"Send my mom home so I can talk to her," I say.

Zeus nods. "I think that's a good idea."

40

Jealousy

I LEAVE THE STADIUM, SHIELDING MY EYES FROM THE BLAZING sun. The row of black clouds still hangs in the west, but it's closer than it was before, and the air almost feels electric. All this is because of me. The seasons are stagnant because of me. It's eternal summer because of me. And now my dad tells me I need to be the one to keep war at bay, too. Why does it have to be my responsibility anyway? My burden. As if my life falling apart isn't enough.

I hop on the first shuttle that comes by the school, heading for home, fighting the anger that runs through me. I get the brief feeling that someone's following me, but when I scan the people on the shuttle, no one looks familiar. It's just a sea of people trying to survive the Global Heating Crisis. A sea of people doomed to slowly incinerate or die in a war if nothing changes.

I've only just turned back to the front when someone taps me on the shoulder. I turn to see the girl who owns the herb boutique, Melina.

"Having a bad day, Piper?"

"Who the hell are you?" I ask.

She puts the most condescending look possible on her face. "You haven't figured it out yet? Oh, come on, Piper. I gathered you were smarter than that."

Melina. Perfect. Beautiful. Eternally annoying.

"Aphrodite," I say. I knew no one could be that perfect on their own.

She pats my cheek like I'm a child who's done well. "Smart little girl."

I want to punch her gorgeous face. "Just shut up, okay."

"Oh, poor Piper. She isn't getting everything she wants for once." Melina laughs. "Welcome to the club."

"You have no idea what I'm going through," I say.

"Of course I do," Melina says. "Who do you think started this whole mess?"

"What do you mean?"

Melina rolls her eyes. "Oh, come on. Let's think back, two weeks ago. It was your birthday. You ate that pathetic cake your mom made. You guys got in some ridiculous argument. And then you got a delivery."

The ceramic jar. "You gave it to me?"

"Who else?" Melina says. "And then you opened it. I watched you. And you know what? You were supposed to die on the spot. There was supposed to be a curse on the jar that whoever opened it died."

I clench my fingernails into my palms. "It was supposed to kill me?"

She presses her pouty lips together. "That would have been ideal."

"Ideal! For who?"

Melina laughs and leans forward on the bench seat so her lips are only inches from mine. I hold my position. I am not going to back down from her. She may be a goddess, but so am I.

"Why for me, of course. What a dumb question."

I glare at her. "What have I ever done to you?"

Scorn flickers across her beautiful face, but she seems to catch herself and erases it quickly, replacing it with her standard seren- ity. "Piper. Persephone. What haven't you done? Here I am the goddess of love and beauty, yet you've taken the hearts of the only two men I could call my own."

"Your own?" My mind processes this. "Ares and Hades?"

Melina mocks my apparent stupidity once again. "Ares, of

course. But then there's my cripple husband, Hephaestus. He pined over the jar holding your identity, worshipping it like a golden idol. I watched him for years, going to the altar, praying for your release. His prayers are the only reason I knew what was in the jar in the first place. The precious secret. Your mother and Apate didn't tell anyone but him—and him only because he crafted the jar and kept it safe. But all it takes is one weak link. So I stole it from him and had it delivered to you."

I fix my eyes on her, trying not to let anything show on my face. I can't believe my mom worked with the goddess of deceit. Apate defines untrustworthy. My mom should know this. "But I didn't die, did I?"

Melina shakes her head. "It seems Apate has earned her name as goddess of deceit. Whoever opened the jar should have burned in Tartarus, but Apate crossed even your mother, allowing that one person would be able to open the jar."

"The person whose identity was stored inside," I say.

Melina nods. "That's right. You. And instead of an existence in Tartarus, which would have simplified my life beyond belief, now here you are once again trying to steal my true love."

"Not Shayne," I say.

"Of course not Shayne," Melina says. "What a bore. Though I'm sure he, like every other guy, would do just about anything to have me. Anything. You do know how guys are, don't you, Piper?"

I'm flooded with relief when she denies wanting Shayne. "How are guys?" I ask.

"They're selfish. And greedy. And all they care about is the conquest. Take your precious Shayne for example. Do you really think all he's been doing for the last eighteen years is pining away for you?"

I bite my lip. Actually this is exactly what I thought. Exactly what Shayne led me to believe.

She must see my answer in my eyes. "Watch this, Piper."

Instantly, images form in my mind of Shayne wrapped in embraces with other girls. Girls who are far prettier and curvier than me, and who have no inhibitions. He's on the beaches in the Elysian Fields, and they flock to him. They pull on his clothes. They trace their fingers over his bare skin. They press their lips against his naked body. He closes his eyes and moans under their touch.

I press my hands against my head, trying to make the images vanish. "You're lying."

"About love? Never, Piper. You know I wouldn't."

The images shift and he's in the meadow of flowers in his garden, and he's clearly making love to another girl. I want to tear the memories straight from my brain.

"Stop it!" I scream, even on the crowded shuttle. Tears spring to my eyes. "Just stop it!"

Melina gives a final laugh, and the images vanish. They can't be real. But no matter how hard I try, they're never going to go away. She's planted them like seeds.

"Don't fool yourself, Piper. Shayne is just like every other guy. He doesn't care about you."

"You're wrong," I say. But what if she's not wrong? What if Shayne really was with those other girls? "You're just angry because Reese wants me."

Scorn fills her eyes. "Reese doesn't want you. And Shayne doesn't want you. You're nothing, Piper. You're a fallen goddess. You aren't worthy of someone like Reese's attention. And if you ever think for a minute that Shayne will be true to you, you're wrong. No one will ever be true to you. You don't deserve anything."

Melina may be the goddess of beauty, but every word coming out of her mouth is filled with ugliness. Her words dig deep and burrow inside me. "Why are you acting like this?" I say. In my past life, I remember talking to Aphrodite on occasion, and though maybe we weren't the best of friends, she never even came close to exhibiting the contempt she's showing now. "I never did anything to you."

Melina's perfect lips press into a perfect smile. And then she leans close to me and whispers in my ear. "Yes, you did, Piper. You didn't die."

I've had enough. I stand up so I can get off at the next stop. How can she possibly call herself the goddess of love? She knows nothing of love. Only jealousy and hatred, both of which seem to be directed at me.

"Oh, guess what I heard, Piper?" she calls out to me.

I take the bait and turn. "What?"

"Your friend from school, Randy Conner . . ."

"What about him?" I ask, and I get a sick feeling in my stomach. Because as soon as I ask the question, I see the answer. I see into the Underworld and into Tartarus. And there is Randy, standing on the banks of the river of fire. He's been moved from Asphodel and put in Tartarus. Guilt for his father's death covers him in a layer of red. As I watch, he steps through the wall of fire which makes up the boundary. He screams in a cry so heart-rending, my own nerves feel like they are on fire. And then he's gone.

Melina smiles. "Yeah. I thought you'd want to know about one more life you've screwed up."

My stomach clenches. She's wrong. She has to be wrong. I refuse to say anything else to her, and I get off the bus.

IN ADDITION TO EVERYTHING ELSE IN MY LIFE CATAPULTING out of control, I now need to save Randy Conner. He can't suffer the tortures of Tartarus. I can't let it happen. I'll go back to the Underworld. I'll talk to Shayne and sort things out. He can clear up everything. This mess with Randy Conner. Melina's poisoned visions of his infidelity. I'm about to call out for him but stop myself as an image of him and the girl in his garden forms in my mind. I squeeze my eyes shut, fighting to force it away. It's nothing but Melina's ploy to get under my skin. But the image persists, and I remain silent.

I look in the direction of the clouds and start to walk toward them. And like they're responding to me, they move closer with each step I take. Closer to me and closer to Austin. I head up the rocky cliff that overlooks the Colorado River, and I watch them. Dare them to come any nearer. Almost in response, lightning streaks through the clouds parallel to the horizon.

It's late afternoon, and there are a few college kids hanging around under a canopy, listening to music. They look over at me, and one of them waves. I wave back, remembering my visit to the Drag with Chloe to get our tattoos. To think I planned on being one of those kids. On leading a normal life. I never had a chance. The Fates have been against me from the start.

One of the guys smiles, and motions me over. "Come join us. We've got plenty to share."

I look to the bottle of liquor he's holding, and honestly, a part of me is tempted. To grab hold of something normal from this world and hang on to it.

"We don't bite," the girl calls. "And anyway, Dylan here needs a date." She points to the boy on her right who gives me an inviting grin. Then she leans over and kisses the other guy full on the mouth until all three of them roll back laughing. Oh my god, they lead such normal lives, even amid the heat and the wars and the chaos. They don't have to worry about any of the craziness filling my world.

I shake my head, and they wave as I walk away. Behind me, I know the clouds follow. The wind picks up, and darkness extends its fingers until it surrounds me on three sides. Lightning fills the sky again, but there's not a raindrop in sight. The storm coming is pure electricity. It's been brewing since my most recent trip to the Underworld, and any minute, it's going to strike.

Once I'm out of the college kids' sight, I sink down to the hard-packed dirt and rocks. I have to save Randy, but I can't bring myself to call for Shayne. I don't want his help for this. I want to do something right on my own. I still hear the music and laughter in the background as I scoot toward the edge of the cliff and look down. The water is so far receded that rocks and sand nearly reach the middle from both sides, leaving a thin ribbon of stagnant brown wetness in between. It's the only way I've known the river. Slow. Dead. Empty.

If I go away, will everything change? Will autumn return and winter come? Will the Global Heating Crisis really end?

"You're Persephone."

I whip around at Chloe's voice, and see her standing there. She must've followed me on the shuttle. But it's not the crazy Chloe who claimed to kill Randy Conner's father. It's the withdrawn Chloe. The one who almost died. And neither of them is the one I really want to see. I want my old Chloe back.

I turn to the overlook, away from her, and watch the sky. "Yeah. So what?"

I feel her sit down next to me, leaving space in between us.

"You didn't tell me."

I shake my head, not knowing if she's looking at me. "You never gave me the chance."

We sit there not speaking for a while. I'm not going to start up a conversation with her, and she seems to be trying to figure out what to say. If she even has anything to say. Lightning strikes again, straight down to the earth this time. It hits the bridge crossing the river with a crack so loud, the whole ground shakes.

"Why did you save me?"

I turn, and Chloe's looking at me. Her eyes contain a sorrow I never used to see. The Chloe I got a tattoo with never showed sadness. She was all fun. And adventure. She is not this Chloe.

I saved you because I love you, I want to say. But it won't come to my mouth. "I didn't save you. Shayne did."

But Chloe shakes her head. "No. It was you. I remember."

I turn back to the cliff, picking up a rock and tossing it over. It clatters on the rocky outcrop, skipping vertically until it stops. Far below, what little water is left ripples in the wind.

"What's going to happen to me when I die?" She sounds like a child asking a random curiosity about the world.

I avert my eyes and pick up another rock. "I don't know. I

don't even know if I'm ever going back to the Underworld." If my dad can be believed, the world could die from war if I do.

"You have to, Piper."

"Really? I'm not sure I read that rule." Why does everyone feel compelled to tell me what to do?

"The Underworld needs you."

I snort. "Please. What do you know about what the Underworld needs?"

Chloe grabs my arm. "But I need you there, Piper. For when I die."

I yank my arm away and toss the rock over the cliff. "You're not going to die."

But she nods. "Yeah. I am. Fate told me so. And I'm scared."

I stand up, walking a few steps away. The wind's blowing hard enough now my hair is flying in every single direction possible. I pull it back with one fist. "You don't know what you're talking about."

"I need you there to help me. I can't handle eternity in Tartarus."

"You don't have to worry about Tartarus. Randy Conner's taking care of that for you. He managed to get all the blame."

Chloe looks at me and blinks her eyes a few times. "He did?" She shakes her head. "But that's not right. It should be me. Not Randy." Chloe stands up now, and fear creeps onto her face.

So what? Let her be scared. "Why don't you offer yourself up in his place then if you think it's so unfair?"

She shakes her head, and her bandana slips off-center. "I told the terrorists I wouldn't join. Said I didn't want any part of blowing up a dome. But they used me anyway, and the next thing I knew, Randy's dad was really dead."

"Randy asked you to kill him."

"I didn't mean to do anything. I swear." Chloe presses her hands against her face. "But Randy shouldn't get the blame."

I shrug. "No, he shouldn't. Maybe if you go explain things, everything will be all right."

Chloe looks up then, taking her hands away. "Yeah, maybe. But I'm scared."

I nod. "You should be." I know I'm not comforting her, but I don't care. My words are true. And right now, the world seems like a very cruel place.

Chloe bites her lip, and my eyes meet hers. "I'm so sorry for everything, Piper."

A gust of wind blows, and she turns away from me, looking out toward the barren water. Before I realize what she's going to do, she puts her hands up into the wind and jumps.

41

Sacrifice

CHLOE FALLS.

I run to the edge, but she's already gone. I'm too slow. My stomach tightens into a knot so hard and full of disbelief, I can't stand it. I lunge out on the cliff, but stop myself, unable to go beyond the rim.

Chloe will die.

I heard the words before and tried to stop them, but it was useless. Chloe is dead, and there is nothing I can do about it. Maybe there was never anything I could really do about it except postpone it.

"No! No! No!" I'm staring over the side, but I can't bring myself to actually look for her body. She's dead. She's gone. And though she's killed herself, I feel like I've pushed her. "Please come back. Don't leave me." I want the old Chloe here with me now. I want us to be friends, before my knowledge of phoenixes or the Underworld or Persephone ever came back to me. "Please, Chloe."

Lightning cracks, and this time, it strikes a building across on the other shore. In seconds, the building catches fire, and smoke fills the air.

Off to the side, I hear the college kids coming toward me. Did they hear me screaming? Did I scream? I can't face them or anyone. Before they can reach me, I run the other way.

Chloe cannot be dead.

Chloe will die.

It was her fate, and she knew it. But what is my fate? To be a curse to everyone I know?

I will not have it.

I direct all my thoughts to the Underworld. Not to travel there, but to command there. I was once the Queen of the Underworld. I should have power. And I want that power now if only for this one decision.

I see the Underworld before me. I rule it.

"Randy and Chloe will be moved to the Elysian Fields," I command. I have no idea if I even vocalize it. But I know I will make it happen with my sheer will. I can't count on Shayne and his rules to do it for me, so I will do it myself.

The ground underneath me seems to quake at my words. I think for a second it will split and swallow me whole. Maybe I will have to take their places in Tartarus. Whatever the cost, I accept it.

"Now," I say. "Put them in Elysium."

The ground trembles one more time, and I feel their souls move from the fires of Tartarus to paradise. My best friend may be dead, but now she's in her rightful place in paradise. It's where she should have been last week.

I shudder from the power I've exerted. I've done it. Chloe and Randy are going to be okay. They'll have paradise forever.

I turn my mind from the Underworld back to the world around me. I run down the embankment, heading out into the street. I love Shayne. And I want to be with him now more than anything. The images Melina showed me have to be false. He wouldn't do that. But I force thoughts of him away for the moment and focus on the Earth because it's my responsibility also.

It's still hot as a sauna, but the wind is blowing so hard, it's almost pushing me over. The lightning is a storm of light and sound, striking everything it can. Sirens explode in the air, and smoke is thick. I run in the direction of the Botanical Haven, because if my mom is somehow responsible for this weather, I have to make her stop. It's killing the Earth.

My legs pound; I run forever. I'm almost there. Sirens and wind are rampant around me, and lightning is striking everything in sight. It cracks so close it feels like it's next to me, and one of the Spanish oaks in our yard splits in half and falls to the ground.

Another branch falls, and it smacks onto the glass roof of the Botanical Haven. I hold my breath even though the glass is shatterproof, because it hits with such force.

The glass holds.

The rest of the world isn't as lucky as we are. I can only imagine how this lightning storm is wrecking downtown Austin. Wrecking the world.

I run across the rocks that make up our yard and pull the door open. My mom is inside, clipping dead leaves off the plants like everything in the world is as it should be. How could she be so oblivious to the Earth outside the Botanical Haven when she's always claimed to love it? The leaves drop to the floor at her feet like the branches outside. I slam the door shut behind me to let her know I'm home. I need to confront her, and it has to start here with her killing everything around her for her own selfish needs.

The wind beats on the glass walls and ceiling, but I try to filter it out. But another branch slams into the roof, and I jump. The glass groans under the weight but holds.

"Why did you do it, Mom?"

She has her scissors in her hand, hanging down at her side, her gloves still on. "What?"

"Kill the phoenix. Why did you take me from the Underworld?"

The smile evaporates from her face like the mist sprayed over our hot Earth. "Who told you that?"

I shake my head. "It doesn't matter. I know—that's what matters."

Her eyes narrow, and her face turns red. "It does matter. Nobody was allowed to speak of it. Whoever told you will go to Tartarus."

"You've lied to me my entire life."

"Ares told you, didn't he?"

"Ares didn't tell me."

Her eyes are wild, moving around the room, looking for something or someone to blame. "He did. I know it."

I uncross my arms and take a step closer to her. "You don't know anything. You killed a phoenix and me at the same time."

My mom shakes her head. "No! I would never kill you. Someone has been lying to you. I love you."

"Love me! You killed me, and then, when I was reborn as Piper, you hid me away from everything I ever knew."

"You're wrong. It wasn't like that at all."

"You never even told me who my father really was."

My mom's hand flies to her mouth. "You know about that?"

I nod. "I know everything, Mom. Everything. I know who you are. Who I am. Who I used to be."

"But how—?"

"I loved Hades, and you took me away. Everything was perfect, and you ruined it all." Tears well up inside my eyes, but I refuse to let them fall.

"Perfect! How can you even say that? I was forced to be away from you for half the year. My precious daughter. And you never even seemed to mind."

"I belonged in Hell as much as I belonged here. My place was as Queen of the Underworld."

"Your place was here with me." She starts cutting again, and her eyes bulge out of her head. They aren't focused on me. They don't focus on anything. There's sweat beading down her face, catching in her hair. "With your mother. Not off in some gods-forsaken place damning souls for eternity. You should have been among the living. Not wandering around underground with no one to keep you company but ghosts."

"I had Shayne." And I want Shayne now.

My mom raises her eyebrows. "Yes, you had Shayne. But that's hardly a reason to spend half the year away from your mother."

"Was he really that bad, Mom? Couldn't you have just tried to get along?"

My mom stops cutting since all the leaves are gone. "Of course he was that bad. He couldn't stand to be around me. He was rude to me and arrogant. He showed me absolutely no respect."

My mouth falls open. I can't believe she's saying this. "But he was good to me. And I loved him."

My mom throws down the scissors, smashing them into the ground. "Good to you? He took you away from me." Overhead, the glass creaks again, and then the branch is too much. An entire section of the roof comes down off to my right, raining glass in a glittering shower.

"Yes, he took me away from you, but he treated me like a queen."

My mom doesn't even seem to notice the roof. "So what? Any god could do that."

My mind flashes to Reese, but I push him aside. I don't need him coming into this conversation.

"I didn't want any god. I wanted Shayne. But you ruined all that." I dig my fingers into the soil of a nearby plant and grab a clump, smashing it in my fist. "You ruined everything. You're selfish, Mom. You've always been nothing but selfish. But let me tell you something. I'm grown up now. I make my own decisions. I will not be under your control any longer. You don't own me."

She meets my eyes then. Her gaze bores into me, but I maintain the hold, not wanting to look away. Refusing to back down.

"You will obey me, Piper." Each word comes out slowly. Methodically. Like she's making a plan even as she says it.

I shake my head. "No, I won't."

"You will go upstairs and pack your things. We're leaving. Right now. We'll hide, and no one will find us again."

"No."

She moves to me to grab my wrist, but I'm faster. I grab hers instead. I clench as tight as I can, hard enough to break it if she were mortal.

"Do you dare to defy your mother? Are you forgetting who I am?"

I grab tighter, holding until I feel the pulse in her arm. "Who?"

My mother stands a little taller. "I am a goddess."

I let go of her hand, thrusting it down to her side. "And so am I."

She stares at me, her mouth opening, but nothing comes out. Around us, the wind from the storm whips through the hole in the roof.

"Mom, do you know what the punishment for killing a phoenix is?"

My mom looks down, picking up the bucket of water by her feet. It's left a wet ring on the tile and drips when she raises it.

"It's life in Tartarus, Mom. Did you know that?"

She nods, still looking down.

I think about my visit to Tartarus. My horrible meal with Aeacus, Tantalus, and Pirithous. A meal that might have been my last. "Have you ever been to Tartarus?"

My mom lets out a bark of a laugh, but it's laced with fear. "Of course not."

"It's the most horrible place imaginable. Even worse, in fact. I've been there—as Piper. I should send you there myself. But even after everything you've done, I will never let you end up there."

The bucket of water falls, and I realize my mom is crying. I stand there, holding my resolve, but her crying tears at my heart. I try to be strong. I try to stay angry. But when I can't listen any longer, I move to her and catch her in a hug.

"I only did what I thought best for you, Piper. Best for us."

She's shaking in my arms. "Well, you screwed up, Mom. And now everything's falling apart."

She stops crying and pulls back to look at me. "I can get help." Her eyes are wide as if she believes the statement. "I can get Apate to help. She'll know what to do."

I stare at her, trying to keep my eyes impassive. "Mom, you can't trust the goddess of deceit."

But she nods her head. "Yes, Piper. I can. She helped me before. With you. I never intended to go through with my end of the bargain. I wasn't going to lose you again. So we came up with the idea of the jar. To hide you from Hades and Ares."

I throw up my hands. "The jar! How could you ever think that was a good idea?" The image of the ceramic jar flashes in my mind, and I get the overwhelming urge to smash it against the wall.

My mom grabs my hands. "It kept you hidden from the gods for eighteen years. Everything was going so well. I stopped using my powers, and your identity was hidden. We had the perfect life. And then you opened it." Her eyes narrow. "Which you never should have been allowed to do."

"But I did, Mom. Don't you see? Apate tricked you. You thought you could tuck away your secrets forever. But she tricked you, and I opened it."

My mom shakes her head. "No. There must have been some weakness. Apate swore to me it would work. We'll get her help now. Get away from here. No one will ever know."

I tear my hands away from hers and meet her wide eyes with a cold stare. "But I know, Mom. And I have no intention of ever being part of your games again."

My mom walks closer to me, but I don't want her sympathy. I don't want anything from her.

"I was just trying to help," she says. "When Ares came to me with the idea—"

My eyes nearly pop out of my head. "Ares! He came to you?"

My mom nods. "Of course. I never would have known about

the power of the phoenix sacrifice if not for him. He was the one I made the bargain with in the first place."

Something clicks far in the back of my mind, but it's nearly silent.

"Ares told you about the phoenix?" My heart has started beating like a drum, pounding so hard I'm sure it'll come out of my chest.

"Ares came up with the idea. We planned it all out. But nobody could be told. Not your father. Not Hades. And certainly not you. Everything had to be just perfect."

Ares knew about the phoenix. It was his idea.

"What happened?" I'm trying to stay calm, but something is building inside me, trying to come out.

My mom pulls off her gloves and tosses them on a plant stand. "We waited until you were due home. And when Hermes brought you back, we acted. We took you to Phoenicia, to the Well of the Phoenix."

"I fought you." I remember this like it was yesterday. Standing by the well. Being forced to drink from the water.

Fear.

Betrayal like I never imagined possible.

And flames.

So many flames.

My mom nods. "Yes, you fought. But Ares managed to control you. He has this way of calming people. Getting them to do what he wants."

It settles on me; I know only too well about Reese's power. It's the power that overcomes me every time he's near. It makes me forget what's real and what's fantasy. "He drugged me."

My mom shrugs. "Drugs. Power. Call it what you want. We needed your cooperation."

How could my mother be a part of her own daughter's abduction and drugging and death?

"I drank the water. There was fire."

"Yes, Piper."

I felt like my heart was being ripped from my chest. My own mother.

"You were supposed to love me and protect me."

"But I was," she says. "Don't you see?" She moves toward me and reaches out, but I slap her hand away. This is not my mother. She's a demon in the body of my mother.

My mom lowers her hand. "Ares killed the phoenix. It had to be done just right. With flames and a knife made of pure gold. Hephaestus himself crafted it, though he had no idea why."

"Reese killed the phoenix?" I say.

"Yes. Without him, I never would have been able to do everything. You were still fighting, but as soon as the bird burst into flame, so did you. And then you were reborn to me and free of Hades forever."

It's like I'm watching my past life through the eyes of someone else. I can't fathom how my mother could have done this. "And Reese's involvement—"

"What? What about my involvement?"

I turn to see the door wide open, and Reese standing there, watching us. Outside, the wind howls, and the air is filled with smoke.

"You're responsible for everything. Everything."

His smile only grows.

"Every single thing that's happened has been your fault. The phoenix. My death. Taking me away from the life I loved."

Reese spreads his arms, like he thinks I'm going to run over and hug him. "But look at everything you have in your future." And then his smell hits me hard, and I know it's a drug.

I can't let it overcome me. I can't let go. I back away, putting distance between him and me, but he takes two steps forward for every step I take back.

"Stay away from me!" I scream it at him, fighting to keep the aroma from entering me.

But he still comes. "You promised, Piper. You said you'd give us a chance." He's close now, and I'm up against a wall.

The memories start to fill my mind. I see us kissing on a balcony, looking out across a sea, telling stories late into the night. But the memories can't be real. I haven't lived them.

I look to my mom, but she's standing there with a dazed look on her face, like she can't process the fact that I'm being threatened. Or she's suffering from Reese's scent, too. Remembering things that aren't true.

"Help me, Mom."

My mom looks at Reese. He's next to her now on his advance toward me. Behind me, I feel the glass of the wall against my skin. The thick scent of wine enters my nose. I force it out but know I need to breathe.

My mom shifts, and I think she's going to do something to stop him. But then she actually presses her lips into a thin line. "Maybe I was wrong, Piper," she says. "Maybe being with him will solve all our problems."

I shake my head. She's under his spell. "Can't you see it, Mom? He's tricking you. You aren't in control. He is."

"Half of the assembly backs him," she says.

I look from her to Reese.

He nods. "Thousands of years, Piper. I've loved you since the day I first saw you. I know you remember."

I do remember. I remember being with Reese. And I see myself with him now. My memories tell me he loves me. They tell me I've loved him. That I could love him again. That he'll take care of me.

But what I see can't be trusted. None of it is real. It's just his scent.

"He'll let us all stay together. We won't have to worry about the Underworld," my mom says. "I can come with you when you need to go away. I can be with you always."

Every word out of her mouth makes me sick. A sudden coldness hits me as reality sinks in. Even my own mother has betrayed me.

"I've waited for you, Persephone. I've waited so long. Forever. It's been worse than eternity in Tartarus without you. Torture every time I see you." He takes a step and then another, until I realize he's only a foot away.

"I don't want you." I force the words out, even against the flood of memories and intoxication I feel seeping through me.

"That's crazy." He reaches out and touches me.

I yank my arm back. "I don't want you. Not now. Not then."

Reese steps close. "You do. You want me more than life itself. I see it in your eyes. I can smell it on you. You want me with every inch of your glorious body." He takes my hand, and though my mind screams at me to yank it away, I don't.

My body is dying to go to him. To give in to the memories. Memories I know are planted by him, but I don't care. Being with him can fix everything. The weather. The world. The situation with my mom.

"Yes, Piper. Come to me. Be with me forever."

My legs betray me, carrying me forward. But some part of my brain stops them, until I'm held rigid by my own internal battle.

"I don't want you." I can only get out a whisper now.

"You can be with me forever, Piper." He traces his fingers along my shoulder, and a jolt runs through me, making every cohesive thought in my brain run off to the shadows. All that's left are the memories of him and me, together.

"Forever?" I repeat. And his scent hits me hard. I fight it for a second, but the smell is powerful, and it takes over. I inhale, and exhilaration moves into my lungs. It reaches every muscle in my body as his scent makes its way through my blood.

He's leaning toward me. His smell is in my nose. In my mouth. His words are music in my ear, lulling me exactly where I want to go. "We can be together like we should have been together so long ago."

"Yes." I whisper the word.

Reese smiles, and his eyes meet mine. And in a single moment of clarity, I see the deception, masked behind sapphire irises. If I don't do anything, he's going to win. And I can't stop him alone.

"Shayne." I call him, praying he'll come. Because I don't think I'll have a second chance.

"He won't come," Reese says. And then his lips are on mine, and I close my eyes.

42

Darkness

REESE'S KISS IS HOT AND HARD, AND I FEEL LIKE HE'S ABOUT to devour me. Crazy memories of desire fill my mind, and even though my brain screams against me, I kiss him back. But then, with a sudden motion, he flies across the room, landing on his back.

The door bangs open, and a breeze blows into the room, clearing away the drug that is Reese. I look around, but don't see anything. And then a familiar hand touches me on the cheek, stroking it gently.

"Shayne?" He's come.

I feel him but don't see him anywhere. And then his lips are on mine, and I know everything Melina told me about him is wrong. He's my perfect soul mate, and I'll never belong with another. The assembly of gods be damned.

"Shhhh," he whispers in my ear. "I'm sorry I took so long."

I still don't see him—he must have the Helm of Darkness on—but he's here, and his invisible presence moves away from me; I know he's heading for Reese.

"Ares!" Shayne's voice booms across the Botanical Haven.

Reese is on the ground, but he jumps to his feet, and a grin filled with anticipation covers his face.

Why did I ever kiss him in the first place?

"Nobody invited you to this party, Hades," Reese says.

I look at my mom, who's glancing around, trying to find Shayne, not looking at me.

"Piper invited me." His voice comes from a different location now. He's moving around. And he's invisible.

Reese jumps out toward the voice, but when he reaches out and closes his arms, they come up empty.

"Looking for something, Ares?" Shayne's voice again, now coming from near the register.

Reese whips around. "Why don't you take off your helmet and fight like you aren't a coward."

"Cowards drug their victims, Ares. If you're looking for a coward, you should check the mirror." And when Shayne finishes talking, a giant palm tree lifts and flies through the air, hitting Reese on the back so hard he slams into the register.

But Reese is expecting it. The terra-cotta pot shatters on the hard tiles, and he spins, flinging my mom's scissors which he's picked up from the ground.

They fly through the air, stick in something invisible, and vanish. And I hear Shayne's gasp of pain. He's been hit.

"Aha." Reese is smiling now, walking toward the spot where Shayne is. "Maybe you can keep the helmet on after all." He punches out, but his fist keeps going, hitting nothing but air.

"I want you to leave Piper alone. Forever."

Reese looks toward me. "Piper wants to be with me."

I shake my head. "No! I don't."

But Reese can't hear the truth. "You do. I see it all over you."

"You're crazy!" I scream, willing him to stop.

He turns away, his eyes roving the room for Shayne. "You were so willing. So excited."

"I wasn't!" I want it to not be true. For me to never have even kissed him. And I don't want Shayne to hear. My face is hot, and everything around me is starting to turn red.

A bucket slams into the back of Reese's head, wiping the smile off his face. He falls to the ground, but lands in a crouched position, like a lion ready to pounce.

"Oh, gods, Piper. Please just give me a chance. I can be everything and more to you than him. I can make you feel like a woman. Let you live aboveground. And what does he have to offer you? Life in Hell? Torturing and burning. Dead souls everywhere. Is that what you really want? If it is, I can give you that, too."

I shake my head. The only person I want—I've ever wanted—is Shayne. "I'll never be with you." I take my own scissors and pitch them at Reese, but he springs off the ground, and I miss him by inches. And then I feel a slight brush on my cheek, and my hair moves aside. I turn, but it's gone.

It's only when I notice the drops of blood on the ground that I know Shayne is in trouble. Each a footstep apart and moving across the room. And before I can warn him, Reese notices, too, and he pounces, landing on top of an invisible form, so it looks like he's levitating in the air.

Shayne pops into visibility, and Reese tosses the Helm of Darkness across the room where it clatters to the ground near my mom, who's still standing there watching like she's placed money on a boxing match and needs to see who will win.

Reese and Shayne fight, rolling around in a battle I fear will end in only hurt. The struggle is a blur of flailing limbs and electricity mimicking the storm outside. I want to go in and stop it but know I can't. Shayne has Reese in a throat lock so tight that Reese's head begins to turn white. He manages to throw Shayne off, gasping for air as he stands up. And then he's back on Shayne, pressing Shayne's head together with the flats of his hands. And Reese turns him to face me.

"You have to love me, Piper. You have to give me a chance. Please."

I watch in horror as I see Shayne struggling to break free from Reese's grip. But it's like a vise.

"Let him go!" I plead.

Reese shakes his head. "I can't, Piper. I can't trust him ever. He'll take you away from me."

"I'm not yours. I never will be. I never was!"

Shayne's face turns redder and redder. His head is being crushed.

"But I need you so much," Reese says. Even as horrible as I know he is, his voice is so pleading. So sincere. I think he really does need me.

Shayne's eyes can't focus. He's losing, and I'm going to lose him.

"You and I were meant to be together. I'll make you so happy."

I shake my head, trying to erase his words, but they won't go away.

"I see it in your face. You want to be with me."

I will my face to be a mask. I want Reese to see he never has a chance. But whatever he sees in my expression gives Shayne the opportunity he needs. He shoves his arms under Reese's and breaks free, rolling away.

And then Reese moves. Not toward Shayne, but right at me. He reaches me, wrapping an arm around my waist. I twist and try to escape, but he's got me too tight.

He turns to me. "Ready?"

"Stop!" Shayne's voice shouts out, and he starts running.

"Ares, catch."

My head whips toward my mother's voice. She picks up the Helm of Darkness and tosses it through the air toward Reese. He catches it, and the last thing I see before I disappear is Shayne coming for me, his hands only inches away, and then the world shifts around me.

43

Fire

I wake up on a sofa inside a room with walls made of rock. When I sit up, all around me I smell something sweet and thick. Like wine.

Reese.

I look around, and even though the scent of Reese is so strong I want to gag and breathe deeply at the same time, the room is empty. I'm alone, and I have no idea where I am.

The room has no doors and no windows. Only grotesque tapestries cover the walls, giving the otherwise dismal room a hint of color. I stand and move to the first tapestry, a bloody scene with bodies impaled on poles, pull it aside, and look behind it. There must be a way out of this place. Behind the tapestry, mortar holds together stones the size of Cerberus. If there is an exit, it's not here.

I move to the next tapestry, a scene depicting an ocean of blood with body parts floating on the surface, but find the same thing—solid construction sealing in my doom. And so I keep moving, circling the room, trying not to breathe in too deeply. Reese may not be in here with me, but his scent—his drug—lingers everywhere.

The next few tapestries turn up nothing better, but when I get halfway around the room, my search is rewarded. I find a loose stone.

I push on it, attempting to shove it through the wall. It wobbles a bit but won't budge; the cracking pieces of mortar wedge it in place. And so I shove harder, fighting to keep the fear building inside me under control. What if there is no way out? What if I never see Shayne again?

"Shayne," I whisper, hoping that Reese can't hear me. Shayne can find me here and help me. But he doesn't come. I whisper his name again and turn to look around the room. It's still empty. Wherever Shayne is, he hasn't heard me.

I try to steady my breathing, but I'm shaking too hard. I shove on the block with renewed effort, but the results are the same. Nothing. I bite my lip, letting my teeth pierce the skin, trying to focus on the pain and not the panic. And then I think to look up.

Overhead, a chandelier hangs, fashioned of wrought iron and human skulls. Their mouths gape open, frozen in screaming terror, and chains wrap through their eye sockets, holding them in place. My eyes follow the chains from the skulls upward where they twist around, knot together, and then continue on to the ceiling. At the point where they meet the ceiling, there is a hole through which the chandelier is raised and lowered. I think I can fit through it if only I can find a way up there.

I run back to the center of the room, to the sofa. It's some kind of antique piece, with a black moiré cushion and a solid wood frame. A frame that should hold my weight. I move to one end of the sofa and rock it forward until it's propped up on its side, perpendicular to the cold slab of the floor. And then I walk behind it where my weight is least likely to tip it, and I climb to the top.

I jump upward, catching the wrought iron of the chandelier with my fingers. I swing my legs up over a couple of skulls and pull myself up. If I can get inside the ceiling, I can get into the skeleton of the fortress and hopefully find a way out. I climb the knot of chains, crunching skulls under my feet. I don't look back. I'm at the hole in the ceiling, and though it's a tight fit, I manage to squeeze my way through. I reach back down through the hole and grab an unlit candle, but there are no matches around. But I remember the match at church.

I have power.

Light bursts around me as the candle ignites, illuminating steel tresses that span a distance tall enough to crawl but nowhere near tall enough to walk. And so, with the candle in one hand, I inch forward, looking for some way out. Some way to get out of this place and get back to Shayne.

I come to a wall blocking my path. A light glows between the place where the wall and the ceiling should intersect. I blow out the candle and lower myself down until stone meets my feet. I walk between the walls, and with each step, the light brightens. It's drawing me closer, and I imagine it's coming from the outside. My escape from this place.

My path ends with a screen which slides when I push it, and I move through. I'm behind a tapestry, but when I peek out, there's a long hallway stretching to either side. On the wall, sconces are lit with blazing candles, and I realize this, and not the outside world, is the source of illumination.

Piper.

My name is an echo coming from the hallway to my left. A whisper that hangs in my mind.

I ignore it and walk to the right, quickening my pace when I hear my name again. There's not a door or window in sight. I'm in a fortress of stone, and my feet slap on the floor so loudly each step sounds like the beat of a drum.

Please don't be afraid.

Reese's voice is soothing, but I'm not finding an ounce of comfort in his words. They're filled with deception.

I need you, Piper.

His voice persists, echoing behind me, never far away. I start running, but the hallway seems endless. It curves around, and the sound of my feet softens. There's now a shadowy carpet under my toes. And at the end of the carpet is an obsidian door. Open and waiting for me.

I have to go through. I see a window ahead. And a window means escape from Reese's domain. And escape means leaving Reese far behind forever.

I move in and shut the door behind me. Immediately, Reese's scent pumps into the room. I scan my surroundings; what I thought was a window is a set of glass doors that open on to a balcony, and I run to them. With a single click, I unlock the doors, hoping to dilute the room with some fresh air. To get rid of the smell of Reese before it overtakes me. And to escape. But as I stand there, I feel eyes on me, and before I open the doors, I turn.

"Where are you?"

Nothing. The eyes are still watching. My skin crawls under their weight, and I glance around, hoping to find him.

Fresh flowers are placed everywhere. On every table, shelf, and chair. All of them are severed at the stem.

"I hate cut flowers." I say it to the eyes I know are watching. To Reese who's here as sure as I am.

He laughs softly—to my right. I whip my head around, but only two wingback chairs and a long sofa table greet me. Above the table hangs a picture—a blood-strewn battle, people drawn and quartered, decapitated heads decorating posts. And high on a mountain, the figure of a man watching it all. A man who looks just like Reese.

"I thought you liked breaking the rules," Reese says. And then he appears on a chair, holding Shayne's Helm of Darkness in his hands. "Or was all that just an act?"

With the helmet off, his smell flows around the room, and within seconds, it moves high in my nostrils and begins its descent to my lungs. Memories of him start to stir. In them, I'm standing with him at the top of the mountain, staring down at the battlefield. We hold hands. We keep the battle in check. My powers of life mix with his desire for killing. We were meant to be together.

The memories never happened. It's just what he wants me to see.

"Take me back right now, Reese. I don't want to be here." I fight the air entering me, trying to will it to go away.

Reese stands and starts walking toward me. "But you are here, and together we're going to change the world."

"Shayne!" I call for him again, praying this time he'll hear. He has to come and get me.

Reese starts laughing. "Shayne can't come save you this time."

I shudder, feeling revulsion mixing in my throat with his odor. I hate him. He's not who I want to be with. My brain knows he is nothing but a liar. A master of deception. It tries to tell my body this, but with each second that passes, my body is refusing to listen because the memories he's feeding me are just too strong.

"He'll come," I say.

But Reese shakes his head. "Shayne isn't allowed here. This is my domain." He's made his way to me now, and he leans in, kissing me on the lips.

I don't kiss him back. I cannot kiss him. Can't go down that path again. Even if I go crazy with my internal fight. I just can't do it.

Reese leans away, but the taste of him lingers on my mouth. I want to lick my lips, to taste the sweetness, but I keep my teeth clenched so tight they might shatter.

"I want to show you something, Piper." Reese walks away, toward the glass doors, and swings them both outward. The wonderful smell of fresh air pours into the room, and I gulp in as much clean air as I can. In this reprieve, my mind clears, and I remember I have to get out of here. I reach to a nearby table and pick up a metal sculpture of two centaurs fighting. It's small enough for me to hold in one hand, and I hide it behind my back. And then the breeze dies, and Reese's smell again takes over.

Outside are the sounds of battle. Guns. Yelling. Screams of men dying. Reese walks onto the balcony and turns to me, holding his hand out, palm upward. His fingers curl in, beckoning me. My legs carry me forward until I'm there next to him looking down on a desert full of men killing each other.

"Do you know what your presence on Earth has done for battle, Piper?"

I try not to watch, but I can't take my eyes off the horror below. These are not dead souls as I'm used to seeing in Hell. These are the dying. Life is seeping out of them one heartbeat at a time. They're in a place between the living and the dead. A place of pain and suffering—like a Tartarus on Earth.

The scene shifts. I look down on a city. Violence sweeps the streets as gangs set fire to food storage facilities and recycling plants. It's like the worst of every news report I've seen in Austin. People inside the buildings try to flee, but the doors are barred shut. They scream as they die . . .

. . . and the scene shifts again . . .

. . . and again, showing battle and violence and chaos across every part of the world.

Reese takes the hand not hidden behind my back. We stand there, just like in my memories, holding hands and watching the battle. Shivers run up my arms, down my stomach. And I know I need to fight them. But mixed with his scent, they just feel so good.

"Men fight over anything these days. Battles can last year-round. They kill each other over the simplest things. Like water. And shelter." He waves outward with his other hand. "And I get to watch it all. Help make it bloodier. Gorier. I get to feed off their miseries."

I look at him then, and want disgust to show on my face, but I have the horrible feeling the only thing showing there now is desire. For the battle. For Reese. For his smell. His drug, which I have to fight.

He lifts his hand, taking my chin in his fingers, and holds it like a fragile flower. "We'll be happy together, Piper. I promise you."

No! I want to scream it at him. At myself. But my voice won't work.

His hand traces away from my chin to my neck, down my chest, to my tense stomach. I want to pull away and run. To leave. Go somewhere. And I want to be with him and feel him always.

"My domain will be yours. I'll keep you safe. Protect you." His hand moves lower.

I shift against the screaming thoughts in my brain and give him room. I have to stop. This is wrong, and he is false. But he's touching me, and for every scream my brain is giving, my body is giving double. His mouth comes for mine, and I meet it, letting the gasp I've been holding behind my clenched teeth escape. His hand moves down. I want it to go on forever. And I want it to stop right now.

"No." I manage the word, forcing it out from inside our kiss. And I swing the hidden statue from behind my back directly at his head.

In a flash, Reese catches my hand midair. He grabs my wrist and twists it, and the statue slips from my hand, falling to the floor.

His mouth is back on mine just as fast, and he pushes me to the floor. He's heavy on top of me, and the air flies from my body, and I'm kissing him again, trying to remember why I want to say no because all my memories are telling me this is what I want. There's a small part of my brain that's screaming at me to stop, but my body has a mind of its own, and it's refusing to listen.

"We were meant to be together, Piper. We should have always been together." His mouth moves to my neck.

"Yes." My body is in control, and my doubts are trapped behind steel bars with no hope of escape.

"So much time has been wasted." His hand roams up my shirt. Down the inside of my legs. "So much time we need to make up for."

So much time. Why hadn't I been with Reese forever? I was with him before. I want to be with him now. Haven't I always? Nothing will ever keep me from him. No one. Nothing.

What kept me from him in the past? Who could possibly do that?

And then my doubts push through the instincts of my body, and it comes to me. I remember Shayne. He's there in my mind. Unable to reach me here in Reese's domain.

It's Shayne I want to be with.

Not Reese.

"No."

Reese doesn't stop. He kisses my stomach, sending shivers everywhere.

"I don't want this."

Reese lifts his head, his fingers and hands still moving. "Yes, you do, Piper. You have to. I need you so much."

And in his eyes, I see his need. My desire. But Shayne's in my mind, and I know Reese's memories are nothing but a horrible deception.

"I want you to stop."

Reese shakes his head. "You're everything to me. Everything I've ever wanted. I'll die without you." His hands are moving faster, trying to pull off my shorts, trying to lift my shirt. They're everywhere, but instead of making me feel good, they are like monsters. Monsters that need to be destroyed.

I'm fighting against him, twisting like a viper, but his body is so strong, I may as well be doing nothing, and I realize he's not going to stop. Not now. Not ever. He's too far gone. I need to stop him, or I'll forever be sorry. His head is down, kissing, trying to draw me back to him, and when he looks up and his eyes meet mine, I remember I am a goddess. I know what I need to do. I don't need to wait for Shayne.

I look at him hard then, and drawing upon the powers of Hell which I know are mine, I ignite him into a mass of flames on top of me.

44

Descent

REESE LEAPS OFF ME, COVERED IN FIRE. HIS FACE IS BURNING. His hair is burning. The harsh odor of his burning flesh hits me, and I suck it in, happy to be free of his drugging aroma. I only watch him for a second; he's moving backward, knocking into a chair, falling to the ground. And then I start running. But when I come in from the balcony, I realize there is nowhere to go. The door I first came through has vanished into the stone wall. I bolt through the doors back out onto the balcony, and leap over the side. Escaping the boundaries of Reese's world. I fall.

I brace myself for an impact, but when I reach the hard-packed sand, I keep falling, moving through the ground and the river of sentient silver. It embraces me on my way to the security of the Underworld, and it delivers me safely.

Shayne is there waiting for me, and I rush into his arms. I don't need to say anything. I can't talk about Reese. Not yet. Shayne holds me until I'm not shaking anymore, and then we turn to the boat, and Charon helps us on board. And in the quiet of the Underworld, I begin to pick through the pieces scattered about in my mind.

"Melina told me things about you—" I start. I try to find the words, but I don't want to voice them.

Shayne pulls me close on the boat. "Aphrodite is a liar."

I turn so I'm facing him, looking into his dark eyes, and I watch the red flashes. "She said there were other girls." I know it's not true, but I have to ask.

Shayne puts a hand on either of my shoulders. "I would never do that, Piper. Never."

"I didn't believe her. I knew it couldn't be true."

"It will never be true," Shayne says. "I would never be with anyone but you."

Relief pours through me. His eyes are so sincere. They've always been that way, even back when I was Persephone. His lips part, and he leans until his mouth is so close to my ear, I'm sure he's going to kiss it. I hold still and wait for the kiss, but it doesn't come.

"Please don't ever leave again."

I feel the words on his breath as he says them. And they are better than any kiss could have been. They erase any and every doubt I ever had. His warmth seeps into me and gives me a feeling of security so strong nothing could tear it away. And then he finally does kiss my ear.

We're still on the boat with Charon moving across the River Acheron. I force myself to pull back and settle into the crook of his arm. The water stretches calm before us, and every so often, a monster nips into the air, causing ripples at the surface.

"What was Chloe's sorrow?"

Shayne is holding both my hands, but releases them. I wonder if he's going to tell me not to listen to the sorrow. But this is Chloe we're talking about, and I want to know.

"You can find it," he says. "You don't need me to show you."

He's right. The Underworld is my domain. I don't need Shayne for this. I turn my head to the right until I'm looking out across the water. And I send my heart searching. Looking for a piece of Chloe.

The water of Acheron is as still as the ice of Cocytus, but I remain focused. The river will listen to me. It has in the past. It will in the future. And so I wait. Something touches the surface from below, and concentric circles grow from the spot. A bubble rises, pushing its way up until it sits on the water, and then it skims along the surface as it makes its way toward me. It grows as it gets closer as if it's a thing alive. And when it reaches the side of the boat, I open my mind and listen.

I never meant to hurt Piper.

There it is. So simple. So selfless. Her final sorrow had been about me. By keeping her alive in the first place, I'd been responsible for her demise on Earth, and here, her last thoughts were concern over my well-being.

There is no better friend than Chloe.

Cerberus greets us on the other shore, and I open my arms to him, letting him knock me to the ground. His three heads fight over who gets to lick me until Shayne finally pulls him away. We say our goodbyes to Charon, and then Cerberus leads us down a tunnel to the safety of Shayne's home.

We're together then, and it's wonderful and perfect. Exactly how it is supposed to be. His touches wake me up in places I never knew were asleep, and his kisses bring back memories I'm only too happy to relive. His memories are real in my mind, and his touches are visceral.

I lean back in his arms on the sofa and look around the room. He's put living plants everywhere. If I never see cut flowers again, I'll live a happy life. Reese and his lies can burn forever.

"I don't ever want to leave." I refuse to acknowledge the fear forming in my stomach. This is my sanctuary.

Shayne kisses my neck and wraps his arms tighter around my waist. "You don't have to."

I shake my head and turn to him, pulling back so I can see his wonderful face. "You know that's not true. The world is a mess."

"It will sort itself out," Shayne says.

"It won't. You know it. If I stay here forever, my mom's going to kill the world. Winter's going to come and it's never going to leave."

Shayne runs his hands through his hair. "I don't know what's going to happen, Piper, just that things have to change. Your mom will have to go before the assembly of gods and stand trial."

My chest tightens. "She didn't kill the phoenix. Reese did.

He's the one who needs to stand trial." Because I know he'll escape the flames. He's a god, and my setting him on fire won't kill him. It'll only stall him.

Shayne lifts a bottle of wine and starts to fill two red crystal glasses. "That's not for us to decide."

I stand up also, moving next to him. "But you're on the assembly. You can help."

"So you're defending her? Even after what she did?"

I shake my head because my mom's actions are just too much. She played a role in sacrificing a phoenix and burning me alive. I shudder at the memories of the flames. And I know that even though I should never forgive her for what she's done, I can't see her be sent to Tartarus. "I never would have thought she'd be so extreme."

Shayne takes my hands and looks me right in the eye. His brown irises are hard around the edges, and the specks of red I love so much dance around inside. "I won't ever let anything happen to you again. I swear it."

I try to push aside the memories from earlier, but they persist. "What do we do about Reese? And about the war? My father said . . ."

He puts a finger to my lips. "Today, we don't do anything."

I shudder, and my eyes flicker upward. "But Reese is still out there. The fighting is going to destroy the Earth. Not to mention he's going to try to take over the Underworld."

Shayne hands me my glass. "Now that you're back, reinforcing it, he'll never be able to get through."

I wish I could be as certain as Shayne.

I take a long sip of wine and let it move through me, washing away thoughts of Reese and my mom. I'll have to face them, and I'll have to help get the seasons back under control. But Shayne is right. I don't have to do anything today.

I look to the table next to the wall, to the empty pedestal there. "Reese still has the Helm of Darkness."

Shayne nods, glancing over at the empty table also. "I know.

And I'll get it back. But for right now, there are more important things to think about."

"Like what?" Though I know what he's talking about.

His face is moving close to mine now. I start to take another sip of wine, but he stops the glass, taking it from my hand and setting it back on the table. And then he kisses me until I can't breathe.

EPILOGUE

Pomegranate

I skate across the River Cocytus and visit the Elysian Fields alone. I've spent countless hours here when my visits are added together, but I never stay very long each time. The job of Queen of the Underworld requires my devotion—a devotion I look forward to every minute of every day.

I visit Charlotte and Chloe and even Randy. I want to tell Randy that his mother and sister are fine, but to do so would only stir up sorrows he left far behind in Acheron. And besides, though Randy's father is dead, I can't guarantee a life of happiness for Randy's mother and sister. That's their life to choose.

I stay with Chloe the longest. When she's not hanging out at the beach parties, she lives in a Japanese garden complete with an arched bridge spanning a pond filled with koi of varying sizes and shapes. Reeds shoot out of the water, rustling when the fish swim through them, and river-washed stones are sprinkled in a bed of sand. Chloe has this whole new Japanese thing down. She rakes the sand and snips tiny limbs off plants, creating works of art in bonsai trees. She's even started a bonsai contest like the sand sculpture contest, and it's becoming the new rage in paradise. Everyone talks about it.

Her eyes light up every time I visit, but she never misses me. Never worries. We talk about anything from my mother to bonsai theory to Hannah Reed's child. All is fair game with Chloe. And our tattoos remain as solid and black as the day we got them.

One day, I visit for over an hour. She has five new tattoos and is trying to convince me to get another. I tell her maybe next time. I ask her if she's met Rhadam yet, but she tells me no, he always seems too busy. If I didn't know Chloe better, I'd guess she's being shy. One of these times, I'll have to make sure to introduce them. It would be nice to go on a real double date, even if it is in the Underworld. I tell her again how perfect they'd be together, and then I leave.

I walk through the hills, heading for Shayne's garden. I haven't visited it since my return to the Underworld. The pomegranate tree has invaded my dreams. It blossoms when I close my eyes, and then flowers, wilts, and dies all in one night. I watch it over and over again. And I can't stop it. It's still dying even with my return to the Underworld—at least this is what happens in my nightmares. I'm afraid that when I visit the valley, my nightmares may be reality. And that maybe I don't belong here after all. Maybe my father was right. And if this is the truth, I don't want to know.

Cerberus joins me near the water. He bounds out from behind the falls, and I wonder if there is a secret passageway there I know nothing about. I make a mental note to investigate it later; maybe sometime when Shayne isn't around. I could find out where it goes and surprise him. Teach him something about the Underworld for once.

I sink to the grass and spend some time scratching Cerberus. He's in no hurry to see the pomegranate tree. Or he just likes to get his tummy rubbed. Thankfully, though he has three heads, he only has one stomach to scratch. Otherwise, the task could occupy an entire day. But soon, he stands and runs off after a bird—in the exact direction I need to go. Toward the garden and the tree.

I wonder if there really is a bird he's chasing or whether he's trying to encourage me. Whatever the case, I think I need his enthusiasm to help pull me forward.

The garden is alive with colors, just like the first time Shayne showed it to me. Electric-blue tulips blow in a breeze, and indigo jasmine hangs from vines twined around large stone columns. It's the image I remember. Shayne's green thumb at work. His hobby. Gardeners on Earth would kill for this kind of skill.

I realize I've been holding my breath. The last time I was here, death and sorrow hung in the air. So I lift my nose and breathe in. And the smell of the pomegranate tree comes to me. At the end of the garden, near the back. I walk toward it.

Cerberus is still at my side. At the edge of the garden, we come to the tree. When I reach it, the sadness hits me, still pulsing through the wood of the trunk. It reaches its tendrils to every branch. To every leaf. And it casts an oppressive aura around everything in its shadow.

I take a deep breath and place my hands on the mucus-covered bark. Under my palms, the tree shudders, fighting against the poisoning sorrow within. It searches for a way to staunch the sadness that permeates it. It opens its pores and soaks in my energy. It gropes for something to make it whole again. And then the pomegranate tree recognizes me, and its searching stops.

ACKNOWLEDGMENTS

I owe a huge thank-you to so many people for making this book what it is today. *Solstice* is where it is because of you all. Thank you!

To Riley, who thinks every idea I have for a new story is a great one. Thank you for believing in me.

To Zachary, who mentioned, when I was telling him about the Underworld, that there would be monsters swimming around in the rivers.

To Lola, who makes art day after day that inspires my writing and my stories.

To Mom and Dad, who supported me during an extra year of college so I could get a History degree and learn bunches more about Greek mythology.

To Jessica Lee Anderson, who drops anything to offer help on subjects ranging from what the smoothest merlot is to how the world would look in a global warming future.

To my agent, Laura Rennert, who shared my vision for this book and has supported my career since we first met at Big Sur. To Lara Perkins for encouraging me to take my story to the next level again and again and again. To everyone else at the Andrea Brown Literary Agency, who helped carry the reality of this book forward.

To my editor, Susan Chang, for believing in me and in my books. I am so grateful that we are able to work together and that you have helped *Solstice* become so much richer than I would have ever believed.

To all my early readers of the full manuscript who helped me shape the myth and deepen the story: Christine Marciniak, Beth Revis, Tabitha Olson, Kim Baccellia, Vivian Lee Mahoney, Stacy Nyikos, and Sarah Rettger. To all those who read portions of the story and offered wonderful feedback: Parker Peevyhouse, Kelly Herold, Patty Palmer, and Cara Frazier.

To my local Writing Group at #THEPLACE for making me feel like I have a life outside of my home office: E. Kristin Anderson, K. A. Holt, Mari Mancusi, Stephanie Pellegrin, Jessica Lee Anderson, Madeline Smoot, Bethany Hegedus, Cory Putman Oakes, and Salima Alikhan.

To Spiderhouse Café for playing the most OSUM writing music and giving #THEPLACE a home.

To my fellow Texas Sweethearts & Scoundrels who share the experiences of being an author and who make marketing so much fun: Jo Whittemore, Jessica Lee Anderson, K. A. Holt, Jeanette Larson, Emma Virján, and Don Tate.

To the Austin writing community, especially Cynthia Leitich Smith, Austin SCBWI, and the Writers' League of Texas . . . you guys make me feel so lucky to live here! The best people. The best events. The best support. The best fun!

To Jen Bigheart, Stephanie Pellegrin, and the Literary Lonestars for being so supportive of the Texas writing and blogging community. You guys make the difference!

To my pals who survived "The Best Writing Retreat Ever" at the lodge. May the words always flow and the taxidermied animals become increasingly eerie.

To the Indie author community for embracing *Solstice* and being such a wonderful support network.

To all the bloggers and readers of *Solstice* for your reviews, your support, and the amazing, selfless gift you give to the Kidlit community every single day!

To Danny and Julie at The Book Spot, and to all the awesome folks at BookPeople: thank you for providing Austin with the best indie bookstores in the world.

To anyone else I may have missed, please consider yourself thanked! I am so appreciative for all the advice and feedback and support I've received on this journey.

Thank you!

BONUS CHAPTER

Dryad

SHAYNE AND I SKATE ACROSS THE RIVER COCYTUS AND SPEND the afternoon in the Elysian Fields. We say hi to Charlotte, and then, while I visit Chloe, Shayne checks in with Rhadam. Afterward, we walk down the grassy path to Shayne's garden. Cerberus follows but chases after a bird once we sit down next to the waterfall.

Shayne runs his hands through my hair, and I push images of the outer world from my mind. I've been hearing reports of everything going on and as much as I don't want to believe it, I know my mom. She's cast the world into an even more deadly stasis. Every tree left alive has dropped its leaves and is hibernating. I don't know what's worse: the images that spring to my mind or the reality. I haven't been back to check. Not yet.

"You're distracted," Shayne says.

I blink a few times and try to bring my mind back to this moment, with Shayne, in paradise.

"Only a little," I say. "It's hard not to think about it."

"Just wait a bit longer," he says. "It will work out."

I'm not sure how he's sure. Nobody can see into the future, with the possible exception of Tanni and her sisters of Fate.

"Do you remember that one time you snuck out?" Shayne says. He traces a finger along the side of my neck, which totally succeeds in distracting me.

I turn so I can focus on him and not on the world above. "Which one? There were so many."

He laughs. We both do, because our first six months of dating had been nothing but me trying to circumvent the strict rules of my mom.

"The first time," Shayne says. "You were so nervous."

I punch him lightly on the shoulder. "You were, too."

"I never get nervous," he says.

"Please. You were so quiet. You hardly said a word."

He pulls me closer. "I was trying to be romantic."

"Romantic! You took me monster hunting."

"Dryads aren't technically monsters," Shayne says. "And I had nothing to do with it."

"You let her out," I say.

"A small mistake," Shayne says.

"Small!" I say. "I'd hate to see your big mistakes."

As my memories flow back, I smile at the image. I kept trying to find ways to get some time to myself. Back then we'd lived out in the middle of nowhere, in a stone temple so small it was more like a cottage. It was my mom's way of making sure I never talked to anyone without her knowing about it. Sure, she let me hang out with my friends, Peisinoe, Aglaope, and Thelxiepeia, but only if she knew where we were going and how long we were going to be gone. Every so often one of our relatives would drop in, and I'd get a bit more contact with the outside world. But absolutely the only time I was allowed to be by myself was when I needed to help the Earth. My mom knew it was my responsibility, and so she'd walk me to a forest or a field or a garden and tell me what I needed to do. And then she'd pick me up when I was done and walk me home. I was pretty sure if she didn't have things to do herself, she would have stayed with me all day. I used to think it was normal, how protective she was. But the more I saw my friends and the freedom they had, the more I wanted that same freedom for myself.

"Maybe I can walk myself today," I said.

My mom finished arranging a bunch of flowers in a vase and

then joined me by the entryway. "Nonsense. I wouldn't want you to get lonely."

"I won't," I said. "And anyway, I was hoping to meet the girls later."

My mom's hand, already pressed on the door, tensed. "When?"

Did she know something was different? Did she know about Hades?

I kept my face as calm as possible. "Oh, you know, maybe in a few hours. I could walk home with them."

I silently willed her to say *yes*.

"Aglaope will be there?" my mom asked.

Of my friends, my mom only really trusted Aglaope, which was funny since she was the one I got along with least. Aglaope always tried to make me feel stupid. I did my best to pretend it didn't bother me.

"Sure," I said, praying the lie wasn't clear on my face. The truth was I hadn't even talked to my friends. They knew nothing about what had happened in the cave. They knew nothing about Hades. It had been over a week since we met, and I'd been clawing my eyes out trying to find a way to see him again. He'd left me notes every single day, hidden behind trees and under rocks, and I'd relished every single one. I couldn't stop thinking about him, and if his notes could be trusted, he couldn't stop thinking about me, either. Even now, I had to replay how we met over and over again to convince myself it was real.

My mom seemed to consider my request as we walked across the fields. I gave her my best innocent smile. I'd always been trustworthy. She had no reason to doubt me now. I reached out and made some flowers bloom for good measure, so she'd know I was serious about my responsibilities.

"You'll come right home afterward?" she asked.

Wait. She was going to agree?

"I'll come home right afterward." Even thinking about how mad she'd be if she found out was scary. I'd never have a chance for freedom again. But scary or not, all I wanted to do was see Hades.

"I'll be waiting for you," she said.

This I had no doubt of.

"I'll be home later this afternoon," I said, and I hugged her.

She hugged me back like I was five. I was sure she'd never let go. But she did. And then she walked away.

I watched as she disappeared in the direction of our house. I watched until I was sure she wasn't coming back. I watched a while longer just to make sure. And then I ran.

His notes had all said the same thing: *Meet me by the side of the lake, under the grove of ash trees.* I'd been trying to get to those trees all week, but they were so far out of my way. Now I had my chance. It took me the better part of a half hour. But when I finally got there, Hades was nowhere to be found.

"Hello?" I whispered.

The breeze picked up in response to my words, rustling the leaves overhead. I placed my hand on the bark of a nearby tree and infused it with life, watching as the leaves grew at my command. And then I moved on to another and then another, passing the time, trying not to feel stupid that Hades wasn't here. Maybe I was wrong. Maybe this wasn't the place. Maybe he'd changed his mind.

A twig snapped behind me, and I spun around.

I was alone.

"Hello?" I said again, louder this time, putting as much confidence in my voice as possible. "Who's there?"

A footstep, this time from the other direction. My heart pounded as I slowly turned. And as I watched, Hades materialized in front of me, pulling the Helm of Darkness off his head. I planted my feet in place and forced myself to stay calm, even though I completely wanted to run over to him. A week felt like forever. I almost forgot how completely hot he was.

"You made it," he said, and his eyes lit up.

I nodded, hoping he didn't think I looked desperate.

"Yeah, there was this whole thing with my mom, and she had all this stuff she needed me to do this week, and I kept trying to come, but there was this forest that needed help, and then some grainfield . . ." My voice trailed off. "I'm babbling, aren't I?"

Hades only stepped closer. "Gods, I've missed you, Persephone."

That's all it took. Every emotion from the week before returned, and the next thing I knew, my back was pressed against a giant ash tree, and we were kissing. I wrapped my arms around him and ran my hands over his back, because I still couldn't believe he was real. I couldn't believe my mom had lied to me about him so completely. Hades wasn't even close to a monster. He was the most gorgeous guy I'd ever seen.

"I missed you, too," I managed to say, and then we kissed some more. And even when we stopped kissing and he finally pulled back from me, I kept my hands firmly in his and rested them on my hips.

"She wouldn't let me out of her sight," I said. "It's impossible."

"It's never impossible," he said.

"You don't know my mom."

Hades brushed a loose curl from my face, tucking it behind my ear. It sent shivers everywhere. I leaned in and kissed him again.

"How long do you have?" he asked.

I glanced at the sun overhead, peeking in between the branches. "A few hours?"

"Ugh," Hades said. "It's going to destroy me seeing you so little."

And . . . my heart sank. "My mom will never let me see you."

Hades shook his head and red sparks flashed in his dark eyes. "There has to be a way."

I'd thought about ways all week, and I'd come up empty. There was no way my mom would ever let me be with anyone, especially Hades. She was convinced he made furniture out of human bones and tortured people for amusement.

"So what are we doing today?" I asked to change the subject. My mom only served to be a mood dampener.

Hades took a step back, taking my hand and pulling me from the tree. "You could come visit the Underworld."

My stomach tightened. The Underworld. Meeting Hades was one thing. Visiting the Underworld was something completely different.

"Um . . ." I said.

"We don't have to," he said quickly. "I don't want to rush you."

I didn't want him to think I was afraid. "No, it's okay. We could—"

Before the words were out of my mouth, something grabbed me. It yanked me from Hades and slammed me into the hard bark of the ash tree. And then it started sucking me inside.

"Hades!" I screamed, trying to reach my hands out for him. But whatever it was that had me wasn't letting my arms move. Something snaked out and clamped over my mouth, and then I was pulled inside the tree completely.

Blackness closed around me. But unlike the small space I expected, the tree was vast. The walls started glowing, and the blackness began to lift, such that when the arms around me released their hold, I could see that they weren't arms at all but tree limbs twisted around the body of a naked woman.

A dryad.

She was draped in green moss enough to cover her more delicate areas, and the branches and leaves were a part of her, growing from her skin. Her hair was a brown darker than the bark that lay scattered across her skin, and leaves grew throughout it.

I took a step backward, closer to the wall. "What do you want?"

I'd heard tales of dryads forever—women whose spirits had been tied up with certain trees. There were all sorts of reasons the gods changed them into dryads. Some of the women begged for it, they were so broken up about love lost. These were normally the ones who helped the Earth. Loved the trees. Blended with nature in the best possible way. But others were forced into it against their will by vengeful gods and goddesses. These were the monsters.

This dryad took a step forward to match mine backward. "Persephone, right?"

I nodded. Held my ground. I was a goddess and had nothing to be afraid of from this tree spirit. "And you are . . . ?"

"Atlanteia," she said, moving closer. One of her branches traced up the side of my body until it twisted under my hair. "And I've been trying to get you alone for a week. That mother of yours doesn't make anything easy, does she?"

As much as I wanted to agree with the dryad—my mom was way too controlling—Atlanteia was my captor, not my counselor.

"I thought you were dead," I said. The last I'd heard, Atlanteia had been banished to the Underworld. She'd killed so many roadside travelers that her tree had been chopped down and then burned while she was in it. The nearby villagers had said her screams were heard for years after. They told their children the stories at bedtime to scare them into staying in their beds.

"Dead?" Atlanteia said, as if she were considering it. "I was trapped in Tartarus. But then the most wonderful thing happened."

"What?" I asked. My stomach tightened.

"I escaped," she said. "Hades opened the gates, and I snuck out."

Monsters had escaped from the Underworld last week, but according to my friends, they'd all been rounded up.

"You should go back," I said.

There was no chance she would listen to me. Go back to her prison when she could stay here and continue where she left off?

"No," Atlanteia said. "I'm never going back. And you want to know the best part?"

I mentally willed Hades to find me. To chop down the tree and get me out of here. But there was no sound. Nothing.

"What?" I asked.

Atlanteia stepped near and twined her limbs around me, pulling me close against her. She must have been able to feel my heart beating. She had to see the fear in my eyes.

"Once I take your soul, they'll never be able to destroy me. I'll have the power of a goddess."

Okay, I had to stay calm. Maybe reason this out. There had to be something I could do.

Her branches tightened around me. She lifted another limb and pressed it against my stomach, forcing the air from my body. My muscles tensed as I tried to pull back from her.

"You don't want to do that," I said.

"I do want to do that." She pushed harder until the bark covering the branch tore at my skin. I felt my blood drip from the cuts.

Think. I had to think. What did I do? I grew things. I gave plants life. I didn't take life from them. That was the job of death. The way to kill a dryad was to kill her tree.

Her hand pressed harder. Blood dripped down my stomach, over my hips. She snaked another hand under my hair and started twisting. I reached for the walls, trying to find some piece of the tree I could connect with, but she held me too close.

"You're the perfect solution," Atlanteia whispered in my ear. "You're exactly what I needed."

"You're crazy," I said, even though I knew there was no reasoning with her. "Just stop."

"Don't worry," she said. "It will all be over soon. I can already imagine how sad your mother will be. How Hades himself will probably pine outside, trying to find a way to destroy me, but knowing that if he destroys me, he'll also destroy you. Because we'll be connected. We'll be one."

She was crazy. I reached farther, stretching my fingers out until I was just able to brush the edge of the tree. And at that touch, I let my power flow. I imagined the tree reaching for the sky, passing every other tree by, growing branches and leaves until their weight became too much for it to bear. And then, as the branches began to fall, I imagined it continuing to grow until it had expended its life and there was nothing left.

Atlanteia released me and stepped back. As I watched, the bark crumbled and cracked off her. The leaves sprouting from her head began to shrivel and fade and fall to the ground. The veins under her skin blackened, and death climbed through her. Within moments, she was nothing but a pile of dust. The dead tree around me fell to pieces. And I was back in the grove.

Hades rushed up, pressing his hands to my stomach to cover the blood.

"Oh, gods, what happened?"

I passed my hand over my stomach and healed my wounds. I brushed dirt and bits of bark from my hair. I looked up into his eyes, and loved the fact that I had done this on my own. I'd rid the world of the dryad.

"Well, there was this dryad," I said, trying to calm my voice. "Someone let her out accidentally."

He swore under his breath. "Atlanteia."

I nodded. "I guess you forgot to recapture one."

"We've had patrols out all week searching for her," he said. He kept looking me over, making sure I wasn't hurt. "She must have known . . ."

I wrapped my arms around his shoulders, stopping his worries with my lips. I'd never felt so alive. Not only was I with the most gorgeous guy in the world, I'd fixed a problem with the world on my own. I couldn't help but wonder what my mom would think, at least about the second half. I figured I could tell her that part. See what she said. Gauge her reaction. But that could wait for another time. For now, being with Hades was all I wanted to think about.

"Is this how your dates normally go?" I asked. "You take girls monster hunting?"

"Only girls I really want to leave a lasting impression on," Hades said.

"Trust me," I said, grabbing his hands to calm the shaking of mine. "It definitely left an impression."

"You sure you're okay?"

"Sure," I said. "And the best part is we still have a couple hours."

This seemed enough to distract him from his worrying.

"What do you want to do?" he asked.

In response, I leaned in and kissed him, and we sank to the ground there in the grove of ash trees until the afternoon had passed into evening and I was definitely late.

Solstice

by P. J. Hoover

About This Guide

The activities and discussion questions that follow are intended to enhance your reading of *Solstice*. Please feel free to adapt these materials to suit your needs and interests.

Writing and Research Activities

I. Solstice

A. Piper's Earth is experiencing an extreme Global Heating Crisis. Go to the library or online to research current scientific studies of global warming trends in our world and efforts being made to combat them. Informed by your research, create a brochure for visitors to your own city or town in 2030. Include information about the climate and landscape, heat-related technologies and government ordinances (such as the cooling gel spray and private car ownerships restrictions in *Solstice*), and additional details about tourist attractions, cooling resources, and activities as you imagine them.

B. Early in the novel, it is clear that Chloe and Randy have never experienced winter. In the voice of one of these characters, write two to three paragraphs describing what you imagine a winter day would be like and what activities you might do on your first day of winter.

C. What does the word "solstice" mean? Create a collage, poem, song lyrics, or other performing, visual, or literary artwork that shows your interpretation of "solstice." Write a short paragraph explaining ways P. J. Hoover's novel helped you interpret the term in a creative way.

    D.   From heat bubbles to hail storms, the elements play key roles in *Solstice*. Make a list of other books and/or films in which weather is a critical thematic or plot feature, such as John Steinbeck's *The Grapes of Wrath* (drought); Ann Turnbull's *Maroo of the Winter Caves* (blizzard); director Wolfgang Petersen's *The Perfect Storm* (hurricane); and The X-Men film franchise (Storm's control of the weather). Choose one book or film from your list as the perfect "companion read/watch" for *Solstice*. Write a paragraph explaining your choice.

    E.   You are a fashion designer in Piper's Austin. Sketch a design for a soccer team uniform, prom dress, or trendsetting high school student's outfit, taking into consideration the weather and conservation/resource situation.

II. Myth and Memory

    A.   Slowly, a mythological world is revealed to Piper. She comes to realize her place therein and the fact that other "ordinary" people are also tied to the mythological world. Make a chart or annotated poster listing all of the mythological characters from *Solstice*. Include their traditional roles in Greek mythology, their names in Piper's Austin world, and the way they are reimagined by P. J. Hoover in the novel.

    B.   Go to the library or online to learn more about the phoenix. Create a PowerPoint or other multimedia presentation examining the phoenix as a central image in *Solstice*, both in terms of the novel's theme and plot structure.

    C.   In the character of Piper, write a poem or song lyrics beginning, "I am Persephone." Or, in the character of Shayne, write a poem or song lyrics beginning, "Persephone has remembered."

    D.   In William Shakespeare's *King Lear*, the character

Gloucester comments, "As flies to wanton boys are we to the gods/They kill us for their sport" (Act IV, scene 1). In the character of Piper, Chloe, Randy, or Zeus, write a journal entry reacting to this "ordinary human" observation.

III. Hell

A.   With friends or classmates, role-play a conversation in which Piper confronts her mother about killing of the phoenix and ending of her past life as Persephone. If desired, expand the role-play to include Zeus, Hades, Ares, Aphrodite or other characters from the novel, to the confrontation scene.

B.   In the character of Piper's mother, write a speech defending your actions and explaining why you feel it is best for the world for Piper to stay out of Hell. Or, in the character of Piper's father, write a speech explaining your absence from Piper's life— despite your power—and your thoughts on what choices you hope your daughter will make for her future. Present your speech to friends or classmates.

C.   In P. J. Hoover's interpretation of the mythical world, Hell is a complex place full of both beauty and horror. So, what might be in Hoover's Heaven? How would Zeus be in charge? Create a world-building outline or multiparagraph description for a Heaven that complements the Hell of *Solstice*.

D.   Once Piper realizes the truth about her identity and rebirth, she must decide how to continue her new life. Write an essay about a difficult choice you have had to make in your own life and the outcome of your decision.

DISCUSSION QUESTIONS

1. Do you think it is important that Chapter 2 begins on Piper's eighteenth birthday? Why or why not? What unusual gift does Piper receive and what does she do with it?
2. What are the Domes? What is the Global Heating Crisis?

Do you think our world is heading toward a super-hot landscape like the one depicted in *Solstice*? Explain your answer.

3. How does Chloe help Piper develop a sense of independence from her mother? Do you think you could handle living with a parent as strict as Piper's mom? Why or why not? What is important about the twin tattoos Chloe and Piper get in the Drag?

4. Compare Piper's first encounter with Shayne to her first meeting with Reese. What qualities do you like and/or dislike about each of these male characters?

5. Who is Tanni? What terrible warning does she give to Piper? Do you think Piper believes her? Is her encounter with Tanni your first clue that Piper may not be an ordinary eighteen-year-old? If not, what are your first clues? What were your first surmises about Piper's identity?

6. How is Chloe's brush with death a critical turning point in the novel? When Piper first visits Hades, do you think she already knows she belongs there—or has a sense of having visited before? Why or why not?

7. Was choosing to keep Chloe alive a selfish act on Piper's part? Do you see a parallel between Piper's choice and her mother's killing of the phoenix?

8. What is your opinion of Piper's father? Do you think he is a better parent than her mother? What argument might you make to Piper to encourage her staying with her mother? Or to suggest she visit her father?

9. Do you feel that Piper is (or will be) able to forgive her mother's actions? Would you be able to forgive Lucia? Why or why not?

10. Which is Hell: life aboveground on a super-heated, violently ruled Earth, or below in the Underworld? Is Hell a state of mind, a state of memory, or can you explain the term in another way?

11. "Solstice" can refer to the longest or shortest day of the year, a time when the sun "stands still." How might this notion

be interpreted in terms of Piper's eighteen years of life, her previous life as Persephone, or the movement of time more broadly in the novel?

12. At the end of the novel, Piper chooses to return to Shane/Hades. Do you agree with this choice? If Piper had asked for your advice about making the choice between Reese, Shane, and her mother's wishes, what pros and cons might you suggest she consider? What decision would you recommend Piper make and why?

13. In what ways can *Solstice* be read as a novel that explores choices—between love and responsibility, between personal desires and the troubles of the world, between sending people to Tartarus or the Elysian fields, between life and death? Has the story made you think differently about the way you make choices in your own life? Explain your answer citing examples from the book.

ABOUT THE AUTHOR

P. J. HOOVER first fell in love with Greek mythology in sixth grade. After a fifteen-year bout as an electrical engineer designing computer chips for a living, P.J. decided to take her own stab at mythology and started writing books for kids and teens. When not writing, P.J. spends time with her husband and two kids and enjoys practicing kung fu, solving Rubik's Cubes, and watching *Star Trek*. She lives in Austin, Texas.

For more information about P. J. (Tricia) Hoover, please visit her website: www.pjhoover.com. P.J. is also a member of The Texas Sweethearts & Scoundrels and The Enchanted Inkpot.